The Scent of Intuition

MIRACLES ON HARLEY STREET, BOOK 2

SARA ADRIEN

© Copyright 2024 by Sara Adrien
Text by Sara Adrien
Cover by Kim Killion

Dragonblade Publishing, Inc. is an imprint of Kathryn Le Veque Novels, Inc.
P.O. Box 23
Moreno Valley, CA 92556
ceo@dragonbladepublishing.com

Produced in the United States of America

First Edition December 2024
Trade Paperback Edition

Reproduction of any kind except where it pertains to short quotes in relation to advertising or promotion is strictly prohibited.

All Rights Reserved.

The characters and events portrayed in this book are fictitious. Any similarity to real persons, living or dead, is purely coincidental and not intended by the author.

ARE YOU SIGNED UP FOR DRAGONBLADE'S BLOG?

You'll get the latest news and information on exclusive giveaways, exclusive excerpts, coming releases, sales, free books, cover reveals and more.

Check out our complete list of authors, too!

No spam, no junk. That's a promise!

Sign Up Here

www.dragonbladepublishing.com

Dearest Reader;

Thank you for your support of a small press. At Dragonblade Publishing, we strive to bring you the highest quality Historical Romance from some of the best authors in the business. Without your support, there is no 'us', so we sincerely hope you adore these stories and find some new favorite authors along the way.

Happy Reading!

CEO, Dragonblade Publishing

Additional Dragonblade books by Author Sara Adrien

Miracles on Harley Street Series
A Sight to Behold (Book 1)
The Scent of Intuition (Book 2)

The Lyon's Den Series
Don't Wake a Sleeping Lyon
The Lyon's First Choice
The Lyon's Golden Touch

Preface

Dear Readers,

None of us exist in isolation and the choices we face in life are often influenced by those we love, are responsible for, or wish to spite. This is the case with Alfie and Bea in the book you are about to read. If you are new to the doctors on Harley Street and this is your first story, keep the following short overview handy so you already know who is coming back from other books. Think of the doctors on Harley Street as a group of friends, almost like in television shows like *Grey's Anatomy* or *Friends*, in which the stories bring everyone back even if the focus may only be one person and his or her love interest.

Philippa "Pippa" Mae Pemberton is the cousin of the heroine in this book, **Lady Beatrice Wetherby "Bea."** In book 1, *A Sight to Behold*, Pippa falls in love with **Dr. Nicholas Folsham "Nick,"** who is one of the doctors on Harley Street. Bea lives with Pippa at Cloverdale House, a large estate surrounded by parks with an abutting orangery, which belongs to Pippa's family, and which will be converted into a rehabilitation center in later books.

Dr. Nicholas "Nick" Folsham is an oculist at 87 Harley Street and the best eye surgeon in London. He studied in Vienna with Alfie Collins and some of the others, including Felix. Nick's story is book 1, *A Sight to Behold*.

Alfie Collins is the apothecary at 87 Harley Street. You are about to read his and Bea's romantic story in this book. He studied in Vienna and completed an apprenticeship in ayurvedic medicine in Delhi, India before he returned to London and opened the practice with his friends.

Dr. Andre Fernando is the orthopedist at 87 Harley Street, originally from Florence, Italy, and he is quite the heartbreaker. Although his past overlaps with that of his friends Alfie and Felix, his future has very different surprises in store. His story is in book 3, *A Touch of Charm*.

Wendy Folsham is Nick's younger sister and the nurse who lives and works at 87 Harley Street. Alfie, Andre, and Felix treat Wendy as their little sister, too, watching over her and keeping her safe. In reality, it's Wendy's wisdom and good heart that help the young men. Her story is in book 4, *The Sound of Seduction*.

Dr. Felix Leafley is the dentist at 87 Harley Street, a master of his craft. He's Jewish and also suffers from a broken heart because he hasn't been able to be reunited with the love of his life. Read his story in book 5, *A Taste of Gold*.

There are several other doctors and nurses who come in and out of 87 Harley Street and who work at the clinic across the street. Find those stories as part of the Lyon's Den series. For more information and a complete list of Sara Adrien's stories, please visit www.SaraAdrien.com.

Prologue

"WHY DO I have to give him the poison?" Bea asked, her voice a hushed yet firm demand in the stillness of the orangery.

Because he was the apothecary, and she was the lady administering the poison. Alfie rubbed his forehead.

"Because nobody suspects you," Alfie replied, his tone intentionally both respectful and urgent.

"Why? Because I'm not noticeable?"

Oh, she was more than noticeable—a beam in every room, a diamond of the first water indeed. Alfie swallowed hard, the hairs on his neck prickling, as Bea stepped closer to the raised bed in the orangery—their makeshift counter—and closer to him. Glad he wore a longer coat to hide the evidence of his physical reaction to her, Alfie tried to remember it was improper to stare at a lady, no matter the lack of chaperones or her beauty, except that this particular lady mattered to him a great deal.

"You're unforgettable," he murmured, his voice barely audible over the nightly hum of the crickets in the park just outside.

She smiled at his response and exhaled just so that a rose gold strand of her hair fell to her forehead. He forgot to breathe. How could she stand so close that he could tuck her hair behind her ears and yet be so far above him in station that he didn't dare?

Alfie Collins had never found himself in quite such a predicament before. Normally, his routine as an apothecary involved the sort of mundane tasks befitting his profession—stocking herbs, organizing vials, and perfecting the elaborate art of customer care, all behind his polished counter, under the bright gas light in his shop at 87 Harley Street. Yet there he was, entangled in a matter of clandestine affairs, in an orangery, using a raised bed with flowers as a makeshift table. He found himself right where he didn't wish to be, doing what he would rather not be doing. Yet, the woman beside him was absolutely the most beautiful member of the gentler sex that he had ever seen. And he'd seen plenty.

Alfie stood spellbound in the shadow-draped orangery at Cloverdale House, where secrets fluttered like moths against the cool windows. Candlelight cast a halo around Lady Beatrice Wetherby—Bea, as her cousin called her—as she navigated the taut atmosphere with the elegance of a seasoned general rather than the delicacy expected of an earl's daughter. That night, she was not merely nobility; she was a mastermind cloaked in silk, wielding a teaspoon as one might a saber.

Alfie's heart thrummed in his chest. Observing her, he marveled at the steady resolve in her actions, her focus sharp as she prepared to administer the ipecac to her uncle, the Duke of Sussex. The idea was simple: the ipecac should purge another more lethal poison from his body, one that made him hallucinate and made his mind weak. That way he'd be sober enough to let Alfie's friend, Nick, marry Bea's cousin, Pippa. But nothing about putting the plan into action was simple.

Even so, Alfie was grateful that the plan brought him closer to Bea because there were so many special things about her that he couldn't quite name them all. Though he couldn't help but try.

She's brilliant and brazen.

A mixture of awe and worry knotted his stomach when he handed over the vial of ipecac, knowing that using it could burn them both.

But as she took it with a daring glint in her eye, he realized he always did have a taste for the spicy ones.

"Why must we resort to this and not something less…" Alfie murmured quietly.

"Effective?" Bea responded, raising a brow.

"Less dangerous." Alfie's words sliced through the hush in the vast room. His expertise as an apothecary had acquainted him with the intricacies of countless remedies, but none so fraught with personal risk as this one.

Alfie tested her resolve and hated himself for it, but if she hesitated and got caught, the consequences would be damning. He may not be the one to administer the poison to a duke, but he'd provided it along with the instructions. For a commoner like him, the law wouldn't allow any excuses.

Her emerald eyes, fierce and unwavering, locked onto his.

"We're doing this for my beloved cousin Pippa, and your dear friend Nick," Bea replied, her voice a fusion of warmth and steel. "Nick can't marry her without her father's consent." Her determination was palpable, a testament to her indomitable will. Her titled cousin had fallen in love with Nick's best friend, a mere oculist—though the best eye surgeon in Britain—and Pippa's father, the duke, needed a nudge to consent, in the form of a little concoction Alfie had prepared.

"You know we must do this, Alfie. After all, you're a romantic," Bea teased Alfie as he showed her how to measure the ipecac extract he'd created and mix it into coffee. Her eyes moved to the vial and a set of additional distractions for the duke: a small chocolate praline and a fruit tart.

Still, the ipecac's scent, earthy and pungent, began to permeate the air, an olfactory herald of the scheme's progression. Understanding the importance of disguise, Alfie leaned closer, his voice a conspiratorial murmur.

"We'll need to mask the bitterness. Perhaps with sugar or rum? Something robust enough to hide its aftertaste."

Bea nodded, her lips curving in a momentary smile that belied the gravity of their undertaking. "Quite right. I assumed as much, and so I brought along some chocolate mixed with sugar." Retrieving a small tin of finely ground cocoa and sugar from her pocket, she expertly blended it with the medicine in preparation for the meeting. The rich, heady aroma of chocolate soon overpowered the ipecac's harshness, creating a deceptive and enticing concoction. "There. See?" Bea seemed pleased with herself.

"Do you always carry cocoa around with you?" The idea seemed quite preposterous.

"You won't tell anyone, will you? It's my weakness. I do love a cup of hot cocoa, so once a month or so I take a bit from the kitchen to keep on hand."

Alfie marveled at Bea's quick wit and resourcefulness, her ability to find light even in the darkest situations. He ached to voice his admiration, to declare his burgeoning feelings, yet the chasm of their social standings yawned wide between them.

"Will he be all right after?" Bea asked, concern lacing her tone. The duke, still blissfully unaware, was, after all, human.

"He'll think he's been through a tempest come morning but will be none the wiser for it."

Her grin at his reply, fleeting and mischievous, was a balm to his worries, but tinder to his heart.

>>><<<

LADY BEATRICE WETHERBY was willing to do anything for her cousin, Pippa. After years of living in her shadows, Philippa Mae Pemberton—Pippa to her—had finally found love and Bea was not going to let anything get between Pippa's and Nick's happiness. Not even her uncle's disgruntled reluctance to let Pippa have his consent.

Granted, Bea hadn't anticipated that the way to her cousin's future bliss would be a conspiratorial administration to poison her uncle, but if that's what it took, Bea accepted the solace of the age-old wisdom that the end justified the means.

Then again, "no good deed goes unpunished" also rang true.

Especially deeds that included Bea being found alone in the orangery at night with a man as handsome as the apothecary, Alfie Collins.

She had to act fast.

Bea steadied her breath. The flickering candlelight cast intriguing shadows, making the room enchanting and conspiratorial. She turned to Alfie, noticing the intensity in his eyes as he watched her.

"Tell me exactly how much to use," Bea said with the measuring spoon in her right hand. Then she dipped her right index finger in the mixture and lifted her hand to her mouth. But before she could lick it off, she noticed that Alfie's mouth fell open, and he narrowed his eyes as she brought her finger to her lips.

"*Ouff*, this is bitter." She tried not to grimace in front of the handsome man but batting her eyes wasn't enough to forget the taste of the ipecac.

Alfie cleared his throat and got to work, blending the concoction in what appeared to be deep concentration.

For the next minute or two, Bea focused on the task at hand, measuring the ipecac extract Alfie had prepared and mixing it into the coffee. She looked up at him, seeing his eyes sparkling with mischief.

"That's enough. Even if you don't like your uncle, don't use more than one spoon," Alfie said, a hint of a smile on his lips.

Her heart fluttered at his gaze, but she quickly pushed the feeling aside.

In Cousin Pippa's orangery, where the scent of orange blossoms mingled with the dampness of wet leaves, Bea found the intoxicating scent of the dashing apothecary by her side much more alluring than even the flowers. She hadn't felt this way since her one and only trip abroad when her parents had taken her to India. There, she'd tried exciting foods, strong spices, and deliciously warming teas. But even the combination of all of those paled in comparison to how Alfie made her feel. There was something about him that sent an exciting shiver through her, unlike anything she'd ever experienced since that long-ago journey.

Warmth radiated from the man, turning to a raging fire deep in her stomach. Perhaps if she helped Cousin Pippa find her happily ever after, she could forge a way to have one of her own?

Chapter One

London 1819.

*T*HE NIGHT OF *the ball at the Earl and Countess of Langley's, after the Duke of Sussex—effectively sobered from the drugs his sixth wife had administered, thanks to the purge provided by a hot, chocolatey drink full of an ipecac mixture Bea had given him—gave his blessings for Pippa and Nick's marriage...*

Bea was alone.

This was new, especially at a ball.

She'd never stood on the sidelines of a ballroom, much less on the sidelines of Society. Usually, Bea was the belle of the ball. Up until that moment, whenever she'd entered a room, all eyes had been on her, scrutinizing her every upswept curl, the stitching of her dress, and the manner of her stride.

And she'd reveled in it as long as there was no sign of the mysterious "beast", the unpredictable and unsightly rashes that sometimes plagued her skin and made her hide in her room. But when Bea could, she owned the attention as much as her cousin didn't. They'd grown up like that, Bea taking the attention and Pippa withdrawing. Over the years, Bea had become accustomed to it.

Not that night, however.

For her cousin Pippa had blossomed.

She'd arrived with several friends to support her and had landed a coup unlike any Society had seen since the winter ball at St. James—when a family who'd hidden that they were Jewish won the competition for official jeweler for the Crown.

Bea touched the diamond collar on her neck and thought about the kind jeweler who'd designed it for her to match the diadem she wore in her hair. He'd been jeweler for the Crown ever since stepping into the light, but threats of losing their livelihoods loomed for anyone who didn't fit in but depended on the Ton. And though Bea fit in—in every conceivable way—she didn't feel terribly welcome. It seemed that fitting in and actually belonging were poles apart.

Earlier, in the golden light of the ballroom, Bea had watched as Pippa floated across the floor, ensconced in Nick's assured presence. It had been a sight to behold, rendering even the most cynical hearts hopeful that there was love for everyone.

Violet, the Duchess of Langley, and the hostess of the evening's soiree, sidled up to Bea in the hall, her eyes twinkling with mischief. "It seems our Pippa has finally managed to do more than just trip over her own feet," she whispered, a smile playing at the corners of her mouth.

Bea smiled with pride. "She didn't stumble into love. They were destined for each other."

Bea's cheeks warmed under Violet's scrutinizing look, the heat akin to the rush she received the moment she saw a certain figure emerge from the ballroom. He was about twenty feet away in the hall, seemingly unaware that she'd seen him.

"And with an oculist, no less. Who would have thought?" Violet chuckled, her gaze following the couple as they twirled. "Only Pippa could turn a mishap into a romance. And to think, it was sealed with the poison you administered from the apothecary's concoction." Violet looked over her shoulder and gave a nod.

Bea felt a flutter in her heart at the thought of the apothecary. Alfie Collins—the man who had unwittingly played Cupid to ensure Bea's cousin's happiness with Nick.

Violet turned her keen gaze onto Bea. "I will leave you to him." Her voice was laced with intrigue.

"Perhaps I ought to thank him?" Bea's question hung between them like a delicate scent, a confession of her fascination with the man that was impossible to ignore.

But after Violet returned to the ballroom, Bea felt the atmosphere changing around her.

She withdrew further into the hall. What else do you do at a ball when your dance card isn't full?

There was a shadow in the hall. The lively string quartet music seemed to fade into a distant echo as she moved toward the shadow that flickered at the edge of her vision.

Three doors down the hall from the main festivities, the corridor was dim, lit only by the occasional sconce whose flame danced in the draft. Here, the air held a hush, a pause in the breath of the night when Bea saw him—Alfie.

Turn away, don't be caught in the hall with a man. Particularly not this man.

From behind, he stood like a column of calm amidst the storm of the night's tumultuous celebrations. His broad shoulders tapered to a narrow waist, outlined against the sparse light. He was a silhouette of masculinity, strength, and grace. Even his rich velvet evening frock, less ostentatious than the sea of brocades and silks in the ballroom, spoke of a man who valued substance over show. And yet, there was a certain allure in the natural fit of his breeches, hinting at a vitality that spoke of both discipline and a life far removed from the sedentary pursuits of the typical gentleman.

Well, he was an apothecary and not a gentleman at all. For Bea, he was as much out of reach as a royal prince.

As if sensing her nearby, Alfie turned and his face came into view, featuring a strong jaw and muscles that twitched before his full lips curved into a smile. His perfect teeth gleamed just moments before the same sparkle appeared in his eyes. Then, he blinked and nodded his head in greeting to her. A flush of warmth climbed her cheeks, an involuntary response to the sudden intensity of eye contact with this dashing man.

Bea looked over her shoulder, checking that they were indeed alone in the hall. A shiver ran down her back, her neck prickled, and she burst into motion, heading toward him to do as she'd been taught: greet politely, and then pardon herself and leave.

Except she didn't want to leave.

With each step she took toward him, Bea felt like she was blooming under his intense gaze, as he watched her approach. As if she were stepping out of her skin, leaving behind the young woman who had entered the ball with no greater expectation than to fulfill her social obligations. Instead, she approached Alfie as one might approach a long-anticipated revelation, dutiful yet tinged with an embarrassment, more about the sudden depth of her feelings than any impropriety.

He seemed like one of those dangerous rakes her mother had warned her about, making women like Bea teeter at the edge of ruination—or at least he was handsome enough to fuel rumors if any existed. However, in the short time that Bea had come to know Alfie Collins, he had the admiration of his colleagues, the respect of his customers, and some sort of effect on her that made her breath hitch.

He was fascinating.

"Lady Beatrice." His voice had a rich timbre that resonated in the air around them. "I did not anticipate the pleasure of your company in such a secluded spot." He cocked his head as if to confirm that nobody overheard their conversation.

His words were simple yet laden with an unspoken understanding. They wrapped around her like a shawl, offering both comfort and a thrilling sense of being bound to him.

Bea barely found her voice but eventually replied with a grace she scarcely felt, "It seems we are both rather isolated this evening." The heat in Bea's cheeks subsided as she remembered the days before. He'd created a mixture from one of Pippa's plants in the orangery, ipecac, to purge her uncle's poison so that he'd be sober enough to consent to Nick's request for Pippa's hand tonight. It had been a deliciously clandestine affair, and now that it was over, Bea feared it would mean giving up something, or someone... Alfie.

ALFIE'S DEMEANOR CHANGED immediately. The music from the ball was in full swing but lightly muted, and Alfie had little interest in dancing in a room full of patients or potential patients. He could keep their secrets but not forget the rashes men hid from their wives nor the tricks the wives used to get their husbands to ... well, that was their problem, and he was here now with the most exquisite beauty in an emerald-green silk gown—the kind he wished to trail his fingers over when exploring her delicate curves.

Absolutely not!

Alfie shifted as if he could switch his thoughts to something more chaste.

But Bea was breathtaking, she didn't need the frills; she had the title, the beauty, and the intelligence to sparkle of her own accord. In the amber light of the hall, Alfie could see her lovely alabaster skin glowing with coveted rosiness. The crystal wall sconces softened the light so that Bea appeared as if she were lit from the inside.

And Alfie was hard with a force that he thought could smash granite.

She was a bit shorter than him, an advantage that allowed him quite the view. He could see the sheer muslin layer sticking out just enough to draw his eyes to the low cut of her bodice. It wasn't her first season, and Alfie knew she could take certain liberties, such as stronger colors and lower necklines. But he had no explanation for why she would be there alone with him in the hall rather than dancing with the aristocrats in the ballroom.

"You did it," Alfie said, in awe.

"My cousin is going to be a bride," Bea sighed, fingering the simple strand of pearls that cast the slightest of shadows on her collarbone.

"They are very much in love, and I am happy that my dear friend has found the love of his life," Alfie said. It was genuine, and he didn't dare deny Nick the splendor of true love.

So why did he feel pity for the beauty before him? Or was pity not the right word?

"How romantic of you, Mr. Collins." She blinked at him for an instant and then looked away. Even in the dim light, Alfie's expert eyes caught the blush rising to her cheeks.

"You were instrumental in ensuring the match, Lady Beatrice." He bowed, considering retreat, lest he cross a line with Pippa's cousin that a commoner like him must not. But he was just a man of flesh and blood, and she was a veritable angel of beauty, licking her lips and twirling the pearl strand around her finger in a way that stirred Alfie's most basic urges. No level of education from the finest faculties of alchemy and medicine could prepare him to cure what he was experiencing.

"I couldn't have done it if you hadn't created the ipecac mixture," Bea said.

"But you administered it, so it would have been worthless without you." *The world is worthless without you.* "Thanks to you, Pippa and Nick can marry. Without your intelligence, none of this would have worked."

She waved her hand in the air, and the pearls fell into the hollow of her neck. Alfie's brow twitched as he looked at the breathtaking interplay of iridescent sheen and the dew of her décolleté. Her beauty was genuinely disarming, even for a man who knew how to live out his urges.

"Will you be back at the orangery for more plants, Mr. Collins?"

He didn't like her calling him by his surname, using *Mister Collins*. So polite. So formal. So distant. He wished she'd consider him just a man, nothing special like an apothecary with the knowledge to mix and dispense medicine.

"If Pippa wishes it, I will be there."

"Why is it you call me Lady Beatrice, yet you call her Pippa?"

Alfie narrowed his brows. Had she read his mind?

"Only if you'll call me Alfie."

"Alfie, I'd very much like to show you the orange blossoms at the orangery. Do you think you could find any use for them?"

"Let them ripen into oranges," Alfie said with a nod as curt as he could muster, hoping she wouldn't know how strongly she affected him.

"And if you were to harvest the petals?"

Oh no, she couldn't possibly ask that. A beauty like her mustn't speak of aphrodisiacs like neroli oil derived from orange blossoms.

"For what purpose, Bea?" That rolled off his tongue far too quickly, bringing the sweetest pink to her cheeks.

"They smell lovely, and I thought you could take a few minutes to craft perfume."

"Neroli oil?"

"Is that orange blossom oil?"

"Yes. And it's an aphrodisiac."

She narrowed her gaze. "You mean it makes people fall in love?"

She was too sweet for her own good—the most dangerous and tantalizing combination of beautiful, smart, and curious.

Alfie surveyed the hall, still devoid of people. Why wasn't there a chaperone around?

He rubbed his neck, trying to remind himself that he was speaking to a member of the Ton. Pippa's cousin, the lovely Bea, had his stomach twisted in a knot, and thinking of her as he did was not acceptable.

Seducing a virgin noblewoman could have devastating repercussions for him. She was the daughter of the Earl of Dunmore, after all, and her parents were away on a diplomatic mission. The suspicion alone would scare his best customers away, and he'd lose the apothecary he'd built for years.

Alfie swallowed. Was there a bowl of ice water in which he could stick his head for a moment?

She blinked at him, still waiting for an answer.

"Aphrodisiacs don't make people fall in love. They tip the balance of desire in a certain direction."

"Toward lust?"

Alfie suppressed a groan. This was not a conversation he ought to have with her. Not here. Not ever.

"Yes. Passion even. Plus, orange blossoms are best picked when the dew is forming—around five in the morning—to capture the most fragrant moments."

She jerked her head back and focused on him so intently that he nearly felt naked. Then she dropped her chin, and her eyes focused on his. "Perhaps then, you can harvest the orange blossoms for neroli oil tomorrow? As a favor to me?"

Chapter Two

HE HAD TO work through an entire day at the apothecary before harvesting the orange blossoms for the neroli oil—an entire day before he could formulate a reason to see *her* again.

Alfie Collins, the apothecary at 87 Harley Street, was as much a dispenser of medicines as he was the keeper of secrets, including his own. His patients, often members of Britain's upper crust, the Ton, had to tell him what was wrong so that he could offer a cure—or at least something to alleviate their symptoms. Sometimes, he merely treated a cough, the pains of a broken bone healing, or ointments to help wounds close without infection.

But there were instances when his professional impartiality came at the cost of his convictions. That was a problem because he wished to tell men not to stray, women to be honest with their husbands, and children not to jump from high rocks. Instead, day after day, problems that could have been prevented presented in the form of well-paying patients, and thus, as long as he had provided the right ointment, tincture, or tea, his business thrived. His role demanded stoic impartiality, and his task was not to pass judgment on behaviors or ponder the morality of the various reasons that led these highborn men and women to his doorstep. Regardless of whether their conditions were of their own making.

He wished he could prevent maladies and injuries as much as

he could help to heal them. Pondering that, Alfie went to the waiting room of the shared practice, as he ought to on a Monday morning. It was where the other doctors gathered around Wendy Folsham, the nurse and younger sister of the oculist, Nick, Andre, the orthopedist, and Felix, the dentist, were already there. Wendy was holding cards with the names of their first patients of the day.

"Twisted ankle from a waltz," Wendy read the card for the Monday morning round-up.

Mornings after large balls were particularly fruitful for Andre the orthopedist, especially during the season when so many of the young debutantes danced on polished and slippery parquet.

"Thank you," he said, taking the note. "I'll get some ice before I see her, it was just delivered from Gatti's ice house." He gave Alfie a brotherly smile, said good morning, and left to find his patient.

"Miss Mary-Ann Portsmouth, governess to little Thomas Jackson." Wendy handed Felix the card. He let out a sigh.

"Drat. Another baby tooth she is making me check to ensure it is in perfect health," Felix said as he took the card. "After it has fallen out!"

Alfie laughed aloud. There was no end to their patients' eccentricities. He and Felix had one thing in common, and even though it might seem trivial to bystanders, it was pivotal to their careers: their skill and expertise had helped them to a position where the country's finest clients sought them out, but their expertise was not always required. More often than not, discretion, or merely listening to their patients' problems was all they could offer... because in reality there was no actual condition requiring a remedy, or an illness to cure. Felix had often told Alfie that he'd rather tackle a complicated gold cast bridge than explain how to angle a toothbrush and how much powder to use for a thorough cleaning. Correspondingly, Alfie much preferred to be stumped by a cure that he'd have to mix than to pick a pre-made vial from his shelf—for one of the many common and predictable ailments, or underlying injuries, usually the result of the Ton's indiscretions. Both Felix and Alfie were capable of innovation and sought to perform medical marvels, rather than drown in daily routines without challenges.

"Pardon me, I'm late." Nick appeared from his second-floor bed chamber, fastening the last button of his shirt and tugging at his cravat. "What have I missed?"

"A few hours of sleep because you were with your fiancée until the early morning?" Alfie asked with a knowing look at Nick's disheveled hair.

Nick glowered back at him, but his eyes didn't hide his happiness.

"Has she slept here?" Wendy's disapproval colored her tone.

"Ahem… we were still loaded with adrenaline after the ball, and talked until it was later at night." Nick cast Alfie a wide-eyed look, waiting to see whether Wendy would approve of the poor excuse for a scandalous night. "Wedding planning," he added for good measure.

"Hmpf!" Wendy crossed her arms as if the argument of a well-planned wedding trumped propriety. "I suppose, as a lady, she has certain expectations for the ceremony?"

"Let them be. They're in love." Alfie gave Nick a brotherly smile.

Only nine hours earlier, Alfie had been standing next to Nick and his fiancée Pippa when they caused a scandal at the Earl and Countess of Langley's ball. Only eight and a half hours earlier, he'd been in a deserted corridor with Bea.

They'd all returned late and got little sleep. Alfie hadn't gotten any, however, because he couldn't stop thinking about Bea. Still, he couldn't let the others know about his infatuation with the beautiful woman far above his station. No matter how much he desired her, the fact was they'd never be together. Even just being seen together could cause her disgrace and that was something he'd never do to her. Better to stay silent about his feelings before Wendy—canny, observant Wendy, obsessed with romance—figured them out.

He gave Felix a smirk. "You know the governess is not here because of the child but for *you*." But Felix didn't pay him any attention. They all knew that he was holding out for the long-lost love of his life, the daughter of his professor.

"And Lady Beatrice is here for you," Wendy said as she turned to Alfie. "I don't have a card."

"Lady Beatrice is here for me?" Alfie rubbed the back of his neck, hoping the pricked-up halls would settle. But at the mention of the gorgeous strawberry blonde's name, everything stood alert, including the parts Alfie rather wished to hide.

"Yes, Lady Beatrice Wetherby, you remember, the wealthy heiress in Debrett's who's already rejected twenty-four suitors and yet, is still a coveted guest at London's most prominent balls?" Wendy's remark was right on point, though perhaps tinged with humor.

Alfie had lost count of how many times ladies of the Ton had come to him and asked for a hair dye that would give that exact shade of light blond with a copper shimmer or a rouge that shone rosily on the cheeks 'just like Lady Beatrice.'

It was true, and Alfie couldn't deny it either: Lady Beatrice was the most beautiful woman he'd ever seen—not just at the ball, not just of the season, not just in England. Alfie had seen, touched, kissed, and pleasured women from Vienna to Delhi, but never had he been caught off guard as he had the night before.

And she was waiting for him.

Chapter Three

Earlier that morning, at Cloverdale House, on Abbotsbury Road, London...

BEA OPENED THE drawer of her dressing table and retrieved her mother's latest letter. Tattered from the many times Bea had read it, it showed as much wear as her nerves.

Singapore, March 11, 1819.

Dearest Beatrice,

We left the port of Singapore, and hearts and sails set toward home. It is with a sentiment most earnest that I entertain the anticipation of beholding you, not merely as the daughter we left behind but as a lady ensconced in the felicitous state of matrimony. Should this expectation be greeted by disappointment, and you find yourself still unattached, pray and allow no disquiet to trouble your heart. Your father, in his boundless wisdom and regard for your future felicity, has pledged his most vigorous endeavors to secure a match of unimpeachable nobility and suitability for you.

With the fullness of time marching inexorably forward, it behooves us to remember that the season for securing such advantageous connections is fleeting. A young lady of virtues and education must seek a husband who both appreciates her merits and can elevate her station. Thus, it is with a mother's urgency and concern that I impress upon you the gravity of this period in your life. I urge you to apply yourself with renewed vigor to this most critical of pursuits so that you might soon grace us with the joyous tidings of an engagement.

I remain, with the sincere expectations for your imminent success,

Your mother,
Lady Claudia Wetherby

No love. No missing her. Just a slur of expectations wrapped in a neat little letter that read more like a warning between the lines despite the seemingly loving platitudes. Her mother's missive was clear: *Marry or I'll see to it when I return.*

A knock.

"Bea, are you there?" Pippa peeked into Bea's chamber from behind the door.

"Come in!" But when Bea saw Pippa, her breath hitched. "You're wearing a veil!"

In nothing but her white muslin nightgown and a bridal veil, Pippa swayed into the room as if carried by a cloud until she stopped in front of Bea. She pushed her spectacles up her nose and beamed. "What do you think?"

Bea tapped her index finger on her mouth and tried to suppress a chuckle. Although Pippa was all grown up, this was rather like in their childhood when they'd wear a crochet tablecloth over their heads and would dance like brides with each other. That had been pretend play, but this was real. Bea's smile gave way to a heaviness in her heart. In only a few days, Pippa would be Mrs. Folsham and move to the townhouse near Nick's practice. She'd never storm into Bea's chamber in her nightgown again; she'd be all grown up and Bea would be alone.

"So the stitching of the crochet hem is lovely, the right shade to complement your complexion," Bea started. Pippa twirled in her nightgown as if it were the finest wedding dress. "But the cinching at the waist of the dress needs work." Bea gave Pippa's side a friendly pinch through the nightgown just like she had done when they were little girls. They both burst into laughter at Pippa's ridiculous dress and then Bea sighed. "It's a lovely veil, dear cousin. You'll be such a beautiful bride."

Pippa dropped her hands to the sides, but Bea didn't want her troubles to cast a shadow over Pippa's happiness and gave her a hug. "I'll move out. I've overstayed my welcome. You have plans for Cloverdale House as a rehabilitation center and you're readying your new home with Nick."

Her cousin tore herself from her arms and took a wide step back. "Where would you go? I didn't plan to do anything with your chambers. You're welcome as long as you like." But Pippa's voice fell as if she realized what she'd said. There'd always be room for the former diamond of the first water who'd been too picky to catch a husband.

"It's all here in Mother's letter. I need a husband to be free from the expectation—"

"But you never wanted your inheritance to fall into the hands of a gentleman of the Ton. You said they'd probably gamble it all away." Pippa's protest rang true. Most men—especially those without wealth of their own whom she'd met in the Ton expected to gain their brides' fortunes. For Bea, that meant losing her independence in exchange for a husband and a life of social pressure among the Ton, not quite a fair exchange in either of their opinions. She sighed.

"It's rather morbid, isn't it? As a lady of station, I have to write my life over to a man to seek freedom, and thus exchange autonomy for something I can't be sure I understand or want."

"Marriage, you mean? How could you not want it?" It was everything they'd been raised to pursue as high-ranking ladies.

"Oh, Pippa! None of the men I've come to know at the balls shall control my life; I want to take charge of myself."

Pippa narrowed her gaze and Bea thought about her mother's expectations. She'd disappoint her even though she'd been a diamond of the first water at every ball—none of which her mother ever saw anyway because she'd been away.

The letter had been sent nearly five months ago. It could be weeks, or perhaps mere days before her parents arrived in London. Bea could not tell how much time she had left before her parents would assign her a husband. If she wanted to have any say in the husband she'd have to have, Bea had to find one posthaste.

Bea inhaled and thought about who she knew, but not a single man in the ballroom of the previous night caught her eye. The most common trait of the men in attendance at this most recent ball at the Langleys was voyeurism and gloating.

"You know," Pippa started, speaking slowly and enunciating every word as if she'd formulated each as it had come to her, "I unleashed quite a grand scandal at Violet's ball last night. You rather relished staging the coup with Alfie, didn't you?" Bea bit her lip as bile rose to her throat at the memories. The supposed "nobility" had systematically singled Pippa out at balls and set her traps with folded-over carpet corners, so she'd trip. Those allegedly coveted "gentlemen" of the Ton had stepped out of the way when Pippa had stumbled. The ladies had been anything but ladylike in requesting the music to stop when Pippa made a mistake, adding emphasis to her embarrassment. Then Nick had seen her—truly seen her, the brilliant, beautiful woman that Bea knew—and he'd appreciated her. Then he fell in love with her and was going to be her husband. Together they'd do more for society—rich and poor—than the supposedly highborn "best people" of the Ton.

"After all these years in which you stood by me when I was mocked, hazed, and even cruelly excluded from society because of my clumsiness—due to my poor vision—you were always there. And if it weren't for your help, I couldn't have gotten engaged to Nick."

"You could have eloped."

Pippa cocked her head. "I'd never want to marry without you by my side."

The irony wasn't lost on Bea. The oculist had seen Pippa for who she was and had fixed her vision with mere spectacles. But he'd also magnified the Ton's cruelty in Bea's eyes. Nick was a contrast to those self-indulgent gentlemen who were anything but gentle in manners to Pippa.

Even though they were always kind to Bea, their hypocrisy was not lost on her. What if she had a double chin one day, grew round with a child, and developed frown lines on her forehead? She wanted a man who loved her for more than her appearance, not one who'd discard her if—or more likely, when—her beauty faded.

Especially not when she always had an outbreak of what Mother called "the beast" looming under her skin. Unexpected, hard to control, and unsightly. It was her fatal flaw, and no one knew about it. Instead, they only saw the beautiful Bea. They didn't know that she often didn't attend balls, not out of pettiness but because Mother made her hide until "the beast" subsided and her skin was once again flawless in others' eyes.

"You could be so beautiful if you just controlled the red-hot beast within," Mother had always said. Never—not once—had she offered help to soothe Bea's itchy skin or suggested a hug to support her while she healed. It had always been a shameful affront to Mother's social sensibilities to have a daughter who could be "so pretty if it weren't for 'the beast'." But Bea had never learned how to control the beast and earn her mother's affection. It just overcame her, and she didn't even know when it loomed under her skin. For as long as she could think, she'd sometimes wake up, face reddened with bumps, and her hair looking like straw atop a feisty strawberry. And then her mother would lock her up in her bedchamber until the outbreak subsided. It usually took almost a fortnight.

Even before her debut season, missing so many social events was an inexcusable offense to Society, and her mother couldn't bear the pain of watching "the beast wallow in self-pity," so she joined her father on his diplomatic mission in Southeast Asia.

And Bea had lost all interest in the Ton.

She didn't want to be the queen at a ball where guests considered shaming her beloved cousin a sport.

Nor did she want to dance with any of the men, first sons or not, who put a coat hanger by the door to look like a butler so that Pippa would take her leave from an object, in front of everyone. And never ever—Bea growled like an angry cat at the thought—would she *marry* any of them.

"I have certain criteria for a husband; I won't just pick anyone." Bea plopped on her bed and folded her hands as if the decision had been made. She'd get married and she knew exactly what the groom would be like. The only question remained as to the identity of her future husband. Didn't that make perfect sense?

Pippa crossed her arms and shook her head as if her veil were an extension of her long blond hair. "Pray tell me the criteria, please! I must hear them."

"So, number one, he has to love me."

"Aha!"

"This is non-negotiable," Bea added for good measure, unsure what her cousin's knowing smirk meant in response to this self-explanatory element. She'd grown up scalded by her mother and envied by everyone else's mothers. Bea had never had love, the unconditional kind from the books and yet, that was what she wanted.

"What's number two?" Pippa gave her such a stern look that Bea thought her mother was in the room.

"Number two, he mustn't be an English aristocrat."

"What?"

"Nick isn't!"

"No, but he's a doctor!"

Bea threw her arms in the air as if that said everything… but she truly hadn't said much at all. Her determination not to marry an aristocrat stemmed from a deeper, more personal motive. She wanted to spite her mother and the other matrons who insisted that a good match was the only way she could have value in Society—as if she had nothing else to offer but her aristocratic womb. Her mother's relentless pressure to conform to those expectations had fueled a deep resentment within Bea. Defying them on this point felt important.

"I'm afraid to ask number three now," Pippa said.

"I want passion. Not just stolen kisses, flowers, and dances at balls with a beau of the Ton. I want toe-curling, hair-raising, scream-out-loud pleasure." Bea swallowed and waited for Pippa's reaction.

"Is this because of what Violet said Henry did to her?"

"No." *Yes, of course it is! How else could I know any of this?* Their friend Violet, now the Countess of Langley, had told the two young debutantes about the benefits of matrimony. "That's what I want—not the dull marriages where love is replaced by suitability, lust by companionship, and passion by quick releases. I want more than women of our station usually get." She sighed.

Pippa nodded. "That's the best of the three reasons."

"It is?"

Pippa shrugged. "When you know, you know. It'll take your breath away, make your heart race, your... *ahem*... toes curl. So, yes."

"Do you have that with Nick?"

Pippa nodded and took the pins from her veil. Then she carefully removed it and held it between her hands. "And I hope you'll find someone who can fulfill all of your criteria. When you do, this will be reserved for you." Pippa held the veil to Bea's hair and Bea gasped.

She held the sheer fabric up and turned her head to see how long it draped over her back. It was lovely, oh so pretty. Bea sighed, dramatically.

"What is it, Bea? What's wrong?"

"Oh Pippa, honestly. Though it's lonely at times, at least while my parents are away, I am free, for a bit, and can act of my own accord. Once they return, Mother is certain to persuade

Father that I should marry before I turn two and twenty." Bea didn't dare think about the matches she might be forced into.

"Your time will come Bea, and you too will find your perfect love," Pippa replied in a singsong voice.

"But first, you will have a lovely wedding, Pippa," Bea said, though when she turned around, Pippa had already left the room, the door still open to the hall, giving Bea the chance to admire herself with the veil just a little longer.

Truth be told, she didn't need any of the pomp and circumstance of a long courtship and elegant balls to announce an engagement. She'd much rather have the sort of love where the man of her dreams couldn't keep his hands off her, and his kisses made her shudder with pleasure and the need for more.

And she was running out of time to find such a man if he existed outside of her dreams indeed. As soon as her parents returned, well, it was best not to think about it.

Bea eyed herself in her dressing mirror and shuffled on her seat, reminding herself of her goal of finding a husband before her parents returned from Singapore, where her father was a diplomat.

She knew his mission involved extensive negotiations with local leaders and coordination with colonial administrators to secure British influence in the newly established colony, and wasn't resentful at all. Her mother had gone with him this time, and she often sent letters and even the newest atlas that finally showed Singapore as a founded state in February. They'd been gone since Bea was sixteen; she hadn't seen them for over three years. Which meant her mother hadn't seen Bea reject twenty-four suitors from the finest families in her first season the year before. But Bea was also aware of the truth.

Her mother had no idea how disinterested Bea had become in the Ton, and the season.

Bea exhaled and looked in the mirror only to see her mother's eyes staring back at her. The same cool scrutiny and strict expectations shot at her.

She walked over to her escritoire, where she kept her stationery, ink, and atlas. She flipped through the pages and found Singapore. Her history books and atlases were friendly companions when Bea was locked away with the vicious red rash—the one they called *the beast*. She'd filled her mind with images of places she longed to visit and the various conflicts of other nations.

Whenever she could find descriptions of disputes, she studied their interests. Father dismissed her as naïve for even considering the opposing views to British imperial interests. "It's not a matter for girls to think about," he would say. "Don't worry your pretty little head about politics and diplomacy." Meanwhile, her mother told her she was developing a double chin from studying the books and maps for too long, or developing frown lines on her forehead when she thought too hard.

Bea knew her time at Cousin Pippa's was growing short. It had been wonderful. She was able to read and study and always enjoyed hearing the latest opinions on matters that the papers only rudimentarily reported on.

When her parents had set sail, Bea had moved to Cloverdale House to live with Cousin Pippa and her father, Lord William Pemberton, the Duke of Sussex. And Bea had been happy there. The large estate was surrounded by beautiful gardens that had been opened up as a park for the public. It was an idyllic setting.

Bea swallowed a lump. She wasn't usually so down. But now that Pippa was getting married and planned to convert the estate into a rehabilitation center, Bea had to find somewhere else to live. She didn't want to get in the way of the newlyweds or become a permanent nuisance for the patients, once the rehabilitation center opened.

All things considered, Bea had been a house guest for too long. Since her parents had left, three seasons had come and gone, and there hadn't been a single suitor that actually stirred anything within her heart.

Not that there hadn't been suitors. As those closest to her

liked to remind her, there'd been twenty-four of record. They had all blended into a blur of uninteresting candidates her mother would approve of. None of them captured Bea's interest, much less her heart. There was simply nothing to recommend them to her. No wit. No intelligence. No spark.

None of them had been worth even the grace of a courtship. First sons, second sons, titles and riches that would make any woman swoon at their mention alone, in combination with the castles, estates, and promises of a lifetime in society they offered—all left Bea cold. She didn't want any of it, because she already had it. What she didn't have was true love and the tingling that Violet had when she spoke about her husband, Henry, Earl of Langley.

So, where would she get a husband from before her parents returned?

One who'd satisfy criteria one and two?

The handsome apothecary came to mind, Alfie Collins. Someone like that would be… *oh,* Bea sighed from deep within.

She'd ask Violet for ideas. If anyone knew how to orchestrate a *coup d'état*, it was Violet, the newly minted Countess of Langley.

Chapter Four

A few hours later, at 87 Harley Street, London.

THE DAY HAD dragged on, but Alfie's mind wasn't in his apothecary. He sorted the paper packets of chamomile, calendula, and fennel teas into the wooden drawer by the strongbox under the counter, where he kept the day's earnings. Though he'd recorded every transaction, he didn't truly take note.

Instead, his mind wandered to the stunning woman he'd encountered at the ball—or outside the ballroom, to be more precise. *Lady* Beatrice. Even though they only worked together briefly to administer the ipecac to Pippa's father, the clandestine operation had quite an impact on him. He couldn't explain it nor rationalize it. Why he was so depressed that it was over—when their mission had been such a success? Alfie found himself unable to return to his usual life—the boring one without her in it—but there was nothing he could do about it.

It made no sense, of course, but it didn't need to, for the feeling to be real.

Alfie had been a lucky man, able to have every woman he'd ever fancied in any way that he'd wanted her. Yet, each woman now faded into a distant shadow in his memory, outshone by the sparkle in Bea's eyes and the quirky asymmetry of her smile. Bea had an innate beauty that had altered something within him, like that whispered tilt of dawn or dusk, when the skies blend seamlessly into one another, and time itself seems to pause in reverence.

It was ironic, truly, as Alfie's medical education had trained him to appreciate symmetry, yet with Bea, he realized that all he ever knew fell short of the perfection she embodied. He was in awe of her. In fact, Bea was so perfect in every way that this tiny quirk endeared her to him even more. He'd noticed it the first time Pippa had introduced her, but at the ball last night, he had the enormous pleasure of watching it build slowly: Her smile. It started first in the corner of her left side, rose to a slight dimple, and then the other caught up, bringing out her rows of immaculate white teeth. Her lips, painted by nature's own delicate brush, promised tender kisses and passionate declarations that could soothe the weariest of souls. She had a million intelligent thoughts but seemed to suppress them, unwilling to share, yet casting an expectant gaze as if she waited to see if he could guess.

And that was the problem.

She was meant to want more and to declare her love to some aristocrat. A titled man of the Ton would one day woo her, kiss her, and—Alfie nearly cast up his accounts—make her his wife. Alfie hated the lucky bastard already.

And he hated himself for standing before her without so much as paying her a proper compliment the night before.

Instead, he'd promised to pick orange blossoms. Why didn't he suggest weeding her garden or fixing her roof while he was already there? It wasn't as though he could ever lay a hand on her.

Yet, he hadn't been able to think of anything else.

The bell over the door rang, and a customer walked in. Alfie sighed and let his daydreams fade into the present.

"Mr. Collins, how do you do?" Viscount Mountbatten-Clyde was nearly fifty, with gentle eyes and a hunched back. Although he suffered from various minor ailments, he'd been generally in good health until his recent diagnosis of palpitations.

"I'm here to try the foxglove," the viscount said. "Is it ready yet?"

"Of course, Lord Mountbatten-Clyde, but I would have delivered it to you myself," Alfie said as he opened one of the little drawers that covered part of the wall behind him.

"You'll learn one thing, son: never assign something to others that you truly need. If you want it done right, there is no better way than to do it yourself."

"Well, I have three dosages here and recommend starting with an infusion of the leaves. No more than three per day to begin."

The viscount accepted the paper envelope with dried digitalis leaves and smelled it. Despite his station, Alfie knew he never sent a servant to pick up his medicine. He also knew he couldn't tolerate anything bitter and always chose the blandest mixtures Alfie could offer.

"Blah! What's the second option?"

Alfie momentarily shut his open demeanor as if drawing the curtains on his patience. He couldn't tell his patient how many hours he'd spent finding just the right teas to mask the taste of the foxglove and how it had affected him tasting a medicine he didn't need so that he could create a palatable version for the viscount. *I know you despise the bitterness. That's why I tasted your medicine.*

"Very well, my lord, the next would be the powdered leaf. This only requires two doses daily." Alfie retrieved a small measuring spoon the size of a ladle for dolls that measured exactly five grams. "Don't exceed two doses per day, one in the morning and one at night."

The viscount uncorked the glass flask with the grayish-green powder and grimaced. "What should I mix this with? Whiskey?"

"Nothing. You may drink tea afterward to help swallow it."

The older man shook his head. "I'm afraid that this won't work, Mr. Collins."

Alfie suppressed the urge to groan and looked at the wall

clock over the shelf. It was already after four o'clock. He'd wanted to harvest the petals nearly twelve hours ago at daybreak when the dew was forming. Now, it was already late in the afternoon, and he hadn't seen Bea—not that he would have at daybreak, but he'd wished to be closer to her than he was now.

He was no fool. He knew he couldn't have her, but he was drawn to her like Icarus to the sun, knowing that his waxen wings would melt the closer he got. But Bea was the kind of woman for which one would plummet into the open sea. She was sweet and intelligent, yet she had a warmth about her that was utmostly feminine. She'd administered the most bitter-tasting ipecac to the Duke of Sussex, and he hadn't even noticed. She was brilliant.

"Mr. Collins?"

Alfie woke from his stupor and shook his head. "I'm so sorry. If you experience anything out of the ordinary, stop using this and come back," he said as he wrapped the vial with the clear alcohol solution of distilled foxglove in a piece of paper and tied it with a string.

"Everything gives me palpitations, so I don't know what would be out of the ordinary." The viscount corked the vial with the powder and returned it to the counter. "Thank you for the liquor version; it'll be easier to swallow."

"You must not take more than one drop. Should you accidentally put two in your glass, throw it out, rinse it, and take another."

"I don't rinse my glasses, Mr. Collins. But all right. What am I looking for in *force majeure* situations?"

"Nausea, vomiting, diarrhea, blurred vision, seeing halos or yellow-green distortions around lights, confusion, or any unusual sensation in your chest," Alfie said, cutting the string he'd just tied and handing the medicine to the Viscount.

"Thank you." The Viscount added it to his tab and left.

Alfie eyed the clock. It was almost time for dinner.

"Alfie!" Andre's voice emanated from the hall, and the bell over his door rang. "I need some arnica ointment for a little patient." He walked in and carried a young girl in his arms. She was no older than six and had two thick, black braids.

"Who have we here?" Alfie said kindly, trying to forget that the time to harvest the orange blossoms had almost passed. There wouldn't be time to see Bea again.

"Miss Charlotte Harrington," a young woman with a dignified accent said as she followed Andre into Alfie's apothecary.

Andre set the little girl down on a chair and pulled the stool from underneath so she could rest her leg on it. "She fell off the swing."

"Oh, that hurts. It happened to me once," Alfie said kindly, tilting his head toward the top right drawer where he had a tin of arnica ointment ready. Andre took it out behind the counter while Alfie squatted before the little girl. "When I fell off the swing, I thought for a moment that I could fly."

"Really?" The little girl sniffled and licked a tear that had rolled onto her lips.

"Oh yes. It was in Austria, in the Alps. When you swing so high in the mountains, the air is thin, and you think you can soar like a bird. Did you feel like that?"

She shook her head and eyed her bruised knee. The skin was barely scraped, but a swelling was building underneath. It would heal in less than three days unless she fell again on the exact same spot—which children sometimes did.

"How did it feel in the moment just before the landing?" Alfie asked.

"I don't know." She sniffled again.

Andre rustled behind Alfie and produced a cold compress, which he carefully laid on the girl's knee. She winced.

"You know, there's glory in the landing, too. Mine at the time was more like a flop." Alfie watched the girl grimace as the essential oils from the compress began to take action. He smelled the witch hazel Andre had applied, which would have been his preferred astringent, too.

"I came upon Miss Charlotte and her nanny at Regent Park

on my way home," Andre explained.

That was the first time Alfie paid attention to the woman who'd watched them. She was pretty, with lush lips and dark lashes. There was a time when he would have invited her for a glass of wine and perhaps more, but that time seemed so long ago. He couldn't explain why, but even last week seemed a lifetime ago—a lifetime before he'd met Bea.

Andre removed the compress, and the little girl hissed. Her knee was bony, but her shins still had such a childish layer of fat that Alfie had to smile.

"I'm sure that you'll heal quickly, and if you ever fall again, you remember that there is glory in the thump you make when you land," Andre said as he opened the ointment and scooped a glob out with a spatula from Alfie's drawer. They worked seamlessly together, as Andre knew where to find the most common medicines he needed daily. Correspondingly, Alfie had learned to make sure the supplies were replenished every morning.

"There's also glory in getting up again," the woman said.

"This is Miss Cassandra Shaw, a substitute teacher at St. George's School for Girls," Andre explained with a man-to-man stare that spoke volumes. Alfie shared a look of his own: *Don't worry, she's yours.*

At the same time, he said, "It's a pleasure to make your acquaintance, Miss Shaw." Alfie inclined his head but then turned back to the little girl. "And if you limp a little until the swelling goes down, remember that anyone who limps has once fallen but has also had the strength to get up."

"So this is a glorious injury?" The little girl said with a half-smile.

"And a most honorable one. A rite of passage, if you will."

"Passing to what?" the girl asked.

"From a child to a professional on the swing. You'll be more careful from now on, but you'll also hold on better and swing higher."

"Like a bird in the sky?" She beamed. "Or the trapeze artist at the circus?"

"As long as you're safe, you can be anything you want." Alfie winked at her.

"Let's put some ice on this now." Andre scooped her back up in his arms.

After Andre and his little patient with the pretty teacher had gone, Alfie shut the door. Ice was an excellent idea. Perhaps he should cool his mind and try not to think of Bea lest he swing too high and plummet most inelegantly to his doom. Getting caught with a nobleman's daughter wouldn't allow him a second chance in life. And becoming the apothecary he was with a practice in the heart of London had cost him too much—he wasn't willing to squander his career and livelihood for a fling.

Then why did the thought of not going after Bea sting so much?

Chapter Five

Meanwhile, at Brunswick House upon Thames…

As usual, in the aftermath of the ball, Bea had taken the carriage to visit her old acquaintance, Violet, the Countess of Langley, who'd hosted the ball and set up the coup that had catapulted Pippa into the epicenter of the season.

The morning sun spilled through the lace curtains of Violet's dining room, casting a soft, golden glow across the array of breakfast foods laid out on the table. Still feeling the echoes of last night's ball in her weary muscles, Bea anticipated a morning filled with light conversation about the event and perhaps some speculation on the coup that had been the talk of the Ton. However, as she entered the room, a different situation occurred. The butler led Bea to the table instead of Violet's drawing room for the usual tea.

"Oh, Bea, I hoped you'd be here in time!" Despite the puffy circles under her eyes that betrayed her lack of sleep, Violet was always the picture of elegance, even at this early hour. She was serving herself a generous portion of coddled eggs.

"In time for what?" Bea asked when one footman pulled a chair back for her to sit and another poured her a cup of coffee.

What was most unusual, however, was Violet chewing with vigor and stuffing half a slice of toast in her mouth. "Hungry?"

she sputtered as if her appetite had left her no time to swallow before her next bite.

Bea tried not to grimace, but her stomach growled at the sight of the lovely display of the breakfast set for guests, which usually didn't include her. The table was covered with dishes of kippers, several tiny white bowls of what she knew to be jams, covered by notched lids and porcelain spoons sticking out of a small hole in each one, as well as racks filled with fresh, toasted bread, and a pot of steaming tea promising to round off the hearty meal.

Yet it wasn't the food nor her hostess' insatiable appetite this morning that caught Bea off guard. Instead, it was the guest who entered the dining room after she'd taken a seat. He was a young man, dashing in a worldly way that words seldom captured, with an easy manner that spoke of good breeding and intelligence that flickered in his dark eyes. His politeness was evident in the slight bow he offered Bea, a gesture of respect that seemed almost from another era.

Or another country.

Bea knew Debrett's well and couldn't recall anyone who'd matched his description, much less anyone of any status whom she hadn't met before.

"There you are. How good of you to join us for breakfast." Violet pressed the napkin to her mouth and nodded toward the seat across from Bea. The guest took his place with all the elegance of a true gentleman, one hand behind his back and a curt incline to thank his hostess.

"Good morning," he said, his voice warm and inviting, filling the space between them with an immediate sense of familiarity.

Aha! He was titled, or else he wouldn't dare forego the etiquette of more formal forms of address when dining with the Countess of Langley.

As soon as he spoke, Bea realized that he wasn't English, but she couldn't pinpoint the slight accent—a combination of a French lilt and the Russian rolling "r," and yet, it was neither.

"I see the preserves from the orchards have arrived," he said, and Violet waved grandly at the little porcelain jam pots.

Oh no, Violet was already plotting something, and Bea hadn't even had time to ask her for help.

"Lady Beatrice Wetherby, may I formally introduce you to our esteemed guest who found himself at our doorstep last night, seeking shelter after the ball?" Violet's eyes sparkled with the thrill of the introduction, a secret pleasure in the orchestration of social connections that was a hallmark of her character.

He was impeccably dressed in cream-colored breeches, polished riding boots, a dark blue waistcoat, and a matching velvet coat. This man was not searching for shelter; he was a surprise house guest.

Then, turning to the young man, whose polite interest had sharpened into keen anticipation at Violet's preamble, she continued, "Prince Ferdinand Constantin Maximilian Hohenzollern-Sigmaringen, this is Lady Beatrice. She is a cherished friend of this household, with a keen wit and a generous spirit that endears her to all who know her."

"A display of sweet delights for me this morning," the prince said, looking at Bea rather than the jams.

Taking the seat across from her, Bea couldn't help but smile, the formality of their introduction melting away in the face of his flattery.

So Violet had a prince in store after the ball.

Cunning.

Smart.

Bea had to give her credit; she was a master manipulator of humankind.

She met Violet's gaze momentarily, and they understood each other perfectly.

"Stan is a Hohenzollern and has traveled widely," Violet started.

"I'm only a Hohenzollern on my mother's side, I'm afraid," he said as he lifted a cup of coffee to his mouth.

"Prince Constantin Ferdinand Maximilian—" Bea started. No, that didn't sound correct. She furrowed her brows.

"Ferdinand Constantin Maximilian Hohenzollern-Sigmaringen," Violet corrected her.

"Right." Bea shot her a *thank-you-for-embarrassing-me* look. There was a reason one had the chance to memorize the names of aristocrats in order before the balls, lest this exact embarrassment occur where one forgot the order of someone else's given names.

"My friends call me Stan; it's part of Constantin," he said with a smile. Bea cocked her head. How did Violet know that misspeaking his name would put her on a friendly basis of using their given names so quickly?

He spooned the strawberry jam onto... that couldn't be right. Before she could say anything, Violet reacted.

"That's jam," her friend pointed out. Apparently, she also thought he was concocting something incorrect for his breakfast.

"I know. Strawberry. Brought fresh in a barrel from Somerset," Stan said, now swirling his teaspoon in a bowl of clotted cream and custard with the strawberry jam instead of layering them on the toast.

The mixture turned into a frothy pink mass. Disgusting.

Then, he brought the spoon with the connection to his mouth and closed his eyes to savor it.

Bea wasn't sure if she'd cringed visibly, but when the prince saw her, he chuckled.

"Where I'm from, we pair foods differently than the English. My apologies if my habits offend you."

"Not at all, Your Highness." Bea inclined her head as was polite and busied herself with the napkin's folds in her lap lest he see disgust on her face.

"Just Stan, please. I don't dwell on formality, Lady Beatrice." As she looked up, he wiped his hands on his napkin and put one hand to his heart. "Sometimes, I miss the simple breakfasts I grew up with at Bran Castle. I had a governess with deep roots in the agriculture of the nearby Braşov, so there was always fresh *brânză de vaci*." He pronounced the Romanian with the distinct ease of a polyglot. She'd heard the language before; it was close to Latin.

"Is it a type of marmalade with custard?" Bea asked.

"No," he chuckled. "It's cow's milk cheese, a very soft and creamy kind. I've had similar in Greece, Bulgaria, Poland, and even in Austria, Lady Beatrice. Just not in England."

"You have reservations toward our country?" Bea wished she hadn't asked when Violet shot her a look filled with daggers—sharp ones.

"I always value fresh cheese and fruit over the hypocrisy of etiquette. When a person means to be respectful, there are ways other than platitudes to show that."

His earnestness was refreshing after all the men she'd met at Almack's, and Bea couldn't help but trust this prince already.

"Bea. My friends merely call me Bea." Heat rushed to her face and neck.

He smiled and ate his odd mixture with a visible appetite.

"Braşov is in Transylvania," Violet explained.

"I know. It's surrounded by the Southern Carpathians," Bea said, reaching for a slice of the buttered toast.

Stan gave her an appreciative nod.

Violet, however, signaled "no" with her head, which meant as much as "don't bore him with your recitation of geographical trivia."

"Stan is the fourth son of a noble family with deep roots in European aristocracy," Violet said with the gravitas of a matchmaking matron and not the young woman she was. "From what I've gathered, the prince has devoted himself to studying international relations, languages, and military tactics, proving himself to be both a scholar and a capable officer. Is that right, Your Highness?"

"You flatter me, Violet." He reached for a slice of toast, too. "But it's true. I've only recently arrived in England."

THE SCENT OF INTUITION

"So you were on the continent during the Napoleonic war?" Bea asked. "How exciting!" She clapped her hands together and immediately regretted it when she felt Violet's triumphant stare. "I mean, it was surely dangerous."

The young man chuckled, the sound rich and inviting, and Bea felt a flicker of intrigue. "I suppose there's an adventure to be had in every new experience," he mused, his eyes meeting hers across the table. "Though I must confess, my own preferences lean toward simpler fare."

As they conversed, Bea learned that he was on a short stay in England, a mysterious detail that lent an exotic allure to his already intriguing persona because he was going to depart soon.

Please take me with you. Anywhere as far away from London as possible.

His observations on English customs, delivered with a blend of wit and genuine curiosity, drew Bea into a conversation that felt as comfortable as it was captivating.

Violet, watching the exchange with a knowing smile, seemed pleased with the unfolding dynamics. Here, under the guise of a simple breakfast, was the beginning of a connection that promised to chart an unexpected course.

"The region of Brașov is caught between powerful forces," Stan explained over breakfast. Me too, Bea thought to herself. "The Austrians, with their relentless ambition, seek to exploit the gold mines nestled deep within the Carpathian Mountains, draining the land of its natural wealth. Meanwhile, the looming presence of the Ottoman Empire casts long shadows over the region, an ever-present threat that seems to press in from all sides."

"Thus Bran Castle stands as a solitary sentinel amidst this turmoil?" Bea asked, and the prince gave her another nod, this time laced with a smile.

Bea felt a kinship with that castle—surrounded, besieged by external pressures, yet standing tall. Her own heart was a territory coveted by the ambitions and desires of others, each moment a battle for autonomy. Just as the mountains hemmed in the region, her choices seemed constrained by duty and expectation. But amid that encirclement, there was a strength within her, a resolve as enduring as the stone of a fortress. She knew she must navigate the treacherous landscape with care, seeking a path that honored both her heart and her obligations. And yet, even though she owned a collection of atlases for physical topography, they didn't show her the path forward when it involved landscapes of the heart.

The distance between London and Brașov seemed like a refuge, but something about it felt wrong and hollow. Why was he so far from the lands he was meant to rule, and could this mysterious prince truly offer her everything her heart desired?

With each shared laugh and exchanged glance, Bea's initial surprise gave way to a realization. With his intelligent eyes and easy charm, Violet's guest had transformed a routine morning into a moment brimming with possibility. As they continued to talk, navigating the nuances of English breakfast traditions and their respective cultures' peculiarities, Bea looked forward to discovering what surprises the day might hold. Perhaps she could check off every criterion of her list and surprise her mother with a betrothal after all?

Chapter Six

A little later that day at 87 Harley Street...

ALFIE HAD TRIED to take a nap before dinner, willing himself not to dwell on missing his opportunity that day to harvest the orange blossoms. It would be too tempting... she'd be too tempting.

But as Alfie lay in bed, sleep eluded him anyway. Every time he closed his eyes, he was transported back to the memories of his apprenticeship in India. He could almost feel the weight of the straw basket in his hands, the small vials inside it clinking softly with each step. His master had entrusted him with the task of bringing daily tea and salves to the daughter of an English diplomat, with strict instructions not to speak to her and to keep his head shawl on, even indoors where the sun didn't burn.

The memory was vivid: the girl sitting alone by the window with an open atlas on the small table and her silhouette framed by the delicate veil she wore. Her hands, peeking out from beneath the fabric, were slender and youthful—no more than seventeen or eighteen years old, just a few years younger than Alfie himself at the time.

Something about her, an intrinsic grace and elegance, captivated him completely. She moved her hands with a silent poise that spoke volumes, an allure that seized his heart even though they never exchanged a word.

Each day, as he placed the basket down and observed her from a distance, he felt a pull toward her. There was a moment, fleeting yet eternal, when their eyes nearly met through the thin barrier of her veil. In that instant, Alfie imagined he saw a spark—a glimmer of recognition, perhaps even a shared longing. It was a simple, unspoken connection that etched itself deeply into his soul.

Those brief encounters became the highlight of his days. He'd linger a little longer than necessary, hoping for another stolen glance, another silent acknowledgment. Her presence filled a void he hadn't known existed, a tender ache that lingered long after he'd left her quarters.

In the stillness of his room now, he could almost smell the fragrant tea leaves, hear the soft rustle of her robes, and feel the heady rush of young love—a love unspoken, unfulfilled, but thoroughly unforgettable. That sense of yearning stayed with him, a bittersweet reminder of a heart once stolen, never fully returned.

Nick burst into Alfie's bed chamber, wearing cream-white breeches, new Hessian boots, a starched shirt, a silk waistcoat, and black tails. "How do I look?"

"Like a penguin," Alfie groaned, sitting up in his bed in nothing but his sleep shirt.

"I'm not going to the menagerie; I'm getting married." Nick beamed. "In just a few days."

Alfie's bedchamber stood in stark contrast to Nick's exuberant entrance and perfect looks. The room, bathed in the soft light of dawn filtering through heavy damask curtains, was in scholarly disarray. Dark wooden paneling lined the walls, adorned with shelves crammed full of leather-bound volumes and scientific equipment—remnants of Alfie's rigorous academic pursuits at the university in Vienna.

The room's centerpiece was a large four-poster bed draped in rich burgundy velvet, where Alfie had been sprawled moments before. On one side, an imposing mahogany wardrobe stood slightly ajar, revealing neatly hung clothes next to a pile of hastily thrown-off garments. The air carried a faint scent of parchment, ink, and a hint of cologne.

Beside the washstand was the door to the shared bathroom.

Nick's arrival injected the room with a burst of energy. Chromius, Nick's mutt, trotted into the room following his master, his tail wagging in excitement as if he approved of Nick's attire. Chromius stopped to nuzzle Alfie's outstretched hand, seeking attention and a morning scratch. Yet, Nick's buzzing excitement truly filled the space as he examined himself in the tall standing mirror near the window, its gilded frame reflecting both his polished appearance and Alfie's groggy dishevelment.

Alfie, still shaking off the fog of restless sleep, moved to face his friend, their contrasting states a vivid tableau of exciting life in the grand chamber.

"I believe I already congratulated you. Isn't it too early to get dressed now?" Alfie got up from his bed and walked to his washbowl, splashing some cold water on his face. Alfie was still preoccupied with Bea... she'd be at the wedding, too. Not sleeping while in bed was oftentimes worse than studying all night, as he used to at university. Alchemy, chemistry, and physiology were some of the most difficult exams at the university in Vienna and yet nothing had prepared him for the way he felt presently.

"What's with you? You look terrible," Nick said, stepping in front of Alfie's wall mirror and fumbling with the cravat. "Help me with this."

Alfie came to Nick's side. "Ballroom knot?"

"No, she wants it tight." Nick squared his shoulders and dropped his hands so Alfie could tie his cravat. "Can you teach me?"

Alfie stood behind Nick and took both ends of the cravat in his hands, crossed the ends, and then crossed them again. "This goes through the loop, over, and then you pull this side out."

Alfie tugged at the longer end. "So she's telling you how to tie your cravat already?"

Nick quirked a brow. "I'm going to miss this, you know."

"You'll live not even a two-minute walk away."

"But I won't burst into your room anymore."

"That's not a bad thing." Alfie gave a wistful smile. It was actually very bad and sad.

"We've lived together since boarding school."

"Nothing was as small as our room in Vienna, though."

"That's not true! The crate we transported Chromius in was—"

"It was bigger!" Alfie jested, and they both burst into laughter. "There!" He tugged at both sides of the cravat, and Nick turned to face him. "You look like a groom a high-born lady would have."

"I'm very lucky to have found Pippa," Nick said with a mix of sadness and relief as he sighed. "But I'll still miss you."

"I'm not going anywhere. You'll see me at work every day," Alfie said. And it was true; he'd never do anything to risk the practice or the apothecary. Whether Nick would leave and live with his wife—as any adult man should—or whether Alfie's heart was being stabbed by the thousands of reasons why he couldn't go after the woman who'd caught his affection, there was nothing he'd do to risk what they'd all built for the past decade. It was a taboo point, risking the practice. There just was nothing important enough—not even his heart.

"Pippa doesn't want me to change my work schedule just because I'm marrying a Duke's daughter."

"But she's transforming her castle into a rehabilitation center." Alfie arched his brows. There'd be much change, whether Nick realized it or not. Commoners like him and Nick couldn't ascertain what it meant to be a Ton member, especially not a diamond of the first water.

Oh, Bea... Alfie tried not to sigh like a smitten green boy.

"One more thing," Nick reached into his pocket and produced a small box upholstered in brown velvet with a swirly gold K embroidered on it for Klonimus, the name of the jewelers. "Could you keep this safe and be my best man?"

"I thought Felix was your best man."

"And Andre. Yes, I need three."

"That's unusual." Alfie flattened his lips and tried to swallow the lump that suddenly formed in his throat.

"We're unusual. Pippa doesn't mind. I need you all close to me."

Alfie's heart plummeted. Nick was nervous. Understandably. He was about to marry a duke's daughter in one of the largest English country estates and she was the richest heiress in the country. Plus, she was kind, intelligent, beautiful, and absolutely devoted to him. Picturing Pippa under a veil with a bouquet in her hands made Alfie strangely proud on Nick's behalf. But then it occurred to him that he'd be right next to them. "Who's her bridesmaid?"

"Bea and Wendy."

"Oh no!"

"Wendy will walk me down the aisle; she's my sister. Will you escort Bea then?"

Escort Bea? In a pretty dress and surrounded by flowers with all their friends and families watching? No!

"It'll be my honor."

So this was his punishment. A lifetime of seducing women, lighthearted trysts, and an easy way with the most beautiful of them all ended in a macabre journey down the aisle with the only woman he wanted more than all the others and could never have. He'd offer his arm, walk her down the aisle, and instead of vowing to love her forever, he'd stand a yard to the side and then watch her from the sidelines. It was too cruel.

"I'll change out of this and come to eat. Felix made lamb with roasted parsnips," Nick said. "Smells good."

Alfie's stomach grumbled. He hadn't eaten since—come to think of it—he hadn't eaten since the ball the night before. A realization dawned on him, quiet and profound. His body might not hunger for food, but his soul... his soul was starved for something far more vital. For connection, for the spark that had ignited between him and Bea. The discomfort in his stomach wasn't from hunger, though; it stemmed from a newfound need, one that craved not just the presence of Bea but the intertwining of their lives.

→»»«««←

AFTER MAKING HIS hair presentable, Alfie descended the stairs. He could hear the friendly voices: Andre's heavy Italian lilt, Felix explaining the spice notes of the marinade he'd cooked up, and Wendy's laughter. He paused for a moment on the threshold, taking it all in. The table was a patchwork of plates and glasses, mismatched in a way that spoke of many hands contributing what they had. Around it sat the people who had become more than friends; they were his chosen family since he'd lost his own in a tragic accident at sea. Each face in the kitchen turned to greet him with smiles that reached their eyes and tugged at his heart.

There was no formal place setting, no sense of ceremony. Instead, an open chair awaited him, as it always did, a silent testament to his place among them. He moved toward it, the weight of the day's worries shedding from his shoulders with each step. Laughter and voices, rich with affection, wove through the air, a melody more heartening than any song. He found his sanctuary within the clatter of dishes and the savory scent of the stew simmering on the stove.

As he took his seat, the conversation enveloped him, easy and unforced.

"Have you noticed the teachers this year are beautiful?" Andre nodded appreciatively. "I wish I could go back to school sometimes."

"After all this time studying, you'd still choose homework

over adult life?" Wendy asked with her motherly tone of the only woman at the table. "I suppose the only true adult here is my brother."

"Hear, hear!" Felix raised his glass. "To Nick, being the first of us to grow up and get married!"

They raised their mismatched glasses and clinked them against each other. After Alfie took a sip of the cheapest wine anyone could ever find and considered pouring it over the vegetables as vinegar, he noticed that Felix was stabbing at the parsnip on his plate.

"Do you have some dispute with that poor parsnip?" Alfie raised an eyebrow. Getting no response, he wondered what had Felix so annoyed. Time for a change of subject.

"So… the viscount came for his digitalis this morning. Seems he didn't like the taste of it after I'd made it completely palatable, so I gave him the dilution," Alfie started, recounting the Latin name for the earlier dose of foxglove he'd sold.

"But that's the smallest dose, isn't it?" Wendy said. "I thought he told me it was the highest in his parcel as he left today."

"Did he now? I must have gotten the order wrong then." Alfie winked at Wendy and shrugged. He stuffed a piece of lamb in his mouth and tore the crust of the bread to soak up the gravy. Until he'd had a taste of Felix's delicious cooking, he hadn't realized how hungry he'd been for actual food, not just Bea.

"You cannot manipulate your patients like that!" Felix said, but it didn't sound like he meant it.

"I needed him to take the smallest dose, and he was intent on taking the largest, which would kill him."

"Tobacco is ruining his teeth, too. Had to turn him down this afternoon," Felix said, poking at his uneaten food.

"You turned the viscount down?" Andre raised his voice. "But he's a goldmine!"

"You mean he needs the medical care, and you couldn't provide it?" Nick cocked his head as if to remind Andre why they were running this practice.

"Yes, I mean that it's obvious how many gold fillings, inlays, and crowns he needs, and that he will pay for this work." Andre raised his brow at Felix. "Turning him down this week could mean we cannot pay rent this month. Have you thought about that?"

Felix dropped his fork. "I have, yes. I don't have enough gold to treat him tomorrow. Why do you think I already spoke to the Klonimuses twice? And the Pearlers?" They were families of jewelers, close friends of Felix, and his suppliers of gold pellets to melt into crowns, gold foil for fillings, and did everything from sharpening his instruments to providing new ones. In many ways, Felix's work resembled that of the Crown Jewelers, even though the crowns he forged were on display inside the mouths of the Ton rather than adorning their heads, necks, or fingers.

"Is this about the gold shortage?" Wendy asked.

"You've heard?" Felix asked.

"Yes, overheard."

Ah, yes, Wendy always needs to know everything, Alfie thought. Whenever she was curious, she'd burst in with a stack of freshly pressed towels and offer her help—typically the meddling kind.

"This is a serious problem, Felix. Can I help with anything?" Nick put his fork down, and the room grew silent. Nick was right. Instead of bickering with each other, they should be finding a solution.

"I don't know. There seems to be a breakpoint in the gold supply chain. If we don't figure out where the gold goes—because it's not going where it should—I won't be able to do more than administer clove oil and henbane and turn my patients away."

Alfie leaned back, his supper forgotten. The fallout could severely impact their business.

Although it was usually his pleasure to supply Felix with clove oil and henbane to mellow the patients' toothaches or pain during treatment, he was well aware that nothing he could offer was, in fact, the treatment for the dentist's patients. The doctors at 87 Harley Street, including Alfie, were symbiotic. He made their work more accessible, the treatment outcomes more predictable, and healing faster with his medicines. Conversely, the patients were his customers, some longstanding if they had chronic conditions. If any of the doctors were missing supplies, Alfie had to help.

Moreover, Felix was the best dentist in London and most devoted to his patients. Taking the material he needed to treat his patients was like taking water from a fish. And if Felix's supplies ran dry, the doctors could soon suffer a dry spell. The risk was too grave.

"I'll help you to get to the bottom of this," Alfie declared.

"How?" Felix didn't hide the hopefulness in his wary eyes well.

"I will find a way."

Chapter Seven

Brunswick House, the home of Countess Langley...

VIOLET AND BEA took a stroll in the garden and later on withdrew into the drawing room for a leisurely afternoon that stretched into the evening hours.

Bea was reeling from having met the new prince. It was nearly impossible to lay sight on an unmarried royal before the matrons of the Ton swept over him like vultures, yet Violet had tucked him away just for her.

Just minutes ago, they'd walked past Henry's study and saw the two men standing over his desk and trailing lines on a map of the continent. They were discussing gold shipments and country lines in Transylvania. Bea was fascinated and wished she could stay and listen, but decorum meant she needed to mind her business. Ladies weren't supposed to show interest in such things. She followed Violet to the drawing room, determined to find out more from her friend.

"However did you keep him here?" Bea asked once the footman had shut the door, and she was alone with Violet. "And what's the talk of gold and shipments and Transylvania?"

"Oh, so you overheard." Violet widened her eyes with excitement and lowered her voice. "He's engaged in a diplomatic mission with Henry. Isn't it marvelous?" She gripped Bea's wrist and squeezed excitedly. "There's a terribly secret and exciting mission he's involved with." Violet leaned closer to Bea as if the walls were spies. "It has to do with gold shipments over the Mediterranean. Thieves, pirates, and lost carriages. Henry has been up all night, studying maps with Stan." Violet spoke familiarly of her husband as if he were anything but the tall and imposing Earl of Langley, but Bea was as intimidated by him as she'd been before Violet married him.

Her friend sat back and folded her hands as if ready for the next act in a play. "So, about you. A prince! And a charming one, too!" Violet cast her a woman-to-woman look.

"Rather charming, I suppose." Bea knew exactly what Violet's mission was, but she wasn't sure she knew enough about the prince to openly set her cap on him. She'd prefer to continue discussing the maps Henry and Stan were studying.

"I asked my staff to keep an eye on Stan, and he's healthy." Violet drew her eyes open and nodded. *"Very."*

Oh dear. "I'm not looking for breeding stock."

"Yes, yes, I know. You're only looking for a husband who can sweep you off your feet and take you to faraway places." Violet gestured as if the thought alone were sheer exaggeration. "He seems capable enough."

"To physically carry me?" Bea frowned. It didn't sound romantic in the literal sense.

"Just imagine, you could be a princess!" Violet stood up and swirled in her morning dress as if last night's ball hadn't ended yet. "You'd live in a castle."

"He said he hasn't been there in a long time."

"Even better! Then you'll travel around the world with a royal escort!" Violet looked out the window dreamily. "Just imagine."

"The distance between England and Transylvania can hardly be considered *around the world*." Although Bea had to admit that traversing the Mediterranean Sea, or the countries spanning from Portugal and Spain via France to the Kingdom of Bavaria, then

Italy, Austria, Hungary, and finally, Transylvania *did* seem rather intriguing. And that's what she wanted just as much as meeting her criteria for a husband—getting away. The farther, the better.

"You look flushed." Violet arched a brow and eyed Bea suspiciously.

Heat had risen to her face and had not subsided. It was probably the effect of the dashing prince and hopefully not a herald of the beast. Now would be a bad time for her condition to appear, especially if she decided to pursue the prince.

He was rather well-built and well-mannered, and his smile was warm and kind. There were worse matches for girls like her among the Ton, and besides, there were hardly any princes available in England.

"This *is* my chance," Bea mumbled, though not with any certainty.

"But he is leaving in a fortnight," Violet warned. "You need to secure the match in a very short time."

"It gives me no time at all!"

Why did you even introduce him to me when the objective is impossible?

"You were considered a diamond of the first water, Bea, until you rejected twenty-four suitors. Still, if anyone can catch a prince in less than two weeks, it's you! He could solve all of your problems."

Violet's words were encouraging at best or a set-up for disappointment at worst. Bea would have to forge her own destiny to choose which way to go. But how was she to navigate between her heart and her mind, especially when—in the end—every one of her thoughts somehow circled back to Alfie.

Thus, the thought stewed in Bea's mind for hours after she returned home, as she considered every aspect. She'd tried to read every magazine that she could find, even *La Belle Assemblée*, throughout the afternoon, but her mind returned to the prince every time—not romantically, as it did with Alfie—but out of curiosity. What she'd overheard when she saw him in the earl's study piqued her interest. She couldn't help but wonder which maps Henry and the prince had studied all night. Trying to distract herself, she'd taken out her embroidery frame, threaded an extra-long piece of green yarn, and began stitching. In and out, the needle went as she stitched tiny green leaves in a circular arrangement.

She couldn't merely express her interest and declare that the prince may court her. Perhaps that would work with a mere baronet or the second son of an earl, but a prince, even if he wasn't in line for a throne, demanded a different sort of finesse.

Bea had honed the skill of letting suitors down easily. But making it easy for them to court her was something she'd never tried.

She set the needle down when the thread was short enough to make a final knot and switch colors. The more she thought about being courted by the prince, the more appealing the idea became. Especially when she imagined the expression on her mother's face if she found out that Bea had married a prince, left, and was on a diplomatic mission on her way to… well, somewhere. Anywhere but London was good. Anywhere but England, was even better.

The farther she could get away from the Ton, the freer she imagined herself.

She certainly hadn't ever wanted to be the best or the prettiest, or the one with the worst secret among the nation's most selfish, vile-tongued, and viciously gossiping aristocrats in Europe—but that's what the Ton had become for her since they'd been so mean to Cousin Pippa.

Red-hot anger flooded her veins.

Hopefully, the Ton would learn its lesson. Perhaps its members had at the ball last night.

Bea fanned herself. It was hot, and she felt the warmth spreading to her neck and she thought about how Violet had mentioned she looked flushed. And yet, now she could feel the burning itch that heralded the emergence of the beast. She'd tried to ignore it in the hopes that it was just her imagination, but not even Bea missed the signs.

Bea touched her cheeks, then her forehead. She could feel the bumps. The beast was emerging. It usually took a week, sometimes two. And even then, pustules lingered and took longer to heal.

"Not again, not today," she said to no one in particular and set down her embroidery as she rushed to her vanity table, then hesitated before daring to look at herself in the mirror.

The telltale red bumps had appeared all over her face, neck, and décolletage. Bea buried her face in her hands.

"It's the toll of beauty," Mother used to say. "A reminder that there needs to be time to hone your other qualities when you cannot show your face in Society until you tame the inner fury."

But Bea had always wished her mother wouldn't focus on the beast so much.

For as long as Bea could remember, when the beast emerged, she would have to retreat for a few weeks, seclude herself, and hone her ladylike skills. In fact, her entire life had been about honing the skills a lady needed. And since her debut, which had been delayed by a journey to India, she had suffered only a few episodes and made marvelous connections at the balls and at Almack's, never sitting out a single dance when she was in attendance.

Bea returned to the embroidery and picked up a new threading yarn, a deep shade of turquoise. Then, she began stitching a second layer of leaves in the circle on her frame.

Waiting for a chance to dance with the prince would take too long. Now that Violet had introduced them, she had a chance to speak with him more freely. The conventional methods wouldn't do; there wasn't enough time.

Pippa was getting married, and she'd be alone. Where should she live once Cloverdale House was converted to a rehabilitation center? Her parents would return—well, nobody could know precisely when. Soon, she'd be shelved among the spinsters while her cousin would have the dashing oculist to dance with at the balls.

No, she'd rested on her laurels far too long, and Violet was right. This was the chance of a lifetime. If only the beast hadn't reared its ugly head. She had to do something, though.

She could be a princess. And with a bit of luck, Stan would take her far away.

But to sweep her off her feet, he needed to love her. Or at least feel a modicum of infatuation beyond mere inclination to commit to her.

Thus, she had to make him fall in love in two weeks.

Bea looked down at her embroidery and swallowed hard. The combination of dark turquoise with green silk shimmered in the light of her chamber in the same colors as his eyes.

Alfie's eyes.

Could *he* help her?

I'll expect you to harvest the orange blossoms for neroli oil tomorrow.

Oh no!

Bea looked at the clock. It was nearly seven in the evening. If Alfie had come during the day, she'd missed him.

She was on a diplomatic mission and had already fallen behind.

As the evening dragged on and night had fallen, Bea had waited for her cousin, but Pippa hadn't returned home. Bea had a good idea of where her cousin was, and she was happy for her.

Later, as Bea lay in her bed, the weight of impending decisions pressing down on her chest like a physical burden, her thoughts churned in restless circles, each one more desperate than the last. Time was slipping through her fingers, and with her parents' imminent return, the noose of an unwanted betrothal tightened. She couldn't afford the luxury of waiting for her rash to heal or hoping for a prolonged courtship. This time, she needed to act swiftly and decisively, juggling the fine line between her duty and her heart's desire.

The thought of her cousin's wedding loomed over her—a deadline not just for celebration but for securing her own future. Bea could see it. Pippa would be with Nick, perhaps strolling hand-in-hand through Marylebone. They would share knowing smiles and be the picture of true love. Bea stared at the ceiling as her thoughts raced ahead.

Her mind played out an imaginary conversation with Alfie, his voice a soothing yet pragmatic anchor in the storm of her thoughts.

"Be practical," he might advise, urging her to consider every option logically. Then she could hear Pippa, whose voice whispered of intuition and following one's heart. Torn between conflicting counsels, Bea got out of bed to study the maps in her atlas once again, tracing the journey to Transylvania and Bran Castle, where Prince Stan was from. Was he the answer?

Bea's eyes flickered over the map's legends, her mind mapping out the journey, even as her heart wavered. She flipped through the pages with a deliberate urgency, searching for more details about Transylvania and its surrounding areas.

Pippa's voice in her head was still telling her to listen to her intuition.

Intuition, Bea thought. If only she could hear it calling to her.

With a sigh, she plopped back onto her bed, closing her eyes in frustration. It wasn't the exotic allure of a far-off land that captivated her thoughts at all. Instead, the intoxicating memory of Alfie's scent from the ball—an earthy, masculine aroma that was distinctly his—embedded itself deeper into her consciousness as a silent plea for clarity amidst chaos.

Finally, exhaustion took hold, and Bea drifted into a fitful sleep, the weight of her worries momentarily lifting.

When she awoke the next morning, a newfound clarity and resolve coursed through her veins as if the dawn itself had rekindled her spirit. Bea couldn't quite name the reckless impulse that drove her feet toward the apothecary's shop, but she'd woken up with the urge to consult Alfie. At about eight in the morning, wearing a veiled hat to hide her disfiguration, she left Cloverdale House on Abbotsbury Road and took the carriage to Marylebone, getting dropped off at the *Patisserie de la Loire* under the pretense of purchasing some pastries. She didn't want the driver to know where she was going lest her courage falter. She couldn't explain why she was going to the practice when she was needed at home to help Pippa with wedding plans.

But Bea knew that Pippa's wedding plans were not hers to worry about. Truly, the choice of flowers or music mattered little now that Pippa's most important choice—her groom—was made. Bea was now one step behind her cousin and running to catch up.

With each minute, the itch worsened, and Bea felt her face heating. It might have been because of the beastly rash or perhaps because of the violent thrumming in her chest. Her heart quickened when 87 Harley Street appeared before her, where the apothecary's shop nestled quaintly. This was no simple errand; it felt more like a pilgrimage to a shrine she hadn't known she worshipped. *Could he... would he... be able to help her?*

Bea pushed the door open; she'd been there a few times to collect Pippa when she visited Nick, so she knew it was unlocked during business hours. She entered the foyer. On the left was Nick's office. Directly across, however, was her destination:

Alfie Collins
Apothecary

She opened the door and stepped inside the room. The air was thick with the scent of herbs and dried flowers, an aromatic combination that soothed her frayed nerves. And there he was, the dashing apothecary, his presence in the dimly lit room both the balm and the catalyst to her anxiety-ridden state.

Chapter Eight

FOLLOWING YET ANOTHER sleepless night, Alfie stood behind his counter and dutifully dispensed the medicines his client needed. He wrapped the bottle in parchment and tied it with string.

"Apply the tincture with a piece of clean cotton twice daily for ten days," Alfie advised a young man with a simple candle burn that would probably heal on its own, when his eyes caught a veiled lady with a narrow waist entering his apothecary.

"And you say that'll heal this, sir?" his patient asked. Alfie had provided him with witch hazel in a carrier oil that would soothe the injured skin until it returned to its original healthy texture. He assured the young man that it would and accepted the shilling he paid, but in truth, Alfie couldn't hear him anymore. His entire focus was on the veiled lady at the far end of his counter. She had turned her back to him and had begun to peruse his display of Parisian cosmetics, and he couldn't take his eyes from her.

She wore a fashionable but subdued travel dress and a thin pelisse with a sash that accentuated her waist. They were of a matching color, though the sash was made of a shiny fabric, while the pelisse was woven. Or knitted. He couldn't be too sure about women's fashions, but he was absolutely certain about women's bodies. And he'd seen this one in his imagination all night.

Unfortunately, she was draped in far too many layers of indiscernible fabric and beyond his reach. *Lady Beatrice.*

His business with the young man concluded, and Alfie walked around his counter and to the window where Bea was smelling the rose pomade and mica powder rouge. Alfie wasn't much of a connoisseur, but it was easy for him to import these creams and powders with matching little brushes from a merchant Felix knew. Beyond displaying these items and leaving one open for his female customers to test, he didn't need to do much. The maquillage almost sold itself. All he had to do was bag it and collect the coin.

"What can I do for you?" he asked when Bea looked over her shoulder, the veil draping loosely over her head and shoulders. She was refinement impersonated like a cultured English rose sparkling with dew drops. Oh, he'd lick every single one of those drops off her if she'd ever let him.

Rein yourself in, Collins. This is Pippa's cousin. She's a lady. No touching a member of the Ton.

He rubbed his temples to wake up his head, considering that all of his blood had traveled elsewhere.

"I heard you speak to the young man about an ointment for his rash. I'll take some of that."

"Why do you need an ointment?"

"Me?" She lifted her head and blinked at him through the veil. True, for the untrained eye, she was fairly well disguised. However, Alfie knew women's bodies and their unique mannerisms in moving and the gentle rocking of their hips when they walked. He appreciated every nuance of their femininity like a wine steward distinguished the high and low notes of good wine. But this was no wine before him. Lady Beatrice Wetherby was more of a prized cognac, a type of brandy made from distilled white wine, and so powerful in its ripeness it could even be used in small doses as a medicinal remedy.

She braced herself, as if she were itchy and yet wouldn't allow herself to scratch. Alfie recognized the symptoms.

"You know who I am?" she asked.

"Yes, of course." *I'd recognize you if you were hiding behind a brick wall, Lady Beatrice. A beauty like you is not easily overlooked.* "I recognize your voice." There was no point in admitting he also recognized her shape and had spent the night fighting thoughts of what it would be like to grasp that waist—or cup those breasts!

"Oh."

"Why have you inquired about witch hazel ointment?" Alfie asked.

"Oh, no reason."

There was always one.

"It is my profession, you know. Patients tell me their symptoms, and I find a cure." He cleared his throat. "At least, I try."

"And are you often successful?"

"Usually."

"What happens when you're not?"

"It may not be a matter medicines alone can cure. Sometimes surgery may be required."

"Surgery?" Alarm pierced her voice.

"Rarely." He fought the urge to lay a hand on her shoulder and comfort her.

Well, truth be told, he fought the urge to lay *her* over his shoulder and carry her to his bed chamber.

Whoa, Alfie, slow down.

"I'll take one of the beige powders, please. The rose-scented one. That'll be all." Her voice trembled and betrayed her withdrawal. Fortunately for her, she wasn't the first lady to work up the courage to seek him out for a medical question and then falter at the last minute.

"Lady Beatrice, if there is anything I may help with, it would be my privilege to offer my assistance. Rest assured that I am in the habit of maintaining the utmost discretion."

She swallowed and blew the air out, so that the veil draping over her face moved as if a light summer breeze brushed the curtains aside. "Even among your colleagues in the practice?"

"Even among them, if you wish."

He heard her inhale deeply now as if she tried to draw the courage from the room to speak; the lace covering wafted in toward her lips, this time. Then she brought both lace-gloved hands to the edge of the veil and lifted it.

Time slowed at the moment her lashes fluttered a delicate dance that caught Alfie's gaze and held it captive. With each graceful bat of her long, enchanting eyelashes, it was as though she struck directly at Alfie's resolve, sending waves of turmoil through his very core. He fought to maintain his composure, to resist the overwhelming urge to pull her into an embrace, to shower her with adoration. Yet, Alfie couldn't help but think that this stirring of the heart, this sweet torment she unknowingly inflicted upon him, was but a minor quandary for a man as well-versed in the art of love as he was.

A constellation of crimson marks had emerged upon her skin, no doubt the silent heralds of some unseen reaction. The blotches were fresh and unmarred yet around them, the skin began to pull taut, mimicking the parched earth's cry for rain.

"I have the pox," she spoke as if she'd taken her last breath. "I get them sometimes."

Alfie tried to stifle a laugh because she was absolutely adorable. "You most certainly do *not* have the pox." His voice came out darker than he'd intended.

"Leprosy?"

"No." He shook his head in suppressed mirth. He didn't mean to sound condescending, but she was just too sweet and seemingly unable to understand how easily her condition could be healed.

"But I'm disfigured."

"Not at all." Alfie squeezed his lips together to suppress the slew of compliments bubbling within him for the unmatched beauty despite the red blotchiness. A true beauty held more in store than impeccable skin. Didn't she know that her condition was manageable even though it seemed terribly uncomfortable? It was harmless. But she was so vexed by the rash, as if she'd had a terminal diagnosis, that he wanted to smile and wrap his arms around her and lift her onto his counter.

She inhaled and eyed him curiously. "My mother keeps me locked up when I break out like this. I usually work on my watercolors and needlepoint to forget that I'm hungry. I mean, so that I keep my shape when I'm waiting for the skin to return to normal. Mother says I'm a blooming nightmare."

Dream. Not nightmare.

He shut his eyes for a moment. He imagined her sprawled naked on dark-purple satin covers with her red-golden hair framing her face as he climbed over her.

Stop! Is this the third way you've thought of taking her in less than five minutes? This is not self-control. Not even a little bit.

"Come to the light, please." He pointed his open palm to the window to get a good look and confirm his suspicion. She followed him and stood facing the pane that led to Harley Street. Alfie made it a habit to keep his apothecary darker than the light outside so that nobody would be able to see his customers. The glass was milky, and even if anyone saw their silhouettes, they wouldn't make out their faces from the outside. Discretion was almost more important to his clientele than the accuracy of a diagnosis or a fair price for the medicines, and Alfie respected that.

She blinked at him, inclining her head so that he could see the redness on her cheeks and forehead.

"It's not too bad," he said, hoping she'd jerk back and not notice that his hand had come to cup her face, and he was almost leaning in. "Is your affliction limited to these red, inflamed patches here?"

She nodded.

"Accompanied at times by itching or even blisters?"

"Itching but no blisters."

"It's what we commonly refer to as *tetter*, or in more severe instances, *salt rheum*."

"You know what it is? You mean... it happens to other people?" A wondering, even relieved, expression crossed her face. Poor beauty, he thought. She'd thought she was alone in an untreatable affliction. "Why does this happen to me?" she asked.

"It is a manifestation of the body's internal imbalance, possibly exacerbated by an external irritant that has come into contact with your body. It is a condition of the skin where it becomes irritated and can flake, weep, or even crust over."

She listened intently, the corners of her mouth curling into a frown. "Is there a cure?"

"There is treatment."

"Isn't that the same?"

"Unfortunately, not. A cure would prevent this from ever happening again. But there are treatments that can speed up the healing process and relieve the discomfort." He opened one of the small drawers and handed her a small glass jar with a metal lid. This was one of the few remedies he always had handy. "Try this ointment. And keep a journal."

"For what purpose?"

"With your observations. There must be a trigger for the condition. Perhaps keeping a record will give us the opportunity to see a pattern or find what affects you and causes your hives to occur. Writing down what you touch or use, what fabrics you wear, and what foods you consume will help us to learn." He paused. "It's like making a map, step by step, to bring us to your 'beast'."

She seemed to ponder the idea for a moment. Her lovely face was bathed in the soft light of Alfie's apothecary, as the potent aroma of herbs and tinctures wove around them, and Alfie's muscles tensed. This was his realm, and he should feel in control, yet it took all of his strength to steady his nerves alone with Bea.

The beauty stood directly across from him, separated by his counter and the cleft of Society; she was virtually untouchable and irresistible at the same time. If she were anyone else but a high-born lady, he'd lay her on the counter and kiss her senseless, pleasure her until she screamed, then carry her into his bed and kiss her until she'd be ready for another round. But he had to suppress any instinct, steady his nerves, and remain calm. She'd come to him as a customer, and he was a professional catering to her needs—whims—*argh!* He'd give her what she asked for. No matter what the nature of her request.

"I happen to be under time constraints and thought myself defeated because of my beast… *ahem*… condition. But if you say it can heal in a matter of days, there may be a way for me to meet my deadline."

"Is this an upcoming ball or something scheduled for a special date?" Alfie asked.

"No," she snapped as if he'd insulted her intelligence. "My parents are returning from Singapore soon."

"How lovely. You must be looking forward to the reunion."

"I dread it more than the plague. Marriage without affection makes me itch even worse."

Now, she had his attention. "And why is that?"

"They expect me to be wed by the time they return, or else my father will make the match for me. I need to make someone fall in love with me first."

Alfie bit his cheek to stop himself from growling in frustration. What he wanted even less than to keep his hands off her was to watch another man get his hands on her. And then she continued, "There's a foreign delegate in London this week. Violet, I mean, the Countess of Langley, introduced us. I need him to fall in love with me and take me to Transylvania."

Alfie was convinced he hadn't heard right. Not only was she intent on marrying some delegate but she also expected to leave England? His chest constricted.

"You'd miss Pippa's wedding?"

Sadness washed over her eyes, and something flickered within her that eclipsed the beautiful exterior, hives or not, with a deep pain that Alfie wished to cure even more than he wanted to soothe her skin.

"I will be there for Pippa. But after the wedding, I might

leave," she said. "There's no solution for my ailment."

"I could give you an ointment—"

"Not that ailment, Mr. Collins. I'm trapped. And my key to escape is going to leave this country when the prince's diplomatic mission is over. If I don't go with him, my parents will marry me to a man I don't even like—"

"Do you like the prince?" Alfie couldn't stop the words even though he heard how pathetic they sounded.

"Well, he's handsome and healthy."

"You didn't answer my question." Alfie couldn't take his eyes off hers. He was locked in an internal struggle. He wanted her for himself, but couldn't have her. And now she was proposing to run off with the first suitable man she could find?

She placed both hands on the counter and leaned forward. So close and yet so far, Alfie felt his insides churning. "Mr. Collins, I'm the belle of each ball, believe me or not. When I don't look like a beast, everyone expects me to make a stellar match, but I've been dragging my feet for too long. It's diminishing my chances. I'm to be a doll, an accessory with as much say as a shiny pocket watch. The irony isn't lost on me. This golden watch is running out of time."

Alfie felt as if she'd punched him in the stomach and cut off his breath. She wasn't a beast, nor was she merely passable. A woman with her spirit didn't qualify as an accessory but as the main spectacle of a lifetime. But he ought not to tell her how much he'd like to prove her wrong.

Yet, his intellect surfaced long enough to dissect the situation: Bea was lonely, caught between her duty as a lady and daughter versus the fire inside her. Her station prevented her from acting on her impulses.

Alfie bit his cheek and considered the matter. There was something familiar about her, a familiarity he'd recognized the day Pippa first introduced her, but now there was something else, too. His stomach twisted at the thought… it couldn't be *her*, could it?

When she was alone with him, she seemed to act more impulsively than at the ball at the Langleys. Even when she'd been at the orangery with him, she seemed freer.

"I'm sorry that nobody sees your true spirit."

She straightened her back and folded her hands in front of her. "Will you help me then?"

"I don't know how I could help you. It's not like I can concoct a love potion."

She growled like a cat about to pounce, and Alfie's cock twitched. This woman had spirit, fire, and zest that he wanted to fuel, not stifle. She needed to be cherished, pleasured, and loved, not locked up like a fury lest she implode into complacency—what a waste.

"How can you help me then, Mr. Collins?"

Against his better judgement, a thought occurred to him, a way to perhaps help this beautiful lady. "I can heighten your natural scents."

"I already have perfume, thank you."

Alfie inhaled deeply, unable to fathom what he was about to do. "A love potion is not what fairy tales say it might be. There's no magic to falling in love. It's purely physical, and that means enhancing the body's natural features that bring about lust so strong, desire so potent, that the heart might follow a person's natural impulses."

"It's too bad you're an apothecary and not a magician. I wish love potions existed." She blinked as if something occurred to her then. "You can't, can you? Is it possible to mix something that induces love rather than lust?"

Not exactly. Alfie wondered how much he should tell this innocent lady. "No. But there are things—herbs, essential oils."

She wrinkled her nose with distaste.

"And things which will stimulate…" he paused. "Certain passions. Not out of love, you understand, but from blood rushing to…places. Irritations that will be eased only from…actions." He took a deep breath. This was awkward and definitely inappropriate. "Things that simulate desire and lust that are mistaken for passion and desire." He couldn't stop himself from talking even though he knew he should. But this was the only way he could see to make her stay near him.

Her eyes widened.

"And there are other ways. Things that are said to heighten one's scent in a way that will attract others."

>>>><<<<

BEA BLINKED WHEN Alfie spoke of love, desire, and lust. His teal-green eyes were even brighter in reality than in her embroidery. Framed by the slight dark line around the green and then offset by the white of his eyes, there was depth and mystery as there would be in the solar eclipses she'd read about. There was so much to see and such joy from looking in his eyes that Bea was momentarily thrown off guard.

"How would you heighten my features then?" she asked.

Alfie rubbed his eyes with the bases of his palms and mumbled something inaudible.

"I beg your pardon?"

"I'd underline your natural beauty, stimulate the imagination of the suitor—"

"He's a prince."

"Yes," he growled. "And then intensify the best features of your natural scent."

"My natural scent?" The hairs on her neck pricked up, and something deep inside her quivered with a blend of glee and curiosity. The notion was scandalous—discussing one's scent with a man was as improper as it was intriguing. She struggled to maintain her composure, but her cheeks betrayed her with a slight flush.

A flurry of emotions danced within her. Nervousness, yes, for she knew the breach of decorum this conversation represented.

Yet, in equal measure, there was a fascination that she could not quell. It wasn't merely the subject matter that held her captive, but the intensity in his eyes, the way his voice dipped into a low, almost intimate tone. He spoke as if he were unveiling a secret just for her ears, making her pulse quicken in response.

She glanced away briefly, her fingers brushing against the delicate fabric of her dress, seeking an anchor to steady herself. How did he perceive her? Did he find her as fascinating as she found him? The thought was both exhilarating and terrifying. This was no ordinary exchange; it felt charged with an energy that transcended mere words.

When she met his gaze again, there was a new resolve in her eyes. She would not shy away from this unexpected turn. Nervous though she was, she would allow herself to be drawn into this unconventional dance of words and meanings. For beneath the propriety and the societal expectations lay a truth that neither could ignore: something profound and stirring was unfolding between them, and it felt distinctly like possibility.

She watched as the apothecary closed his eyes and seemed to inhale deeply. "Right now, you use soap with rose oil, but it clashes with the spark of vivacity and energy in your nature. Rose is subdued. I'd use sandalwood and cinnamon to heighten this aspect." He opened his eyes and squinted. "The copper tones in your blond hair give a richness that only the darkest of berries can emphasize. Sherry would be a suitable base, and it would also invite a lingering kiss wherever you applied the mixture. I won't use anything that aggravates your ailment. The oils must first soothe your skin, then heighten your natural scents."

Bea's face heated and she wanted to fan herself but was too mesmerized by him to move as much as blink her lashes. His words painted her in scent, and he looked at her like an artist with a trained eye—or rather nose.

"You have a bounce in your step when you're happy, like when you come to meet up with your cousin, but when you're sad, like today, you drag your feet. I'd mimic this with the rare note of fir, uplifting at best, or intrusively clearing the sinus when not properly welcomed."

Oh my!

"The richness and depth of your eyes would best be captured by the closed blossoms of lily of the valley, maintaining the grassy and grounding undertones of the petals that shroud the fragrance within."

"And what about the neroli oil? I wanted to apologize in case you came to harvest some orange blossoms, and I missed you."

"I'd be happy to make the neroli for you but it's not the citrus notes that would capture your essence and heighten it, but rather, apple blossoms."

Bea felt light-headed and needed to sit. The description and nuances with which Alfie saw her made the room spin. Something told her—intuition perhaps—that he saw her. All of her.

And she wished nothing more than to fall into his arms. "Can I watch you make it?"

Chapter Nine

LATER THAT NIGHT, Alfie was at his usual place behind the counter of his apothecary shop, a sanctuary of bottles and botanicals, each with its own story and secret life. But all of this paled compared to the beauty standing opposite him, a distraction bigger than the Kanchenjunga mountain—which stood at twenty-eight thousand feet in the Himalayas.

"Thank you for helping me," she murmured as she leaned over the counter to watch him at work. Bea needed his help, and if the purpose weren't to drive her into another man's arms, Alfie would have gladly helped. Yet here he was crafting the instrument to break his heart under her watchful gaze. Never had Alfie been defeated by his knowledge. He was no better than an artist sketching his tomb.

The dimly flickering light caressed the room, casting long shadows that danced on the walls as the gas lamp breathed life into the space. Alfie moved with a purpose, his every action deliberate, his hands reaching for the tools of his trade, but his heart sank lower with every motion.

He tried to convince himself that it was the best course of action: giving Bea what she wanted, the elixir to heighten her essence. But how could the prince be worthy of her if he failed to capture her essence? How dull the prince was to overlook her allure? A woman like her stood among others like a flowering magnolia amid bare trees in March—overlooking the blossoms was akin to ignoring life.

He looked at her for an instant. Their eyes locked and for a flicker of a moment he felt just like the apprentice he had been all those years ago when—but it just couldn't be—or could it? She reminded him so much, somehow, of the young woman in the veil that he'd helped in India. Then she shifted and the fabric of her dress rustled in the quiet of the apothecary. She leaned on the counter on her elbows and tugged off her gloves, finger-by-finger. He'd never seen Bea's hands ungloved.

Alfie's heart stopped. He recognized her hands—those elegant, delicate fingers that had once brushed against his own in an almost accidental communication. The memory of those days in Delhi surged back, vivid, and unbidden, filling him with astonishment and longing. The girl under the veil, alone by the window all those years ago…

It *was* her!

His mind raced but his body remained frozen, caught in disbelief and an unexpected wave of emotion. It had been years since he last saw those delicate fingers, yet every small gesture and unspoken word they had shared came rushing back as if no time had passed. Her hands were exactly as he remembered, moving with a familiar and achingly beautiful grace.

A part of him wanted to speak, to bridge the years and the silence that had stretched between them. But another part held him back, fearing that words might shatter this fragile moment of recognition. He watched as she turned slightly, her veil fluttering with the movement, revealing just enough of her profile to confirm what his heart already knew.

She was older now, as was he, but the essence of her—the elegance, the quiet strength—remained unchanged. His throat tightened, the rush of long-buried feelings overwhelming him. He had never forgotten her, nor the way she had unknowingly captured his heart with her poise and presence.

As she glanced up, their eyes met again, and for a brief, effervescent moment, the world seemed to hold its breath. He saw a flicker of recognition in her gaze, a shared history that spoke louder than any words ever could. The connection between them, forged in silence and distance, felt as palpable as it did all those years ago.

Alfie felt a sense of completion in the quiet space between them, as if a missing piece of his soul had finally been restored.

If he had a chance to capture her essence, to feel the caress of her lips and drive his fingers through her hair, he'd never let her go. But it was forbidden to hold her as he wished; that could not only end his career but also risk the reputation of the practice.

He repeated to himself that the best course of action was to make the elixir for her and let her go. Perhaps he could forget the unforgettable woman; he certainly couldn't touch the untouchable lady who was so removed in station that he shouldn't even look, much less overreach his position.

She dropped her eyes to the bottles on the counter and the moment was over. "Sherry, cinnamon, and apple blossom essential oil?" Bea picked up several of the vials on his counter in turn and read their labels.

"These notes already exist within your natural scent." He'd sensed it in India and noticed it the first time they'd met in London when he gave her the ipecac to help Pippa's and Nick's coup. But there was more to her now that he knew her a little better—*remembered* her a little more strongly.

"I have to capture her scent and enhance it," he mumbled when he retrieved a notebook from the shelf behind him that he'd started on a journey in Morocco. He glanced at his scribblings and the sketch he'd made of a glass beaker with three layers. Oriental perfume theory dictated a symphony of high, middle, and low notes to overpower the human defense to resist, like a knock on one's memory, a push through the door, and then a step inside with no intention of leaving.

He closed his eyes and thought of the woman whose essence he had to capture, amplify, and highlight only the most seductive, tantalizing allure of her femininity. But when he looked at her, his entire body reacted. Thus, with his eyes closed, he tried to draw her essence out. Alfie tried to concentrate but a flurry of thoughts prevented him from focusing. The golden-red curls, silky skin… the dress she'd worn at the ball, and the sweet breath when she spoke to him. She exhaled and waited, and he wished the world would be different when he opened his eyes. If only she knew—but she couldn't. He'd never spoken to her in India, and he'd always kept the head scarf on. Did she know it was him? Could she even remember him?

Alfie swallowed hard.

Back to the task.

He opened his eyes and looked at the sketch in his notes and the top layer in the picture of a beaker, a combination of essential oils floating to the top of the mixture. "The high notes greet first, light and fleeting, an initial whisper of an invitation," he read aloud. If the potion worked, at least he'd make this last encounter with her last.

He reached for the second little drawer on the left in his wall and took out a bottle with a cork stopper. "Almond oil is a sweet carrier oil with a slightly nutty aroma, to welcome the vanilla and apple blossom oil as the high notes."

"Oh!" Bea watched him as if he fascinated her, and he tried not to think about whether she'd recognized him, too. Alfie carefully selected the vanilla, choosing plump and glossy pods, their fragrance rich and inviting. "Are these Pippa's vanilla pods from the orangery?"

"No, I have a supplier because I use them often to mask other scents. Vanilla usually adds a touch of sweetness, a hint of warmth that draws the other scents together." However, it was still too pale for the woman he was trying to describe, not with the sketches of a brush but with the layers of scents. The apple was too tangy, and he needed something to round the highest notes off.

Peach.

No.

Plum. Dark and ripe plums like her cheeks when she was flushed—like now.

He slid a mortar and pestle across the counter to her. "Would it be too much trouble for you to crush some of these vanilla beans for me?" Alfie retrieved a parchment from the drawer under the counter and pulled out two long glass vials filled with the bean paste he'd scraped out of the pods that had come in yesterday's delivery.

Bea's face lit up. "I'd love to help."

Oh, how he'd love to kiss her.

But he knew he mustn't.

"Pardon me for a moment, please." Alfie needed to collect his thoughts and calm his body. He groaned when he walked to the kitchen and exhaled in relief, seeing the fruit bowl bearing one little dark purple plum. The cutting board and knife were still there from dinner. He sliced the last plum open and watched the dark juice flowing onto the light wooden board. The red and orange hues of the flesh reminded him of Bea's hair, and he thought the dark tinge of the plum's skin represented the mysteries of the night. It was tart, but the aromas from just beneath the skin were precious, so he collected the pieces, left the pit, and brought them to his apothecary, where he began to boil the plum on a low flame in alcohol. While it cooled, he considered the next layer, one that would bring the hydrophilic and lipophilic parts of the mixture so that it wouldn't take more than a little shake to create a uniform tincture to rub on her wrists or pat on her collarbone.

Bea had finished with the vanilla. She'd done an impeccable job.

She was perfect.

Alfie sucked his cheeks in. "Thank you."

Bea set down a vial she'd been testing, wiping a droplet off her nose. "The almond oil smells lovely."

No, you do.

Alfie tried to concentrate on the potion. He read his notes in the open book on the counter: *The middle notes emerge, the heart of the perfume, where the actual character is revealed in rich, lingering melodies.* Bea's deep laugh came to mind, the uncontrolled one she'd kept hidden at the ball but that he'd heard when she was alone with her cousin Pippa. The only trace of it had been the rising and falling of her chest when she eyed him in the hall at the Langleys' ball, hiding her thoughts in a well-practiced poise.

He started with the musk, its rich, deep aroma filling the air as he opened the vial. The scent was powerful and primal, evoking an instinctual response that was hard to define but impossible to ignore. Alfie knew its value, the way it could serve as the cornerstone of his creation, grounding the other scents with its earthy base. Too much, and the entire mixture would smell like the cheap perfumes one could buy at the fair.

"What's ambergris?" Bea asked when she read the label on another vial he uncorked.

"A very rare and one of the most precious ingredients," Alfie began, then thought it might be better to let her smell it. He held the beaker in front of his face and waved from the opening toward her face.

She leaned forward to take a whiff and was so close.

Almost close enough to kiss.

The ambergris was just like the woman whose essence he was painting in scents.

"It's amazing, is it not? Do you know it makes its journey from the belly of a whale to our fingertips, transformed by time and tide into something magical." Its scent was complex, a mingling of sea spray and earth that spoke of ancient mysteries and the deep, unfathomable ocean.

"That's marvelous! You know, I've seen whales," she said, her voice reverent. "I was on a ship for a few months when I was sixteen, and then later, I turned eighteen on a schooner in the middle of the Indian Ocean."

I know.

But his heart sank. Of course, she didn't remember him. How could she? He'd always worn the scarf on his head.

"So have I."

"And did you know blue whales are the biggest animals in the world?" Alfie was impressed at her knowledge and enthusiasm. Just another layer to peel back.

You are the most beautiful—and intelligent—woman in the world, do you know that?

"Yes." He chastised himself for the brevity of his conversation. Why was he suddenly tongue tied in front of her? "Where did you travel?"

"Oh, here and there." She waved in the air. "My parents have tried to find a cure for my beast—*ahem*—tetter."

I know that, too. I've been there.

"Do you know that I had to drink a dreadful tea for almost a year that smelled exactly like the ointment you gave me?"

"Hmpf!" *I made the ointment here in England, from the extract of the same tea I brought you every day.*

"It was dreadfully bitter and smelled rather medicinal." She sighed. "But there was this kind young man in India who brought me honey to sweeten it."

That was me, Bea. I brought you the honey. I'd bring you everything you desired in this world if I were allowed.

But he wasn't.

"Do you wish to go back?" he asked.

"To India? Oh, yes, well actually, anywhere! The farther the better!"

"Why?"

She furrowed her brows, and she opened her mouth to explain, but then seemed to think the better of it, and instead she said flippantly, "To get away from the beast. Or what causes it."

She must think that the trigger for her condition wouldn't follow her—or perhaps she didn't want to admit it to herself. How could she? She called it "the beast" and it was slumbering within her.

His heart sank with pity. Oh how he wished to explain that he'd been there before and that he didn't mind what she called "the beast"—nobody was less beastly than her. If only he could tell her that he'd thought of her every single day since he'd left India. And yet, he'd vowed discretion to Master Varier, and he was only an apothecary. She was a lady. He wasn't allowed to cross the line.

Back to the task at hand. He suppressed a deep sigh and waved his hand over the beaker containing his mixture, sniffing the scent that wafted up to his nose. So far, it was but an approximation. More work was needed to capture the irresistible essence of Bea.

He considered his notes and the lowest part of the sketched beaker.

"The low notes, deep and resonant, anchor the fragrance, infusing the senses with a bouquet that persists, a lasting memory of the experience." He turned his notes over to her and she trailed her finger over his writing.

The fir was next, its delicate fragrance rising like a whisper from the distillation apparatus standing proudly on the wooden counter. According to the flower girl who'd delivered the fir, the needles had been picked in the cool, early morning when their scent was most potent. Alfie poured the fir distillate carefully, the refreshing notes bringing a lightness of a gentle breeze to the blend.

Finally, he turned to the lily of the valley, the preserved buds dried to perfection, retaining their essence and promise. He crushed them gently in his mortar and pestle that was always ready on his counter, releasing their oils and fragrances into the air. The scent brought the promise of better times, and the warmth of spring to the mixture. Perfect, just like Bea, for she was the promise of a better life.

Except that she wasn't meant for him.

Alfie worked precisely, measuring each ingredient on his scales before combining them in a crystal flask. He mixed them with a practiced hand, stirring the concoction with a glass rod, watching as the colors and scents melded into something new, something extraordinary.

As he worked, the light played across his tools—the gleaming scales, the polished mortar and pestle, the array of vials and bottles—each reflecting the light in its own way, each an essential part of the alchemy taking place. The carrier oils he chose were as important as the scents themselves. Jojoba and almond oil provided the perfect medium, their own subtle aromas adding depth without overpowering the delicate balance he sought to achieve.

After he'd filtered the mixture and poured it into a simple glass vial—a British understatement to the potency within—a drop of it got onto his right index finger, and he rubbed it in and smelled it.

"Does it smell like me yet?" She reached for his hand and brought his finger to her nose.

His breath hitched, and he couldn't take his eyes off those delicate fingers wrapped around his wrist. Oh, how he fought the impulse to open his palm and cradle her lovely cheeks in his hand—but it was prohibited. Plus, she trusted him to create a potion for her; she was there as a customer.

"It's close, but not wholly you."

She furrowed her brows and let go of his hand as if she'd been burned.

Perhaps it was for the better because they'd left every modicum of propriety behind this late in the day at the apothecary, creating a way for her to entice a prince... he mustn't think about it.

Something unique and exotic was missing, the spirit she'd stifled as a lady, but that Alfie knew all too well a good lover could bring to the surface.

From the bottom right drawer of his wall of treasured substances, he retrieved a thin tube with a waxed cork.

"May I see?" Bea reached out again, her curiosity seemingly

getting the better of her.

"This is irreplaceable. I've saved it for a special mixture." With great care, he held the tube upright and removed the cork, then let the dark orange drop fall into the vial—oil of guava.

When the potion glowed amber in the candlelight, its scent a complex tapestry of desire and longing, of earth and sea and blooming gardens and ripe fruits of womanhood, Alfie sealed the flask carefully, his fingers lingering on the glass, feeling the warmth of the liquid inside. He knew this was not just a perfume but a weapon of femininity. He'd used his understanding of the natural world and its hidden language to give her something so powerful that the prince couldn't resist.

Then why did it feel so bad and unsatisfying to create this masterpiece?

Still, Alfie surveyed his counter and was rather pleased that he'd worked with such precision and skill, following the teachings of his mentors from years ago with great diligence. He'd captured the essence of seduction combined with Bea's unique spirit.

He'd created a key to unlock the heart's deepest desires. After years of dreaming of the veiled girl in India, he hadn't even known that he found her until he sketched her scent with nothing but his intuition.

She was so precious that his chest constricted at the thought that another would hold her.

"Let me smell it," Bea said as she reached for the beaker.

"It needs to come together for a few hours, and then it's ready."

The shop seemed to hold its breath, the air charged with anticipation, as if it, too, recognized the power of the potion Alfie had crafted when she inhaled it. In that moment, he was more than just an apothecary; he was a weaver of dreams, a conjurer of love's most elusive magic.

And now it was time to give it away.

Chapter Ten

THE NEXT MORNING, Bea sat alone in her bedchamber at Cloverdale House. The soft glow of a single candle cast flickering shadows across the room. In her solitude, she noticed how profound the silence around her was now that Pippa was busy with Nick and preparing to move to another house with him. Only the occasional rustle of leaves outside her window and the distant creak of the house settling interrupted her thoughts.

She rested her hands on the small escritoire, its mahogany surface polished to hide the scratches that betrayed its age. Before her lay the journal Alfie had given her, its pages filled with her neat, precise entries of everything she'd consumed and what she'd applied to her skin, exactly as he'd instructed.

Breakfast: Toast with butter and a cup of tea, with a bit of sugar.

Luncheon: Cold chicken, bread, and a glass of milk.

Afternoon tea: Raisin scone, halved, with clotted cream. Tea.

Dinner: Roast lamb, peas, and potatoes, a slice of apple tart. Tea. Sherry.

She rifled through the pages, evaluating how much she'd eaten and wondering what Alfie might think. For some inexplicable reason, it mattered more to her what he thought than all of her mother's friends of the Ton combined.

Next to those entries, she had recorded her skincare routine in meticulous detail. Morning: Rosewater tonic, followed by a light application of almond oil and the medicinal ointment.

Evening: Lavender-scented soap and a touch of chamomile balm. Then more ointment.

Soon the journal was no longer just a ledger of meals and lotions. She'd thought of Alfie so much that the journal had transformed into something more personal, an intimate conversation with Alfie. Bea dipped her quill into the inkwell and began to write, the words flowing freely from her heart.

> *There was a boy, once, in India. A young man. He was very kind and my only friend during those days. We never spoke a word, not one, but he reacted to everything that happened around us as if he understood every nuance of my situation. I often thought he could comprehend English, though I never dared to ask.*
>
> *For an entire year, he brought me tea and honey every morning, along with salves and other remedies. Sometimes, he would leave a flower—bright and vivid like the land beyond the walls I wasn't permitted to visit.*

She remembered the first time he laid a blossom on the table next to a small copper container with dry tea leaves, his eyes meeting hers for a brief moment. It was a simple flower, yet it felt like the most precious gift she had ever received.

Bea paused, her heart aching with the chance she'd lost to speak to the young man in the headscarf. Out of fear of disappointing her mother before her first season, she'd obeyed her mother, never uttered a word to him. She'd never even thanked him for the honey or the flower.

Bea put the quill down and brought a hand to her chest. She'd vowed herself never to allow an opportunity like that to go by again.

She reached for her old atlas, the one with the Indian Ocean map. Opening its worn cover, she turned to the back where she had hidden the pressed flower—a *Nagapushpa*, rare and delicate.

The petals were still remarkably intact, their pale beauty a testament to the passage of time.

Her fingers trembled slightly as she touched the fragile blossom, memories of her travels with her parents flooding back: the scent of spices hanging in the air, the vibrant colors of the market stalls, and the warmth of the young man's presence beside her. Pippa didn't even know of this secret keepsake or its significance.

She wrote again, her quill scratching softly against the paper.

Even now, I can see his silhouette so clearly, the way his eyes crinkled when he smiled—shyly—whenever our eyes met. He never needed words; his actions spoke for him. That year offered me a respite from the loneliness, a quiet companionship that I cherished deeply even though I was locked away at the mansion all that time. Would he remember me if we met again?

Bea closed her eyes, letting the memories wash over her. The young man's half-visible face seemed to meld with Alfie's in her mind, two figures from different times and places, yet both holding a piece of her heart. The young man's eye color had been the same.

The weight of unspoken words and unrealized possibilities settled around her like a heavy cloak.

She carefully placed the pressed flower back into the atlas, closing it with a reverent finality. The journal, now imbued with her innermost thoughts, found its place in her reticule. The act felt symbolic, a merging of past and present, a step toward a future where she could embrace her experiences and the emotions they stirred.

As Bea stood and made her way to the window, she looked out at the moonlit garden below. The night air was cool, and the stars glittered like diamonds scattered across the velvet sky. She felt a sense of peace, a quiet resolution. Whatever path her life would take, she carried with her the strength of her memories and the knowledge that friendship from this young man had touched her deeply. And she had a feeling she'd have to free herself from the shackles of her station before her parents returned if she wanted to ever experience it again.

The next morning, Bea received a note from Pippa. The butler presented it to her after she'd had her breakfast. Bea had been summoned to 87 Harley Street.

Wedding preparations. Be at Nick's at four o'clock, please.

Pippa's notes had grown shorter, and she'd been spending less time at Cloverdale House, giving Bea ample privacy and time: to rub Alfie's ointments on her face and chest, and to record everything she'd eaten and been in contact with in a journal per his recommendation. She brought the small journal with her, which was less than ten centimeters in length, and it fit in her reticule as she left to meet Pippa. On the way out, Bea examined her reflection and flashed a mirror image of the curt smile that her mother had trained her to produce at the ready. But then she stuck her tongue out, laughed open-mouthed, crinkled her nose, and raised her chin at the beast within. Alfie's ointment had made it bearable to overcome the hives and return to normal life—whatever that meant among Pippa's wedding preparations and Bea's mission to capture the prince to gain her freedom. Bea was ready to act. The bumps had gone, and she covered the remaining redness with powder. He was correct; there was treatment, and the beast had been tamed. She was healing.

What else could Alfie be right about?

Less than half an hour later, Bea stepped from the carriage and entered the front door at 87 Harley Street feeling more alive than she'd ever been. The bustle in the hall and the energetic voices coming from the back kitchen reminded Bea that she was young, that life brought excitement. That there was more to life than dull balls where she was expected to suppress every emotion, opinion, and her soul. After all this time in near-seclusion, she was ready to burst with energy and was excited to see Nick, his colleagues, and—yes, admittedly—Alfie.

"Do you know what this is about?" Andre asked when Nick had called everyone together as the grandfather clock in the waiting room chimed four times.

Bea shook her head as Andre opened the door to the kitchen for her, and she entered ahead of him. "Pippa asked me to meet her here and made a great fuss about punctuality." Bea cast Pippa a look as soon as she saw her standing solemnly in front of something that looked like a cart. Bea couldn't be sure; it was draped with a white cloth.

"Alfie, it's time!" Nick's voice resonated from the hall. "Wen-de-e-e!"

Wendy appeared within the minute, and Nick looked smug and proud—just like a groom ought to. Although Bea was happy for her cousin—it was a rare treasure to marry for love—Bea worried that she herself may never have such luck. Even if she managed to woo the prince, she didn't fool herself into believing that a love potion could make him actually love her. Lust her, perhaps, but love was rare and special.

A blur of memories of the young man from India, Alfie's kindness and his expertise in crafting the potion for her, and the breathtaking dexterity with which he'd made the potion nearly made Bea sway. *Alfie, Alfie, Alfie,* her mind thrummed. He'd captured her essence and seen her in a way that nobody else ever had. Was that what Pippa had meant when she said that Nick had seen into her heart? But before Bea could sort her thoughts, he appeared in the doorway. Her heart skipped a few beats.

"I'm here!" Alfie entered behind Nick, wiping his hands on a white towel, and looking just the right amount of disheveled. Bea could imagine him standing over the complicated distilling contraption with the little round glass containers and doing whatever it was with the small gas flame. The combination of danger, intrigue, and intelligence had stirred Bea's insides. Correction: the mere thought of Alfie had her stomach fluttering most unusually. It couldn't be healthy, and Bea wanted to speak to Pippa about it.

"Is this an impromptu wedding?" Andre jested, but Nick shot him a look with daggers around his head like a knife thrower at the circus.

"In preparation for the wedding, Andre." Pippa smiled just as proudly as Nick. "We need your opinions."

"Where's Felix?" Wendy asked.

"On a house call. We will save him one of each," Pippa said as she picked up the corner of the white cloth that hung over the cart. Nick picked up the other end, and they lifted it off together to reveal an intricately decorated selection of small French cakes.

"Oh my!" Wendy clasped her hands together in glee. "How very unusual to have anything but fruit cake!"

Even Bea couldn't help but marvel. "I think it's completely unique and a lovely idea!"

"These are some of our favorite selections," Pippa stated with such severity in her tone that it was as if she were choosing a boarding school for her firstborn son. "We've already ruled out two flavors."

"And the *Pâtisserie de La Loire* has combined some of our *most* favorites since they played such a special role in our union," Nick added. It was where Pippa and Nick had met by accident, but they were fond of calling it *fate*.

"We need to decide on the wedding cake by tomorrow. The pastry chef needs two days to gather the ingredients and ensure it is ready," Pippa said.

"He can assemble it at Silvercrest Manor," Wendy added.

"The wedding is not in London? Are you sure you want everyone to travel to Silvercrest?" Alfie asked. Pippa's and Bea's grandfather had left the manor to Pippa, but Bea had spent nearly as much time there as her cousin had. It was more of a castle than a manor, but they'd only ever used it for short periods.

"It's our grandparents' estate," Bea replied to his inquiry then turned to Pippa. "Grandfather would be so proud if you got married there."

"Oh, I see," Alfie blurted out, looking at her with an intensity that made her insides jump again, but then, as if he'd chastised himself for being so overt, he looked away.

"So this first one is strawberry and vanilla custard—a classic," Pippa said.

"Boring," Andre added.

Bea frowned. "It's one of their best tarts."

"But it's not special enough for a wedding," Wendy added.

"Well, that was easy." Pippa opened her eyes wide, and Bea understood. The wedding wasn't merely about Pippa and Nick; it involved them all. Plus, enlisting her friends' assistance in the decision-making process allowed Pippa to focus on some of the changes that would soon convert Cloverdale House into a rehabilitation center.

"Here we have almond torte," Nick said as he picked up a plate with a square cake entirely covered in meringue and sugar-glazed almond slices. He set it down, and cut a few pieces to serve everyone.

The nutty aroma of marzipan enveloped Bea's senses, and she liked the combination of the brittle meringue and the crunchy bite of the burned almond slivers. "This is delicious," she said.

"Yes, but look at the decoration on this one," Pippa said with sparkling eyes as she lifted a narrow but tall cylindrical cake. "He used a little of my last pineapple and has enough for another larger layer of cake if we choose this." Pippa cast Alfie a warm smile. "He sent his compliments for your rose oil and said it was a lovely balance to the tang of the fruit."

"Rose and pineapple?" Andre licked his fork clean and held out his empty plate. "I'm ready to form an educated opinion on the combination."

"Certainly you are," Nick chuckled.

"It does look rather pretty." Bea admired the rippled creamy edge and the piped rosettes around the perimeter of the cake. Miniature pink marzipan flowers were set between the rosettes, and chocolate leaves stuck out from the sides. The top was a shiny layer of a bright yellow mousse, likely the pineapple.

Sliced, the cylindrical creation revealed about twenty thin layers of cake and alternating yellow and pale beige custard. It was a work of art.

When everyone had a piece on their plates, Bea set the edge of her fork onto the yellow cream. It sank through the layers effortlessly, and she lifted her fork to her mouth just as the faint scent of rose cream reached her nose. She tasted the tangy pineapple first. But what she felt most of all was a shiver down her back. Alfie was watching her.

⇶⇷

THERE WAS NO cake, not even the pretty ones with creamy rosettes and sculpted marzipan, that could rival the beauty standing no more than three feet from him. Bea had let out a moan and an elegant little sigh when she first tasted the almond torte. But when she licked her lips and opened her mouth for the pineapple cake, Alfie knew he'd lost his wits. It was the only logical explanation, since envying a piece of cake was stupid.

Nonsense really.

Yet Alfie couldn't peel his eyes off her mouth.

At first, she touched her lower lip to the yellow mousse and darted her little pink tongue out just long enough for Alfie to turn rock-hard instantly.

He looked to Andre and Nick, hoping they'd be busy with the cakes as he shifted uncomfortably, restrained by his tight breeches.

But Andre gave him a knowing look.

Alfie turned away, but his gaze was drawn back to Bea's mouth. He was a mess by now, ogling her like a starving man.

She took a tiny bite from one of the marzipan flowers on her fork, then she tilted her head and licked the bottom drop of the heavy cream off before it fell from her fork. Alfie observed the elegant curve of her neck, and with his eyes, he traced the wispy curl that lay so lightly on her skin as if it had landed there with the lightness of a down feather.

Alfie's infatuation with her wasn't going anywhere. He'd have to learn to manage it.

Andre elbowed him.

"Ouch!" Alfie mumbled but Andre shook his head in admonishment. It didn't matter anymore, for Alfie was lost in the beauty of Bea's sensuous mouth.

Her lips were moist and pink.

She chewed and closed her eyes. Even her fanned dark lashes were beautiful.

"Good cake?" Alfie croaked, trying to stop her from moaning lest he have to take an ice bath to cool himself off.

She blinked at him, her face flushing that adorable shade of pink. "Delicious." Her voice came out raspy and a bit hoarse.

And even…seductive. Who knew that wedding cakes could be the thing that undid him?

Chapter Eleven

AFTER THE DECISION to choose the pineapple and rose cake for the wedding was made, Alfie informed Bea that her order was ready. She followed him to his apothecary shop while the others went back to their usual business. Alfie secretly cherished the opportunity to be alone with her again—before the prince swept her off her feet and whisked her away to a faraway country. This time, he knew, he wouldn't be so lucky as to be the apprentice catering to her. His place in life was in their London practice, with his friends.

"This is what I promised." Alfie slid a fluted vial with a light-rose golden glow from the liquid inside illuminating the delicate grooves running vertically along its form. The glass stopper fit snugly to preserve the precious contents. "I have warmed it, and the scents all come together quite harmoniously."

Bea took the vial and pushed the stopper down with her thumb. Then she looked at the small bottle in her hand and at Alfie, then back at it. Of all the containers, flasks, and boxes in his apothecary shop, he thought sadly, the one in her hand had the power to alter her life. And his. "What if it works?" she whispered.

He wasn't sure whether he should answer, but his heart lurched when her eyes searched his for something he mustn't give. But he couldn't stop himself.

"Then the prince will get the best bride in all of England," Alfie said heavily. "He would not be able to stay away."

"What do you mean?"

Where to begin?

"He will want to kiss, woo, and marry you. I don't know in which order, though I can suspect."

"Out of that order would be improper." She blushed an adorable shade of pink. "Although…"

Her eyes moved as if she remembered something, but she remained silent. As much as he knew it was inappropriate to ask, that he was risking everything, he couldn't stop himself from asking the thought that weighed on his every thought. "Bea, pardon my directness, but have you ever been—"

"Kissed?" She cut him off with vigor as if the word had exploded between them. Then she narrowed her gaze. "Did Pippa tell you about my reputation?"

"No." Only you are the belle of every ball; your dance card is always filled, and suitors trip over each other in the mornings when they bring you flowers. She didn't have to tell me the rest; you're the sweetest, loneliest, and most intelligent woman I've ever met.

She cocked her head in disbelief. "I've been to many balls and danced with every eligible bachelor of the past three seasons."

"Until the ball at the Langleys."

"Indeed." She said the word as if tasting something sour. "So if this works, if the prince wishes to kiss me, I'll do what my mother taught me, and it will go by soon enough."

Now, it was Alfie's turn to blink incredulously. "It will 'go by' soon enough?"

"Yes, you know: Keep your lips pressed shut, count to twenty, and then push him away."

"What *is* that exactly?"

"Well, it's how to kiss. I thought you ought to know."

"In fact I do. Know how to kiss. And what you have described is something else, something dreadfully awkward."

"Kisses are intimate contacts with another person's mouth; they are supposed to be dreadfully awkward."

"But that is not... you see... it's just that is not at all how it works." Alfie was stunned to say the least.

She shifted her weight to the other leg and put a hand on her hip. "Are you jesting?"

It was too good to be true, wasn't it?

Except, what if she'd recognized him from India? Was this a test?

He shook his head, trying hard not to stare at her lips. "Most certainly not. I can show you if you'd like," Alfie said.

Loudmouth. It didn't help to chastise himself, the words had been uttered.

"Are you suggesting that none of the peers of the realm who have kissed me did it correctly?"

"If it was how you described, they did rather poorly indeed." He quirked a brow.

"And you are certain you can do better?"

"Yes." Alfie's heart was pounding, and he couldn't catch his breath. *What was he thinking?*

She narrowed her eyes and gave him a once-over. "That's very magnanimous of you."

He shrugged, trying to appear nonchalant.

"Prove it," she said.

"You want me to kiss you?" Alfie couldn't believe his luck. This had been too easy, and he needed to be absolutely sure that it was her wish—it was undoubtedly his.

"Mother says twenty seconds is enough. So, in twenty seconds of lip contact, show me that you can do better," she said, her chin raised high, and her neck stretched in his direction.

Alfie took a steadying breath.

His pulse raced as he stood before her, the air thick with anticipation. He had a mere twenty seconds, a brief window to eclipse all her past kisses, to make them pale in comparison. He couldn't merely take her with all the vigor shooting through his veins; it had to be for her. He'd gladly make everything about her. Confidence surged within him—he was more than capable.

The first step was simple yet intimate; he reached forward, his fingers deftly untying the ribbon that held her bonnet and veil in place. As they fluttered to the ground, a cascade of curly strawberry blonde locks tumbled around her shoulders, framing her face in a wild, natural beauty.

Carefully, he gathered those errant strands, tucking them behind her ears. The simple action drew a visible shiver from her, goosebumps blossoming across her skin in a silent affirmation of their effervescent connection. Her breath hitched, growing heavier with the anticipation that Alfie hoped matched the pounding of his own heart.

In her eyes, he found silent questions and whispered hopes. This was his moment, his singular opportunity to prove the depth of his desire. To prove the sincerity of his affection. Though he couldn't say it to her lest he betray her trust as a client, and as Pippa's cousin. What was worse was that he'd led her on a path that could assure her of her prince, while she was like a princess to him, and he wasn't allowed to chase her. The daughter of an earl could be with a prince—not an apothecary.

Yet, he'd take a kiss. Nobody would be for the wiser if they never mentioned it to a soul, and Alfie could lock it deep in his heart to cherish forever.

He needed the perfect angle, the ideal proximity, to ensure that this kiss would be equally imprinted upon her memory, forever casting a shadow over any before it. *Or after.* But Alfie didn't dare think of the same effect for the future, even though he wished he could lay a claim on Bea.

With a tenderness born of genuine care, Alfie placed his right hand upon her left cheek, his thumb softly tracing the delicate curve of her reddened cheekbone. Her skin was irritated and flushed from her condition and demanded a gentle touch. He obliged, applying enough pressure to stir her senses without causing discomfort.

At this moment, the world fell away, leaving only the two of them suspended in a bubble of their own making. The air between them crackled with an unspoken promise, a prelude to the passion and connection that hovered on the brink of realization. Alfie leaned in, guided by an instinctive knowledge of the contours of her face, the sweet anticipation of her lips.

This kiss was an admission, a declaration without words that spoke of nights spent longing, of days filled with hidden glances and unspoken yearnings. He was about to cross a threshold, to venture into the uncharted territory of her embrace, driven by a desire that had simmered beneath the surface far too strong and far too long, to remain contained.

⇶⫸⫷⇷

SURPRISE. THAT WAS the first sensation that washed over Bea as Alfie leaned in, close enough for her to feel the warmth of his breath against her skin. It was an immediate, tangible connection, a prelude to the contact that hadn't yet happened. His proximity was an invasion of the space around her, yet not unwelcome. The freshness of him—his clean, crisp scent with the earthy undertones, reminiscent of a dense, ancient forest just after the rain, and mixed with a spicy edge that hinted at hidden strength and resilience—filled her senses, drawing her in, making her crave more.

In previous encounters such as this, she'd braced herself and started counting, eager to break it off. Not this time.

Not with him.

She pursed her lips in anticipation, a silent invitation, a readiness for the touch she assumed would follow.

But it didn't come. Instead, Alfie held back, his lips a mere half an inch from hers, lingering in the space between promise and fulfillment. Her breath hitched at the audacity, the deliberate tease. It was a dance on the edge of desire, a test of patience she hadn't known she possessed.

With his lips so tantalizingly close yet not touching, Bea became acutely aware of every detail—the heat radiating from his body, the steady rhythm of his breathing, the faintest hint of stubble along his jawline. Time seemed to stretch, each second elongated by the intensity of her focus on these minute sensations.

The absence of contact, the deliberate pause, heightened her awareness to a level for which she hadn't been prepared. Bea's heart pounded, a rapid drumbeat echoing in her chest, reverberating throughout her body. The urge to close the distance, to initiate the contact he so purposefully denied, was almost overwhelming. Yet, she remained still, caught in the spell of anticipation he'd woven around them.

And then there was the realization, a dawning understanding that this moment—this deliberate withholding—was itself a form of intimacy. In his restraint, Alfie communicated trust, a willingness to let the moment unfold at its own pace, to savor the build-up as much as the culmination. It was an unexpected form of seduction that spoke to a depth of feeling Bea hadn't dared to consider.

When should I begin counting if he hasn't touched my lips yet?

Then he did, softly at first. His fleshy lips sank onto hers, and a jolt of heat shot through her.

One.

The sensation was unexpected, like the first ray of sun breaking through a persistent winter cloud. It was warmth and light, and it spoke of promises whispered in the dark, now brought to life in this single touch.

Two.

His lips moved against hers with a gentle insistence. This was an unfamiliar yet welcome territory. She kept her lips pursed but felt them growing hot against his. There was no rush, no demand, only an unhurried quest for connection. The sweetness of the moment unfolded slowly, like honey dripping from a spoon, thick and golden.

Three.

Her senses were alight, each one heightened to an exquisite degree. His taste was intoxicating, a blend of mint and something that made her feel like a fairy dancing from one mossy rock to the next in the sparkling dew of a forest after a summer rain. Their breaths, mingling and hesitant, became the only music she wished to hear.

Four.

The feeling of his hand, at first tentative on her waist, tightened, drawing her closer against his broad chest. His other hand cradled the back of her head and pulled her closer. This wasn't merely a meeting of lips; it was a melding of souls that had longed for this reunion, even if they hadn't known it until now.

Five.

And as they deepened the kiss, Bea felt herself unraveling, layers of reserve and caution melting away under his tender assault. There was a surrender in this, yielding not to defeat but to discovery, to the joy of finding and being found.

Six.

She exhaled through her mouth, and a moan escaped her.

Seven.

His tongue flicked over her lower lip.

This was where Bea usually skipped to twenty, but she wished to stop counting now.

Another gentle flick of his tongue and a pause followed, his warm lips nudging hers apart.

Eight.

Bea parted her mouth, unsure whether she needed to say something or stop him, but she let it happen. She let him conquer her in a way nobody else ever had.

Nine.

A wisp of cool air touched her mouth when she opened to him, and he inhaled just before he plunged his tongue into her mouth. Just a little bit. But enough for a sudden spark of delight to ignite inside her.

Ten.

Oh no, half of the kiss was already over. Bea's heart sank when she realized it.

Then, she decided to make the most of the next ten seconds. Unsure at first how she wanted to draw him in.

Hands, yes, good idea.

Eleven.

She brought one hand to his neck and then let her fingers crawl to his dense, curly hair. It was lush, soft, and yet thoroughly masculine.

Twelve.

He let out a deep but silent growl that spurred her on even more. So Bea opened her mouth wide and sucked his tongue in. He changed the angle, and then she changed it, too.

Thirteen.

Her tongue entered his mouth, and she felt his velvety warmth and then his slightly cooler teeth in a perfect row.

Fourteen.

The pleasure was intense and immediate, but she was beginning to learn. There was giving and taking in kissing, and then there was this. A oneness.

Fifteen.

Heat.

Sixteen.

Depth.

Seventeen.

Urgency.

Eighteen.

Bea felt light-headed and nearly forgot to count. His hands, firm on her waist, anchored her to the present, to him.

Nineteen.

Her senses were alight, and every touch and breath shared amplified the feeling of completeness that enveloped her. It was as if they were discovering a secret language, one spoken not through words but through the meeting of souls and the gentle exploration of hands.

Nineteen and a half?

Was he keeping count, too? She mustn't ask for more than the twenty seconds he'd been willing to give.

But the pleasure was a wave so powerful it threatened to sweep her away; it drove her to cling to him, her fingers tangling in the fabric of his shirt as if he were the only thing anchoring her to the earth.

"Twenty," she whispered. The time allotted was up.

He immediately let go of her waist, broke the kiss, and stepped back.

Bea swallowed hard, her lips swollen as if they'd doubled in size. She was dizzy.

The room went dark around the edges.

Alfie cocked his head and said something, but he sounded like an echo far away.

And then there was blackness.

Chapter Twelve

Bea drifted in a haze that wrapped around the edges of dreams, softening reality into mere whispers. Voices floated to her, muffled and distant, as if she were underwater and the voices on the surface were discussing her fate.

"Why did she faint?" A man's voice asked. Perhaps Andre.

"I didn't even know she was with you." Pippa's voice rang familiarly. "Thank you so much for preventing her fall and carrying her here."

But as Bea lay there, the voices sharpened, clawing their way through the fog of her consciousness. The bed beneath her felt unfamiliar, not the comforting embrace of her own but something foreign, too firm, and yet oddly yielding, like sinking into a cloud that refused to let go.

"Tell me exactly what happened," a male voice said, and then Bea felt something cold, and round on her chest—a stethoscope. Then, someone touched her wrist and waited. "Her pulse is quick but stable," the voice said.

"Thank you, Andre," Pippa said.

For a moment, she imagined she was adrift in a dream, one of those vivid ones that felt tantalizingly real yet slipped away upon waking.

"Was she flushed or pale before this happened?" Andre asked.

"Flushed." Alfie's voice sounded grumpy but had the same

effect his kiss had previously had. Bea felt her knees weakening again, and she was glad she already lay flat on a bed, for she'd swoon again.

The scent in the air was different, too; it lacked the comforting notes of lavender, chamomile, cloves, and alcohol from the apothecary.

"Is that a bad sign?" Pippa asked.

"Flushed before fainting means that she swooned," Nick said but his voice sounded a bit farther away. Were all the doctors surrounding her and Pippa with them?

Another growl came from the room's far end, but Bea couldn't see anything. Her eyelids felt heavy as if weighted down by the remnants of sleep, but curiosity—or instinct—urged them open. The blur of colors and shapes that greeted her slowly coalesced into a room she did not recognize: stark white walls, a window with curtains that fluttered slightly with an unseen breeze, and shadows of people moving just beyond her line of sight.

A pang of fear knotted in her stomach, sharp and sudden. This wasn't a dream. The realization hit her like the first breath after diving deep underwater. Real. Too real. The voices weren't figments of her imagination but actual people, talking about her, discussing her as if she weren't there, or perhaps as if she were nothing more than a problem to solve.

Then she remembered the last thing before she felt her vision going dark. The last thing she'd seen—the last person—had been Alfie.

She licked her lips.

"She's coming to," Pippa announced. Then Bea heard the trickling of water and a cold compress on her forehead. A gentle hand came to hers and gave her a reassuring squeeze. "I'm here."

Her throat felt parched, her voice a mere whisper lost in the expanse of the room. Panic fluttered in her chest like a bird trapped in a cage, seeking an escape that seemed all too elusive. This was no dream. This was reality, and she was caught in its unyielding grasp.

"Please leave us," Pippa said, and footsteps followed. The floorboards creaked, and a door clicked shut. The compress came off Bea's forehead. There was more trickling of water, probably in a bowl, and then the compress returned cold and jarringly wet.

Bea reached for her head and frowned. She opened her eyes and saw her cousin's concerned look.

"You swooned," Pippa said.

Bea blinked a few times, and her cousin's concerned frown turned into a scandalized curiosity usually reserved for girl talk or gossip over tea.

"Where am I?"

"The patient room. Alfie carried you here."

He'd carried her in his arms; all she cared about was that she'd missed relishing the sentiment. Heat rushed to Bea's face, and she inhaled deeply as she surveyed her surroundings. The window was slightly open, blowing the sheer curtain into the room as if fairies were trying to dance inside.

"So, my dear cousin, what happened?"

"I had a flare-up," Bea said as she slowly propped herself on her elbows and sat up. "So I came to ask Alfie for powder to cover it up." She didn't want to admit to the love potion, for it was too embarrassing for a diamond of the first water to resort to such measures to land a prince.

"Like the maquillage Violet had?"

"Yes. He had similar ones in his apothecary."

"Hm!" Pippa narrowed her eyes. "*Aaand?*" She drew the word out and arched a brow. When had she become such a wizard of women's secrets?

"And he recommended an ointment."

"Did it help?"

"Yes."

"So you came back for more?"

"No."

Pippa pursed her lips and crossed her arms. "Why were you

in the apothecary with him instead of staying to eat cake with me?"

Bea nodded. "I had placed an order and came to retrieve it."

"An order for more ointment for your skin?"

"No. It was for a love potion." Bea always told her cousin the truth, which would be no exception regardless of how painful it was to admit it.

Pippa shut her eyes momentarily and sank onto the edge of the bed. Then she turned to Bea. "Why do *you* need a love potion?"

"Why?" Bea felt heat rising to her face, but it passed the level of a lady-like blush and went straight to red-hot anger. "Why, you ask? Because the coveted 'belle of the ball' is apparently all too easy for a prince to resist."

"Prince Ferdinand of Transylvania?"

"How do you know about Prince Stan?"

"Violet told me. You already have a nickname for him?"

"*Hmpf*! He told me to call him 'Stan'. It's part of his name. Anyhow, he's my chance to leave."

"Go where?"

"First down the altar and then to his castle. Far away."

"Where nobody knows about your flare-ups?"

"Yes. And where the Ton isn't so mean to you and there's no threat to my reputation all the time."

"So a love potion is supposed to make him want to take you to his magic castle like in a fairy tale?" Pippa sounded skeptical.

"I don't know about magic, but I hear it's a large medieval construction with turrets and much green landscape surrounding it. You can see the mountains from Bran Castle."

"Aha, well then, it's a must that you devote your life to living there. Especially since there are no castles and green landscapes here in England."

Bea's eyes snapped to Pippa. She was making fun of her now. At least it distracted her so Bea wouldn't have to tell her what else had happened.

That's what Bea got for playing by the Ton's rules, seeking the highest-ranking bachelor she could find before her parents returned. She was beginning to hate the rules and the expectations. Bristling against the requirements of her station, Bea had finally had enough. This ploy had to work; she must be on a ship in the Mediterranean Sea before her parents returned.

Only... she'd received a bone shattering kiss from the apothecary.

If she had any sense at all, she'd distance herself from him, or else he'd turn her resolve to a powder finer than his medicines.

Her cheeks tingled and a flash of heat flushed over them. A burning itch sparkled across her face, making her want to rake her fingernails over her skin. *The beast.*

Bea touched her face, and it was hot.

Oh no, not again!

Chapter Thirteen

ALFIE HATED HIMSELF for knocking the wind out of Bea and slumped onto his chair behind the counter, the only place where he felt in command and control. After she'd awakened, he'd started working in his apothecary and by the time Pippa took her home, Alfie had already polished his beakers, recalibrated the brass scale, cleaned the window, and sorted the tea sachets. Again. But there was no amount of tedious work that could take his mind off the kiss.

It was a kiss of a lifetime with the woman of the century.

"Alfie, someone is waiting for you." Wendy burst into the apothecary shop and placed a stack of crisp white towels on the kitchen table. She leaned on her elbows and waited.

"Yes, Wendy?" Alfie knew that look. He'd known it since she was a little girl. It always worked.

"Why is he here?" She opened her eyes wide and gestured to the kitchen door.

If he engaged, she'd trap him. He knew it. And yet, Alfie had to ask. "Who is waiting for me?"

"Prince Ferdinand Constantin Maximilian Hohenzollern-Sigmaringen."

"What?" Alfie shot up from his chair and let it fall back with a screech. He stormed to the door and found a tall, dark-haired man in a very expensive-looking coat tapping on the wall in the waiting room as if he owned it.

Alfie stopped in the doorway, suspicious of the prince's intentions. He couldn't possibly have already found out that Alfie had kissed the woman destined for him, or could he?

Wendy was at his heel, and he turned around, shaking his head "no." Wendy deflated and dragged her feet as she left and disappeared out the door.

Alfie turned back to the prince and cleared his throat.

The prince turned and gave him a superciliary once-over that immediately irritated Alfie. He gave the man a similar, dismissive once-over in return.

Tall, young, strong. Impeccable tailoring. Excellent shave.

He'd make a handsome husband for Bea.

Alfie instantly hated him.

"Are you Collins, the apothecary?"

Alfie eyed the prince's tapping fingers on the wall, and the prince stopped. Slower than he intended, Alfie walked back around the counter to the spot where he was in charge. From there, he could reach every drawer behind him, easily able to tell what was where without looking. This was his realm of expertise. Where he reigned.

"What do you need?" Alfie tried not to growl, but what else would two wolves do when fighting for… well, they weren't fighting. The prince had won.

But something in his heart hadn't given up yet.

"The Countess of Langley tells me that you are well-versed in non-traditional medicine."

His rolling 'r' had the same effect as a wolf's warning growl, and Alfie crossed his arms.

"Who?"

The prince laughed. "Very good. I like your discretion. But I was there, you know. I saw you at their ball a few days ago, and I'm well aware of the bonds you share."

Alfie shrugged. Whatever His Highness may or may not know, he wouldn't confirm.

"You've come with a requirement for a salve?" *I hope you're itching and burning. Go sit in some nettles.*

"No."

"Then what can I do for you?" Alfie put his hands on the counter and leaned forward, taking up as much space as possible. He was just as tall as the prince, and as far as Alfie was concerned, a title earned by way of studies was worth as much as one inherited. Whether the prince would live up to his title was yet to be seen.

Except that Alfie hoped that it wasn't Bea who would be testing the prince's virtues and merit.

"I need something highly concentrated and undetectable."

Don't they all?

Earls who needed salves of a certain slippery nature, dukes with a preference for elixirs to harden the muscles, while others preferred some for relaxation... Alfie's list was endless and secret.

He could fill volumes with how many times ladies had come for a poison that could solve their marital problems by ending their husbands' lives. Sometimes, they wanted their husbands to suffer. Other times, they wanted to rid their bodies of the evidence of sidesteps. But Alfie never catered to such requests. He wanted to help heal ailments, practice medicine with honor, and not sell his integrity for charlatanry or the dispensation of justice where it wasn't his place to serve it.

"No poisons. Sorry! I'm not dealing with this kind of—"

"Not a poison." The prince *tsked*. "A little something to erase traces of questions I cannot freely ask." He drew circles in the air as if the effect were self-explanatory. "Violet said you could make anything."

"A truth serum?" Alfie shook his head.

"A mixture that masks the effects of something nobody knows exists, an untraceable potion?"

"Never."

The prince dropped his shoulders and looked Alfie in the eyes. "Why not?"

"There's no such thing as a truth serum. Perhaps if you find a specialist in witchcraft or charlatanerie, they will sell it to you."

"Then invent one! You're the best, aren't you?"

Argh! Alfie hated nothing more than a challenge from the man he wished to surpass.

"Let's see. If there were such a thing, and I'm not saying there is, there are several problems. First, the dosage is problematic because I cannot give you a medicine for a third person whose weight and physique I don't know."

The prince inclined his head. "Fair enough. I can obtain this information for you."

Alfie narrowed his eyes. "And I don't make anything that could harm my clients. Or anyone."

"Very good. I'd be the client and wouldn't take it, so there would be no harm."

He was smart and uncomfortably direct. If he were anyone else, Alfie would almost respect the prince. But he didn't. He hated him because Bea liked him.

"How do I know that you won't use this to manipulate a woman to do what you—"

"I would never!" The prince hit his fist on the counter and looked appalled. "That's preposterous! Criminal! Immoral!"

Alfie cocked his head.

"Look, I'm not in line for anything; I'm merely trying to accomplish my mission."

"Which is what?"

"Preventing harm to my people."

"At the hands of?"

"An enemy I know of whom you are aware."

Alfie quirked a brow. "You know nothing of my enemies." *You're ranking at the top.*

"I understand that you are friends with the Jewish jewelers at St. James."

Alfie crossed his arms again and raised his chin. "So what?"

"The Klonimuses, Pearlers... Felix works in this practice with you, right?"

"Yes, Felix is the dentist here. His name is on the door." *Why was he pointing out the obvious?*

"He uses gold. That gold comes from my country. And many want to subvert it without paying."

"Thieves?"

The prince brushed the words aside as if they could be swept away like dust. "When countries clash with each other, it's not theft. Not even a crime. An annexation is not a repossession in diplomacy. Persecution is not a manhunt, either. The bigger the scale, the more harmless the words."

Even though he has a moral compass, I must hate him.

"Who's your target?" Alfie asked.

"Richard Nagy."

The man was the worst sort of scoundrel and nasty, with vile motives. If anyone had perfected the art of being a perpetrator of crimes against minority groups, Richard Nagy was the ultimate master. On top of that, he had an awful mannerism that made him seem like the victim—after he preyed on people based on their ethnicity, religion, or wealth.

"I beg your pardon?"

"And Baron Wolfgang von List."

The only person worse than Nagy was von List, a Prussian baron on a self-appointed diplomatic duty to sully the waters in the English parliament, so that no equality would be given to the Jewish citizens. If the prince had anything to do with either of these people, Alfie rather wished to stay far away from him.

"Leave my apothecary."

The prince chuckled, widened his stance, and sucked his lower lip in. "I'll bring you their weight and sizes from their tailor, but I take it you know who they are?"

"I can't say." Alfie sucked his cheeks in. Of course, he knew the no-gooders who never got caught abusing their stations and inflicting harm upon his Jewish friends. The temptation to extract information from the Prussian Baron von List and his lackey,

Bailiff Richard Nagy, would give the Pearlers, the Klonimuses, and Felix more than mere ammunition to defend themselves. Helping under these circumstances would be a good deed and a big step toward justice where the authorities were misguided.

"Can I pick it up tomorrow morning? They're playing cards at Langley's house, and I'd like to show my generosity with a round of whiskey."

Henry was the Earl of Langley, one of the best and most prominent patrons of the practice at 87 Harley Street. So he was involved, too. This information reassured Alfie because it meant that the prince was on the right side of the conflict.

Alfie didn't want to admit it to himself, but the set-up at the Earl of Langley's house would be perfect.

He didn't want to help the prince, but his mission was worthy and in the spirit of justice and equality indeed. Plus, it was helping his friends who'd been victimized by Baron von List and Nagy for long enough. "Cognac."

"What?"

"Whiskey doesn't mask the bitterness. Cognac does."

"So you'll make me a truth serum?" The prince didn't hide his hopefulness well.

"I didn't say that."

"Can you make it undetectable, so he won't suspect anything?"

"No. Medicine always smells or tastes a certain way."

The prince furrowed his brow.

"But if I run a test, I must be there to detect its effect."

"It's dangerous to do this at my friends' home, the Earl and Countess of Langley."

"I'm a man with integrity," Alfie said, raising eyebrows. "Thus, I need to be sure you don't use this on a woman."

"So come and watch me."

Chapter Fourteen

HER HEART BETRAYED her station, Bea thought. The kiss hadn't been proper.
But oh, had it felt wonderful.
Alfie was—she sighed—like a revelation of what the world could be if two halves came together, the male and the female. She'd been only half, and since she'd kissed him, she knew there was completion to be attained, yet getting there eluded her.

In the quiet sanctuary of her chamber, Bea leaned against the window frame, staring out at the moonlit gardens that stretched beyond Cloverdale House. The night was still, save for the occasional whisper of wind through the trees. Her thoughts were anything but calm and refused to be quelled.

She touched her lips, still tingling from the memory of Alfie's kiss. In her mind's eye, she could see the softened edges of his rugged face, the way his eyes had darkened with desire as he leaned in. The moment had been electric, an unexpected jolt that sent her heart racing and left her breathless. She hadn't planned it, hadn't even considered it a possibility, yet there it was—searing and unforgettable.

Bea knew she was playing a dangerous game. She was meant to woo the prince, weave her way into his good graces, and secure her family's position while escaping the grip of London's elite. She'd outgrown the Ton in the course of her seasons and wished to leave their gossip and superficial values behind like an old gown. But she was racing against time, unable to see exactly how much she had left until her parents' return. She'd rely on her charm and a vial of love potion now hidden beneath her pillow. The potion was supposed to ensure the prince's devotion, a foolproof way to bind his fate to hers. But now, the very thought of using it felt like a betrayal—not to the prince, but to herself.

Her heart skipped just thinking of Alfie. He was everything the prince was not: grounded, genuine, and utterly irresistible. His touch had ignited something within her, a fierce longing she didn't know she was capable of. It was as if he had seen through the layers of pretense and expectation that cloaked her, reaching the core of who she truly was. With him, there were no masks, no need to perform or pretend. It was a raw, unfiltered connection, and it terrified her.

Bea sighed, turning away from the window, her fingers reaching for the small vial of potion under the feather pillow. It was supposed to be her ticket to security, to a future where she needn't worry about her family's precarious standing. But now, it felt like a burden, a reminder of the lengths she was willing to go to achieve her goals.

From her vantage point, she caught a glimpse of her reflection in the dressing mirror. Her heart grew heavy as she noticed the telltale signs of another outbreak—a smattering of red, angry patches creeping across her cheeks and jawline.

She ran her fingers lightly over the inflamed skin, wincing at the tenderness. The rash seemed to flare brighter with every anxious heartbeat, spreading like wildfire.

Desperate, she rummaged through the drawers, searching for the salve Alfie had given her the last time. Her hands shook as she uncapped the small jar, scooping out a generous amount and applying it to her face. The cool ointment offered immediate relief, but it couldn't erase the underlying cause of her distress.

She sank onto the edge of her bed, the soft down comforter softening beneath her weight. Could she really go through with it? Could she look the prince in the eyes, knowing her heart belonged to another? The stakes were too high, and the consequences were too severe. Yet, the thought of never feeling Alfie's kiss again, never hearing his voice or seeing his smile, was almost unbearable.

A tear slipped down her cheek. She was trapped between duty and desire, between what was expected of her and what her heart yearned for. It was a cruel twist of fate to find love where it was forbidden and to be bound by obligations she could not shirk.

Bea lay back on the bed, clutching the vial to her chest as if seeking solace from the very thing that caused her turmoil. The choice before her was impossible, each path fraught with its own perils. As she closed her eyes, the echo of Alfie's kiss lingered, creating a bittersweet reminder that some things, once felt, could never be forgotten.

Chapter Fifteen

AFTER THE PRINCE left, Alfie remained in his apothecary shop and thought about where to start. Then he heard footsteps.

"What did he want?" Felix asked as he and Andre walked in, arms crossed, and looked out the window. They had seemingly been waiting outside the apothecary's door until the prince left.

"Langley said he was on a diplomatic mission. He doesn't look sick to me," Andre said, poking at the truth in his telltale Italian method of interrogation. Whoever credited the Greek philosopher Socrates for investigative methods hadn't met Dr. Andre Fernando from Florence, Italy.

"I can't say." Alfie squatted under the counter to pick out the beakers and flasks for the mixture he needed to make.

"We are a practice, so in fact you *can* say," Felix said. "Patient information is held closely among us."

There was even more to it and Alfie knew that. If anything could harm one of them, they'd all be affected—not merely if their business suffered but because they were like a family. Secrets shared between the five of them—Alfie, Nick, Andre, Felix, and Wendy—were sacred. And they'd protect each other, their patients, and the confidentiality of their patients, but that didn't mean that they couldn't consult with each other and help. That was the thing with the doctors at 87 Harley Street. They weren't just collaborators or colleagues; they weren't merely friends. They were family. They'd lay down their lives for one another. And what was worth even more than life itself, they'd sacrifice their licenses to practice for one another.

They had an unwritten code of honor dictating that they'd share delicate questions of ethics, medicine, or even life itself. Like in a family, the others might get upset and admonish him for his mistakes, but they would always come to his rescue. Not telling them about this was too big, too dangerous.

"He's not a patient," Alfie mumbled behind the counter.

"Then tell me what you're making." Andre leaned forward and tried to peer over at him. "I worry that it's dangerous or else you wouldn't make such a secret of it."

Alfie got up and placed three small glass vials on the counter along with the glass flasks to boil his concoction over the burners. He cast Andre a look and pinched his lips; he wouldn't say. That didn't mean he couldn't show.

And yet, he had a duty to preserve his customers' secrets.

"Indian pennywort, belladonna, and henbane," Alfie said. "Then muskroot and valerian. I cannot tell you any more."

Andre cocked his head. "Isn't henbane what they poured in Hamlet's father's ear to kill him?"

"The Greeks poisoned their arrows with a decoction of henbane. Vikings even took the seeds to their graves," Felix added. If it weren't helpful for a muscle ache or to clean wounds, an ordinary orthopedist wouldn't know. Felix, however, had studied in Delhi with Alfie. Even if he didn't know how to mix the medicines, Felix knew what to ask for, given various symptoms.

"If you had a patient with earaches, rheumatism, sciatica, and insomnia, you could tell me. If it were for a toothache, you'd have already sent him to me. That leaves only one use." The dentist opened his eyes wide. "Hallucinations, the inability to withhold the impulse to speak, and unconsciousness." Andre leaned forward. "Who's getting the truth serum?"

Alfie held Felix's gaze momentarily and then surveyed Andre's expression. It was stern and unforgiving, with a gravity unusual in the man's expression.

"Someone who deserves it," Alfie said. *We all know him and yet I can't say.*

"Alfie, we swore the Hippocratic oath. You mustn't administer poisons that could alter a person's perception of reality without their consent." Andre, usually the first to joke and promote mischief, had lost the benevolent Italian lilt, and now his accent sounded rather strict.

"I'm not doing anything like that."

"Ayurvedic medicine should be used for cures and treatments, Alfie. You promised never to act in bad faith," Felix said. "You're not above the law and you can't take justice in your own hands. We both promised to Master Varier when we completed our apprenticeships in India. You even stayed an extra two months until you earned your fare back to England!"

"Yes! We promised not to use it for evil or to manipulate people. *That's why* I agreed to make it."

Felix's eyebrows shot up, his mouth slightly agape as he blinked rapidly, seemingly struggling to comprehend Alfie's words.

"Some people use their influence to manipulate and twist the truth, to create hurdles for the people I love and respect. I'm hoping to extract some information to make it stop," Alfie added.

"By poisoning them? It's not your job to bring justice to where you believe it belongs," Andre said.

Alfie swallowed hard. He knew that.

Yet, this was necessary.

He pulled out the vials and little paper packets of dried herbs from his drawers, then uncorked the belladonna extract from the drawer of his counter. Felix grabbed his wrist.

"Who's this for, Alfie?"

"What if I told you it was for the enemy?"

Felix let go of his wrist. "My enemy or yours?"

"Does it matter?"

"If it's incriminating you on my behalf, I don't want it," Felix said. "You don't need to commit crimes to protect me, I never asked you for that!"

It went without saying that Alfie and Andre were upset about the fact Felix and their other Jewish friends didn't have the same rights as the gentiles under British law. Even though England was more progressive than the nations on the European continent, they were all trained to see all people as equals—which they were, from a scientific perspective. Why not from a legal one?

"I didn't offer it to you. And someone else asked."

"But it serves Felix's purpose?" Andre sounded exasperated and started to pace the room. "Please don't tell me you're taking on the baron."

Felix froze and stared at Alfie, who lowered his head and poured plain alcohol into a beaker.

"Did the prince ask you to poison List?" Felix whispered.

"Prince Ferdinand... with the long name," Alfie murmured.

Felix stared. Andre stopped by the window and turned to glare at Alfie.

"It's something to do with gold. A trade route in the Black Sea involving the Pearlers and the Klonimuses... and the metal exploitation of Transylvanian territory."

"The prince is seeking leverage to stop Nagy and List from ruining the suppliers of the gold?" Felix combed both hands through his hair. "Arnold and Caleb have a trade route for gems, so they are going after the gold."

"Yes, they are going after the Jews' Achilles heel—yours, too, Felix. Without gold from the Klonimuses, you can't work."

"And without gold, the *Crown Jewelers* will lose their commission," Andre said.

The Pearlers and the Klonimuses were a renowned Jewish family of jewelers, the Crown jewelers to Prinny. They had created the most distinguished and luxurious pieces and were now producing pieces for the Royal Grand Service. They needed gold and Baron von List intercepted it to weaken their position. Something wasn't right.

"It's not just about the golden goblets, platters, and tureens, is it?" Andre clenched his mouth shut so that the muscles of his cheeks protruded. He looked angry.

"If Prinny cannot maintain his honor and show off the English riches, England will lose its influence."

"And the Russians can swoop in with the idea to segregate the Jews in constricted areas of the land, just like they do in the Pale of Settlement under the Czar?" Alfie knew, as the others did, that it would cut off their supply for gold and the ability to trade freely, a privilege Jews had under English law. If he were isolated, Felix didn't need to explain it because Alfie knew just as well as Andre that Felix was the only Jewish doctor at their practice, and that he alone brought in more money with gold fillings than all the others combined.

"Yes. They want to undermine the entire path that fuels any chances the Jews have to establish a meritocracy. And international political stability might be the collateral damage." Alfie arranged the bottle of alcohol and set a brass weight on his little scale. "I'm not ready to let that go by without doing something about it. The law has never protected Jewish minorities, nor anyone who's different, you know that. Prinny can't act either, without corroboration of the threat, and he would have to give other jewelers a chance to cater to him."

"Without Felix's income, we'd be quickly in debt and the practice would—" Andre inhaled sharply, unable to speak it. They had all worked too hard to lose their livelihoods and reputations.

"How can you get their consent to take the serum?" Felix asked. "Don't do it without that."

"I don't know yet."

"They have to want it," Felix said.

"You have the right dosage?" Andre asked with the air of a co-conspirator. Anyone who'd met Baron von List wouldn't question the need to poison him—he was the kind of entitled nobleman seething with venom, and possessing the self-centered smugness of a criminal who continued unpunished thanks to his title.

"I'll be there to ensure the prince doesn't go too far." Alfie set another small brass weight on his scale and spooned a brittle dry mix of leaves on the other scale tray.

"I'll be here if you need me," Andre declared and left.

Finally, Felix's shoulders drooped; he seemed to fight with himself a moment more before he raised his head and asked, "What can I do to help?" Without waiting for a response, he stepped around the counter and pulled a white apron from the shelf. He shook it, and the unfolding of the freshly starched white cotton produced a breeze in the apothecary—a breeze that brought on change.

And Alfie hoped it would be a good one.

Chapter Sixteen

WAKING IN A fog, from bad dreams which featured a certain prince, Alfie gathered a wicker basket filled with large glass bottles of plain alcohol and a knife. His heart felt heavier than his shoes as he prepared to leave for Pippa's orangery. Bea had invited him to pick some of the fragrant orange blooms, and as they'd discussed, that was best done in the early morning. If he waited another day, the blooms may be past the height of fragrance. The sun had hardly risen in the sky and the air was damp with dew. The perfect time for harvesting.

With a click of the door latch, he stepped onto Harley Street and waved for a hackney, pausing to glance back at his home. An odd sensation gnawed at him, like an undiagnosed ailment lurking beneath the surface. Others seemed to fit into their lives seamlessly, like doors closing gently into their frames. But Alfie felt misaligned as if his latch never quite engaged with the strike plate. Something didn't click into place.

As he contemplated his situation, a painful churn twisted his stomach. If he helped the prince, he'd be betraying everything Nick, Felix, Andre, and Wendy stood for. Yet, aiding Felix and their Jewish friends when no one else would stand up for what was right—didn't that count as heroism? The authorities wouldn't help Jewish citizens; they had no protection under the law. List was on a mission to weaken even the little protection they had and stifle the supply of the precious gold they needed to earn their livelihoods and their prestige. It wasn't right.

Or was it foolishness to pursue the wrong people based solely on a stranger's word? Even though this stranger was a prince, carrying innate credibility? Even though he held the potential to wed Bea and take her away forever? The conflicting thoughts left Alfie grappling with his conscience.

Once he'd gotten into the hackney and taken a seat on the forward-facing bench, the carriage traveled the span down Harley Street, past the stone facades of Marylebone, and toward the busier, more colorful section of London toward Cloverdale House on Abbotsbury Road, Pippa and Bea's home. The mares snorted; they were overworked and tired.

Alfie remembered the tall white horses at Vienna's prestigious Spanish Riding School. He'd been there often, delivering buckets of clay mixed with essential oils for the horses' joints. The gleaming Lipizzaner horses were the cream of the crop for the specialized Viennese riders and had unparalleled grace training. What a contrast London offered. Alfie frowned at the hodgepodge of brown, grey, speckled, and black horses pulling carriages through puddles on the slick cobblestones. The Spanish Riding School horses would never haul anything behind them.

Of course, their "stables" had chandeliers. Within its storied walls, centuries-old traditions blended seamlessly with masterful training as the majestic horses performed breathtaking maneuvers that epitomized the art of classical dressage. Alfie had seen them; he'd brought them salves. He'd looked up to the royals among horses and had served them.

He mustn't do any more than that with Bea either. He was only allowed to serve her because he was so far below her in station. She was a Lipizzaner mare living under crystal chandeliers and he was only a speckled grey cob in a hired hack, on the way to collect his flowers for oil extraction. And just like that, his profession, his calling, and all that he'd studied seemed shabby. He hadn't realized how low he'd sunken because starting the practice and establishing his clientele had just been so much work. Now, if word got out that he'd kissed a client—an earl's daughter—he'd have to leave. Oh, and how he'd kissed her.

I'd do it again in a heartbeat.

Perhaps he could help Nick, Felix, and Andre maintain appearances if they made a big scene of letting him go to protect their patients.

Alfie knew he'd gone too far. Kissing an aristocratic woman was above and beyond anything he could get away with. And yet, his friend Nick had gotten away with it, hadn't he? He was engaged to a duke's daughter.

Alfie loathed himself.

You are the lowest kind of cad.

Even scolding himself, however, didn't erase his guilty conscience. Not only was Bea Nick's fiancée's cousin, but she was also a client. She'd come with the distinct request of a love potion, so a prince—*a prince!*—would fall in love with her. And it wasn't far-fetched because she was a diamond of the first water, a beauty inside and out. She didn't merely fit into the ballgowns and squeeze herself into the corsets or pile her hair atop her head to impress others at the balls. Alfie had seen her. It was all just accessories because her beauty shone brighter than any diamond ever could. She was the main attraction. She wore the dresses gracefully because she was that refined, that precious! Like the Lipizzaner, she'd been bred to achieve more than others, and she did.

He'd seen her.

And she'd taken his breath away.

The hackney stopped, and Alfie stepped out, basket and bottles in hand. He paid the driver and walked toward the park's gates adjacent to Pippa's castle, where Bea lived.

Of course, she lived in a castle, and not in a seventy-five square foot chamber overstuffed with books about alchemy, chemistry, and plants as he did.

She was beyond his reach.

AT CLOVERDALE HOUSE, Bea didn't feel particularly pretty. That morning, though the salve had greatly eased the burn of her rash, and she almost looked normal, she was anxious to get out of her chamber. So she put on a less-than-stellar dress so she wouldn't need to ring for her maid, and left. She was glad she didn't need to stay locked away for two weeks with barely any food, something her mother had insisted upon, to ensure she maintained a slim silhouette while she confined herself until her skin healed.

She'd dress for the Ton later, but first, she longed for a brisk walk before the park was filled with watchful eyes, scrutinizing her every move and finding out about her beast. She had to hide herself until it was all healed. Bea couldn't explain its appearance and had leafed through the journal of her meals that she brought with her in her reticule. She'd read her notes about her catalogued uses of cosmetics and even her bath oils. Since she'd sampled so many wedding cakes with Pippa, Bea hadn't even had dinner. What could have possibly brought on her beastly rash again? Oh what had Alfie called it? *A tetter. Salt rheum.*

Her choice of gown was one of her softest and most-washed, which was champagne colored muslin with pink embroidery. She felt like herself in this old but soft dress and not as a piece of decoration for parlors and ballrooms. It even let her forget the red hives. In the dim light of dawn, Bea wrapped herself in the warmth of her gown, the chill of the early morning seeping through the thin fabric. She shivered, her breath visible in the cool air of her chamber after the fire had gone out. The floorboards felt icy beneath her bare feet as she padded across the room to her wardrobe. Pulling open the doors, she selected a woolen shawl. Then she brushed her hair and powdered her face, wrapped the serviceable scarf around her shoulders, and snuck out of her room, down the corridor past Pippa's room, and downstairs toward the side door.

Just as she touched the cool metal of the door, the grandfather clock chimed five times.

Orange blossoms are best picked at five in the morning to capture the most fragrant moments.

The dashing apothecary was on her mind like a constant companion, and she remembered everything he'd said—and especially everything he'd done. He was the kind of man who could sweep her off her feet.

But there was more to him—he was a man of substance and principles. He didn't merely kiss her senseless; he'd caught her and carried her to safety. How else could a man so young have accomplished so much in his life if not through hard work, and integrity?

Bea pursed her lips as she walked through the door, consumed by her circling thoughts, which were dead ends for someone who knew maps as well as she did.

For the first time in her life, Bea thought about the consequences of her actions… for another person. She'd be jeopardizing his career if she asked Alfie for another kiss, or more. She mustn't be so selfish as to think that her father would let him escape his punishment for touching her and—if anyone found out—compromising her reputation. She wouldn't be a prize to parade about to go to the highest bidder, or at least, the richest bachelor in the Ton. She'd be soiled, ruined, destined to be married off to whoever would accept her father's wealth in payment for the acceptance of a "used" woman.

And Bea didn't fool herself into thinking that Alfie would ever receive her father's approval.

It left a sour taste in her mouth just thinking about it.

All those rules from the Ton were supposed to give her life structure and order in Society—yet they accomplished the opposite. If it wasn't for the cleft that Society had placed between the aristocracy and hard-working, brilliant people like the doctors on Harley Street, she could follow her heart rather than suppress emotion. Yet, as a lady, her destiny was not to marry for love, but for another supposedly good reason, and love wasn't it. Title, and the wealth and power that went along with it, was.

Bea stood in the misty courtyard that connected the main house and Pippa's orangery. The chill of the morning sent a shiver down her spine, and she wrapped herself in the scarf more closely.

Then she saw a shadow through the fogged-up glass wall of the orangery. The only person who frequented it was her cousin.

Could Pippa be awake at this hour?

It would be wonderful to speak with her cousin about the dilemma in her heart.

Chapter Seventeen

ALFIE HAD COME days later than promised to collect some orange blossom petals. Hopefully, he wasn't too late, and the blossoms hadn't lost their scent.

He'd been to the orangery at Cloverdale House only twice before, once to harvest the ipecac and the second time in a great hurry to show Bea how to administer it. This time, he had a chance to admire the neat rows of plants. It was so early in the morning that he didn't expect anyone to see him. He'd collect a few blossoms, and take them back to make the neroli oil. It would end up being a typical Wednesday even with the unusual start. Thus, he pulled the side door open and entered.

"Alfie!" Pippa appeared from behind a tall, potted tree, scrambling to thrust her spectacles back onto her face.

"I didn't know you'd be here." Nick appeared behind her, tucking his shirt into his breeches. "We were... um... harvesting... I mean, Pippa was... I was helping."

Oh, please! The sun's barely up. Don't pretend that I don't know what you're doing.

"Bea asked me to harvest some orange blossoms, but I couldn't get here before this morning." Alfie cast Nick a man-to-man look, but Nick shrugged, put his arm around Pippa, and gently kissed her hair. That must be love if a man is happy to kiss the woman's hair atop her head, Alfie thought.

"Well, it's good to see you because we needed to speak with you," Pippa said, seemingly unashamed that her buttons were misaligned.

"Why me?" They couldn't have known that he'd kissed Bea.

Unless she'd told Pippa.

And Pippa had told Nick.

Uh-oh!

Nick opened the buttons of his shirt sleeves and began to roll them up slowly as if readying himself for a fight.

Alfie deflated. He deserved a punch in the gut for kissing Pippa's cousin.

Well, he wouldn't even duck away.

But Nick had a unique skill in aiming for the face, and Alfie wasn't willing to take a punch for that kiss. It had been glorious, and the beauty loved it; he knew that. Women didn't moan when they were bored; they *did* moan with pleasure as Bea had when he'd kissed her.

"So!" Nick said, and Alfie took a step back and squared up.

"Let me, please!" Pippa stepped in front of him.

Oh no, now he couldn't duck. If a woman felt the need to deliver a punch, all Alfie could do was take it in stride. He dropped his head. Chances were that Pippa didn't know to aim upward for the chin and might hit his forehead. Perhaps his eye.

It wouldn't be the first time he'd had a black eye; it was a manly rite of passage, and he'd earned it when he'd tupped… *never mind*. That had been long ago.

These days, it was unbecoming to welcome his clients to the apothecary with a black eye, but he could explain it away. What he couldn't explain was his bruised heart.

"It's about the wedding, Alfie," Pippa started.

"None of it would have been possible without your help." Nick beamed, his arm snaking around Pippa's waist again.

"You found each other; I really cannot take any credit," Alfie said, trying not to look at Nick's hand on Pippa's waist.

"I disagree." Nick kissed Pippa's head again. It was starting to be odd. Alfie had never seen Nick smitten with a woman, and it was just too bizarre to witness their public displays of affection. Especially now, when he'd expected a bruising. Where was it? And what was going on?

Perhaps the secluded passages between the tall plants in Pippa's private orangery were not exactly public. And considering that he and Nick had grown up together, there wasn't much that distinguished them from being brothers. But still...

"We have the special license, but we would like you to be one of our witnesses," Pippa said as she folded her hands and looked at him solemnly.

He was already the best man and wouldn't miss their union for anything.

"It would be my honor," Alfie finally said, reaching to pat Nick on the upper arm. But his friend wouldn't have any of it and let go of Pippa to give Alfie a tight, brotherly hug. The glass bottles in his basket tinkled together like little bells.

"It means you'll sign the papers *and* be my best man," Nick said.

Yes, it was an honor indeed. It was a special privilege in the lives of his dear friend Nick and the woman he loved.

And I kissed her cousin. Alfie's heart dropped.

But they didn't appear to know about that. Nick explained that he'd come to help Pippa collect a few things for her coachmen to transport to the new townhouse she'd bought, one within walking distance from the practice, which was why they'd been "harvesting" in the orangery. They left him with an empty terracotta jar in which to collect orange blossom petals and left to speak to the coachmen while he remained in the orangery. It would take a long time to convert Cloverdale House into the rehabilitation hospital Pippa and Violet had planned, he mused, but it would be worthwhile.

Alfie had always harbored the utmost respect for all soldiers, not merely British ones. He didn't subscribe to the usual heroism of sacrificing one's body or health for international conflicts. No, those were better solved with treaties and ink on paper rather than blood spilled in the fields. But all soldiers were brave, facing unimaginable danger for a cause greater than any of them alone. That was something Alfie respected.

If the rehabilitation center came into being, he'd be the primary supplier of ointments, tinctures, and any medicines needed unless he risked his reputation, and they lost the practice. The rehabilitation center could not function without them, and Pippa's generous plans would falter. He was hopeful that he could provide more than the usual laudanum to dull the patients' pain, and instead create more proactive and effective medicines to cure and treat their injuries and ailments. He'd maintain the plants at the orangery in Pippa's absence, and with her help, they'd create their own steady supply of medicinal plants.

Now, the purple and pink rays of the morning cast a lovely glow over all the plants in the orangery. Alfie moved to the little orange trees that stood, ironically, like soldiers at attention in a row. The waxy white blooms shone against the pruned green leaves. Carefully, he cut the blossoms below the sepals to ensure the same branch could regrow at the same spot. Then, he plucked the white petals off, placed them in the jar he set down on the raised bed of orchids and little pineapple palms.

"P-i-i-p-a-a-a-h!" A voice sounded from outside. Then, the courtyard cobblestones leading away from the orangery betrayed rushing footsteps. "Pippa! Are you here?" And then he saw Bea as she threw the glass door open and rushed into the orangery. "Oh!"

Alfie nearly dropped the jar with the precious petals at the sight of her. She was even more beautiful in the morning than later in the day.

⇛⇚

"I DIDN'T EXPECT you here," Bea croaked when Alfie rose from the crouched position he'd been in between the little orange trees in a line of pots. She covered her cheeks with her hands, unwilling to let Alfie view her reddened cheeks. Even though he'd healed her only a few days ago and knew all about her affliction—indeed, he'd diagnosed it for her—she didn't want him to see her this way. Not after he'd kissed her.

She wanted to be beautiful for him. But in spite of her disfigurement, she didn't want to leave him now that she knew he was here. The door shut with a click behind her, and she stepped forward, careful to remain in the shadows and not reveal her reddened face.

"I've been here for a little while, almost finished." Alfie shook a small terracotta jar, and a few white petals bounced out lightly in the air. "Please accept my sincere apologies for the tardiness of my visit. I meant to come days ago."

"Why didn't you?"

"I couldn't be here before but I am now. "I've been here less than a half hour. To harvest the blossoms of course." He shook something off his hands and rolled his white shirt sleeves back down, covering the muscular arms with the slight veins that Bea could see even from her spot in the shadows ten feet away.

She didn't know how to respond. In truth, she'd been distracted by the way the tendons in his arms had moved under his skin and hadn't actually listened to his response. She felt her face heat even more than it did from the beast.

"There was too much work; I didn't want you to think that I'd forgotten, but—"

"No, please!" She held a hand out, and the light illuminated it while she was careful to remain in the shadows so he couldn't see how flushed she was. "It's all right. Thank you for coming to harvest the blossoms."

"My pleasure. But I won't take any more lest there remain no oranges to harvest." He turned the lid of his jar. "Now Bea, about the neroli oil. It's very potent." Alfie took a few steps toward her.

"I'll come to pick it up." She turned her back to him, afraid that he'd come closer and see her inner beast on her reddened outside. "Thank you."

She pushed the door open and ran away.

He mustn't see me like this. Not again.

Of all the people in the world, for some reason, Alfie's opinion of her mattered more than any other's. She wanted him to appreciate her and see her as beautiful even though she didn't know what to make of the feelings surging within her.

Tears pricked her eyes as she rushed back into the house and through the corridor when—*bam!*—she collided with something. Or some*one*, since whomever she'd collided with called out. "Oh!"

Pippa! She scrambled back in surprise.

"Bea!" Pippa frowned and rubbed her arm vigorously. "Why are you awake? Were you outside? What's wrong?"

"Nothing," Bea was eager to go back to her chamber and cry in her bed upstairs—far away from the orangery and its heady, flowery fragrances.

"Bea?" Pippa had followed her upstairs and knocked, but then she'd just entered anyway. Perhaps some things would never change, and she and Pippa would always be like sisters. Though Pippa was all grown up and almost a bride who'd move to a different house in London.

"Don't look at me," Bea mumbled into the pillows, closing her arms over her head.

"I won't. But I do need to speak with you," Pippa said in a voice that was too calm, clashing with the upheaval in Bea's chest. She pressed something into Bea's hand. Her journal! "I noticed this. You left it at the breakfast table."

"*Hmpf!*" Bea frowned into her pillow. She'd dropped it onto the table on her way out to the orangery, never imagining that anyone—except one of the servants—would see it. She peered at Pippa from under her elbow. "Did you look at it?"

"I didn't read it, but I'd like to know what's so important that you keep it with you most of the time otherwise."

Bea sighed. "It's a record of my diet and cosmetics." And my memories of the young man in India with eyes who looked exactly like Alfie's.

Wait! Could it be that she'd recognized more in Alfie than a newly-forged bond? Was it more than a coincidence that Alfie's eyes were like the young man's?

"Why are you recording everything you eat and put on your body?" Pippa asked.

"Alfie told me to." Bea released the pressure on the pillow. Sobbing required a lot of extra air; everybody knew that.

"Why?"

"To find out what triggers my beast to break out."

"He knows?"

Bea lifted her head and nodded at Pippa.

For a prolonged minute, Pippa stared at Bea. She did that when she had to formulate a thought that required finesse. "What do you want to say?" Bea asked.

"How is it possible that you hide from me, but he was allowed to see you when you were red and blotchy?"

Interesting question. And not one Bea had an answer for. Plus, she'd let him see it before the kiss. Since then, something had changed. Bea sat up and crossed her arms to hug herself.

"It's just that you must trust him a great deal if you didn't merely expose your fury to him but are also keeping a detailed record to discuss with him what could have triggered it," Pippa said. She furrowed her brow.

"Medical information," Bea mumbled.

"Aha! It's a test!"

"What kind of test?"

"A vision test, like the one Nick gave me. He knew immediately that I'm shortsighted and merely had to examine my eyes to determine exactly how much."

"So?" Bea didn't think much of that. Nick was an oculist, and it was his calling to measure people's vision and make up the loss of correct lens curvature with lenses.

"So? Don't you realize? He saw me for who I was before even I did. He'd cured my clumsiness before I ever knew it could be cured," Pippa said, and Bea could hear in her tone that she was marveling at her handsome future husband's brilliance.

"You're in love, Pippa. I'm happy for you. But I don't expect to ever marry for love like you."

"Perhaps you'll have a chance."

"With Stan? No." And it wasn't love he could offer her... so did he fail her criteria? Could the fact that he could take her far away outweigh the lack of love?

"Why not?" Pippa sat back and eyed Bea as if she'd sprouted an orange tree on her head. Was it that absurd that she'd marry Stan?

"He's too aware of his value. If he offers for my hand—and I will say yes, of course—then it's a transaction to fuse my connections in London and his royal bloodline."

"That's not very romantic." Pippa grimaced. "It's transactional."

"No." Bea straightened her back, her eyes cast low. "It's a logical continuation of my destiny."

Pippa remained silent again. Looking deeply into her eyes, she gazed at Bea as if she didn't see the red-hot blotches. Perhaps she could see something with her glasses that Mother never had, for her eyes only ever skimmed the surface of Bea's skin, worrying that the hives would leave scars and reduce Bea's value as a noble bride.

"Perhaps you need glasses," Pippa said.

"My eyes are fine."

"Figuratively speaking, cousin. You must look at life through another lens and sharpen your senses."

"Why should I?" Bea mocked Pippa's idealistic response. "It's a husband I'm looking for. Quickly, before my parents return. The duller my senses the better, because it's not love I'll have."

"You're on a hunt for love, not merely a husband."

Bea sighed. "Pray tell, dear cousin, how am I supposed to

sharpen my senses in this quest then?"

"Use your intuition," Pippa said, giving her a sisterly hug and an added squeeze. "Why did you run away from the orangery if Alfie already knew about the hives?"

Bea withdrew from the hug and folded her hands in her lap. It was a good question. "I was lightheaded and suddenly felt the urge to run away."

Pippa pursed her lips and gave Bea the same grave look Violet had given her at the breakfast with Stan. Except that Pippa's intention seemed driven in another direction. "What made you feel that way?"

"I'm not certain," Bea said but then the scent came back as if she could still smell it. A combination of sweetness, something like musk, the flowers, and the freshness.

"Think," Pippa leaned forward and nudged her. "I know you know, deep down, and just don't want to admit it to yourself." Then she gave Bea a gentle pat and left.

Befuddled by her own feelings, Bea sat on the edge of her bed, her pulse echoing in her ears. The room felt smaller, the walls closing in around her as she struggled to understand the tumult within. She clutched the embroidered pillow, tracing the delicate patterns with trembling fingers. Her thoughts drifted back to Alfie. His smile, always so genuine, played at the corners of her mind.

She shut her eyes and could almost feel his presence beside her, the warmth of his hand just inches away. The memory of their kiss and then the way he'd looked at her just minutes ago in the orangery, his eyes lingering on hers a moment longer than necessary. A shiver ran through her, not from the cold but from the realization that had been dawning slowly, like the morning sun breaking through the mist.

The scent of the orange blossoms and the early morning crispness in the orangery filled her senses, intertwining with the memory of Alfie's cologne—woody and refreshing. It was the same scent that had enveloped her when he leaned in close before their kiss, making her shiver and forget the world around them. Bea's heart raced faster. She could see now what Pippa had tried to reveal.

A pang of longing swept through her. She remembered the way Alfie had looked at her in the hallway outside the ballroom, his eyes full of a softness she hadn't dared to interpret until now. Every shared glance, every fleeting touch—they all painted a picture she had been too blind to see.

Bea stood, crossing to the window. Daybreak stretched out before her, serene and unchanging, yet everything felt different.

She pressed her forehead against the cool glass, her breath fogging up a small circle. The realization settled over her like a warm blanket on a chilly evening.

I fell in love with Alfie.

The truth settled in her chest, both terrifying and exhilarating as the thought of him brought a smile to her lips, and for the first time, she allowed herself to imagine a future where there were more than stolen moments.

How had she missed it? The way his presence made her heart flutter, or the comfort she found in his laughter. There was no denying it. She was in love, undeniably, irrevocably in love with Alfie. And now, she had to find the courage to act on it.

Chapter Eighteen

MEANWHILE, ALFIE STOOD agog in the orangery, fingers curling tightly around the jar of orange blossoms. The fragrance that once promised serenity now suffocated him. The memory of Bea's sudden departure played over and over in his mind, like a cruel jest he couldn't escape. The woman who had swooned in his arms, her breath mingling with his in a moment that felt as inevitable as the sunrise had fled, as if from a specter. A leaden weight settled in his chest, and self-recrimination gnawed at him. What had he done to frighten her? The thought that he might have caused her discomfort twisted his stomach. He was a cad, an idiot. Every rational bone in his body told him he should apologize, set things right. Yet, the words seemed impossible, blocked by a wall of societal expectation and personal doubt.

His mind churned with a torrent of conflicting emotions. If only he could explain how he truly felt, lay bare the storm raging in his heart. But he was a commoner, tethered to a world where such declarations were discouraged. Bea was a lady of standing; their worlds were not meant to intersect in such intimate ways. The kiss, the desperate need to make her understand—it was not acceptable for a man of his class and a woman—a true lady—like her. Yet, inaction felt like a dagger twisting inside him.

The impossibility of it all left him aching, each breath a reminder of what could never be. He needed to act, to speak, to bridge the divide between them, but how does one defy the very fabric of society? The ache in his chest persisted, a constant reminder that some emotions, once awakened, could not simply be forgotten.

Alfie methodically placed the jar of orange blossoms into the leather bag he had brought, his movements slow and deliberate. He was bracing himself to leave Cloverdale House and never return. He should stay away from Bea. And his retreat would do her a favor.

Alfie sighed.

The orangery felt oppressive now. He tightened the straps on his bag, each pull echoing the tension in his chest. With a heavy heart, he moved toward the door, his thoughts still tangled with Bea and the kiss and the question of what he'd done since to send her fleeing.

The creak of the door broke the heavy silence as Alfie grasped the handle to leave. Just as he swung it open, Pippa stepped through, her expression a mixture of curiosity and concern. She paused, seemingly reading the turmoil in his eyes.

"Alfie," she said gently, closing the door behind her. "What's happened?"

"Oh, I gathered enough petals for about two ounces of neroli oil. It's very potent, truly, this shall suffice—"

"Between you and Bea." Pippa took two steps forward and Alfie had to take a step backward. She was cornering him. This was an interrogation, and he had little choice but to speak the truth.

"She ran away from me."

"I know. She's crying in her chamber."

Alfie squeezed his eyes shut. He'd made her cry and loathed himself for that even though he didn't understand *why* she cried.

He hesitated for a moment, then let out a weary sigh. "I don't know why she's crying exactly but I'm afraid it is because of me."

Pippa nodded, her eyes softening with understanding. "Bea can be… complicated. But I've never seen her respond to anyone the way she does to you."

He leaned heavily against one of the raised beds, his head bowed, the weight of his confusion and heartache pressing down on his shoulders.

"She let you see her."

"I know."

"I mean, she let you see her when she's having an outbreak, Alfie. She never allows anyone to see her, not even me."

He narrowed his eyes. "I'm an apothecary."

"I don't think this is why she allowed it. I think it's because she trusts you. And she's ashamed at the same time."

"She can trust me. I will never recommend a treatment that won't help."

"Not with an ointment or a salve, Alfie. She trusts you with her heart." Pippa spoke slowly as if she was only just realizing what she'd said when she heard her own voice. "Don't toy with her. She's not just anybody."

Alfie shook his head, his voice tinged with frustration. He had a reputation as a rake before he'd moved to London, but he wasn't a cad. Nor had he ever experienced such torrential agony when he couldn't have a woman.

No, she's not just anybody. She's everything to me and has been since I brought her honey every day in India.

"I'm a commoner, Pippa. Whatever feelings I have, they don't belong in her world. I shouldn't have kissed…" He trailed off, unable to finish the thought.

"Is that why she swooned?" Pippa's eyes locked with his and she wasn't letting the question slip away unanswered. So, Alfie nodded.

Pippa took a step closer and raised her chin, her gaze unwavering. "Listen to me, Alfie. Social standing might dictate where we ought to belong, but it doesn't dictate who we love or who we belong with. You need to follow your heart. If Bea means something to you, don't let fear or society's rules keep you from pursuing what's true."

He looked at her, a glimmer of hope flickering in his heart. "And what if she doesn't feel the same? She ran away from me. What if I've only made things worse in kissing her?"

Pippa smiled, a hint of mischief in her expression. "You'll never know unless you ask her. Bea is stronger than she appears. Give her a chance to decide for herself."

"She's set her cap on someone else."

"Ah, the prince. Yes. She thinks she has. He's a great man, I am sure of it." Pippa spoke without regard for Alfie's feelings and his mood soured as she sang the prince's praise. "He will make some woman very happy someday, Alfie. But that woman is not going to be Bea. They don't love each other."

Oh? Love? Did Bea love him and not the prince she was trying to capture?

Suddenly, he had no doubt that he loved her.

He blinked at Pippa, and she gave a crooked smile, a knowing one.

Alfie agreed, her words resonating deeply within him. "Thank you, Pippa. Nick is very lucky to have you by his side."

She tipped her head and smiled.

As he turned to leave, Pippa touched his arm lightly. "Remember, Alfie, courage isn't just about facing danger. Sometimes it's about facing the unknown. You have to speak your heart."

With a determined breath, Alfie left the orangery, the leather bag heavy on his shoulder but his heart lighter with newfound courage. Perhaps this wasn't as impossible as he'd thought?

Chapter Nineteen

ANOTHER DAY HAD passed, and the practice had been a flurry of activity but not the usual sort. Sample flower arrangements, wines for the ball following the wedding, and embossed invitations had come and gone alongside a blur of patients and other deliveries. The only constant was the image in Alfie's mind of the moment in the orangery when Bea had turned away from him and run away. A flicker of hurt had washed over her features, and he hadn't seen her again. There hadn't been an opportunity to seek her out, and he couldn't approach her father and ask if he may court her. First, because her father was somewhere in Singapore or someplace else and out of reach. Second, her father would never give permission if he knew Bea stood a chance of a marrying a prince.

But neither of those concerns mattered if he didn't get permission from Bea first.

Still, Pippa had been right. History didn't allow him to rewind time, so there was no alternative but to go forward. He hadn't decided how to accomplish that yet. He had to tell her he loved her… but could he tell her he'd known her all this time—since their days in India?

He wished he could not merely offer his heart, but also present a solution to their greatest problem, their differing class status. One could say "love was love" and that was all that mattered, yet the issue of gentry joining aristocracy was not a small one. He knew he had to be cautious, and absolutely sure, that it was what Bea wanted.

And that's where doubt gnawed at his resolve because she had asked for a love potion to use for the prince.

He wanted to tell her of his feelings but if she was determined to woo—or worse, seduce—the prince, then Alfie had no right to attempt to change her mind. Especially if he loved her; he had to respect her desires for her decisions—even if they hurt him.

He was stuck and that made him angry… at himself or the world, he wasn't sure.

Alfie walked out of his apothecary door during a lull in business, and saw a swish of a white apron disappearing into the back corridor, followed by an unsettling gasp. *Wendy.*

He'd known her since she was a girl, and even though he'd tried to alert Nick to the fact that his little sister was a grown woman, Nick only shook his head and didn't want to hear the truth. Perhaps she could find out for him?

"What's the matter?" Alfie asked in a hushed voice when he found her pressing her back against the kitchen wall, hands in fists, and her thumbs pressed to her mouth.

She reached out and grabbed his waistcoat to pull him out of sight of the door.

Sneaking around, hm!

Her shoulders lifted in tension, and Alfie ducked under the slant of the stairs leading up so he could get a good look at her.

Her pupils were enlarged, her hair stuck up, and she looked rather unraveled, which was entirely uncharacteristic.

She shook her head and held his eye contact.

Yes, I'll be quiet.

Then, the voices from the kitchen came into focus.

"You were right about my intuition, but it's guiding me to where I cannot navigate." Bea sighed. "It's just that I cannot stop thinking about him." Bea's voice came as an exhale of desperation. "My chest feels constricted when I think about him, but when I'm near him, it beats so wildly that I fear it'll jump out of my body and into his arms."

"Because that is where *you* wish to be?" Pippa asked gently.

Fabric rustled. He could imagine Bea nodding.

"Did you tell him how you feel?" Pippa asked.

More fabric rustled. Alfie wondered why Wendy was interested in Bea's and Pippa's private conversation but then thought better since there must be a reason why and how Wendy always knew everything. Sneaking around explained it all. She was a natural investigator of human nature and its secrets.

At that thought, Alfie's chest constricted, and he inhaled but couldn't sigh.

"If you want the prince to take you with him to his castle and away from here, as much as I would miss you, dear cousin, you'll have to tell him how you feel."

"I don't think he cares," Bea whispered as if it were a revelation. "And he has to leave in four days."

Wendy gasped and put both hands and not just her thumbs over her mouth. She looked at Alfie, her eyes red-rimmed, and then she ran away, up the stairs, and a door slammed shut. He didn't know what had gotten into her, but he was already upset and preoccupied with his own thoughts.

Alfie didn't know what to make of this news, but he had to deal with his own pain. He walked slowly down the hall and back to his apothecary, tugged at his cravat to loosen it, and buried his face in his hands.

Bea wanted the prince, not a mere apothecary.

He'd never see her again; if he did, she'd be a princess accompanying her royal husband on a diplomatic mission.

Alfie gripped the edge of his wooden counter and squeezed until his knuckles turned white and his fingers burned.

Impossible.

Yes, he'd start to keep his eyes open for more than just a fling over the summer or an affair in the gardens.

No, I don't want just flings anymore.

Bitterness crept up his throat and spread in his mouth.

He had never been like this about any woman. Not even back at university. But all his previous encounters were forgotten now that he knew the veiled girl in India was Bea. She had been an unknown he couldn't chase, and now she was a known he mustn't.

He brought a hand to his forehead. Not feverish.

Selective amnesia was a condition he'd heard much of and not one he had any cures for—not that he wanted one, really—though it was known to happen after a blow to the head.

But a blow to the heart?

No matter what, it was the future that counted and not the past.

He'd never have a wedding to plan like Nick and Pippa one day. He'd never take his bride cake-tasting like Nick had done with Pippa. If his bride wasn't Bea, he didn't want any of it.

He'd imagined his wedding, with the veiled girl, and how he'd carry his bride over the threshold into a newly appointed bedroom with elegant silk sheets and the curtains drawn shut. There would be water pitchers, trays of biscuits, cured meats, sparkling wine, fresh fruit, and anything else they'd need for a few days of sustenance. Because once he could, he'd take a very long time to worship her body as much as he did her heart.

Now, he could imagine every detail as if the future had been painted clearly before him. His bride had long, curly hair in the exact shade of a drop of molten copper falling into gold, swirled to create a rich hue of rose gold. And she had the perfect alabaster skin, rosy cheeks, and a narrow waist that he'd grab just firmly enough to bring her into the ideal position beneath him. When he'd kiss his way from her navel up toward her perky breasts, Alfie's imagination stumbled as if there'd been jagged rocks in the way. He looked up at the face of his bride and saw Bea. It had always been Bea.

IN THE KITCHEN at 87 Harley Street, Bea turned the teacup between her hands and stared at the barely-eaten cakes. After several hours of wedding planning, embossed wedding invitations and an open bottle of wine remained on the table.

"The drapes will be delivered to the new house around the corner. I should go soon," Pippa said.

"Will you ever forgive me for failing to meet you at the dressmaker?" Bea had a bad conscience for leaving her dear cousin alone at the fitting for her wedding dress, but she had such a heavy heart that she'd forgotten. Pippa's wedding planning from Nick's practice was as unconventional as their union but it also made perfect sense, because between his patient appointments Nick came in to be with Pippa.

Pippa looked at her with understanding, yet there was a spark of a question in her gaze. "It's him, isn't it?" Pippa whispered barely audibly.

Be nodded and deflated. "It's just that I cannot stop thinking about him. My chest feels constricted when I think about him, but when I'm near him, it beats so wildly that I fear it'll jump out of my body and into his arms."

"Because that is where you wish to be?" Understanding colored Pippa's voice.

Bea clasped her hands over her chest and nodded. She mustn't feel that way, and she wished she could cure herself of the incessant longing to see him. She'd even contemplated staying in the sun too long and then seeking his help with an ointment against sunburn, a paste to cover the freckles, or perhaps just a scented soap—any excuse to speak with Alfie.

"Did you tell him how you feel?"

"Of course not!" Bea jerked her head back.

"If you want the prince to take you with him to his castle and away from here, as much as I would miss you, dear cousin, you'll have to tell him how you feel."

Oh, Pippa thought she meant the prince.

Then why did she drag out the word "prince" so much?

Bea's heart plummeted even further.

It ought to be the prince; he was everything she needed.

Just not what her heart desired.

"I don't think he cares, and he has to leave in four days."

"It doesn't take very long to follow through once your heart is set on the right person," Pippa said.

She didn't want to admit her cousin was right. Instead, she pushed that suggestion away. "Do you remember how we put curtains over our heads and danced in the nursery?" Bea asked Pippa.

"We pretended to be brides and danced to our own song." She gave her a wistful smile.

Bea felt the tension of the frown on her forehead. "How was it possible that we thought about everything from the dresses to the cakes to the music and even the chandeliers?"

"You planned the chandeliers for your wedding?"

Bea narrowed her gaze. "You haven't planned the chandeliers for *your* wedding?" Her expression was a mix of disbelief and intrigue. Perhaps she had plans to travel and strict criteria for a husband, but what did that have to do with her dream wedding? Some women left every little detail for the last minute, but Bea preferred not to leave anything to chance. What good were the flower arrangements, cakes, or even the bride's dress if the chandeliers didn't put it all in the best light?

"Sprays of white and yellow ranunculi are complementary to the atmosphere in the ballroom at the estate." She meant their grandfather's country home, where she and Pippa had always planned to have their weddings.

"You truly have thought of everything." Pippa chuckled.

Except for the groom.

"Of course, I did! Venetian glass, white candles reflected in polished brass and carved drip panes shaped like tulips are bunched together at the center with golden brass bows from which crystals fall. The vines of *emaille*—the divine French enamel—twist around the center, and each chandelier resembles a bouquet of tulips in the morning, with the crystals dripping like dew into the sparkling sun. Fresh flowers draped over the brass branches."

Pippa raised her eyebrows. "That's very detailed. But what about your criteria for a husband who will whisk you away to Transylvania?"

Bea's heart dropped. It was just a broad stroke of the detail in her imagination. She just couldn't quite picture the groom and his far-away castle in the Southern Carpathian Mountains. She knew exactly that the height of the castle, the trees in the surrounding countryside, and even the distance alone would suffice to let her breathe away from the Ton, away from her reputation. She could be free and herself.

That's what she wanted. Her freedom by way of a groom who'd sweep her off her feet.

Preferably before her parents returned.

And yet Prince Stan's image was not the one in her mind. It was Alfie.

"I want to do as I please, not merely plan it." The words spilled out before she could understand the depth of their meaning. "I can see him so clearly!" She let go of the teacup and put her hands in the air as if she held something between her hands. His eyes rose before her, along with the warmth of his mouth, his taste, the scent of him, the feel of his rough, shaved skin against her own as she pressed her lips to his. "I just want to grab his face and kiss him. I want to hold him until this… this starvation in my belly goes away." Surprised at her declaration, Bea blinked. It was as if she'd opened her eyes to the truth for the first time and really seen it.

Bea sighed. She'd opened up more than she'd intended, but this was Pippa after all. She'd always kept her secrets, and if Bea kept this growing and overwhelming feeling locked in her chest any longer, it would burst open like a cabinet overstuffed with sparkling crystalware. Because it felt like that—sparkling rainbows reflected on shiny delicate vessels, and the idea Alfie could fill them with effervescent sweetness was like wine that went to her head. But at the touch of the wrong man, Bea feared the crystals would shatter into lumps of sand on the ground. "Do you know what I mean?"

Pippa pursed her lips and swirled her cake fork in some leftover whipped cream on the plate before her. "Perhaps."

Bea gripped her hand, and Pippa dropped the fork. "Tell me!"

"When you say you want to feel *him* because of the deep hunger, is it desire you speak of?"

"How would *I* know?" Bea asked, after a pause to consider the matter.

Pippa cracked her neck. "I must say, I never imagined to be the one to tell *you* about making love. It always struck me that you'd be the first one to…"

Bea tightened her grasp on Pippa's arm. "You've already…?" She gave Pippa a once-over. "With Nick?"

Pippa nodded. She blushed. Not in a flattering way, but she turned red like a lobster in boiling water.

"Tell. Me. Everything."

Cakes were forgotten, the wedding plans had quickly turned to something much more decadent, and Bea's curiosity prickled with what she now knew to call *desire*. Time passed—Bea wasn't sure how much—but the whipped cream had grown soggy, and the sponge cake had dried unappetizingly. She wasn't hungry anyway, not like that.

"I want it all," Bea mumbled when Pippa finished her clumsy explanation. "All of that!" Then Bea shook her head as if she had to shoo a fly away, "Not with Nick, of course."

It hadn't been long, and apparently, Pippa thought she was still learning from Nick.

Interesting.

Pippa said she felt like she couldn't take the pleasure, but there was a point to push past, and then it was more spectacular than anything she'd ever imagined.

I want that, too.

And when Pippa said nothing could bring two people closer than to hold one another after reaching their climaxes, Bea was ready to storm out and request precisely that. Of course she wouldn't; that was not how she'd been brought up. Without a proposal from a titled gentleman, she couldn't even begin to consider it... and yet, that was exactly why she itched to do the unexpected. She'd had enough of the rules of the Ton that made her lock her feelings up... Alfie did the opposite, unleashing her essence in a way nobody else ever had. She felt as though she'd known him a lifetime and could be more open with him than even Pippa.

And there was the problem. When she thought about where to run and ask, it was merely down the hall to the first door on the right and not to a castle in a faraway country.

But then Pippa took both of Bea's hands as they'd done as little girls when they shared secrets. When it was just them, just after Pippa's mother had died and Bea's parents had sailed off to Singapore.

"It's precious and strong. Don't get me wrong, dear, it's marvelous. But there's something you need to know." Pippa pulled Bea closer. "This doesn't work if you don't love him. And he must love you, too."

Must imagine Stan in Alfie's place. Bea repeated the thought in her mind, hoping it would take root and overgrow the images of what she didn't dare admit to herself.

Bea's eyes shot from Pippa's left to her right and back several times. "The mechanics work."

"Not the feelings."

"B-but..."

"Hear me out, please. If you close your eyes and imagine it, it's more chaste than when you do it. The act can turn into a wild fumbling, and the heat of the moment is overwhelming for all of your senses. So make sure you see yourself with the man who can give you all that *and* his heart. My darling cousin, you deserve all the pleasures and every level of intimacy, but it has to feel right. You won't have anywhere to hide in the heat of the act." Pippa slowed down at the last few words and squeezed Bea's hands gently for emphasis.

Bea swallowed hard. She closed her eyes and imagined. She'd have a wedding under the sparkling chandeliers and a dress with so many layers that she'd feel like a blossom swirling on the parquet. And when her groom, in a narrowly-tailored frock, picked her up and carried her to a room with elegant bedding and a fire crackling in the hearth, she'd let desire reign free.

She didn't want to hide.

And as she imagined the scene, her groom held her tightly and gave her a warm smile.

It was Alfie—the prince of her heart and not the prince of a country. She had enough of the exhausting superficiality of the Ton and Society's rules. She'd follow her own heart and rules from now on. All she had to do was figure out how.

Chapter Twenty

ALFIE RETURNED TO the kitchen to boil water and clean his beakers when he heard dishes clattering. As soon as he walked in, he knew he should turn around and leave her alone before she saw him.

"Oh, hello!" Bea looked over her shoulder with a shy smile, one so sweet Alfie's insides cringed as his body went hard, and his brain liquefied as if she'd melted his resolve. She was irresistible, and he wanted to be close to her as much as he wanted to breathe air.

Pippa had warned him, and he knew he should speak with her, but this wasn't like the other times. He couldn't find a few smooth lines to convince her to let him kiss her. If he did kiss her, he'd lose his heart forever. Perhaps he already had. He wasn't sure, but he knew this was unchartered territory for him.

"Bea!" Alfie said, immediately chastising himself for not being more courteous. What he should do was bow to her and return to his apothecary. Or better, lock himself in his bedchamber until she was gone so he wouldn't have wicked thoughts near the virtuous and most definitely virginal aristocratic lady who was— what was she doing?

"I wanted to put these back," Bea said as she used the hand towel to wipe the rims of the teacups. Did she know how to dry dishes?

She has servants for these tasks.

"Why are you cleaning the cups in our kitchen?" Alfie asked, and she flinched.

She closed her eyes momentarily and inhaled as if she had to restore her courage. Then she sniffled. "I spoke to Pippa, and then she had to leave. Given that there were no maids or footmen to call on, I thought I should tidy the kitchen up before I leave."

Alfie didn't believe her. A lady didn't just clean up other people's kitchens; they didn't even clean their own. Judging from most ladies of the Ton he'd met—and he knew many, including their secrets—they probably didn't know where their teacups went after use.

"Why are you still here?" he asked.

Bea looked intently at a cup in her hand, polishing the handle as if it were a diamond set in gold. "Perhaps Pippa will need me for the wedding plans when she returns."

"Didn't she go to the new house with Nick?"

"*Yes-s-s?*" Bea drew the word out as if she dragged her feet toward a poorly conceived lie.

"So they won't be back today."

Reading between the lines was one of the skills an apothecary honed over the years. When patients spoke of symptoms, they tended to leave out the most embarrassing bits or lie about the sources of the infection or injury. Simply put, Alfie could detect when people lied to him, and Bea was not telling him the truth about why she was there.

"Lady Beatrice?" Alfie stepped closer. "Bea?" She was "Bea" in his mind, especially when they were alone, and he had a sinking feeling that her title and station were the source of her distress.

"I was hoping to see you," she whispered, her back turned toward him.

She was so preciously shy.

You can trust me. But you should stay away from me because I don't trust myself around you.

"There are workers at Cloverdale House. They've come to

retrieve some of Pippa's things for the new townhouse on Harley Street." Bea turned her head as she spoke, raising her brows and taking on a placid expression. It was an act of pretending to be stronger than she was.

"Pippa will move out, which upsets you," Alfie said.

Bea's lips flattened into a line but quickly drooped into a frown. "You must think me a terribly selfish person. I apologize if I disappoint you." She said it with such ease as if she'd often been told... *wait!*

"How could you ever disappoint anyone?" Alfie asked.

She faced him now, waved in the air, and inhaled. "I disappoint everyone. I'm not good enough. It's why my parents left, why Stan doesn't want me or else he would have called on me or sent flowers, and it's probably why you will leave me alone, too."

Alfie took another step toward her, still keeping a safe distance so he wouldn't wrap himself around her and kiss this nonsense out of her mind.

"Why did your parents leave for China?"

"Singapore." She corrected him. "It's not part of China."

"Why Singapore?"

"They are representing the Crown's interest. It's supposed to be a trading post to expand the tea trade routes and other goods." *They're trying to multiply our fortune and avoid me at the same time.*

Opium came to mind. It was the most coveted good the English wanted to import, even though tea masked the shipments perfectly. Alfie knew this well from his apprenticeships in India, which was a frequented port for the English ships on their return.

"They are ashamed of me," Bea murmured.

"Ashamed. Of you." Alfie felt the bitterness in her voice like a punch in the stomach, yet his mind could not grasp the absurdity.

"It's because of the beast. The inner fury, Mother says. No virtue can mask it when it comes out, and they think it's why I haven't had any offers yet."

Ridiculous. It was nothing but a rash. It wasn't a punishment or a result of her lack of...whatever it was that her parents thought she lacked. But that's what she had been told, enough times that she believed she was at fault for the affliction that plagued her. "But you have, haven't you?"

"Four-and-twenty. Mother doesn't know I turned them all down, but Father won't allow me to turn another down when he returns. Which will be soon, and I'm not wed." *And I'd rather run away than accept one of the aristocrats at Almack's who'd lock me up when I have the hives—perhaps even when I don't. I won't let them keep me in a gilded cage.*

Alfie's heart plummeted. She was so far out of his reach; he'd known it all along. But the beauty of the Ton had already rejected several titled men, most of them probably handsome, young, and rich—there just wasn't any ground for Alfie to compete.

"Can I help you?" Alfie asked when Bea dragged a chair to the cupboard.

"Yes, tell me where this plate goes, please." She juggled three cups, precariously perched atop a tower of saucers in her hand. When she stretched, the hem of her dress rode up, and Alfie could see her slim ankles as Bea raised up on her toes to reach the shelf. The fabric of her dress lay in folds over her bottom, accentuating the perfect curve in a way that left little to the imagination and yet stimulated the most tantalizing thoughts in Alfie's mind.

Suddenly, the dishes crashed onto the tiled floor with a merciless clatter, shards of porcelain scattering on the dark tiles. As each piece skidded before Alfie's feet, the jarring crash echoed off the walls—a harsh reminder of how easily something whole could come apart, leaving nothing but scattered pieces in its wake. That's what would happen if he laid his hand on Lady Beatrice. *Bea.*

No! He mustn't think of her as Bea. But since he'd kissed her, he couldn't help it. She was as out of reach as the cups on the top shelf, and if he overreached, shards with sharp edges would make him bleed.

One saucer spun away, twirled on the tiles, rolled on its edge, and fell over.

"Oh, look!" Bea darted toward it, probably attempting to retrieve it. But she stepped on a sharp piece of porcelain and slipped.

With the spontaneous surge of a lion jumping to catch an antelope in mid-air, Alfie lunged forward, wrapped his arms around her, and pulled her close and away from the broken dishes.

The safety of his hold contrasted sharply with the chaos around them. Holding her felt so right that order was restored. They stood around the ruins of their mishap, her breath quick in the silence that followed. In that moment, amidst the shards of their accident, something fragile yet unbroken passed between them.

"I'm so sorry," she whispered, her breath light and sweet.

Only then did Alfie realize that his hands were on the small of her back and his arms closely wrapped around her body. It would have been scandalous if anyone had found them like this. Nick would probably never speak to him again if he knew how little restraint Alfie showed around Pippa's cousin.

But then, why did she relax in his grasp?

Alfie felt more complete and at ease with her in his arms than when she was out of reach.

Like burned sugar turning into caramel, the moment thickened, and the sweetness of their contact developed a unique flavor that neither had until they came together—sweetness and heat that became a sticky mess—yet one that was delicious and irresistible.

Alfie flexed his biceps, and Bea met his gaze, making no effort to escape his grasp. Although she blushed and batted her lashes quickly, she remained in his arms.

Several of the curly flyaways that framed her face as a rose-golden halo had fallen in her face, and Alfie shifted her weight in his left arm, let go with his right, and brushed a strand of her soft hair out of her face, along her left cheeks, and then he tucked it behind her ear.

She sucked in her lower lip, and her gaze fell to his mouth.
She wants another kiss.
I want to kiss you, too.

⊱⊰

BEA'S HEART BEAT so fast in her chest it was as if it were an orchestra of percussions. It wasn't until his gaze fell to her mouth that the cymbals slammed together.

Now that she knew how he kissed, she didn't dare breathe lest she miss the moment his lips met hers.

His eyes, deep pools of longing, lingered on her lips, tracing the curve as if committing it to memory. Bea's breath hitched, anticipation tightening its grip. She stood frozen, a statue poised on the brink of an awakening when Alfie leaned in again, erasing the distance.

Just as their lips hovered on the edge of touching, a voice cut through the kitchen's enchanted silence.

"Alfie!" Wendy's insistent and urgent call from the other room pierced the magic bubble they'd wrapped themselves in. It spoke of reality crashing back, of duty and demands that waited for no one, not even for two hearts teetering on the cusp of surrender.

Alfie's response, a murmur barely audible, carried a weight heavier than the words themselves. "She can wait," he said if he were speaking about his little sister and not Nick's. Determination laced his tone, a declaration that nothing would drag him from this precipice—not duty nor expectation, for this sliver of time.

"Alfie, quick!" Wendy's voice sounded closer.

Bea's pulse soared. His words, a vow in the quiet of the evening, promised her everything. That she mattered more than the call of responsibilities, that this moment—they—were worth every second stolen from the world outside.

Their eyes locked, and the unspoken understanding of the

kiss that didn't happen flooded her senses like a rapid opening of a floodgate of emotion. In Alfie's gaze, Bea saw the reflection of her resolve. She no longer saw the girl who hesitated and feared the fall. Instead, she recognized the woman who dared to leap, heart first, into forbidden pleasures.

With courage fueled by his assurance, Bea closed the gap. She didn't care if she got caught, she was burning for Alfie. Her lips met his in a kiss that spoke of yearning held at bay, whispers shared in the quiet, and promises made under the cloak of night. It was a kiss that defied interruptions and honored the truth in their hearts.

In that kiss, time ceased to exist. There were no calls to answer, no world beyond the space they occupied in the kitchen. There was only Alfie and Bea and the realization that some moments were worth every risk.

"Alfie!" Wendy's voice was an exhale as she arrived at the door.

Bea tore herself from Alfie's mouth and dropped her head.

To her astonishment, instead of stepping away from her, Alfie held her and placed a kiss on her forehead.

"Yes, Wendy?" he grumbled when he finally melted away from Bea, his reluctance as obvious as the broken cups on the floor.

Wendy frowned, but Bea didn't dare hold her gaze. She'd been found out.

Perhaps Wendy would tell Pippa.

Bea should be ashamed—but she wasn't. Kissing Alfie was as necessary as letting her heart beat. It was the elixir of her essence, and when she was near Alfie, she was more herself than she'd ever been. No love potion or truth serum was necessary, for Alfie brought her nature to the surface without any chemistry support.

And she liked that version of herself.

Even if Wendy gave them a stern look.

They were caught.

Chapter Twenty-One

Bea took a step back. So many rules of decorum had been broken that they made her head spin.

Or was it the fact that Alfie was still holding her hand?

"What happened here?" Wendy asked in the exact tone of Bea's mother. For years, Bea tried to imitate her strict tone, and all it took was getting caught kissing Alfie so that Wendy could produce a perfect impression of Mother's worst tone. If Bea weren't still tingling all over from Alfie's kiss, it would be funny.

Alfie squatted to collect some of the larger shards on the floor. "We dropped some cups, and I was just looking for a broom."

"In her mouth?" Wendy narrowed her eyes but didn't seem upset with Alfie; it was Bea who had seemingly irked her somehow.

"No, Wendy." Alfie had the tone of a big brother, annoyed with his surrogate younger sister. Bea knew that Alfie had known Wendy since she was a child, but there was a level of closeness as if they were siblings. "Why did you call for me?"

"A patient is here with a baby," Wendy said, staring at Bea so thoroughly that she broke out in goosebumps.

"Who?" Alfie rose, tossing a stack of shards in a bucket near the door and wiping his hands.

"She didn't say." Wendy stepped aside, and Alfie passed her, turning around to give Bea one parting I'm-so-sorry look, but then he was gone.

Wendy shifted and watched Bea.

Her impulse was to ask for a broom to clean up the mess, but instead, Bea lifted her chin and gave Wendy a superciliary glance. To Wendy, she was Lady Beatrice, not a kitchen maid. For some reason, Bea's instinct told her to raise her guard.

"Why are you kissing Alfie if it's the prince you're after?"

Ah! Wendy was excellent in her roles as Hestia, the goddess of domesticity at 87 Harley Street, and her family's protector, including that of her brother Nick and even all the others, Felix, Andre, and Alfie.

"It's sweet that you are trying to protect Alfie's heart, but I think he can look out for himself."

"He could lose his customers for seducing you, and yet you're toying with his life. I know your kind, Lady Beatrice, and it's not fair that you take advantage of hard-working people for your own fleeting amusement while you are after a royal prince." She hissed the word "prince" as if it were pure venom. "Don't toy with Alfie, he's like a brother to me."

Bea's heart dropped, and she searched for something to hold. When her left hand finally touched the back of a chair, she brought her right hand to her stomach. That was what she'd always worked on; it was nothing useful like the doctors or the nurse, just her reputation.

"You must think I'm terribly shallow based on what you've seen of me." Bea was suddenly acutely aware that her simple day dress had more brocade than fit the setting and that Wendy merely wore a white apron over a grey muslin gown. Only now Bea noticed that the nurse's front had several buttons because she dressed herself, and that her hair was tucked under a bonnet. She didn't have a wardrobe designed to be laced by lady's maids, nor did she have ribbons braided into her hair as it was pinned up. Bea sank onto the chair and stepped on a few shards that clattered under her feet.

Wendy cringed at the sound of the broken porcelain on the tiled floor, but she seemed too proud to bend down and clean it up in front of Bea. But then the moment was interrupted by Alfie's call. "Wendy!" His voice rang out. "Come here!"

Both Bea and Wendy darted to the hall and toward Alfie's apothecary shop.

Bea stood at the threshold, the sharp scent of herbs and remedies pricking her nose. Her heart tightened at the sight before her. There on the countertop lay a baby boy, red-faced and wailing, his tiny body writhing on the pristine white towel and his knees pulled up to his belly. He was covered in an angry-looking rash. Alfie leaned over the infant, his brow furrowed in concentration as he gently dabbed at the child's skin with a damp cloth.

A nursemaid hovered nearby, her hands fluttering uselessly, her face as pale as milk.

"How did he come in contact with the nettles?" Alfie's voice was calm, steady, but Bea could hear the undercurrent of concern. The nursemaid stammered, explaining through tears that the baby, no more than ten months old and eager to explore, had slipped from her watchful eye for only a moment.

"What were you doing if not watching the child?" Alfie asked but the nursemaid broke into tears, and he stopped his line of questioning.

Bea noticed that she was scratching her wrist, and the backs of her hands were covered in red bumps. Well, at least she'd taken him out of the nettles.

The baby's cries pierced the air, his tiny fists clenched in agony, his head turning an alarming shade of purple. Alfie handed the cloth to the nursemaid and motioned for her to hold the baby still. He reached for a small jar. With practiced ease, he unscrewed the wooden lid and scooped out a dollop of salve.

With gentle precision, Alfie smeared the soothing balm onto the baby's inflamed skin. Alfie's large muscular hands contrasted with the baby's smooth pink skin, but Bea couldn't take her eyes off the glistening salve on Alfie's hands. He rubbed the baby with as much gentleness as precision. Bea watched as the child's screams ebbed into whimpers, then silence, replaced by hiccupped breaths and wide, teary eyes. The transformation was immediate, almost miraculous.

Bea's chest swelled with an emotion she couldn't name—admiration, perhaps, or something deeper. In that moment, Alfie was more than just an apothecary; he was a healer, a savior. And in the quiet aftermath, as the baby's sobs faded into soft murmurs, Bea felt her pulse begin to steady, finding solace in Alfie's capable look when he cast her a glance as he wrapped the baby in the towel and handed him gently to Wendy.

Bea's heart twisted as she observed Alfie, the resolute set of his jaw as he handed the nursemaid the jar of salve, the calm assurance of his hands as he placed the lid back on and wiped his hands on a white muslin cloth. Here was a man who moved through life with a purpose, a healer whose touch brought peace to the suffering. In this small shop, surrounded by jars and tinctures, herbs and oils, he was in his element, performing miracles with every patient he attended. The realization struck her like a hammer: if she pursued him, if she pulled him into the tumultuous world of balls and gossip, she'd be dragging him away from this place where he was needed most. Nick had to move, even if it was only two minutes away, he wouldn't be there around the clock. Alfie should be there. And she shouldn't be.

The thought gnawed at her, a relentless ache that refused to quiet. She didn't want to be selfish, to prioritize her longing over the well-being of those who depended on Alfie's skill. Yet the desire she harbored for him was an inescapable force, powerful and insistent. It pounded within her, throbbing in her stomach, a constant reminder of the connection she yearned to deepen. The conflict within her mind was like an open wound, raw and painful. Torn between her love for him and the undeniable truth of his calling, Bea stood at a precipice, uncertain which path would lead to something whole.

What she did know with certainty was that she didn't want to lose Alfie.

Chapter Twenty-Two

ALFIE HAD WATCHED Bea leave, and he'd had several more clients before he could shut the door to his apothecary shop and work on the truth serum. It was imperative that he help Felix and his friends, but he hated that the man who'd recruited him on a mission that pushed Alfie's code of honor was the man Bea was supposed to marry. He'd heard her with Pippa, knew that in spite of their interlude in the kitchen, she longed for marriage with the prince.

Could he dare dream that she cared for him with such longing instead of the prince?

Alfie couldn't rid the image of Bea from his mind, her presence lingering like a ghostly touch even as he worked. The shop was quiet now, the baby's cries replaced by the steady rhythm of his own breath. He leaned against the counter, his fingers absentmindedly tracing the grain of the wooden surface, replaying the softness of her lips against his.

The memory of their kiss surged through him, both exhilarating and confusing. It wasn't the first time she had kissed him, but each encounter felt more intense and impossible to ignore. Her unexpected tenderness contradicted the disciplined life he had built within these walls. For every herb he ground and every oil he mixed, thoughts of Bea invaded his focus, unraveling his carefully maintained composure.

He knew he should have resisted and maintained the boundaries society imposed. And yet, he regretted nothing more than keeping to those rules for a whole year when he brought Bea tea, honey, and her ointments. Now that he had the rare chance to be with her, he wasn't going to squander it. But Bea was a force of nature, her affection seeping into the cracks of his resolve. The world needed him here, rooted in his apothecary, serving those who relied on his healing hands. Yet, a selfish part of him longed for her touch, craved the brief moments when the world outside vanished, and it was just the two of them, wrapped in an unspoken promise.

Alfie pressed his fingers to his lips, as if to capture the lingering sensation of her kiss. The conflict within him was a constant battle between duty and desire, and he realized with a jolt that he was losing ground to his heart's wild demands.

He tried to focus on his work. One step at a time, he layered the potion to elicit the truth and erase the memory of the baron who was supposed to receive this. He put his little finger to the rim of the beaker and licked a drop off. He grimaced. The mixture needed something to mask the bitter taste of the truth serum. He tried honey, and it was a little better, but it was far from good.

Then he tried aniseed. *Awful.*

Orange peel oil with clove?

Alfie dripped it carefully into another beaker, added some water, then the truth serum, and … oh no! It smelled like the dried ornaments for a Yuletide dinner at an inn.

Time slipped through Alfie's fingers like grains of sand as he immersed himself in the meticulous process of crafting the masking liquor for the truth serum. The familiar scent of herbs and tinctures filled the room, grounding him in his work even as his thoughts occasionally drifted to Bea. Here, in the quiet sanctuary of his shop, he found solace in the rhythm of his labor, the steady progress of his creation a reminder of his purpose.

"Taste this," Alfie said when Felix came into the apothecary for some mint tooth powder for a patient.

"I'm not taking your truth serum." Felix shrugged.

"Just dip your finger in it and tell me if it tastes odd."

Felix picked up the beaker and swirled the light liquid, sniffing the air that emanated. "Smells like a lady's cordial."

"But it tastes so bitter; I cannot find anything to mask the taste," Alfie said, pointing at an array of vials and flasks on the counter.

"Then don't mask it." Felix found the toothpowder and made a note in the ledger so Alfie could track what was taken and what he had to reimburse him for.

"You're not helpful."

"It's the same as with teeth. Sometimes, you can't hide the gold, so you polish it, and the patient has to lean into the restoration of a broken tooth. It's better to restore it than to lose it." With these words, Felix left.

He was all about teeth, teeth, teeth. Regardless of his work's brilliance, Alfie's old friend sometimes annoyed him.

Polish and lean into… *wait a minute.*

Alfie picked up the beaker with the concentrated truth serum and waved his hand over it.

Then he closed his eyes and focused on the high notes, the first to reach his nose and evoke an image. At first, he couldn't concentrate all his attention on the olfactory experience. But then, he slowly tuned out the bustling in the hall beyond the closed door of his apothecary and the clip-clopping of hooves from the horse-drawn carriages outside. Suddenly, even the noise of the voices in the hall disappeared.

Time to focus.

Alfie tilted his head and acknowledged the tightness of his starched cravat around his neck. It didn't matter, and so he ignored it.

Concentration.

Light flickered when people passed by the window of his apothecary or when a large carriage stopped near the building and blocked the light. No more, he decided to turn his inner eye away from the distractions.

He squeezed his eyes shut.

He'd learned this in India but hadn't practiced genuine moments of introspection to catalog scent notes since he'd started his apothecary. The array of pre-mixed ointments, salves, and tinctures had dulled his senses, and he may not have acknowledged anything nice about the prince, but he'd given him a new challenge, and Alfie cherished that more than the noble cause for which he was making the serum.

Alfie inhaled deeply and observed the scents in his apothecary. Crisp burns from the alcohol he used for dilutions, a faint powdery rose from the stand with women's rouge in the far left corner of the room, mint and chamomile mixed with some dust from the dry tea on the scale. He inhaled again.

His polished counter's dry, woodsy scent hung low, but he could notice it now. A clean, soapy smell from his apron and the cocoa bean oil he'd rubbed on his hands and hair after the morning shave. All those scents were noise.

Now, he swirled the concentrated truth serum and inhaled deeply, stopping just the moment before his chest stretched uncomfortably. From the initial impression to the lingering afternotes, he needed to figure out the highest notes first.

Invigorating, pungent, and slightly bracing. *Lemon.*

Something sharp but clean. *Ginger.*

As the fragrance notes began to register, an image started to form in his mind. Lemon and ginger could be associated with a strong winter tea, but that was not right.

They had been mixed with other fruits in India for curries.

He inhaled again, and images of mountains... no... forests—in high altitudes came to mind. Crisp and cool water flowed in the late afternoon when the air heated with sunlight, but the trickling of a tiny creek preserved the dewy freshness of morning mist.

Alfie exhaled and then inhaled again. *Mint.*

Not just peppermint, but several kinds.
Even citronella could link the minty notes to the lemon.
Yes.
Then, there was a sharpness so intense in the middle notes that the high and fleeting ginger almost paled.
Spicy and woody... *rosemary.*
Alfie swallowed hard. There had to be more in the bouquet of scents, and he brought the beaker closer, keeping his eyes carefully shut.
Something earthy was needed but not leafy. Aromatic herbs, perhaps.
The depth of the lingering notes was the most important one. Once the alcohol's burn was gone, he had to ensure that the aftertaste invited the sharing of secrets, invoking a feeling of being huddled on a soft carpet near a blazing fire while it was cold outside.
He had figured out what was there and how he could heighten the notes to draw attention to the scents inherent in the concoction rather than mask it. Felix had been right; he had to build on what was there and lean in the direction he'd been given. Only a master of his craft could manipulate the most bitter mixtures and create something so delightful that the recipient would request more.
Every novice knew that a medicine had a more significant effect on a receptive patient—even if the medicine was an involuntarily administered truth serum.
Alfie blinked his eyes open, and the sounds of the bustling Marylebone streets outside, the bright afternoon sun shining through the window, and the chaos of flasks on his counter anchored him back in the present.
Then he got to work.
First, he tempered the bitterness with rich and robust molasses, dark but sweet like the secrets he hoped to draw out of Baron von List. Those were best complemented by a woody, slightly bitter undertone from the roots and barks, such as gentian or

angelica root, lest a seed like anise create a cordial rather than a strong digestive liquor as the one he was creating. It had to be masculine and sharp, yet not overpowering so that the person drinking it could feel strong and cocky, so much so that he'd be reckless enough to tout truths and give away secrets rather than guard his clandestine motives.

Confidence.

Relaxation.

Power.

That's what this drink had to imbue in the recipient.

Alfie added a hint of oak-ripened whiskey for the honesty from the cask aging process, which brought to mind layers of vanilla and a touch of smokiness, but didn't quite offer either.

He swirled the mixture around, and the bitter undertones were minimal.

Good.

Then he tipped the beaker to about a 50-degree angle, touched his finger to the oily film on the glass, and tasted it.

Something else was missing.

The woody elements were there; the scent was fresh, but it wasn't relatively high enough or crisp. It didn't beg for seconds, which was what he needed.

Alfie pulled out his old botany book and turned to the needle trees. Coniferous forests usually existed at higher altitudes, but some evergreens had similar notes and more promising medicinal uses.

He didn't need the camphor notes or the sinus-clearing pine tree effects. What he needed was broad and heavy but light enough to linger like the crisp and cool air in the mountains, demanding to be inhaled deeply, reaching down to the lowest spots of List's darkest secrets.

Myrtle.

And he knew just where to find it.

Chapter Twenty-Three

At the orangery at Cloverdale House, later in the day...

PIPPA LIFTED THE buds of her orchids and eyed them critically. "They won't blossom in time for the wedding."

"Not every beauty can keep up with the breakneck pace you and Nick have," Bea said, trailing her hand over the new waxy leaves of the orchids. She always admired the long but robust leaves of these plants, which were so at odds with the delicate layers of the blossoms. Several times, when Bea was confined to her room during a flare-up and worked on perfecting her watercolor skills—an activity her mother always highlighted to mask the true situation—she'd found herself thinking about Pippa. Unlike Bea, Pippa could freely spend time in her orangery, unburdened by society's expectations and the relentless pressure to be the belle of the ball for whatever event her mother deemed important next.

In those moments of solitude, Bea had time to think and often let her mind wander while her hands controlled the pencil for a loose sketch and then the paintbrush for precise movement of the colors. Even though many debutantes were not terribly fond of watercolors, Bea always enjoyed them, especially painting flowers and plants from Pippa's Orangery.

There were the prickly tops of the pineapples, like palms

growing without a trunk. Long pigment-laden brush strokes lent themselves to the sharp-edged dark-green leaves. The same colors but different strokes were required for the busy ferns, which consisted of many-layered dots with just enough space between them to give them the plant's shape. And then there were the orchids, with burned sienna around the edges of the underpainting, layered with blues for the fleshiest parts of the leaves on either side of the center thread. For the blossoms, however, Bea barely touched the brush to the paint and almost let the pigment flow to the edges of the delicate petals.

"How can I help the orchids bloom in time for your special day?" Bea asked when she'd counted nearly forty dark pink and purple buds.

"I think we need to ask the footman to light the coal stove he installed. There's still not enough heat." Pippa surveyed the room. "It's humid enough but not quite warm enough yet. I'll ask him on my way to deliver some of these things to the new house." She eyed the plants near the stove. "Should we move those, do you think? I don't want them to get overheated or scorched."

"I'll do it," Bea offered. She and Pippa said goodbye and once her cousin had left the orangery, she began moving the pots closest to the stove.

A figure came to the side door, the glass one that had gotten foggy with the humidity.

Bea squinted.

Then, two hands pressed against the glass, and a face followed, looking in.

He knocked.

Bea straightened, sure it was Nick who'd come in search of Pippa and ready to greet him politely.

It would be all right to be found alone for a moment with her almost cousin-in-law.

Thus, Bea tugged at her dress and walked to the door. She turned the key on the inside, and it clicked open.

"Pippa, hullo," Alfie said as he stepped in. "Oh!"

Bea blinked at the apothecary, dressed in a simple dark brown coat the same color as his chocolate hair. He looked sinfully delicious as always. Her heart skipped a beat.

"I beg your pardon, Lady Beatrice. Ahem... Bea... I thought Pippa might be here."

"She was, but she left."

He surveyed the Orangery and the rows of raised beds, and his eyes stopped at the furnace behind Bea. "Why is there a coal oven?"

Bea withdrew from his proximity, an act that demanded every ounce of her willpower. The space between them felt like a gulf she dared not cross, yet she couldn't stop her mind from wandering in that direction.

"The wedding is in two days, and Pippa wanted her orchids to bloom. We're trying to warm the space so the buds will bloom."

Alfie followed her through the path between the raised beds and around the end of one to the mossy bed with tree bark that housed an array of white-laced orchids with delicate stems and little buds in the shapes of lanterns hanging from thin stems.

"Pippa and Nick will be very happy together. I hope they get their orchids for the decorations," Alfie said in a low voice.

"Why does that make you sad?" Bea asked, instantly chastising herself for sounding like a ninny.

Alfie shook his head. "It doesn't. Not at all. I couldn't be happier for Nick. He's always been there for me, and if I had a brother, I would have wished it were him." Yet Alfie avoided her gaze and looked over his shoulder at the plants. "Do you know when Pippa is coming back?"

Bea shook her head, shy to admit it but reveling in being alone with Alfie.

"I hoped she'd allow me to pick a few leaves from the myrtle," Alfie continued. Then he looked up at the tall potted trees near the furnace. Its stems, woody yet slender, converged into a singular trunk, and the canopy, loftier than a man at full height, sprawled outward in a lush display of greenery, casting a cool, dappled shade beneath it.

"I've always wanted to see how tall these could grow naturally in the Mediterranean region—Sardinia, Corsica, and the Aegean Sea islands have myrtles, but this one is from Morocco," Bea said, trailing her hand along the jagged bark of the myrtle. "What will you do with it?"

"Well, if Pippa lets me take a few leaves, I'll steam distill the essential oil and use it," Alfie said, tilting his head backward to look at the canopy of the myrtle just over his head. So that's what the expression meant: a man standing tall as a tree. Bea could see his Adam's apple bobbing as he swallowed and the muscles of his neck, which probably led to an even more muscular chest, and… was the furnace working? She'd started to feel overheated.

Wait, *she* was hot, not the space around her. The coals were still cold; she didn't know how to light a fire in a furnace.

"I'll let you take as many leaves as you need," Bea said, eyeing the metal cylinder with holes and the tray of coals. "I'll be here anyhow, trying to light the furnace."

"I can do that for you," Alfie smiled at her for a fleeting moment, but quickly looked away as if his eyes were not allowed to linger on her anymore.

"I would like that very much." Stupid ninny, what's there to like? Glowing coals? "I mean, I'd be most obliged for your help." Bea curtsied politely to express her gratitude, but Alfie caught her elbow and gently pushed her up.

"Don't do that with me," he shook his head and furrowed his brows.

Taken aback momentarily, Bea looked at his hand on her arm. She liked his touch, but why wouldn't he accept her gratitude? It would have been rude if his gaze weren't so sincere.

"You never need to thank me. Especially not for something simple like lighting a fire."

"Oh!" That wasn't rude, it was direct, and kind, so she gladly accepted this help. On second thought, nobody had ever done anything for Bea without expecting her to pay them or thank them profusely. Alfie was refreshingly unaristocratic. Yet, he wasn't like the servants either. He was educated and had an air of certainty about his profession that Bea hadn't quite experienced before.

Most men of the Ton relied on their social standing and connections to get their way, or on bribes, threats, and perhaps even worse. Not Alfie. He only needed to rely on himself, his knowledge, and his mind.

"Thank you." She shook her head. "I mean, not thank you… ahem… just—"

"It's my pleasure," Alfie said as he set aside a glass bottle he'd been holding and unbuttoned his brown coat. He shrugged out of it and then untied the white strings of his simple white shirt sleeves. He rolled up his cuffs.

Bea licked her lips.

His wrist bones were visible, and a vein formed a long line over his shapely arms, giving Bea a trail to follow with her eyes until the shirt blocked its destination—but she knew it led to his heart, to the strong chest, and, most likely, to the athletic body underneath.

All she'd ever seen were the marble statues at the British Museum.

But now her curiosity was peaked to explore such artistry in flesh and blood.

His flesh, to be precise, brought her blood to boil so much that her vision blurred.

Alfie bent down and stacked the coals within the belly of the small metal furnace. Bea retrieved a candle from a box under one of the raised beds and handed it to him. After lighting the candle with flint and steel, he carefully held its flame to the coals within the furnace until they caught fire.

"This is the best method, actually. Gradually lighting the coals makes for a controlled and steady flame," he said, igniting the small black shapes one by one.

Bea felt like one of them, feeling the heat rise in her chest as if she were sitting on a furnace, imagining it was Alfie—for he lit her senses on fire.

<hr />

THE COALS HEATED quickly, emanating a wave of warmth that Alfie hoped was not due to his hard cock, but the furnace.

"Who is the myrtle oil for?" Bea asked.

"I cannot say."

"Oh, it's not a surprise, is it?"

"No."

She frowned most adorably, pouting a little.

So kissably sweet.

"I'll just pick twenty leaves and a few twigs if you don't mind." The tree had at least a thousand little leaves, and Alfie only needed a few.

"We have so much here, Alfie. If you think it can be useful, please take what you like."

He flinched at that.

"I often wish I could do something with my station, my privilege. Oh, I admire you so!" Bea's hand shot to her mouth, and she clasped her lips shut, turned her back to him, and walked toward the large potted tree.

She admired him?

"My work or me?" Alfie wished he could have suppressed the urge to ask a lady that; it was beyond improper, and yet the question burned in his chest. He'd had such an overwhelming sense of knowing her that he couldn't stop asking.

Bea faced him but she was several steps away. "Both?"

"Are you asking me?" Alfie took a step toward her, but only one.

"I don't know much about your work as an apothecary. I met some ayurvedic healers when I was sixteen, but they didn't speak with me."

It couldn't be... did she remember?

"Where did you meet them?" he asked carefully, trying not to let his mind join his heart in that elusive space where he hoped for more than he ought to have with Bea. But if they had a past, or at least a shared encounter... would anything change?

"I... ahem... nobody must know but you already do. I've never told anyone where we were when I was sixteen. My parents searched for a cure for my beast." She frowned. "Or rash, as you call it."

"In Delhi? With Master Varier?"

Bea's eyes found his and her pupils grew wider as her mouth fell open. "Who told you?"

"Nobody." But it all made sense now. He shouldn't have recognized her veiled in his apothecary, but he'd seen her that way in India and now he followed his intuition. There was no doubt in his mind that he'd seen her like this before. "I was there."

Bea jerked her head back. "Where?"

"At the British Residency, the British Resident in Delhi was Sir David Ochterlony."

"Did you work for the East India Company?"

"No, for Master Varier. I was an apprentice." And considering how many people there were in India, it wasn't just a coincidence that he'd seen Bea before. It was fate.

She cleared her throat, furrowed her brow, and crossed her arms. Alfie was unperturbed because the tension in his stomach had ebbed away, replaced by the serene certainty of newfound knowledge.

"I was two-and-twenty, and I had completed my apprenticeship. Felix was there, too. He worked in the town. I continued to work with Master Varier until I had enough to pay for the passage to England."

"What does that have to do with Sir Ochterlony?"

"He had guests. A family from London with a daughter who

always sat by the north-facing windows, away from the sun. She was always veiled."

Bea narrowed her eyes. "Did anyone tell you this?"

"No! Who would tell me that your veil had small yellow flowers embroidered along the edges and a few white tassels in the back to hold it down? Or that you always had stacks of books and maps before you?"

Bea gasped and her arms drooped to the sides.

"How would I know that the apprentice—also veiled—brought you honey to sweeten the awful-tasting tea that Master Varier had delivered to you every day?"

"That was you?" She closed the distance to Alfie and surveyed his eyes as if she could find a glimmer of her past in them.

He nodded.

"Why didn't you tell me before?" Confusion mixed with anger pierced her voice.

"I didn't realize it had been you all along. We never spoke until Pippa and Nick wanted me to make the ipecac for your uncle."

The flicker of recognition in Bea's eyes ignited into a full-blown blaze of enlightenment.

"Y-you spoke English!" Bea clasped her chest with both hands. "You knew about my beast!" The color drained from her face. "Did you understand everything my mother said?"

Alfie pinched his lips. Patient confidentiality turned into a rather muddy area if one was speaking to a patient who'd been treated by one's master… *oh drat*! This wasn't a conflict of interest but a conflicted love interest.

"I wasn't supposed to speak with the lady, but I was chosen for the task to ensure that I understood and that I could comply. Most of what I did was carry sacks of dried herbs, berries, and leaves at that time. Master Varier only let me mix in his *rasashala*, his laboratory."

"So you know about my beast? How long have you…?"

"I didn't know it was you. My residency was confidential and there were so many rules I was required to follow. I wasn't allowed to speak with you, for one. I was supposed to be as invisible as the servants fanning the air around you."

"But you did speak. I remember it."

Alfie couldn't suppress a slight smile. The fact that she remembered meant more to him than he ought to admit. "I brought you honey, and I snuck cinnamon into your tea to make it taste a little less bitter." *I also remember that time my thumb accidentally brushed over your hand and the jolt I felt.*

It was nothing compared to kissing you.

Bea stood seemingly puzzled under the myrtle. The foliage overhead had the shape of a large umbrella made of many elliptical leaves. But the woman standing under the canopy took his breath away. She sucked her lower lip in.

He'd given her much to think about and he wasn't yet sure what to do with the revelation of their shared encounters more than three years ago. All he knew was that he wanted to hold her now.

Distraction.

Good idea. He had to distract himself.

From what exactly? He'd nearly forgotten why he was alone in the Orangery with the girl he'd admired from afar and dreamed of for all this time, only to find out that she was the same who'd let him steal some of the most sizzling kisses he'd ever... *I want to kiss you again.*

The simple muslin dress accentuated her cleavage, and even though there was nothing more exposed than a lady ought, the light layers of dusty pink fabric brought out the copper hues in her hair and the flush on her cheeks. A cream-colored layer of something delicate stuck out of her cleavage, and Alfie imagined the sheer layers of a chemise, how he'd lift it slowly and bunch it over her hips.

He reached up and tried to pull a myrtle branch down to pluck off some leaves, but he was just a few inches too short, perhaps three.

>>>><<<<

THE ONE TIME she'd been allowed to travel with her parents, Bea had been isolated from the locals. After months on the schooners with Father discussing diplomatic relations with the captain and her mother forcing Bea to practice her watercolor and embroidery in her cabin all alone.

She'd been forced to wear a veil even though it had been stifling hot at the Residence. Her mother had wanted to hide the rash, but he knew… he'd seen her… and somehow, Bea wasn't ashamed anymore.

This explained everything.

"So you completed your apprenticeship, came back to England, and started a practice?"

"That's making it sound rather simple, but yes." Alfie followed her.

"And the ointment smells like the tea! I recognized it right away but thought it was a coincidence!"

She turned around and Alfie's face had already lit up with a bright smile. "I combined some of the skills from our western chemistry with ayurvedic herbs. It's the same combination of herbs, but I made a more concentrated essence and mixed it with soothing oils."

"It helps," Bea said.

He beamed. "I'm glad." He bowed and her breath hitched. She didn't want that distance her parents had put between them. He wasn't a servant. Alfie had become so much more for her.

She just couldn't quite formulate the thought in her mind at the time, yet now she could. She loved him. And she always had because he'd been her only friend, and they'd communicated without speaking and… oh she wanted Alfie and not the prince! But she'd been raised to wait for a man to woo her and didn't know how to act around him anymore.

Bea led Alfie to the raised beds, her heart thudding in her

chest as she revealed the set of wooden crates hidden beneath. She was aware of his gaze washing over her like a summer rain. With a nod, he hefted the largest crate and carried it over to the tree, positioning it carefully before climbing on top. Bea's breath caught as she watched him, his movements graceful yet strong. The Orangery transformed into an intimate shrine where she found herself in awe of Alfie's quiet strength and unassuming presence.

His shirt bunched up as he reached to gather the myrtle leaves, revealing a tantalizing glimpse of his lean, chiseled abdomen. Bea couldn't tear her eyes away, mesmerized by how his body moved with such effortless elegance. Each stretch of his arm sent a thrill through her, and she marveled at how this simple task could become a moment of pure reverence. In that secluded, sun-dappled space, Bea's admiration for him deepened, her emotions swirling like the fragrant air around them.

But as Alfie descended from the box with a handful of leaves, his eyes met hers, holding her gaze with an intensity that took her breath away. Bea's pulse quickened, and she felt an urgent pull to act on the longing that had simmered within her for so long. Her courage to touch him was as fragile and potent as myrtle's scent, leaving her teetering on the edge of indecision.

Thus, she decided.

Her hand shook and grew a little wet, but she reached for his belly where she could see the skin exposed. His muscles twitched and she wanted to withdraw. Perhaps she'd gone too far.

For certain.

But then Alfie bent down slightly, put his hands under her arms and pulled her up onto the crate. Bea forgot to breathe the moment she looked into his eyes. As if he could smile with his gaze alone, Alfie's bright green eyes were so much lighter than the shades of the leaves overhead. And then everything blurred but his face.

"I've been dreaming of the girl under the white veil for so long that I never thought it possible that I'd hold her in my arms."

Bea nestled against him. She was the beastly girl whose first season had to be postponed, whose parents traveled across the world in search of a cure for her affliction. She'd been locked up and hidden behind veils but somehow Alfie didn't see any of that. He was the only person in the world who knew everything about her darkest secrets—yet he held her with such reverence that she had trouble believing her good fortune.

"And you say I'm the dream," Bea whispered as she wrapped both arms around him. "It's been you all along."

There, on a wooden crate under a potted tree that should only grow on the Mediterranean coast, the apothecary who could take a sack of twigs and leaf dust and turn them into a healing tincture had lifted her heart into a realm she didn't know existed.

And when his lips touched hers, Bea knew that everything would change.

Chapter Twenty-Four

LATER THAT NIGHT, no matter how hard Bea tried, she couldn't banish the image of Alfie's chiseled abdomen from her mind. She turned restlessly in bed, wishing she had found the courage to kiss him more. The idea to wrap herself around him and hold him close became the central point of her thoughts and the image of Alfie reaching for the myrtle—his arms stretched high, muscles taut under his shirt—made her heart race. She longed to comb her hands through his hair, take his mouth with hers, and feel his body's strength against her. Again and again.

Bea's desire for Alfie was an itch she couldn't scratch, an insistent desire that left her skin tingling. His ointment wasn't enough to soothe the burn within her—she needed not the apothecary, rather the man behind the counter. She sat up and reached for her journal, scribbling feverishly about how much she wanted to touch him, to kiss him. Each line was more fervent than the last, her private musings pouring onto the pages in a flurry of longing.

> *My heart trembles with desires too bold to be spoken aloud for I must not ask to satisfy the cravings deep within. Tonight, I find myself overwhelmed by thoughts of Alfie. His mere presence stirs within me a yearning so profound that I scarcely recognize myself for I cannot be whole without his touch. I was too timid to reach for him at the orangery when he left with the myrtle*

leaves, and now I regret the chance that I let pass.

Would he have allowed me to caress the taut skin on his stomach?

How I long to feel the warmth of his embrace, to trace my fingers along the firm lines of his body, and lose myself in the depths of his eyes. The thought of pressing my lips to his, tasting the sweetness of his breath, sends shivers through my soul. I imagine the strength of his arms around me, holding me close, our bodies entwined in a tender dance of passion and affection.

To run my hands through his dark hair, to feel each silken strand slip through my fingers, and to whisper my love into his ear—these are the dreams that haunt my waking hours. Oh, to lay beside him, the world fading away, leaving only the two of us in a cocoon of shared warmth and whispered promises. The flame of my desire burns bright, and I wonder if I shall ever have the courage to ignite it into a blaze of reality.

How cruel the paradox of my existence as a lady! I know well that I must not ask for what my heart so ardently desires; propriety and decorum demand my restraint. Yet, it is precisely because I am a lady, with all the passions and yearnings that accompany such a station, that I long to follow my heart's true desire. The societal expectations that bind me feel like chains, forcing me into silence while every fiber of my being cries out for the freedom to love openly and without reservation.

Bea sighed. She was being ridiculous, she could never have that sort of connection. Leaving her journal as usual on her desk, she clambered into bed and tried not to dream of Alfie Collins. She had to think about how best to help Prince Stan with his plan and her role in it. Step one was to attend the card game at Violet's and Henry's townhouse the next evening, and impress Prince Stan to … what did she want? Bea's head was spinning; she needed to impress the prince and work with him, and yet her stomach churned with longing for Alfie. She let out a mournful murmur, resonating from the depths of her being, as if her very soul had decided to speak its truths through the language of breath.

But she had her own plan and knew what step two would be: Marry and move away from the stifling rules of the Ton, the hypocrisy, the ever-looming threat of scandal.

But she couldn't say goodbye to Alfie and leave after Pippa's wedding as she'd originally planned. Sometimes in life, plans had to change.

Bea's eyes grew heavy, and she put her head down on the pillow.

"Alfie," she sighed and drifted off to sleep.

⇶⇷

When the first light of dawn crept through her window, Bea woke up with the journal lying beside her pillow.

She knew she had to see him. Determined, she took her carriage to 87 Harley Street, asked the coachman not to wait for her, and made her way to the apothecary.

Bea knocked. It was Saturday and the front door was locked. She used the knocker and cleared her throat. Her neck had begun to itch. Everything itched, actually. Could it be because she was overstepping every boundary of propriety? She stopped speculating as the door opened.

"Alfie!" She exclaimed, as if she didn't expect him to open the door of the building in which he lived. Yet, the warmth of his smile sent a flutter through her heart. His presence seemed to fill the space with a quiet strength and gentleness that made her feel better just by virtue of being near him.

"Pippa's just left, everyone's on the way to Kent," he said as he stepped aside and gestured to invite her in as if Bea's only reason to visit 87 Harley Street were to meet with Pippa and Nick for wedding planning. Well, that was not an excuse she could use this time.

Except for Chromius barking and jumping on his hind legs to

greet her, the practice was eerily quiet indeed.

"Why didn't you go with them?"

"I have an important meeting tonight," he said eyeing her intently and then he looked out the door. "Are you alone?"

"Yes." Bea knew she shouldn't have come unchaperoned, especially knowing that Pippa had already left for Kent. But she didn't want a chaperone, and Violet would cover for her if needed. She could let her know later that evening, as Bea had planned to attend with Prince Stan. When Bea's parents had left for their trip, and Pippa's father remarried, they'd changed the instructions of their lady's maids, and both avoided being chaperoned whenever possible. It had been an enormous risk to their reputations but also an exciting and liberating sense of control over their own lives. And that's how Bea viewed what she'd done that morning—taken control.

Plus, since her uncle had suffered sobering at Violet's ball, there wasn't much heed paid to propriety. Good! Perhaps Bea didn't know how to ask for what she wanted but she was certainly not going to ask for what she didn't want.

Alfie glanced up, his eyes warm and questioning as he noticed her scratching her arm.

"Can I help you with something?" he asked, his gaze flicking to the journal while he turned his back to the door and shut it.

"I've been itchy all night," Bea admitted, hoping her voice didn't betray the true cause of her restlessness. "I can't seem to… soothe the burn… inside of me."

THE BURN INSIDE *of her…*

Alfie suppressed a groan. It was Saturday morning and he'd just drawn a hot bath for himself, trying to ready himself for the task of the evening of helping Prince Stan. Oh, who was he fooling? He was going to soak in the hot water and think of Bea.

Who was here.

Now.

Standing before him.

Then he noticed Bea scratch at her arm again, and concern etched his features. "You really have irritated skin? Perhaps an oat bath would help soothe it," he suggested gently, trying not to think about the itch in his breeches that must not be scratched.

Bea hesitated, biting her lip. "Pippa's maid has gone with her and most of the house has been packed already. I appreciate the suggestion, but drawing a bath seems like such trouble with the move to the country estate and the wedding preparations."

"Nonsense," Alfie replied, a reassuring smile spreading across his face. "Let me prepare one for you here. It won't take long, and with everyone else already off to the country, there's no need to rush. Only Chromius and I are here."

Her eyes widened slightly, a mixture of surprise and something more flickering within them "If it's truly not too much trouble…"

"It's not," he assured her, his voice steady and warm. "Come, follow me."

As they walked upstairs toward the large water closet next to his bed chamber, Alfie couldn't ignore the way his heart quickened. The moment's intimacy was undeniable, and he couldn't shake the feeling that this simple act of kindness held far more significance than either dared to acknowledge.

He'd gone too far and offered a service that was far beyond his apothecary shop. In fact, he was taking Bea upstairs. If anyone found them, it would be scandalous. But a bath had been drawn and Bea could benefit from it more than he would.

"I promised to soothe your skin, so let me." Alfie's voice failed him when Bea's mouth fell open, and she glanced up the staircase.

It was exactly as bad as it sounded, and yet, an oat bath would soothe her skin.

And it would aggravate the burning desire inside of him, Alfie thought, but he didn't dare speak anymore.

Bea let out a puff of air as if she'd had an entire conversation with herself in her mind. She placed a hand on the railing and took the first step. "This way?"

Alfie nodded and followed her.

This was different from how the day was supposed to go. Alfie had prepared to assist the prince that evening—a mission that could elevate the prince to heroic stature—yet he felt a pang of inner conflict. The prince's daring actions tonight could change their lives, solidifying his place on a pedestal of royal virtue unattainable for an apothecary. Alfie knew well that he must not compete with the prince, for his role was one of service and loyalty and Bea was destined to make a noble match. However, as he watched her hips swaying gently as she walked upstairs ahead of him, her allure so intoxicatingly close, he couldn't quell the burgeoning sense of rivalry that stirred within him. He knew she was interested in the Prince, he'd overheard her speak about him.

But Alfie was not going to let her get out without putting up a little fight at least. Although he knew he could never have her, she ought to know what she'd miss. An aromatic herbal bath seemed like the perfect battleground if she allowed it.

Determined to focus on the moment at hand, Alfie turned his attention to preparing the hot bath for Bea. The water steamed invitingly, and the scent of oats mingled with the air, creating a soothing sanctuary. He added a few essential oils to mask the nuttiness of the oat scent.

"What is this for?" she asked, her arms crossed, hugging herself and eyeing the tin tub she'd step into. Naked. Soon. Alfie suppressed a groan.

"This is rose water, it's a hydrophilic moisturizer and balances irritations of the skin because it mixes with the warm water." With every word, his head throbbed even more, and he corked the bottle and retrieved a smaller vial with walnut oil. "The walnut oil here is an oil-based moisturizer, so it makes a film on the water's surface and coats—" he swallowed hard, "your sin…

skin… ahem…" He shut his eyes and tried to concentrate but the thought of anything coating her bare skin besides his touch blurred his vision and cut off his breathing. Alfie never thought he'd be jealous of a half cup of walnut oil floating on hot water, but he'd stooped that low in that moment.

"Why do you have these in your bathroom cabinet?" she asked.

"We share this bathing room. Nick, Wendy, and I." Alfie avoided her gaze. She was a lady and probably had five bath chambers to choose from every day.

And she chose yours today, he told himself as his breeches grew too tight and he tried to turn away from her.

"I should disrobe before the water cools," she said as she tugged at each finger of her gloves and set them on the stool next to the tub.

Alfie should have nodded and taken his leave politely. He would have if his feet hadn't been heavy as anvils and his mind throbbing in the same rhythm as his middle.

Bea removed some pins from her hair and put them in her reticule, where Alfie still saw the journal peeking out. His eyes went to the hook on the wall behind her and she followed his gaze, leaving him frozen like a besotted green boy as she hung her reticule on the hook.

His mouth was dry despite the steam in the room, which Alfie hoped came from the tub and not his breeches.

"It's getting cold," she said, pulling the string that tied her pelisse open.

He'd seen her décolleté at the Langley's ball, then why couldn't he stop watching as she removed her pelisse?

"Here's a stack of towels," Alfie croaked as if he were no more than fifteen again and he left the towel cabinet open for her. With all the power in his body, he dragged his heavy feet, and himself, to the door. It was tortuous to leave Bea undressing in his bathroom—as if he'd been climbing a mountain in the Himalayans on a hot summer day.

"If you were not a lady, Bea, and if I didn't know any better, I'd—" but he knew better than to finish the sentence. Her mouth fell open, and her eyes grew wide. She was a lady, a virgin, and not anyone else.

"Would what?" She whispered, seemingly holding her breath as a pink flush spread on her sweet cheeks.

He couldn't say.

And he couldn't stay. Lest he do something irrevocable.

Bea watched him leave with a curiosity that mirrored his own unspoken thoughts, and when he stood in the door, she didn't protest. Of course not. He was a commoner, and she was a lady—a virgin lady with her cap set on a prince.

Alfie's heart sank. "Take as much time as you wish." He tightened his grip on the doorknob. She simply nodded, gratitude and something deeper swimming in her eyes. The intimacy of the act, performed in the quiet solitude of the small room, spoke of the unvoiced sentiments that lingered between them.

As Alfie shut the door behind him, leaving Bea alone, a rush of heat surged through him. His heart pounded with an intensity that surprised even him, each beat echoing the forbidden nature of his thoughts. He imagined Bea undressing, the delicate fabric of her gown slipping from her shoulders to reveal the soft curves of her body. The thought of her standing there, vulnerable and trusting, sent a thrill coursing through him that was both exhilarating and disquieting.

His mind raced, torn between his duty to suppress his need and his burgeoning desire for Bea. It was all so private and charged with emotions that it left him feeling both honored and tormented. He knew he should focus on the mission ahead and ready himself to help the prince later that night—his priority should be the practice and saving Felix and his friends. But the image of Bea, bathed in the milky foam of his bath, lingered in his thoughts, a tantalizing distraction that he couldn't easily dismiss. It was even stronger now than all those years ago in India. He knew how it felt when she kissed and how she felt in his arms.

Nothing would ever be the same again.

Was this his chance to show Bea how he felt, or would he abuse her trust beyond repair if he did?

Chapter Twenty-Five

B
EA STEPPED INTO the hot bath, her sigh echoing softly in the dimly lit room. The warmth of the water spread from her legs up to the rest of her body, relaxing muscles that had been tense for far too long. She held onto the edge of the tub as she pulled her other leg in, then slowly melted into the water. The scent of rose and walnut wafted around her, enveloping her senses. It felt like she was immersed in a decadent dessert, a luxury she rarely allowed herself.

The milky water, infused with oats, soothed her skin, but it did little to ease the throbbing in her middle. Her thoughts wandered back to her last conversation in this very building. Downstairs, when Cousin Pippa had spoken of pleasure in a tone both conspiratorial and enticing. Bea finally understood it, and yearned for it, an ache that pulsed more insistently with each passing moment.

Leaning back in the tub, she let the warm water cascade over her shoulder. She lifted her hair, allowing the heat to penetrate the knots in her neck. A shiver of relief ran through her, momentarily easing the tension that coiled deep inside her. Instinctively, her hand moved to her middle. It wasn't allowed, but who would know? Who could possibly check? She found power in defying her mother's rules, the constraints imposed upon her at finishing school—she had enough and yet none of what she wanted—or who she wanted. Alfie.

Bea closed her eyes and spread her fingers and brushed over her skin.

In just a few hours, she was to meet with the prince. The thought should have filled her with anticipation, but instead, her mind drifted to the man in the room next door. This was where he bathed. His chiseled neck, his muscular abdomen—images of him towering over her in the Orangery that brought her senses alive came to mind and the idea of his being naked in this very tub.

As she reclined further, the water lapped gently at her skin, creating ripples that mirrored the sensations within her. Her fingers brushed lightly across her abdomen, exploring the forbidden territory. She closed her eyes, recalling every detail of Alfie's form. His presence stirred something deep within her, something that Pippa's words had awakened but hadn't fully ignited.

The sound of footsteps outside her door broke her reverie. Bea quickly retracted her hand, her heart racing. The footsteps faded, leaving a silence that seemed louder than before. She exhaled slowly, trying to calm the erratic pounding in her chest.

Her thoughts returned to Alfie, lingering on the way he looked at her with a mix of curiosity and something more primal. His gaze had lingered a bit too long on her lips before he'd left her for the bath, and she remembered the way his breath had hitched when she'd accidentally brushed against him on the way up the stairs only minutes earlier. Did he feel the same pull she did?

She couldn't afford to think this way until they could speak freely again. Not with the meeting tonight, not with the responsibilities that lay ahead. But alone in the bath, surrounded by the comforting scents and warmth, it was hard to focus on anything else. She wanted him in every way imaginable.

Bea's fingers trailed through the water, drawing patterns that dissolved almost instantly. The sensation was calming, yet the tension in her middle remained. She thought again of Pippa's words, about finding pleasure. Was it wrong to seek it? To want something just for herself amid the duties and expectations that constrained her every move?

The warmth of the bath was beginning to dissipate, but Bea stayed submerged, unwilling to leave the cocoon of solace it provided. She glanced at the small window, where the last light of day was fading, casting a soft glow on the walls. Evening was approaching, and soon she would have to prepare for her encounter with the prince. He would check off all her criteria except for the one she cared about most: love and passion.

So for now, she allowed herself a few more minutes of indulgence. The floral and nutty scents continued to surround her, a sensory embrace that made her feel cherished, if only briefly. She thought of Alfie again, imagining his hands where hers had been, his touch igniting a fire that no amount of warm water could quench.

A FEW MINUTES later, Alfie heard a clatter coming from the bathroom. The lush, creamy scent of rose wafted into his bed chamber. He could feel the warmth of the oil, an enticing note of a soft, ripe fruitiness, and the undertone of nutty sweetness.

Alfie pinched the bridge of his nose with his index finger and thumb, hoping he could ground himself in the task at hand. Folding.

Yes.

Good idea. He had to fold his bed sheets.

Easy.

He pulled a corner of the sheet over to the other side, pairing it with its counterpart to... what was that?

A slight splashing and a moan?

He stilled and listened.

Another light moan—no, more of a sigh.

He knocked on the door. "Is everything all right?"

No answer.

He knocked louder.

"Bea?"

Another little splash and much louder moan.

Oh no! Could she be in trouble? In the bathtub?

He'd never heard of a grown woman drowning in the tub, but his years of medical training taught him to expect anything.

Had he made the water too hot for her?

Could she have grown dizzy? He'd made her swoon once before and caught her, but this time, she was in water.

Perhaps she was in trouble after all.

"Bea?" Alfie called, laying his hand on the door as if he could feel her pulse through the thick wood. Yet another feminine sigh escaped the bathroom.

Without thinking of propriety, he turned the knob and went in. The aroma of the bath oil enveloped him like a spell he'd laid upon the room. Even though it was just a small room, furnished to be functional and without decoration, it was a clean canvas for the most sensual image he'd ever seen.

Bea's head was leaning on the rim of the tub, her hair dry except for the temples. She must have brushed her hair out of her face with wet hands. From his angle, he saw her delicate neck and nothing more; only her perfect profile came into view. She hung one elegant leg over the top of the tub, pointed foot twitching.

Her eyes were closed, and she let out another moan.

Then, a little splash.

Had she not heard him calling? Or knocking?

"Bea? Are you alright?" Alfie asked again, taking three steps forward and then swallowing hard.

She lay in the tub, his tub, with her gorgeous legs spread wide. Naked. One hand on her breast, the other immersed under the foamy water. He could imagine what was under the lucky little bubbles and envied them. Soapy balls, just filled with air, and yet so fortunate as to caress the most beautiful female body he'd ever seen.

She moved her hand, but her eyes remained shut.

Alfie cocked his head.

He ought to turn around and give her privacy. But he couldn't. If she allowed him to be there, he wasn't going anywhere.

It was only a fleeting moment, yet a million thoughts swished through Alfie's mind—a sin he'd watched her for a long time, admired her like an oil painting at the museum.

"I can't figure out how to… ah…" she said, her eyes still pinched closed. A few adorable layers of skin wrinkled just over the bridge of her nose, showing how tense she was and that her face was stretched with the most even gorgeous skin.

Then her hands came to the rim of the tub, and she dropped her leg in the water. She blinked her eyes open, and Alfie reached for the towel hanging on the wall just behind her head. He held it out, and she dried her eyes, but a small bead of the foam remained on her long lashes, making them sparkle like the sun's rays on a dewy spring morning. Why wasn't she shocked that he'd entered?

"My apologies, I shall go. I feared that you needed help because you didn't respond when I—"

"I do need help, if you offer." She spoke matter-of-factly as if she were seated in full dress on a settee and not lying naked in the bath, covered with only a layer of foam.

"With what?" Alfie asked, scanning the room. A stack of towels was there; her clothes hung on a chair, and the gas light flickered warmly. What could she want?

His mind raced. What did women need in the bath?

A scene came to mind: a servant holding a towel up for a princess so she could step safely out of the tub. His mouth went dry, and he bristled against the idea. He was not her servant and could never be. After all the years of work, Alfie didn't want to remain shrouded in a head scarf like the apprentice he'd been in

India. This time, he wanted to show her exactly how he felt. He certainly could wrap her in a towel, but it would not be merely to ensure that she was dry.

"I need a hand," she said, raising her head and looking at him straight. "A hand that's not my own."

"What for?" Alfie's right hand twitched, and he put it in his pocket to contain it. As if his hand knew where she wanted it, and he wouldn't allow it such an escapade, he held back.

"I'm trying to figure out the point of all this. It occurred to me that the scent of seduction is in the air, so how can I know when I succeeded?"

Alfie blinked several times to make sure he was awake, and she hadn't merely said all this in his imagination or dreams.

"What do you mean?" He knew what she meant. Even his hand knew. But he couldn't allow it.

"I can't figure out what the finish is. The great finish that everybody is talking about."

"Who's talking about it?"

"Oh, everybody. My cousin Pippa. Violet."

"Lady Langley?"

"Yes."

A moment of awkward silence punctured the lovely scent in the room. The air was hot, and the rose hung lower than the nutty walnut. Of course, it would, Alfie thought; it's a much heavier oil. That's why the lighter rose wafted out of the bathroom first, sending for him like a calling card.

"Do you remember the pavilion? From the ball at the Langleys?"

Of course, he did! He'd heard what occurred there and he was quite certain it was where he'd seen Nick and Pippa wander off that night at the ball, just before Bea had come to speak with him. He'd imagined the pavilion. He pictured himself with her in said closet uncountable times. This was not something he could easily forget. "Faintly."

"There was something I heard. 'No woman ever failed to

finish in this closet.'"

"Hm!" Good to know. Except that he didn't want to know. He'd rather find out how Bea finished. She'd probably do amazingly well, considering that she had no scruples about conversing with him stark naked from her vantage point in the tub—his tub. Even the tub was lucky, just like the bubbles. What Alfie longed for was what was between the tin of the tub and the lovely layer of bubbles, the body sheathed from his view.

"I should go."

"No, please!"

"Do you need anything, a towel or a bar of soap?" Alfie turned toward the door. He couldn't just stand there and look at her. It was too hard to hold back. He put both hands in his pockets and stood there, not allowing his hands to go where his mind had already ventured.

"I am two-and-twenty years old. I've never managed to reach this finishing point. I'm certain I know nothing of how it's done."

He had not heard right. This was his mind playing tricks. The scented oils lured his imagination so he couldn't discern reality from wishful thinking.

"Please! You know so much of the human body. You studied medicine and pharmacy. You, you—"

Alfie swallowed again; his Adam's apple bobbed and suddenly his cravat was too tight.

He tugged at it to loosen it just a bit. His eyes searched for the window, but it was all fogged up. The steam from the hot water had shrouded them in privacy, so even the dim sunlight couldn't find them.

"What are you asking me exactly?" He was just a man, after all, in heat. Unforgivably so, actually. And yet, he had to hear it. He'd bring her a towel if she said she needed it. If she said she needed a cup of tea, that's what he'd get. There wasn't much he wouldn't give for the beauty in his tub blinking at him innocently with the expression of a student about to embark upon a science experiment.

"I wonder if you'd be inclined to show me."

"Show me?"

She arched her back and brought both hands to her breasts. The foam parted, and he saw the perky round mounds, her hands covering her buds. "I can't manage it when I know the next motion. It mustn't come from my own hand."

"So you want mine?"

"Yes. Do you know how to make a woman finish?"

"Yes," Alfie croaked. This could not be real. He pushed his hands into his pockets, hoping he'd burn them on something and wake up. This dream was too dangerous for him; he couldn't continue down this path unharmed.

"Alfie?" Her voice echoed faintly in the room. "Alfie?"

He heard her well, but had he heard well?

"I'm sorry," her voice was low now. "My apologies if I embarrassed you." She heaved for air and slid down in the water. The bubbles closed over where she'd gone down, closing the layer of foam. Her knees were all he could see, two islands in the foam.

Wait, wasn't she coming up for air?

"Bea?" Alfie called.

"I'm here," she said, emerging with wet hair and foam on her face. Her eyes were closed.

Alfie reached for the towel she'd hung on the rim of the tub. Half had been immersed in the water and was soaked, heavy with moisture. She reached for it and dried her face, then dropped the towel on the floor next to the tub. She brushed both hands over her face and hair, stroking it out of her face. The long tresses in the water floated in elegant curls.

Alfie's body was so hard he could be a beam holding up a house. What he couldn't hold was his composure.

"Thank you. I'm sorry if I embarrassed you."

"You did not."

She shrugged, and the foam parted over one of her breasts. Alfie tried not to look. Not to stare, but it was impossible. The little pink nipple couldn't have pulled him more if he were wrapped in a rope and brought ashore to the gorgeous floating island that was this bud.

"I want to be kissed. I want to know what it feels like to finish like other women told me. I tried to manage it myself, but it's not working."

Alfie cleared his throat and scratched his neck. It wasn't itchy; he just needed to know this was not one of his many dirty dreams.

"I've... ahem... Bea." His mouth was too dry to speak.

He reached for a towel from the stack on the stool to wipe his hands.

But this was a virgin daughter of a duke. She had set her cap on a prince from another country, and he sighed and gripped the towel hard as if it could absorb not just the water from his skin but also the desire throbbing in his body.

He didn't dare turn back around to see her, but there was a slight gasp.

Alfie hung the towel on the hook on the wall. "Call me if you need anything."

"I need you to show me how it feels."

Alfie hung both arms limp beside his body. Her words were about to defeat the restraint he'd tried to flex around her like a muscle, but he wasn't strong enough anymore.

"Violet said it can be done with the fingers. I want your hand, Alfie. Just this once, without any consequences."

Impossible.

And impossible to resist.

Alfie shook his head, his back still turned to her.

He unbuttoned the sleeves and rolled them up over his elbows.

Then he turned around. "Bea, I like you too much for this to be inconsequential."

She nodded, seated upright in the tub. "Me too."

Her breasts were above the water, both of her little pink

nipples exposed and bright pink.

"I don't want to wait anymore. I want you to show me."

"This is reserved for your future husband. It can't be me," Alfie hoped he'd said it aloud. It was certainly the right thing to do but then she arched her back, and his restraint evaporated.

His tongue twitched in his mouth at the sight, his appetite for her overpowering.

Bea's gaze was dark. He took two large steps to the tub and knelt on the side.

When Alfie put his right hand in the water and leaned his left on the rim of the tub, he gave her time to stop him.

But she didn't.

"This won't leave traces on your body, Bea, but it is not something you can forget you've experienced once you have."

"I don't ever want to forget anything I've ever experienced with you. Not now, not ever."

Alfie narrowed his eyes. "What?"

"I have a flower that I received many years ago. Someone gave it to me, and I kept it pressed in paper. It's a constant reminder of the time I didn't speak because I wasn't supposed to. But I never forgave myself for not even asking for his name."

Alfie's heart leapt. That was him! But before he could find a way to phrase it, she took his right hand and pulled it to her center.

"I'm not going to not ask for this," she said, looking down at her middle, hidden under the foamy water, instead of at him.

He'd missed a year's worth of chances when he wasn't allowed to speak to her. It was worse now and he mustn't do what he wanted.

"I'd give you anything you want, Bea. Pleasure, if that's what you want."

My heart and soul are yours if you want me.

Alfie looked at her, but she leaned her head back again and shut her eyes, sucking in her lower lip.

He wanted to kiss her. Stroke her face and her lips.

He wanted to hold her in his arms, not just be a helping hand. But even now, she was a lady and out of his reach.

So he did all he could, all he was permitted. This time, he did what she permitted, not the circumstances or the people commanding their lives.

He quickly found his way and parted her folds. She helped with both hands.

In just a moment, his index finger slipped in. She arched her back and pushed against him, but she was so tight. So precious and so hot.

He knew how to move but started slowly. Only when she moaned and relaxed a little did he insert a second finger.

"Faster," she whispered, her eyes still closed.

Alfie's heart dropped. This was not how he'd imagined this to go.

He was serving her.

That was his station as an apothecary.

Although this was going above and beyond his job description.

And yet, it could never be more, could it?

He could never love her openly. It wasn't permitted.

And she was most likely simply curious and overcome by the fragrances in the warm bath. Could she feel more? He mustn't allow himself to hope.

His heart was breaking as he picked up speed. She tensed and arched her back, pushed against him, and then she opened her eyes.

She blinked at him, and he froze.

There was something in her gaze that took him off guard.

Her gaze shot to his soul, and he couldn't hide his feelings.

Then she reached for his collar and pulled him to her face.

"Alfie, I've wanted you for so long." Her breath came hot on his lips.

Alfie leaned in. Their eyes exchanged a serious glance. For a moment, nothing happened.

Everything happened.

Her eyes darted from his left to his right eye and back as if she were calculating something in her mind—or recalling a memory.

She knew who he was, not merely here, but also all those years ago in Delhi.

And then she opened her mouth and pressed her lips against his.

He was too far gone to make this a chaste kiss; she pulled his collar, and a slight ripping sound echoed in the distance. All he could focus on was her hot mouth, the heady combination of the fragrances, and her throbbing middle.

"Take me out of the bath!" she whispered and then plunged her tongue into his mouth. Alfie opened up and received her so willingly that he couldn't but suck a little. Her lips were swollen, and he knew all too well how slick and ready she was—yearning for him.

Alfie stretched his arm and took another towel from the stool without breaking the kiss. He didn't remove his right hand from her center but wrapped his left around her back. She rose, her mouth still on his, and then he had to pull his hand out of her.

She gasped in protest.

He wrapped her in the towel, feeling the heat loss from the water on her wet skin.

He took her in his arms and picked her up, carrying her to the table by the wall.

The table on which he usually folded towels was sturdy, modest, but smooth.

Her mouth was on his, unable to let go, and he certainly didn't want her to leave him. Ever.

He set her on the table, so the towel fell off her, a layer between her soft skin and the hard wooden surface.

Alfie spread her legs, and she complied. He took a position standing between her legs and put his right hand back. She fell back as he inserted his middle and index fingers at once, so his thumb could find her pearl. With his left arm, he caught her just when she gasped with pleasure.

She arched back and cupped his face, pulling him in for the deepest kiss in his life. He could feel her in his bones, so passionate was her kiss. Her tongue was clumsy, fresh, innocent, needy, and ready for him.

⇉⇉⇉⇇⇇⇇

HE KISSED HER with vigor as if he were speaking to her insides. She could feel a ripple of emotion through her entire body when he flicked his tongue and his hand... oh his hand... coherent thoughts left Bea's mind. This was forbidden, and it should be. Now that she felt him like this, she was addicted. She wanted more of him, and she wanted him entirely.

"Deeper!" She cried into his mouth, unable to stop exploring his mouth with her tongue. She felt his large, sharp teeth.

She leaned back and let her wet hair fall back. Propped on her elbows, she freed his left hand, and he grabbed her breasts. Oh, how marvelous. Magical tingling rushed through her.

His hand covered her breasts. Then he kissed her jawline. Then, her chin. And he went down to the nape of her neck, along her décolletage, and down to—oh!

He took her nipple between his teeth, and... her heart nearly jumped out of her chest.

She felt his hand so deep, as if it were in her throat, reaching through her body to her heart and enchanting her. This was a life-changing experience, and she grabbed his head.

Driving her right hand through his hair, she tried to remain propped up on her elbow, but when he let go of her right nipple with his mouth and brought his free hand there, he took the other nipple in his mouth and did the same thing.

The same magical kiss.

She collapsed onto the table. Her legs spread wide as she was offering herself up. He was dressed and feasting on her body while giving her something she never knew existed.

And then she tensed.

For a moment he paused. "Do you want to finish?"

She didn't know. She was certainly not done. Her lips were swollen, her nipples hard, her center throbbing for him to resume.

"If you like this first finish, we can start anew, and you can have another."

"Another?"

He nodded.

"Promise?" Urgency colored her voice.

"Yes," he panted. "Any time."

And with a swift motion, he did something with his hand that filled her more, stretched her more, and then he moved. His hand on her breast, he kneaded her nipple most expertly, anticipating the sensations she'd need before she even knew. And he came down with his mouth, further down, until his thumb flicked her bean up and he took it in his mouth.

A scream pierced the silence. It was hers.

He exhaled, and heat overcame her as he sucked, stroked, and whatever it was that he did; Bea's vision failed. Her skin tingled where he touched her in the best way imaginable. With his gentle kisses, she discovered new sensations her body was capable of. Somehow, he knew her body even better than she did, and she wondered if it could be true for her heart.

Then it happened.

She forgot to breathe, and a tremor shook her from the center through her body, from the inside out like a ripple of the water when a rock plopped in. She could feel it like a cramp in her body, curling her toes and prickling at the base of each hair on her head.

She let it wash over her and then she heaved for air. But what she really wanted was him.

Disheveled, eyes black, his mouth glistening with her slick desire, he came up from there.

His hand exerted gentle pressure.

It was so good. And he felt so right.

She hadn't known her body could do that. And she knew then she was made for this—for him.

She reached for his gorgeous face and pulled his head up. He complied after removing his fingers and just laying his hand flat on her hot throbbing center. It was soothing her in a way she wouldn't have known to ask for. He was everything she'd wanted and needed yet never knew to request.

And when he came to her face, he stilled and looked into her eyes.

She knew he wanted to say something but didn't. There was a certain sadness, a vulnerability in his gaze. He looked younger than ever before, raw.

Then his eyes fell from her eyes to her mouth, and he lowered his face.

Just before his mouth touched hers again, he closed his eyes so tightly, as if he were about to dive into cold salt water and wanted to shield his vision.

And the kiss was unlike the one a moment ago.

He was slowly feeling her lips with his, pressing to intensify the touch and then releasing her to bring his tongue to her cupid's bow. He was telling her something.

Without words, just with the tenderness of his touch.

And there was that special color of his eyes…

His hand left her middle and he trailed both hands along her sides, over her breasts, along her shoulders and arms. Then he inserted both hands behind her back and supported her while he kissed her so deeply that she thought she was dreaming and yet it was an awakening.

He pulled her up, supporting her back with both hands and he wrapped her in the towel.

Still kissing her.

Next, he crossed the towel over her breasts, and she instinctively held it over her shoulders like a shawl.

And then he broke the kiss.

She could tell he did so reluctantly.

He dropped his forehead onto hers and turned his head sideways as if he wanted to say something and didn't dare again.

Then a bark. *Chromius.*

He was outside the door, scratching and whining. It was time for his walk and meal.

Bea's eyes grew wide. "This never happened."

"What?" Alfie whispered.

He inhaled as if he needed to tell her something and it appeared that courage failed him.

"Shh!" Bea put a finger on his lips. She was too embarrassed about her feelings but this... she was a wanton woman. She would embarrass Pippa in front of her almost sister-in-law if anyone were to find out.

Alfie deflated, slumped his shoulders, and then he dropped his head.

Bea's heart pounded as she found herself back in the dimly lit room, a sense of disorientation washing over her. She was sitting on the edge of the table, wrapped in nothing but a damp towel, the remnants of their encounter still clinging to her skin. A cold shiver coursed through her, and she began to tremble.

Her middle was sore and hot, a poignant reminder of the intimate moment she had just shared with Alfie. The realization struck her with the force of a tidal wave—she had allowed him to touch her too intimately, far beyond the bounds of propriety. Panic surged within her, and she scrambled to gather her discarded clothes and her reticule with her journal, clutching them to her chest as though they could shield her from her own reckless desires.

"I have to go." She looked left and right, trying to ensure that she wasn't leaving as much as a hairpin behind. Tears blurred her vision as she stumbled out of the room and into what she hoped was his bedchamber. She reached for the door with desperate hands, slamming it shut behind her and turning the key in the lock. The sound of the bolt sliding into place echoed in the quiet room but on the inside, her thoughts grew into an unbearable cacophony. She'd wanted this, him, all of Alfie more than she could say. She was supposed to have the prince, but would he even want to have her? Did it matter anymore? And what about when her parents returned?

She leaned against the door, her breath coming in ragged gasps. Her eyes burned with unshed tears, and she felt a sob rising in her throat. It had been so good, his touch, his kiss. The memory of his lips on hers sent a fresh wave of heat through her, mingling with the cold fear that gripped her heart.

Alfie. The gorgeous apothecary. She licked her lips and could still taste him, could still smell the heady mixture of herbs and sweetness that seemed to permeate the air around him. Even now, as the steam from their shared moments began to settle, the aroma lingered, tantalizing and intoxicating.

Bea's shoulders shook with the force of her sobs as she sank to the side of the bed, clutching her clothes to her chest. She cried for the sheer wrongness of what had happened, for the breach of propriety she had committed. But more than that, she wept for the realization that had dawned upon her with startling clarity.

She had been so wrong before. Her daily visits to the apothecary had not been driven by a need for his concoctions or remedies. No, she had wanted to see him, to be near him, to bask in the warmth of his smile and the kindness in his eyes. She had wanted Alfie, the man behind the apothecary, and there was no other explanation for the longing that had taken root in her heart.

And she recognized the familiarity now… she'd ignored it far too long.

The tears flowed freely now, each one a testament to the confusion and desire that warred within her. Bea buried her face in her hands, feeling the weight of her emotions pressing down upon her. How could she have been so blind? How could she have let herself fall so deeply, so irrevocably, for a man who was beyond her reach again after all this time?

She'd recognized his eyes, the color was too unique with the specks of teal and the lines of deep and light hues of blue. He was Mater Varier's apprentice.

Bea clasped her stomach, nausea bubbling within her. She'd loved him all these years.

The muffled sound of Alfie's gentle and concerned voice reached her ears. "Bea? Are you all right?"

She choked back a sob, unable to find the words to respond. What could she possibly say to him now? How could she explain the torrent of feelings that had overwhelmed her, the fear and desire that intertwined so tightly within her? He'd been her friend, and she'd let him do… oh she had no words. She should be mortified and yet, even though she knew it was too scandalous, she wanted to do it again.

"Please, Bea," he called again, his tone softening. "Let me in. I just want to know you're well."

The tenderness in his voice only made her cry harder. She pressed her forehead against the bunched-up fabric of her clothes, wishing she could disappear, wishing she could turn back time and undo the moment that had changed everything. But the past could not be undone, and she was left to grapple with the consequences of her actions.

Slowly, hesitantly, she stood, walked to the door, and reached for the key and unlocked it. The handle turned, and Alfie stepped into the room, his expression a mixture of worry and relief. He crossed the threshold cautiously, as though afraid one wrong move might shatter the fragile connection between them.

"Bea," he said softly, his eyes locking onto hers. "I'm sorry if I frightened you. That was never my intention."

Her tears welled anew at his words, and she shook her head. "It wasn't you," she managed to whisper, her voice trembling. "It was me. I didn't know how to handle… this."

"I didn't handle it well either."

Bea looked at him, searching his eyes for some reassurance, some promise that everything would be all right. And in his gaze, she found it. The way he looked at her, with such tenderness and understanding, soothed the raw edges of her panic.

"I still have the Nagapushpa." She heard her voice say the words before her mind had made the decision to utter them. "It reminds me of the time when I wasn't so alone." But now that it was out, she had to wait. If it was him, and she knew in her heart, it must be, he'd have to react. Would he admit it and give her permission to love him this time?

Alfie reached out, his fingers brushing against her cheek in a gentle caress. "You're not alone any more if you don't want to be," he said.

Bea's heart stopped. He'd seen deeper into her, recognized her, and he knew her heart better than she did, just like her body. He had always known what she needed.

"It didn't work last time."

Alfie jerked his head back. "Last time I wasn't in the position to ask for your hand."

"You abided by the rules of Master Varier, didn't you? You were not supposed to speak with me."

Alfie furrowed his forehead and made wide eyes. "but now you know it was me."

"I didn't know at first," Bea said, blinking as she pulled his covers around herself. "But I'm right, aren't I? And why you gave me the rare flower?" A new-found intimacy of not merely passion, but a shared past, enveloped her more than Alfie's scent from his covers. He'd been in her heart all this time; the physical aspects were the bonus.

ALFIE'S HEART THRUMMED so strongly that he could feel it in his throat. "Why didn't you tell me sooner? Why didn't you come to find me?"

"Why didn't I? Why didn't you?"

"Because I'm below you, again. Still. I was your servant and then you came to ask me for a love potion for a prince! I'm not supposed to feel this way, it's not allowed."

She furrowed her brows and stood so absolutely beautiful in his covers that his chest could burst with the love for her. "I can't love a lady. Couldn't then and can't now."

"I see. All I am is my title and my station."

"No. That's not what I said."

"But it is more important than the truth? What is it that you expect me to say? I recognized you but it took me some time to put the pieces of my only true friend in life together?" She waved in the air and nearly dropped the covers that kept her decent. "I'm the poor aristocrat in the gilded cage and you're free to roam the world, why pick me? I'd anchor you to the scandal, the Ton, the hypocrisy of the noblesse. With me, you'd be chained to so many rules that they'd stop you from breathing."

Alfie shook his head. "I never said anything like that. I'd drag you down, Bea. I'm nothing. My parents died on a merchant ship, and I had to work to pay for university. The room I shared with Nick in Vienna is smaller than your closet. I couldn't even pay for the fare to come to England when my apprenticeship ended, and I had to work off the cost to leave India." Alfie combed both hands through his hair. "There's nothing I can offer you but my heart! You can't raise a family on love alone, I know that I can't overreach to hold you, but somehow, I can't stop myself."

She pressed her lips into a flat line and two large tears ran down her cheek.

He cocked his head. "It's not my privilege to pick you. I wish it were, Bea. I wish I could speak freely and tell you that I've loved you since the day I brought the girl in the veil honey, but it would be silly. It was an infatuation. Now that I truly know you, the person you've become, I know it's the kind of bone-shattering love that I will never recover from."

"Why should you need to recover?"

"Because I can't have you, Bea. I'm just an apothecary."

"And you were just an apprentice in India?"

"Yes." Alfie dropped his head.

"So what was this? Practice? A test?"

He shook his head. "Untraceable."

A long awkward pause followed. Alfie wanted to fall to his knees and propose to her, declare his everlasting love and devotion—but it wasn't his place. She was worth a prince, not merely an apothecary.

She heaved one more time, then wiped the tears from her face and straightened her back. "As I said, it never happened." Her voice cracked. "Leave me, I must dress and go."

Yes, Alfie thought. He'd given her the love potion to take the path she ought. At least she now knew what she was missing.

And so did he.

Chapter Twenty-Six

BEA LEFT BUT Alfie had the gnawing sense that he shouldn't have let her go.

She was on her way to the prince with the love potion and he'd mucked everything up.

The little that remained of the day passed and the scent of rose, walnut, and oat from Bea's bath hung in the air at 87 Harley Street like a raincloud over Alfie's head. He didn't know where she'd gone but he imagined her with the prince. Alfie's stomach hurt and he was nearly sick with a mix of rage and frustration that it couldn't be him. He didn't begrudge the prince anything, his motives were noble, and he was obviously a royal with a pure heart—but that didn't mean Alfie was willing to let Bea go. He couldn't because he loved her. She was a part of him, even if he could never be a part of her world.

After he'd walked Chromius a second time, Alfie had shut the apothecary and dragged himself upstairs to his bedchamber. What had he done?

He shouldn't have... oh, there was no name for what he had done to Bea—but he could lose his practice for touching a well-bred lady in this manner if anyone found out. The damage was done...even though he'd ensured it was undetectable.

What a stupid notion—undetectable. As if the passion they'd shared had not been ingrained in his soul. As if he could ever forget her moans when he'd touched her where nobody else ever had.

As if it could be undone.

Or at least she had an inkling that Alfie had so much more he wanted to show her.

He knew that women had such a thing as a sexual awakening.

And he was an idiot for serving the most beautiful and intelligent woman to a prince—as if a prince needed any help attracting a woman of that caliber.

Alfie balled his hands into fists until his palms hurt from the pressure of his fingertips. Sometimes, he loathed his job. He should have just told her there's no such thing as a love potion; none could be made, and she'd have to find other ways to attract his attention.

Her beauty initially, then her warm smile, sweet voice, and sharp mind.

Yes, that had been enough for something to dislodge deep within him. Now, he was no more than a clock with the most important gear missing—the one that made everything else turn, the one called Bea.

Then he heard a yelp and whining.

Chromius, Nick's dog, came into Alfie's room and hopped onto his lap.

His furry, warm body nestled into Alfie's arms, confiding that he needed love.

"I know how you feel, old boy," Alfie cooed to his fuzzy friend. Chromius wouldn't have known but Alfie was to bring him well-groomed and ready to be the ring bearer for Pippa's and Nick's wedding. "I'll bring you to Nick soon."

Of course, Chromius didn't respond but shifted, eager to jump back down. Alfie let him go, and Chromius led him downstairs.

He followed, and Chromius stopped in the kitchen, next to the back door where Nick usually hung the leash on a nail on the wall.

"You want to go out?"

Chromius wagged his tail and went in two circles around Alfie's legs.

"Alright, let's go," Alfie said, picking a hat from the shelf.

And so he walked behind Chromius, who was pulling the lead. Alfie had known him since Nick first brought Chromius to their shared student quarters.

It was a long time ago, but Alfie thought about the small room he'd shared with Nick at university in Vienna so fondly that his chest hurt. Everything would change soon.

Chromius tugged at the leash, and Alfie only paid attention to the carriages and traffic but not where they were going. He could barely follow his thoughts, much less decide where Chromius was taking him.

It was the same in life, Alfie thought. He'd been adrift.

Perfecting his craft hadn't been a direction for his life. Perhaps it had brought him to 87 Harley Street, but it had also become why Bea had found him and ordered a love potion from him.

Alfie tasted acid. He'd been so consumed with impressing her with his skill that he hadn't considered that he'd handed her the instrument to achieve her goal with a man that wasn't him.

While he'd be here, heart bleeding for her, rinsing beakers, corking flasks, and at a complete loss of what to do with the rest of his life; if Bea left with the prince, she'd take his heart and leave him a shell of what he had been before he met her... before he kissed her.

She was the girl sitting by the window, veiled and lonely. She'd never been allowed to speak to him, a mere servant at the Residence in Delhi, but she'd communicated with him. All these years, Alfie thought he'd made more of it in his mind than it had been, that he'd wished for his feelings to create memories of events that had never happened. But they had.

And Bea remembered.

They'd found the missing explanation of the puzzling attraction between them, a shared connection from the past. She was the forbidden fruit he'd kissed in the Orangery—the irony wasn't lost on him. And yet, the closer he wanted to be with her, the more absurd his idea was. A noblewoman didn't marry a commoner... except that Pippa and Nick were about to do just that.

Chromius had led Alfie to Green Park, across the cobblestones to the linden-lined path, where the bushes provided squirrels with ample hiding spots.

Of all the women he'd kissed and tupped, the only face he could conjure up was Bea's now.

He saw her everywhere.

Her lovely copper-colored tresses under the bonnets of the women walking with a parasol.

He heard her voice—or imagined it.

He smelled her perfume and sensed her closeness.

Even though he stood under the fragrant linden trees, he smelled Bea.

Alfie sucked his lips in, for he could even remember the lush softness and the eager pressure from her lips.

A kiss wasn't enough anymore, and he longed for more now. He longed for her.

Alfie chastised himself for being unable to think of anything but his self-pity for falling for the aristocratic cousin of Nick's bride. He hadn't meant to let it happen; he knew it was not wise.

Alfie closed his eyes and slumped against a tree.

He'd fallen in love.

Despite better judgment, he'd contracted the one condition he had no remedy for—lovesickness.

Then, Chromius tensed, his body straight like an arrow.

Alfie looked toward where Chromius was staring, and then he froze.

Bea was riding in a carriage along the path and next to the prince.

Alfie stepped around the tree trunk and into the shadows lest he be seen.

THIS WAS HER chance to forge her future. The love potion smelled lovely, and she hoped it would work because she couldn't wait to start a new life after Pippa's wedding—just not the way she'd initially planned. With only hours left in her old life, Bea never felt more ready for a change.

After Pippa's wedding, Bea would start a new chapter in her life. The new plan was in motion.

Bea blinked and then narrowed her eyes.

Alfie had crafted an intoxicating perfume that lingered on her skin. It was a unique blend that reminded her not just of his alchemical talents, but of his tender touch. Each moment spent with Alfie had imprinted itself upon her senses, and now, enveloped in this new fragrance, she felt a profound and novel energy within herself. She wasn't just wearing a different perfume; she was blossoming with a newfound sense of identity, one that resonated with confidence and clarity.

"That's why the gold mines are such a fruitful target. We have four in Alba County, *Zlatna*, *Abrud*, *Baia de Arieș*, and *Roșia Montană*."

"I know, they date back to the ancient Romans. But there's *Brad*, too. In the Hunedoara County." Bea remembered the pages in her atlas when she'd studied Transylvania. But it didn't appeal anymore.

"You know the names of the counties?" He asked but she couldn't follow the conversation. Her heart was in turmoil and instead of hoping the love potion would work, she now feared that it would work in the way she'd originally hoped rather than what she now wanted. It had been too late to cancel the carriage ride with Prince Stan, but Bea had put on the love potion for Alfie. She'd changed into a more elegant gown and decided to tell him what she wanted—him! Alfie!

As the carriage rocked gently along the path, Bea couldn't

ignore the growing dissonance within her. Sitting beside the man she had briefly envisioned as her future husband, she realized how wrong her plan now seemed especially when she couldn't deny her feelings for Alfie. The ambitions and dreams she had held onto so tightly suddenly felt like remnants of another life—one in which she hadn't yet discovered who she truly was or what she truly desired. Shifting slightly on the bench, she moved further away from him, creating a physical distance that mirrored the emotional rift opening up between them.

"Zlatna has many other precious metals, too. It's a flourishing city." Stan talked and talked, and Bea thought he might be homesick. She would be, too. Her desire to travel were naught now if they didn't include Alfie. All the longing to see the world had been something else entirely and she understood that now, she'd been on a search for him all this time.

Alfie occupied her thoughts, and the realization struck her with startling clarity. The man beside her, though perfectly amiable, could never ignite her soul the way Alfie did. It was Alfie's touch, Alfie's voice, Alfie's very presence that had awakened something deep within her—a passion and a purpose that she'd been stupid to attempt to deny. She wasn't the old Bea in Alfie's eyes, and wanted to grow into the adventure of the new woman she became when he held her in his arms. The plans she had made now felt like a constricting corset, one she was desperate to shed in favor of the freedom that came with being true to herself. As the carriage carried her onward, Bea knew that her heart had already chosen, and it was leading her straight to Alfie.

Bea tried to pay attention to what Stan had explained to her, and the county borders and the political impasse between the Austrians, Hungarians, and Prussians would be fascinating if she didn't have a sense of urgency to speak to Alfie again.

"So, I said, not all citizens have the same protections under the law, and it's not how justice was meant to be. Even the ancient Greeks recognized the need for equality among men and a balance of power between those who govern and those who are governed." Stan seemed to talk to himself as much as her—although he was so consumed in his lecture that she could have been anyone—even a tree.

Bea turned her head and held her bonnet to keep her eyes shaded. It was unseemly to roll her eyes at a prince, especially one who'd agree to stroll in the park with her when he was so busy with himself otherwise.

Alfie had never done that, she thought. He'd never talked on and on about things that only interested him without considering her an equal partner in the conversation. Even when he'd explained the workings of his connections, he'd stopped and asked for her opinion. He'd given her a vial to smell. She sighed and let her eyes glaze over with tears.

Holding her, pleasuring her... it had been the most wondrous experience and she had never felt more wanted and desired.

Bea shuddered at the thought that she'd lost control as she had, letting Alfie lift her naked out of the bath and... oh, what a wanton he must think of her for even accepting his offer of bathing in his quarters.

Bea squinted. She could have sworn she saw a man who looked just like him under the Linden trees.

No matter, for she mustn't allow the inner hunger for him to take over her mind.

No, Alfie had first taken over her mind, and now her body wanted to follow suit.

She tilted her head back and groaned.

"Oh, I'm sorry, Lady Beatrice. Have I overstepped?" Stan asked, his brows furrowed.

She blinked at him, but the sun hung low and was too bright, making Stan look like no more than a dark silhouette. The carriage turned around a curb, and Bea glanced again.

Then her stomach lurched.

It *was* Alfie.

With a shaggy brown dog. Chromius.

She'd recognize the dog anywhere.

And the man with those strong shoulders, narrow waist, and the way he combed his hands through his curly hair.

"Lady Beatrice?"

Bea turned to Stan and eyed him curiously. He was handsome in the classic sense, clean-shaven, with dark eyes, she suspected had seen more of the world than he'd care to admit.

But he wasn't Alfie.

He didn't have the same turquoise eyes that sparkled like emeralds around the obsidian circle of his pupils when he looked at her.

Why did Stan look at her so intently?

Bea jerked her head back and withdrew when Stan leaned in, closed his eyes, and—*oh no!*

Chapter Twenty-Seven

CHROMIUS TROTTED AHEAD, his leash taut between Alfie's fingers, when suddenly, through the break in the trees, Alfie saw a carriage approaching. His heart leaped into his throat as he recognized Bea inside, deep in conversation with Prince Stan. The prince's refined profile contrasted sharply with Bea's animated expression, her eyes focused and bright. Alfie's grip tightened on Chromius' leash, knuckles whitening, as a wave of jealousy and sorrow crashed over him.

Hours ago, he'd held her in his arms and now she was in this carriage pursuing her plan with the prince as if he was naught.

Alfie swallowed bile but the bitterness crept up his throat; he couldn't even speak to Chromius.

His stomach twisted into painful knots, and he felt a profound sense of loss as he watched Bea with the prince.

He should have been in that carriage with her, not standing amidst the linden trees, an outsider looking in on the life he desperately wanted to share with Bea.

And wasn't he the stupid man who'd handed her the rifle to shoot him by giving her a potion that would make her irresistible to the prince.

How could he face the prince later that day?

There he was, ready to help the prince fight the good fight, but his true calling felt missed, slipping through his fingers like sand.

Alfie tugged gently on Chromius' leash, signaling the dog to turn back. The weight of what he had just seen pressed heavily on his chest, yet he knew there was nothing he could do about it now. Bea's place was in that carriage with Prince Stan, but Alfie couldn't allow himself to become paralyzed by his heartbreak. He had a duty to fulfill, one that transcended his personal desires. Felix's future depended on uncovering Baron von List's secrets, and Alfie couldn't let his friend's fate hang in uncertainty.

As he walked, the warm air brushed against his face, providing a fleeting comfort amid the turmoil within him. He squared his shoulders, steeling himself for the task ahead. It didn't feel good, but it was the right course of action. Perhaps in aiding Prince Stan, Alfie might find some semblance of redemption or clarity. The mission was fraught with danger and intrigue, but it was one he had to see through. If there was any chance that the prince could help him—whether through influence, information, or sheer force—then Alfie was determined to seize it. His love for Bea prevented him from getting in her way but his loyalty to Felix compelled him forward, igniting a flicker of purpose within the darkness of his despair.

※※※

BEA HAD COATED herself with much more love potion than Alfie had advised.

She was burning for Alfie, but she had to find a way to leave England before her parents returned and found a husband for her who'd keep her tied to the Ton forever. And if anyone knew about her wanton misstep with Alfie, she'd be ruined.

And Bea was getting hot.

She was ruined.

But she wanted more.

She was too hot for her taste and eager to escape, for this

wasn't the same sizzling warmth that spread throughout her as when Alfie was close; it was the type of heat that made you cringe when you burned your tongue on too-hot tea.

The sort of burn that hurt for a whole other day.

The prince was going to kiss her. *No!* This would be akin to a proposal and everything she'd set out to accomplish but didn't want any more.

Bea put her hand on Stan's chest and tried to stop him, but he'd shut his eyes and laid his hand over hers on his chest.

Oh no, oh no!

All she could do now was to turn her head away and let him press a kiss on her cheek. At that exact moment, her eyes drifted to the linden trees, and she saw Alfie in the distance. He dropped his head and turned his back to her, his body slumped as if he'd been injured.

"I'm going to tell you, Lady Beatrice," Stan whispered. "I love it here in London and wish I never had to leave." Then he withdrew and looked grave as if he were expecting something. Not a kiss, that was for sure.

He hadn't tried to kiss her; he'd leaned in to whisper a secret.

Why hadn't the love potion worked? It was made to enhance her essence... didn't Stan like her?

Of all the men she'd met, neither Stan nor Alfie was like anyone else she'd been taught to know. Technically, neither were in the group of men she'd been trained to learn to understand. Stan wasn't British aristocracy and didn't seem to fit into the Ton.

And Alfie was—Bea sighed—a commoner, but couldn't be more uncommonly brilliant, handsome, and kind.

Her insides twitched.

"Why don't you like me?" She knocked on the side of the open carriage to signal the driver to halt. "Don't misunderstand, I don't wish to be rude. I'm only curious. I've done nothing but indicate that you could have me. Something many men would wish for themselves." Bea smiled ruefully. "Here I'm quite a catch and jumped straight into your net."

The carriage slowed, and Bea leaned forward. Looking over her shoulder, she saw Alfie's back. He was walking with Chromius in the other direction.

Stan pressed his lips into a knowing smile, and looked at Bea, then followed the trail of her gaze. "Like you, Lady Beatrice, I need to keep up appearances. But there's no chance to fool the heart, now is there?"

"You mean... there's someone else?" Bea stuttered. Again, she could have felt hurt, but the only part that stung was that he was right. She'd set her cap on him to keep up appearances while pretending she could fool her heart. But it had been in vain, and she wasn't fool enough to continue the ruse.

Stan nodded. He instantly looked different. If she didn't know any better, he looked like a young boy who'd been vexed.

Her heart lurched.

She'd seen that exact look on Alfie when she took the potion and left.

The carriage had come to a stop, and Bea rose to climb out when Stan blocked her way.

"Please don't tell anyone. *She* doesn't even know yet."

She blinked, for she was frozen with fear and couldn't even manage a nod. Then Stan pushed the door open, and Bea ran.

She ran as fast as she could, her dress catching between her legs. She had to tell Alfie what she wanted and how she felt.

Her lungs burned as she gasped for breath, tears spreading over her temples as the wind brushed them out of her eyes.

Where had Alfie gone?

She reached the row of linden trees, but they all looked alike once she'd gotten closer. There was no sign of Alfie or Chromius. She looked around and brought both hands to her head in desperation.

And the tears came, pouring down her cheeks as she ran from tree to tree.

She couldn't call him; he was not there. Too many people knew her in this area, and she didn't want to run screaming the apothecary's name. What else could the Ton accept him to be for her but a man offering his service?

Nobody could ever understand that she'd offered him her heart. She hadn't even told him.

Bea stood alone, her lungs constricted at the thought of Alfie turning his back on her.

The vibrant greens of the grass and trees seemed almost surreal under the high noon sun, ignorant of Bea's pain. What appeared to be a vivid backdrop to the leisurely promenades of ladies and gentlemen, their laughter and chatter weaving into the fabric of the day, was jarring to Bea. Didn't the world stop its activity when Alfie wasn't there for her?

It struck her, then, how seamlessly he had become a part of her world. In mere days, Alfie had transformed from a stranger to someone she sought out, not out of necessity but from a desire that fluttered softly within her chest. His laughter had become a melody she yearned to hear, his approval a balm to her uncertainties.

The carriage approached, and Stan waved at her. "Are you coming back in?"

Bea held her hand to her forehead to shade her eyes, but there was no sign of Alfie. She was too far from Cloverdale House to walk back.

"Yes." She hesitated at the carriage door and looked over her shoulder again to see if Alfie had reappeared. She couldn't see him, and the longing in her heart became painful. She hesitated to grasp the polished handle of the carriage door, though Stan offered his hand. A delicate shiver cascaded down her spine, betraying her outward calm, when she accepted his help back into the carriage, then sat back next to him.

"Is it Mr. Collins, then?" Stan asked.

Bea nodded, folding her hands on her lap. As the carriage passed through Green Park, the light dappling through the trees cast intricate patterns upon the path ahead, mirroring the complex weave of emotions threading through her heart. Bea realized she no longer pictured her days without Alfie's companionship, without the spontaneous conversations that filled her with warmth, without the silent understandings that said more than words ever could.

"You like him?" Stan asked in a low voice.

Bea blinked at Stan and narrowed her gaze. "Not quite," she tasted the words because she'd never uttered them. "Like is not right. I like you." She acknowledged the tender tendrils of affection taking root within her, a connection she couldn't—and no longer wished to—deny. Somehow, Alfie had, in bold and subtle ways, claimed a place in her heart.

"So you love him?" Stan didn't sound upset nor was he impatient as most men of the Ton were, especially when Bea hadn't agreed to allow them to court her yet. Well, she'd never allowed anyone.

"You could be a little more upset you know." It hit her as strongly as the revelation that she didn't wish for his affection even though he appeared like the perfect match for her. But what seemed perfect from the outside often felt different on the inside. And Bea's heart beat for the apothecary.

Stan inhaled slowly and twisted his upper body to her to speak with her directly. "Lady Beatrice, you are the perfect woman, as Violet said. She sang your praises, and I wholeheartedly agree with her."

Bea matched his polite smile. They agreed the external factors would have been ideal but neither of them wished for more than friendship.

"I'm not upset that you don't want me to be yours."

He shook his head. "My life is perilous right now, and I am not able to keep a woman safe."

"Safety is not what I was looking for."

"What were you looking for with me?"

"Everything. You seemed to have everything to offer that I could ever wish for in a man but then I discovered my feelings for someone I have known a while."

A slow smile built on his face, and sincerity was in his gaze, which she had only seen a few times. It wasn't desire, lust, or love—it was friendship. "You are very generous, Lady Beatrice. I hope to be worthy of your compliments."

"How did you know I was in love with someone else?" she asked.

"I had a suspicion when you climbed into the carriage today. Most women use this as an opportunity to fuel a courtship."

Bea jerked her head back.

"Yes, and then you looked at me exactly like that when I wanted to whisper in your ear. Horrified." Stan gave a wistful smile. "I would never take a kiss if it weren't given freely, Lady Beatrice."

She dropped her gaze to her gloved hands and plucked at the lace on the cuffs. "It's not right, you know. Nobody should take what isn't given freely."

"That's exactly why I am in London."

"Is it about your country? And what the Austrians are trying to take?"

"Yes." Stan's smile faded, and he stared into the distance.

"The Habsburgs must give you a constant reason to fear, right? Or are you from the area under the Ottoman Empire's rule?"

Stan's eyes shot to Bea.

She continued, "Last I heard, the Austrians were interested in the regions of Transylvania, Banat, Crișana, and Maramureș, areas rich in resources, including forests, agricultural lands, and minerals."

"You know our geography?"

"Only from the atlas I studied. But there's so much gold in the Carpathian Mountains, especially in regions like Transylvania, right?"

"Yes." Stan's eyes widened, and Bea thought they were rather shapely, dark, and intelligent. He was an intriguing man, and she was eager to be his friend. But it was Alfie she ached for.

Bea sighed. "I've had much time to perfect all the skills my mother deemed necessary for a lady of the Ton. I also read a lot of atlases and maps, and things about the gold mines in places like Roşia Montană. Have you ever been there?"

"Yes, it's under Hungarian rule now."

"They rarely do anything without the Austrians, I'm afraid."

"You know about the Prussians and the Czar's intention with Transylvania under the rule of the Holy Roman Empire?"

Bea nodded. She was sorry that the regions were in such conflict and that so many parts of Europe were controlled by people like Baron von List, a Prussian whom the Earl of Langley, Violet's husband, despised—for good reason.

The prince studied her speculatively. "Speaking of the Holy Roman Empire, tell me, Lady Beatrice. Would you, perchance, speak Latin?"

"I studied it, yes. Nobody truly speaks it, I suppose. They call it the Holy Roman Empire, but the language is Italian, even in Rome. I speak a little German and French."

Stan blinked. "Then forgive me if it's not what you initially set out to achieve, but I have a proposition for you."

Chapter Twenty-Eight

Eight o'clock in the evening at Brunswick House upon Thames.

ALFIE STOOD AT the entrance of the Langley's elegant house, feeling as though the grandeur of the place threatened to swallow him whole. The elaborate stonework, the towering columns, and the lush greenery whispered tales of wealth and privilege far beyond his grasp.

Violet, the Countess of Langley, greeted him with a smile as cunning as it was lovely. "Welcome, Mr. Collins," she purred, her voice like silk brushing over steel. "Do come in. The gentlemen withdrew to the drawing room after dinner."

Yes, the gentlemen might very well have been there, but Alfie wasn't one of them. He had only the title he'd worked for and none that had been passed down to him for generations. Coming here felt as if he were a child playing with tools that were too pointy and sharp. He was bound to get hurt.

Still, he needed to support Felix, and the jewelers; this was no time to focus on his status. Instead, he'd focus on his purpose here tonight, one initiated because of his craft and his skills. Alfie followed Violet and the butler down the same hall in which he'd spoken to Bea only days ago at the ball, though it felt as if a lifetime had gone by. Just as he remembered it, the Langley's entrance hall was a cavernous space dominated by an imposing marble sculpture of the Roman emperor Lucius Verus. Alfie felt as if the cold, stone eyes of the emperor were judging him, measuring his worth and finding him wanting.

"This way," the butler intoned when Violet entered ahead of Alfie. The man stood back, ushering Alfie through a double door to the parlor room. A blazing fire in the hearth seemed a mere decoration, offering no warmth to Alfie's chilled nerves. The room smelled of polished wood, expensive cigars, and the subtle tang of spirits.

At the card table, he saw Henry, the Earl of Langley, standing beside Baron Wolfgang von List. Both men held crystal tumblers filled with a dark amber liquid that caught the firelight in its facets. Their conversation halted as Alfie entered, their gazes shifting to him with curious intensity.

"Ah, Mr. Collins," the earl said, his tone dripping with false formality. Of course, he couldn't betray how close he was to Alfie since a mere apothecary was so far below his station. The trust of a patient must never be betrayed, and Alfie never would break that confidentiality. "We've been expecting you."

"Thank you for inviting me to play cards with you, my lord. As you know, I've wanted to learn the game for some time." Alfie nodded and exchanged polite greetings, carefully bowing low and long enough to the earl and the baron to show his status before the aristocracy.

"You've helped me so with my…needs, Mr. Collins. It would be poor form of me not to give you this opportunity in exchange for your services," the earl told him. It was all for the baron's benefit, of course. He couldn't question his host's choice of guests; decorum made that impossible. But giving a reason for Alfie to be there would hopefully put to rest any of the baron's doubts and suspicions. And of course, his opinions didn't matter to either the earl or the apothecary.

The butler reappeared at the double door and cleared his throat as if he'd been waiting for fanfare that never came. "Prince Ferdinand Constantin Maximilian Hohenzollern-Sigmaringen and

Lady Beatrice Wetherby, daughter of the Earl of Dunmore."

Alfie turned his face toward the door so fast his neck cracked and his heart plummeted. What was she doing here? And with *him*? Surprise widened his eyes, for he had not expected to see her tonight. It was a pleasure and yet, it was pain. His breath hitched, and a cold sweat prickled at the back of his neck. She stood close to Prince Stan, their heads bowed together in a conspiratorial whisper and her arm hooked into his. The warm glow of the chandelier cast a golden halo around them, making her look ethereal and further out of his reach. A pang of jealousy shot through him—had their intimacy meant nothing to her? Was he simply a stepping stone in her quest to win the prince's favor? And then, for a flicker of an instant, she made eye contact with him. It was meaningful and deliberate as if she tried to tell him something.

And then something worse bit into Alfie's already somber mood: Bea could be in danger this evening.

The room seemed to blur. The aristocrats' lively chatter and hollow greetings were a farce because he knew this was not a friendly social gathering. Clinking glasses faded into a distant hum. Alfie's mind raced, each thought more frantic than the last. He could still taste the lingering sweetness of Bea's kiss, feel the softness of her lips against his. But now, seeing her so close to the prince, a man of power and prestige, he felt the crushing inadequacy of his station. He was the one people consulted for his opinion and advice when he stood behind his counter, commanding the world of medicinal plants, serums, tinctures, and salves. Here, he preferred to—he was expected to—remain silent, a mere servant in the grand tapestry of their world.

He clenched his fists, the rough fabric of his coat scratching against his skin He couldn't put up a fight for the love of his life, not against someone like the prince.

Alfie blinked and tried to focus his vision, pushing the anger aside when Bea stood close to Stan when speaking to Violet. The scent of her perfume still hung in the air, mingling with the rich aroma of wine and the musky scent of the ballroom. Her familiar and yet distant laughter echoed in his ears, intertwining with the voices in the elegant drawing room. The air grew stuffy, constricting Alfie's chest as if his shirt were metal armor. Instead of fighting for his love, his role was reduced to a mere footnote.

"Shall we begin?" Prince Stan's voice cut through Alfie's thoughts, sharp and commanding. He turned to see the prince watching him with expectant eyes.

Alfie moved to the card table. Next to it was an elegant mahogany cart with a silver platter and a decanter, four crystal glasses, and a deck of cards. The instruments for their interrogation lay ready. The decanter with the truth serum glimmered ominously in the firelight.

After the men settled around the card table, a footman poured four glasses from the decanter. As the first dose was administered, Alfie watched the baron's reaction intently. But the man's cold, pointed stare remained unyielding, his pupils mere pinpricks of defiance. Stan dealt the cards, his hands steady despite the growing tension.

"Shall we play whist?" Prince Stan's tone was deceptively casual. "For those unfamiliar, the game is simple. Each hand comprises thirteen 'tricks', and whoever wins the most tricks wins the game," he said, obviously for Alfie's benefit but when Alfie nodded to signal his understanding, he stopped explaining the rules.

Baron von List gave a slow nod, his eyes glinting with something unreadable. "Of course," he said smoothly. "I'm well acquainted with the game."

As the cards were passed, Alfie couldn't help but glance at the baron, whose aloof demeanor never faltered.

From where Alfie sat, he could see Bea without lifting his gaze from the cards too much. She stood near the fireplace and watched the men intently, her eyes flickering with curiosity and suspicion. She adjusted her shawl, the warmth of the fire contrasting with the chill in the room. Violet, seated on a plush chair by the fireplace, served Bea and herself tea with genteel grace, her gaze occasionally lifting to observe the players.

The earl shuffled the remaining deck and put it aside. "Let's begin," he said, his voice deliberately light.

As the game commenced, Alfie watched for any sign of weakness in the baron. The first few rounds were uneventful, each player taking a polite turn. Alfie won a trick with a well-timed Queen of Hearts, while the Prince played an Ace of Spades, securing one for himself. The baron remained unperturbed, his strategies sharp and calculated.

Alfie had only lifted the glass with the truth serum to his mouth but not wet his lips with it. The earl had finished about half of his, and List the first glass. The prince had left his untouched, reaching for it occasionally but then appearing—cleverly, Alfie had to admit—to be distracted by the game.

Meanwhile, Violet had signaled the footman to top off List's glass from the same decanter. The second dose was underway.

"How do you like the digestive?" The earl asked, taking another minuscule sip but smacking his lips as if he'd gulped down a whole glass. "It was a gift from a friend who'd visited the Bavarian Alps."

"It burns," Stan said, seemingly intent not to meet Alfie's gaze.

"It's a fine concoction, indeed," List spoke as if he meant something else. The room grew silent for a second that stretched.

Alfie watched as Bea and Violet cast each other a look.

"I've never had anything with this level of bitterness. You know, Maximilian I Joseph has sent me a bottle of his *Almgebräu* every Christmas since he ascended to the throne."

Alfie knew he was speaking of the first King of Bavaria in 1806, when Bavaria was elevated to a kingdom during the Napoleonic Wars. "It has a different taste every year, depends on the herbs the monks use in the distilleries." He took another swig. "I like the burn better than the ones with too much honey. Sweet ones remind me of cough mixture my governess forced down my throat."

"Is this the same King Max whose daughter was promised to…" The earl began as he shuffled the cards to deal them again.

"*Och ja, ein herziges Mädel.*" Oh yes, a nice girl. List wriggled his fingers, demanding the cards. "I should deal this time."

"Who might that be?" Alfie asked, unwilling to betray that he'd understood German exactly since he'd studied and worked in Vienna for several years. Except that he felt out of his depth with the political intricacies that seemed to mean much to Prince Stan, Bea, and the Langleys. No matter. His job was to make sure the truth serum worked well enough for List to give away information that would help his friends. But it was also to ensure List didn't take too much. There was no way to know how much he could tolerate; even the best of Alfie's calculations based on his size were mere approximations.

"His daughter, Princess Sophie of Bavaria, is supposed to marry Archduke Franz Karl of Austria as soon as she's old enough," the earl explained.

"This marriage will link the Bavarian royal family with the Austrian Habsburg dynasty," Stan added, raising his brows appreciatively. At this, Alfie perked up. Weren't they rival families for Prince Stan?

List nodded. "Very important alliance."

Stan cast Alfie a short look, and Alfie signaled "no." List's pupils were still small, his face had the usual pallor, and his language remained clear. He was certainly a man who could hold his liquor, given that he'd already had the second glass of the strong alcohol laced with the truth serum.

The earl waved to the footman and List received his third glass.

"A coffee for me, please," Violet said, exaggeratedly loud in the background, as if she meant to tell her husband that it was enough truth serum for him.

"Me too," Bea nodded to Violet.

The women had obviously grown nervous about the amount

of Alfie's serum that had made the rounds.

During a lull in the game, Stan must have decided to up the ante. "Tell me, Baron," he said, examining his hand. "What brings you to our kingdom? Surely, it's not just for the pleasure of our company."

Baron von List's smirk was almost imperceptible. "Ah, various business dealings," he replied. "Trade routes, alliances... you know how it is."

The earl interjected, his tone now lacking the earlier friendliness. His pupils were enlarged, and his face flushed. "Interesting, considering we've heard rumors of more...*nefarious* activities." He tugged at his cravat, loosening it. Alfie could see the carotid artery pulsating on his neck.

List's hand hesitated above the table, a fleeting sign of uncertainty. "Rumors are the currency of the weak," he said coolly, playing a King of Diamonds.

"So, nothing to do with the smuggling operations near the Prussian borders?" Stan pressed, his eyes never leaving the baron's.

List let out a soft laugh. "That's quite the accusation. But I assure you, I have no involvement in such matters whether they are underway or not."

"Forests along borders are the most fertile grounds for smugglers," Alfie said, picking up his glass and swirling the dark liquid in it. The whiff of the potent mixture reminded him of the smells in his apothecary. It was an infusion of courage to press on. With each trick won or lost, the game revealed more about the characters involved. The baron's composure held, but tiny cracks began to show.

Alfie watched as Bea shot a glance toward Violet, a silent communication passing between them. Both women came to the table, Violet assuming a position behind her husband and Bea—to Alfie's chagrin—between the prince and him.

Matters were made worse when her scent—the one he'd created for her to capture her prince—wafted to his nostrils, making it hard to focus on the baron, even as the footman came and administered the fourth glass to List.

But then a vein popped up on the baron's forehead and it began to beat vehemently. It took all of Alfie's willpower not to leap up to check List's pulse. But then he noticed that there was a glimmer of evil in List's eyes that was more pronounced as he grew increasingly uninhibited. Finally the serum was working effectively to reveal what usually lay hidden.

Alfie wasn't proud of himself for supplying the serum and helping the earl and the prince administer it without List's consent in spite of Felix's and Andre's protests. What was worse was that he'd given Bea a similar potion to woo the prince. What should have been a skill set to create healing mixtures had become instruments of intrigue and manipulation.

Alfie couldn't help but loathe himself. Nothing should be worth betraying his integrity as a man of medicine and science, even though List's political games were endangering his Jewish friends.

Perhaps Alfie had helped the prince and the earl to take justice into their own hands, but that wouldn't have been necessary if the authorities had done it. In a way, they were stepping up for those who didn't have rights and protections under the law, because their Jewish friends, Felix included, had scarce legal standing in England. None in continental Europe, Alfie remembered from his classes at his university. And if people like List and King Max of Bavaria received more sway, they would skew injustice even further in their favor. It wasn't right.

Still, even if the ends justified the means, Alfie wished he'd never gotten himself into this tangle. He'd become an apothecary to help people with their health, not poison them and never to engage in political intrigue. Or, potentially, murder.

List brought the glass to his mouth and took another swig.

Alfie focused on the dosage—too little, and Baron von List could still weave lies; too much, and the man's heart might race out of control, leading to death.

Chapter Twenty-Nine

Bea's gaze met Violet's as she nodded subtly, her fingers tightening on the back of her husband's chair, when the footman placed the crystal stopper on the decanter. Only a small amount, perhaps a glass and a half, was left. Bea should have been astonished at List's composure; he certainly held his liquor. Was it time to push him to talk?

But as the game of whist continued, the serum barely seemed to take hold. While List's German accent became stronger, his breaths came faster and sweat beaded on his forehead, tracing a path down his temple, he wasn't giving the impression of losing control over his composure. It didn't appear he would say anything incriminating yet—nothing useful for Stan.

The room was filled with the low hum of haughty chatter and crystal glasses clinking. Although the setting was lavish—golden chandeliers casting a warm glow over the opulent décor, the scent of rich tobacco and expensive liquor mingling in the air, Bea had not yet had the chance to prove her worth as an associate for Stan's espionage. She took a deep breath, forcing herself to focus. This was more than a game; it was an opportunity to gather vital intelligence. For the first time in her life, Bea felt a purpose for all of her years of mingling among the Ton and a use for making small talk and meaningless, polite chatter.

Though now, List's words echoed in her mind, heavy with

the weight of their implications. The conflict along the borders was far more nuanced than simple territorial disputes. It was a complex web of personal vendettas, long-standing feuds, and a hunger for power that drove the Prussians and Austrians to such lengths. Understanding this required not only a keen awareness of the geopolitical climate but also an ear to the ground for the latest gossip that could change alliances overnight.

"What benefits the Bavarians in forming an alliance with the House of the Habsburgs?" she asked, feigning a prim smile and the naïvety of a debutante. It was a role she'd perfected.

"*Och, immer das selbe*, always the same. It's what Max said before, everything costs more and more."

Stan raised his chin, and Bea noticed that he'd missed his turn to play a card when he turned to Alfie and cast him a questioning look. "What do you think he's referring to?"

Alfie nodded at his cards. He didn't betray the undercurrent of communication between them.

But he also didn't make eye contact with Bea again, and that stung.

"Max has done so much for Bavaria already; it's flourishing these days. *Ein Schlaraffenland*! A land of milk and honey." He chuckled. "And beer!"

"Bavarian beer is rather different from our own," the earl said, apparently for good measure. Bea understood right away that he was gearing the conversation away from food and drink and toward national interests. They were on course to explore where exactly the collision of interests would occur.

And hopefully, List wouldn't remember any of this on the morrow.

"*Nicht hier!*" *Not here!* List cursed and hit the table with his fist and lay his cards flat on their faces. He was losing his poise.

Bea held her breath at the outburst—did he mean the cards or international relations?

"The beer in England doesn't deserve the name." He shook his head, beads of sweat making their way down his hairline to his eyes, the only part of him that had remained pale. "You know how much an acre of hop costs these days? And the workers harvest so slowly on the hills."

Stan narrowed his eyes. "Where does the money come from for the new crops?"

"Och," List turned the corners of his mouth down. "Here and there."

"I heard about the issue with the Carpathian Mountains," Bea said to Violet with a nod that meant *play along*. On their perch behind the men they were in view of the baron and yet, as women, they could speak any amount of nonsense without incurring any suspicion of their intent. This was a great time to take advantage of List's prejudice against women, it was good to go underestimated. She knew he didn't have a magnanimous view of her gender; he hadn't even greeted her when she'd entered the drawing room.

"You don't say!" Violet let go of her husband's backrest and put a hand on her mouth. "You heard about it at the masquerade ball?"

Bea nodded gravely. It was all a ruse, but List didn't know that. None of the men did. But when Bea and Violet had been at finishing school together, they'd used the term "masquerade ball" as a code for the-event-that-I'm-making-up-right-now. It was a way to pretend and glean information from someone, though never in a situation with as much importance as this.

She noticed that neither Henry, nor Stan, or even Alfie paid her any heed. Instead, they too eyed List intently. Her heart warmed because it meant that they trusted her and knew she was setting a trap.

"Well, I didn't think much of it at first." Violet inclined her head and put a hand on Bea's elbow. "But you know what they say, where there's smoke…"

"What have you heard?" List asked, his open vowels strongly enunciated.

"Oh, I'm not one to spread rumors, my lord." Bea shook her

head and flattened her lips into a line. She fluttered her eyelashes prettily for good measure, like any vapid debutante might; at least, in what she imagined the baron thought.

"As you shouldn't, Lady Beatrice," Stan said kindly. "It's never good to fuel a scandal."

Violet harrumphed. "I dare say, this one would be explosive and there's not much we can do. It's a matter of time really until she shows…"

"Shows what? Who?" List put both hands on the table. They were bluish-purple and his nails looked unhealthily white.

Bea cast Alfie a look. She could tell from his expression and his focus on the baron's fat fingers that he had noticed it, too.

"I don't know the man but from what I was told, he's rather dashing," Violet said, raising her eyebrows at Bea.

"Yes, and the family owes him so much." Bea watched List as she tried to come up with a rumor that could just be plausible enough and provoke List the right amount. "He's been a royal surveyor for years now. Ignatius… no… Ivan…" She cast a look at Stan. *Help me.*

"Ionel Petrescu?" Stan asked credibly confused.

"Yes!" Bea lifted her hand. "Exactly, Your Highness."

List had followed their exchange intently.

"Your move, baron," Alfie said, his voice pulling her—and List—back to the present. It was the first time this evening his eyes had met hers. He smiled, but the look in his gaze was serious as if urging her to stay focused. She nodded, her mind racing as she considered her next step but in the delicate dance of espionage and alliance.

"*Moment mal.*" *Just a moment.* List leaned back and crossed his arms. "What do you know about the royal surveyor?"

Bea shrugged as if there were so much to say. In reality, she had to think something up quickly. But there was too much she didn't know, even though they'd finally found a topic that irritated List enough to lose his temper. Perhaps he'd lose control over his words, too.

"She's a woman and doesn't know the half of it," Stan said as if he were the only one leveling with List. But Bea realized that she'd opened a door for him, and he was taking control. "You'd have to be there to understand just how important his reports have been."

"So you know?" List asked, raising his chin and eyeing Stan.

"I beg your pardon? Are you trying to insult my intelligence or my rank?" Stan was buying time and eliciting information. Bea had to give him credit. She was no expert, but even she could tell that he was good at his spy craft.

Her eyes flickered to Alfie, seated across the table. He was effortlessly professional, his casual posture masking his sharp intellect. His eyes—for those who knew how to read him—showed that he was watching List closely, counting how much he drank, and how he reacted.

Bea's heart ached with a longing she couldn't afford to show. Alfie was astoundingly talented, a master at reading people and situations, but she had to hide her admiration—especially from Violet. Violet's eyes were ever watchful, and Bea was supposed to be with Stan. The thought of Stan brought a wave of guilt, but she quickly pushed it aside. There would be time for remorse and explanations, hopefully later, but for now, she needed to prove her worth if her plan to achieve her freedom was to succeed.

"I'm certain my guest is doing neither. Are you?" Henry asked List and put a friendly hand on his shoulder. but then List hit it away and rose. His face was red, and the paleness of his eyes made them look like ice cubes about to succumb to the heat of his rage.

"We take the virtues of our daughters very seriously. She wouldn't risk the alliance for a mere surveyor! The rumors cannot be true!" List raised his voice. It was working; gossip about Princess Sophie's virtue provoked him.

"Much has been said behind Princess Sophie's back." Bea kindled the flames of List's fury.

"Time will tell. It always does," Violet added in the same tone she used among women. She was a master at eliciting gossip. "And even if it's true, the Archduke will have his pick—"

"No, he will not! He must not!" List stomped on the floor.

"Why do you care so much about the connection between the surveyor and Max's daughter?" Stan asked.

"Because! It must not happen!" For it was a connection at the heart of List's evil power and Alfie needed to have one thing he could stand up against, the baron threatening his friends.

Chapter Thirty

List stood and surveyed the room. "Where's the *diener*?" He'd mixed English and German, calling the servant a "diener."

"You haven't finished the round," Alfie said, playing another card. He needed to see if List could still follow the rules of whist.

A footman came to the card table and picked up the decanter.

"Another!" List commanded.

The footman reached for the decanter and lifted the stopper out with a *"pop."*

Five *doses? No, no, no.*

There was nothing else to be done. He needed to keep the baron from receiving another dose. Alfie downed his glass in one large gulp. "I haven't had my second yet!" He held his empty glass out to the footman.

The servant froze, and his gaze darted to the earl who, as the host, decided who should get the last precious pour of the drugged digestive.

Violet's hand came to the earl's shoulder, gripping it tightly. "Isn't there enough to split the last bit?"

"No!" Stan rose and buttoned his coat. "I've had enough, and I think the baron should get it all." Then he turned to Alfie. "I'm sorry, but he's a visitor from abroad and ought to enjoy the remainder of his time in London."

"No." Alfie took the decanter from the footman. List's hands were purple, which meant that his blood was not pumping enough blood through his body. He was sweating profusely already; his pupils were large, but he didn't blink. Any more and he could—and probably would—die.

"How dare you?" List thundered, trying to rip the bottle from Alfie. But Alfie was swift and withdrew it from his grasp. "I want that!"

Oh no. List had begun to slur audibly and bowed over the card table, propping himself up on his arms like a tiger gasping for his last breath.

"I'm sure he doesn't mean to overstep." Bea came to Alfie's side and tried to take the decanter from him. "Here, let me pour."

But Alfie shook his head when Bea's eyes caught his.

"Do it," the prince insisted, his eyes hard and unyielding.

Alfie hesitated, his hand trembling as he clasped the decanter. "No!" He was a healer, not a murderer. The weight of his Hippocratic Oath pressed heavily on his conscience. Finally, he made his decision. With a swift motion, he lifted the bottle to his own lips and drank the remaining serum.

The room fell silent, the only sound the crackling of the fire. Alfie's pulse quickened, not from the serum, but from the realization that his career—the one thing he had always clung to—now felt like a consolation prize. Bea was unattainable, and the truth of her feelings eluded him. Surrounded by the luxury at the Langleys and next to Prince Stan, Alfie felt meager. Yet, he wasn't going to let his shattering heart stand in the way of his career—nor could he let his mixture be the cause for a man's death—regardless of how much he knew List deserved to suffer.

The delicate intricacies of the political landscape were daunting, but Alfie had been privy to plenty of his aristocratic patients' secrets not to underestimate the power of gossip among the Ton. Yet, Bea and Violet were surely better-versed at making the connections.

"I don't know what any of this has done for you, but I'm

finished," Alfie said as he jumped up and made for the door. The others followed close behind, leaving the baron slumped over the table. When he got out of the baron's earshot—not that the man was capable of listening and comprehending at this point—he said, "Don't come back to me for any other sort of hocus pocus. I'm a man of science and none of this is part of what I usually do." He saw the butler approaching but couldn't get out of there quickly enough.

"When you get to your practice, let Felix know that he can expect new shipments of gold," Bea said quietly. "I know where the friction point is and can resolve it."

Alfie froze and turned to her slowly. All eyes were on her.

"What do you mean?" Violet asked.

"He gave away too much." Bea smiled. "Didn't you catch what he said?"

As if on cue, everyone narrowed their gazes, but Stan was the only one who gave a slight shake of his head. "What exactly?"

"Isn't it obvious? Austria under the Habsburgs and Prussia under the Hohenzollerns vied for Central European dominance for so long and now that Napoleon's threats are gone, they are engaged in every sort of power struggle."

Silence followed, and Alfie tilted his head back. During his time in Vienna, he'd heard all the names of the royal line that was the Habsburg-Lorraine dynasty. The head of the family and the ruler at that time was Emperor Francis II. After the dissolution of the Holy Roman Empire, he became Francis I, the first Emperor of Austria, reigning since 1804.

"The Vienna Congress?" Stan asked.

Bea nodded slowly. "My father was there. It shifted everything."

"I don't understand," Alfie muttered. Even though he'd still rather be leaving but he might as well hear Bea out. Especially since perhaps this would be one of the last times he'd see her at all.

"Well, King Max of Bavaria allied with Napoleon Bonaparte,

which led to its elevation to kingdom status in 1806 in the first place. This alliance was primarily driven by the Bavarians' desire to reduce Habsburg influence in their region and gain territorial expansion." Bea spoke as if this were as plain as day.

"Oh dear!" The earl sank onto the armchair. "The Wittelsbach Dynasty."

"But if this were the friction point, then List should be on the side of the Prussians, shouldn't he? The Austrians and the Prussians are rivals over the territory." Stan rubbed his chin and started to pace the room.

"King Max is a Wittelsbach," the earl said. "And he promulgated the Bavarian Constitution last year and introduced a bicameral parliament," Bea said.

Alfie was still not following. "Like the House of Lords and the House of Commons here?"

"No, because there's a key difference." Bea lifted her right index finger as she explained, looking more like one of his professors than Alfie ever imagined possible. "The Bavarian system limits voting rights to wealthier citizens with inherited titles."

"Aha!" Violet sank onto the settee and reached for her husband's hand. Alfie noticed through the corner of his eyes that the earl placed a gentle hand on Violet's stomach as if to check for a heartbeat.

Good for them.

"So List plays both sides?" Alfie asked.

Stan pivoted and came to Alfie's side. "He only wants to serve his own purpose."

"But you still cannot prove it, Stan," Bea intercepted.

"Prove what?" Alfie asked.

"That List is exploiting the gold mines in Transylvania, and then he is blaming the shortage of gold on the Prussians when he speaks with the Austrians."

"And when it's the other way around, he blames the Austrians, so the Prussians are upset," Stan added.

"*Streiten sich zwei, freut sich der Dritte*," Alfie said. "It's an old German proverb. This means that when two parties are in conflict, a third party may benefit from their dispute."

"He's exploiting my country! My land!" Stan combed both hands through his dark hair. "And he's getting away with it!"

"Well, then, I should present this information to the prince regent and—" the earl rose and seemed eager to end the evening, assuming a thank-you-for-coming-but-go-now-pose.

"If you do that, you hurt my friends," Alfie said as a wave of queasiness twisted his insides. How much of the concoction did he drink? Two and a half glasses?

"Why?" Violet asked, joining her husband.

His normally steady hands trembled, fingertips brushing against his clammy forehead as he leaned against the wall for support.

"Because if you are all correct, then the Jewish Crown Jewelers are List's scapegoats. They have a trade route and can supply everything except for gold. Diamonds, rubies, emeralds, sapphires... but no gold. They don't have access to the mines because they can only trade freely in the Pale of Settlement," Alfie said.

"Which ends much farther north," Stan confirmed. This was even worse: List's plans were to isolate the gold mines and keep them permanently out of reach for Felix, the Klonimuses, and the Pearlers—every bit of List's effort was driven by the hatred of the Jewish Crown Jewelers and any other Jews who needed gold. Since they supplied Felix's gold foil for the practice, cutting off their trade access meant the practice couldn't remain financially viable. Most of all, it was unfair that a single man could cause such damage to the livelihoods of hard-working, talented people. Especially those like the Crown Jewelers because they were the best and not because they were Jewish. The unfairness of it all brought his blood to boil. He wanted to help Felix and the others, and at least the truth serum had brought clarity to List's motives.

>>>><<<<

BEA WATCHED ALFIE from across the room, her concern growing with every passing second. His face was flushed, with a fine sheen of sweat glistening on his forehead under the soft glow of the chandelier. He tugged at his collar, his movements agitated and restless. It was clear to her that he was in distress, though he valiantly tried to mask it. The truth serum was taking its toll, gnawing away at his composure, and she could see the strain etched into his features.

Henry, ever vigilant, stepped forward and placed a firm hand on Alfie's shoulder. "You can't go home in a hired hack in this condition," he said, his voice laced with authority and concern. "I'll send you home in my carriage."

Bea felt a surge of determination. She needed to speak with Alfie, to understand what was troubling him so deeply and to offer whatever comfort she could. Crossing the room with purposeful strides, she approached the men. "I'll go with him," she announced, her gaze fixed on Alfie's fevered expression. "I need to get home as well."

Violet inhaled sharply and Bea knew her friend was no doubt worried that Bea's virtue could be compromised if she were traveling alone in a carriage with him, but she shot the countess a woman-to-woman glance and Violet shut her mouth with a snap.

Alfie glanced at her, his eyes flickering with an emotion she couldn't quite decipher. For a moment, it seemed as though he might protest, but then he simply nodded, his resistance melting away under the weight of his exhaustion. However, as they moved toward the door, Bea noticed his reluctance. His steps were hesitant, as if he was trying to maintain a distance between them even within the confines of the carriage.

Once inside, the carriage jolted forward, and Bea found herself seated beside Alfie in the dimly lit space. She turned to him. "Speak to me."

"No," he croaked and turned away, looking out the window.

This was new. It was awful, for he usually never took his focus from her. Gone were the hungry eyes from that morning.

"I saw you at the park with Chromius," Bea started.

"I saw you, too." He glanced at her, but Bea could see hurt in his gaze even though the carriage's cabin was dark. "Glad it worked." He turned away, watching the streetlights pass by as if they held a truth he couldn't find in her face.

"It didn't work. The potion, I mean."

His snorted. *Hmpf!* was the only response she got. "It will."

"I don't want it to work anymore. Not with him."

"Then don't use it."

He shifted as if he was uncomfortable, and his gaze fixed on the passing scenery outside.

"Alfie?"

He didn't respond but she noticed his body tensing. "It's nothing, Bea. Just... not tonight," he replied, his voice rough with an edge of desperation.

"Tell me what's the matter with you or is it such a terrible secret?"

"Everybody has their secrets." He gulped.

The pain in his voice pierced her heart. She reached out, placing a gentle hand on his arm, but he flinched away, his body unyielding. Bea withdrew, feeling a mixture of hurt and frustration. She longed to bridge the divide that had opened between them, but Alfie seemed determined to keep her at arm's length.

Chapter Thirty-One

The next day at Silvercrest Manor. The day of Pippa and Nick's wedding...

THE SUN HUNG high in the sky, casting a golden glow over the garden of their grandfather's ancestral estate, where Pippa's and Nick's wedding was taking place. Bea had donned her best gown, but she'd never felt worse. Alfie hadn't spoken to her on the ride home from the Langleys even though she'd showed him that she'd risk everything to be with him just for being in the carriage with him. She felt his rejection like a saber in her chest.

The medieval castle stood majestically, its ancient turrets seemingly smiling down on the joyous occasion unfolding in the garden below. Pippa's and Nick's wedding was a vision of romance and timeless beauty. The grounds were exquisite, under a brilliant canopy of white silk festooned with garlands of fragrant roses and delicate ivy. The canopy fluttered gently in the soft breeze, its elegant drapes framing the scene with a sense of aristocratic grace.

A pristine white carpet had been laid out, stretching from the castle's grand chapel to the heart of the garden, where the couple would exchange their vows. Each step along this aisle was adorned with petals from freshly picked blossoms, their colors a vibrant contrast against the pure white path. The perspective of the entire setup was carefully aligned to look onto the orchard beyond, its rows of fruit-laden trees offering a picturesque backdrop of natural splendor.

Guests, seated in neat rows on either side of the carpet, looked on with anticipation as Pippa appeared at the entrance, her arm hooked into Alfie's, her gown shimmering like a cascade of moonlit water. She moved forward, each step measured and graceful, the soft rustle of her dress mingling with the gentle murmur of the gathered witnesses. Bea's breath hitched as Alfie led Pippa down the aisle. She wasn't jealous of Pippa for there was no better man to escort her beloved cousin. But Bea realized that she wanted to be a bride. She was ready to be a bride. Alfie's bride.

And yet, he avoided her gaze, blinking profusely.

Nick waited under the canopy, his eyes locked onto Pippa with an intensity that spoke volumes of his love and devotion.

When Pippa had arrived at the altar and handed Bea her bouquet, Bea stood beside Pippa, her heart heavy with unspoken emotions as she witnessed her cousin's moment of bliss. The sun bathed the entire scene in a golden glow, casting dappled shadows through the trees and adding a touch of magic to the air. The scent of roses mingled with the faint aroma of ripening fruit from the orchard, creating an atmosphere of serene enchantment. It was a perfect wedding.

And one of the worst moments in Bea's life.

The orchids in Pippa's bouquet were lovely, and a smattering of fuchsia orchids had been braided into her blond hair. Bea felt the soft rustle of her dress as she stood beside Pippa, the fabric whispering against her skin with every slight movement. She tried to focus on the beauty of the moment—the delicate lace of Pippa's gown, the way Nick looked at his bride with absolute adoration, and the melodic strains of the string quartet playing nearby.

Bea's heart ached with each passing second. She could feel Alfie's presence next to her, a silent, impenetrable wall. His refusal to speak to her since last night gnawed at her, turning every breath into a quiet struggle. The sight of Pippa and Nick exchanging vows, their faces radiant with love, only made the pain sharper.

"I, Nicholas Folsham, take thee, Philippa Mae Pemberton, to be my wedded wife, to have and to hold from this day forward, for better, for worse, for richer, for poorer, in sickness and in health, to love and to cherish, till death us do part." Nick spoke clearly and with reverence, as if Pippa were the only person there.

They were standing before an altar, much like Bea and Alfie were now, but the emotions in her heart were a convoluted mess of joy for her friends and a deep, searing sorrow for herself.

Bea's breath hitched as Pippa began to speak her vows, her voice trembling with emotion. The words hung in the air like a delicate thread spun from the deepest parts of her heart. "I, Pippa, take thee, Nick, to be my wedded husband, to have and to hold from this day forward, for better, for worse, for richer, for poorer, in sickness and in health, to love and to cherish, and to obey, till death us do part."

Pippa's voice cracked on the word "obey," her eyes glistening with unshed tears. Bea felt the floodgates within her own heart burst open, hot tears spilling down her cheeks as she watched her cousin's raw display of love and vulnerability. The beauty of the moment was almost too much to bear, magnifying the ache in her own heart.

She glanced around, seeking solace in the familiar faces of friends and loved ones. Wendy stood nearby, dabbing at her eyes with a delicate lace handkerchief, her face soft with empathy and shared joy for her brother's bliss. On either side of Wendy stood Felix and Andre, their expressions solemn yet touched by the moment's significance. Felix's arm was comforting Wendy as she hooked hers into his, while Andre held his hands clasped in front of him, a small smile playing at the corners of his mouth.

Only Alfie stood apart, a solitary figure, his posture rigid and unyielding just like in the carriage the previous night. He faced

Bea, his eyes locked onto hers with an intensity that both shattered her and held her together. The distance between them felt insurmountable, a space filled with all the words left unsaid. The sight of him standing there, alone and silent, amplified the pain in her chest until it was nearly unbearable.

Alfie's presence was a silent echo of the turmoil within Bea. As the ceremony began and the vows were spoken, the world seemed to hold its breath, captivated by the profound declarations of love and commitment. Bea struggled to maintain her composure, the beauty of the moment only heightening her inner turmoil. She glanced toward the guests and suddenly had to blink. *Oh no!* She looked again. *It couldn't be.* But it was true, she saw her parents amid the sea of faces.

When they arrived home, the servants must have told them about Pippa's wedding, and they'd rushed—just in time, she was sure they told one another—to see it. To see her. Their sudden appearance after three long years felt like a fresh wound, reminding her of how far she still had to go to find her own happiness.

The gasps, then thunderous applause, that followed the couple's kiss was a chorus of joy that resonated through the garden and beyond. When Pippa and Nick kissed, Bea caught Alfie's eyes, and what she saw there was pain.

Her parents looming in the rows of guests meant her time was up. The world around her continued to celebrate, but inside, her heart ached with unresolved longing and new uncertainties brought by their unexpected arrival.

Bea allowed herself to fully feel the weight of the moment, each tear that fell a testament to the torrent of emotions coursing through her. She wanted to reach out, to bridge the gap between her and Alfie, but something held her back—perhaps it was pride, perhaps fear. Instead, she stood there, amidst the sea of joy and celebration, feeling as though her world was crumbling. They'd caught her at a wedding ceremony that wasn't her own and she was nowhere near the goal they'd set for her.

After Pippa and Nick sealed their vows with a kiss, the garden erupted in applause once more. Bea clapped along, but her heart wasn't in it. She could see the happiness on everyone's faces, yet her own sorrow painted everything in the gray shades of despair. When she met her mother's gaze at the edge of the crowd, her heart sank even further. Her parents had arrived just when she felt most vulnerable and farthest from achieving her dreams.

The juxtaposition of the joyous wedding and her internal turmoil was almost too much to bear. Bea tried to steady herself, to focus on the happiness of the occasion, but the presence of her parents and the unresolved tension with Alfie weighed heavily on her soul. She stood there, feeling both part of and apart from the celebration, as the world around her continued to move forward, leaving her to navigate the labyrinth of her own emotions.

She turned her eyes to the sea of wedding guests, seeking distraction, and then she saw them—a sudden bustle at the edge of the crowd. Her parents were coming toward her. Bea's breath caught in her throat. She hadn't seen them in three years, and there they were, looking exactly as she remembered though perhaps a bit older. Her mother's hair was still neatly pinned as always, and her father's stern yet loving gaze scanned the gathering as if he was in charge. They were here, at Pippa's and Nick's wedding, but all Bea could think about was how far she felt from finding her own happiness and how much she'd surely disappoint her parents.

A wave of panic surged through her. She wasn't ready for this reunion, not now, when she felt so broken and vulnerable. She tried to steady herself, to push back the tears that threatened to spill over. The joyful celebration around her felt like a cruel contrast to the turmoil inside her heart.

She ran.

Chapter Thirty-Two

ALFIE STOOD RIGID, his eyes fixed on Bea as she watched Pippa and Nick accept a flurry of well wishes as the crowd came to congratulate them. He could see how her shoulders trembled slightly and how her hands clutched each other as if she were holding herself together by sheer willpower. The sun cast a golden halo around her, illuminating the tears that glistened on her cheeks like diamonds. His heart twisted painfully in his chest. He wanted nothing more than to reach out, to offer some solace, but something held him back—a barrier constructed of society's rules and ranks imposed upon people.

He knew it meant nothing because all people were ultimately made of flesh and blood and yet he didn't want to ruin her chances for success in Society by making a claim. If there was anything Alfie respected, it was the future and her independence.

Among the guests and his closest friends, he couldn't act on his desire. He was painfully aware that he was too far below her station. The world wouldn't let him have her, he was just an apothecary and didn't deserve Lady Beatrice Wetherby no matter how much he loved her. He just wasn't enough gentleman for a lady of her station.

As Pippa accepted a handkerchief from Nick, Alfie saw Bea's composure shatter. She began to cry, quietly at first, but then more openly, unable to hold back the tears. He noticed Wendy discreetly wiping away her own tears while Felix and Andre stood protectively at her sides. Yet it was Bea's raw, unfiltered pain that gripped him. Her tears weren't just for the beauty of the vows; they were an outpouring of deeper pain that only he, apparently, recognized.

Alfie felt a pang of guilt, knowing he was partly responsible for her distress. Unsure what he had said in the carriage and astonished at how much the truth serum had affected him, Alfie feared he'd said something terrible. All day, he had avoided her since during the night before, his own insecurities and fears created a distance between them. Now, standing here amid the celebration of love and commitment, that distance felt insurmountable. He wrestled with the urge to go to her, to bridge that gap, but his feet remained rooted to the spot, his body betraying his heart's deepest desires.

And then, suddenly, Bea moved. It wasn't a gradual retreat but a sudden, desperate flight. She turned and ran, her dress billowing out behind her like a white sail caught in a fierce wind. Alfie's breath caught in his throat as he watched her flee, the sight of her retreating figure searing itself into his memory. Each step she took away from the ceremony felt like a cleft between them.

For a moment, everything seemed to freeze. The joyous bustle from the guests, the gentle rustling of leaves in the orchard, even the light seemed to dim around him. All he could focus on was Bea, disappearing into the distance, her pain now echoing his own. Alfie knew he had to do something, but he was paralyzed, trapped in his own hesitation and regret.

Finally, spurred into action by the realization that he could not let her go like this, he started to move. The world around him slowly came back into focus, and then all that mattered was reaching Bea, finding a way to mend whatever had broken between them. As he began to follow her, he was determined. He would not let this moment slip away; he would not lose her without a fight.

The applause and cheers from the wedding ceremony faded

into a distant hum as he sprinted across the garden, his eyes locked on the path she had taken. The orchard loomed ahead, its rows of fruit-laden trees casting dappled shadows on the ground. He pushed past branches and leaves, his breath coming in sharp bursts as he navigated the twists and turns of the orchard.

The scent of ripe apples filled the air, mingling with the earthy aroma of the soil beneath his feet. Alfie's heart pounded in his chest, each beat echoing the urgency he felt. He caught glimpses of Bea's dress through the gaps in the trees, a flash of white amidst the greenery, guiding him forward like a beacon.

"Bea!" he called out, his voice strained but resolute. There was no response, only the rustle of leaves and the distant chirping of birds. He quickened his pace, his thoughts a whirlwind of regret and again, of determination. He couldn't let her slip away, not like this, not when so much was left unsaid.

He rounded a corner in the orchard and finally saw her ahead, her pace slowing as she neared the edge of the trees. She glanced back, their eyes meeting for a brief, heart-wrenching moment before she turned and continued running. Alfie felt a surge of desperation, his legs burning with the effort to close the distance between them.

Bea reached the side of the main house, her movements now more frantic as she fumbled with the door handle. Alfie was close behind, his hand reaching out as if he could catch her by sheer will alone. She slipped inside just as he reached the threshold, the door swinging shut behind her with a soft thud.

Undeterred, Alfie pushed the door open and stepped into the dimly lit hallway. The cool, air of the old house enveloped him, a stark contrast to the bright, sunlit garden outside. He could hear Bea's footsteps echoing through the corridor, leading him deeper into the labyrinth of rooms and passageways.

"Bea, please!" he called again, his voice softer now, tinged with a pleading note. He followed the sound of her footsteps, his own steps measured but urgent. The walls around him seemed to close in, the antique portraits and ornate wallpaper blurring as he focused solely on finding her.

"Oh, *now* you will speak to me?" Her voice wobbled and he looked up the staircase, seeing her more than twenty steps above.

He took two steps at a time and caught up with her just when she slipped into a bed chamber. Bea stood in the center of the room, her back to him, her shoulders rising and falling with each ragged breath. Alfie took a hesitant step forward, his heart breaking at the sight of her so vulnerable and distraught.

"Bea," he said softly, his voice barely above a whisper. She stiffened but didn't turn around, her silence speaking volumes.

"Get out of my room!"

Alfie saw a bed, an open trunk with fabrics. The journal on her vanity table. This was a room in which she'd spent much time before. It was a home for her, her grandparents' estate. And he was an intruder.

"I'm so sorry," he continued, his words rushing out in a desperate attempt to bridge the cleft between them. "I've been a fool. I should have talked to you, should have told you—"

"Why now, Alfie?" Bea interrupted, her voice trembling with raw emotion. She finally turned to face him, her eyes red and glistening with tears. "Why are you here now, when it feels like everything is already falling apart?"

Alfie took another step forward, closing the distance between them. "Because I can't stand seeing you in pain. Because I care about you more than anything, and I can't see you like this."

Bea shook her head, her expression a mix of anger and sorrow. "You don't understand, Alfie. I've been trying so hard to hold everything together, and now... my parents are here. I failed at the one thing they asked me to succeed at, because of you!"

"Why me? I gave you the love serum. I stepped aside so you and Prince Stan can—"

Her eyes flashed at him, full of emotions he didn't dare identify. "I don't want you to step aside! Why would you even?"

Alfie jerked his head back. "Why? Because you're a lady and I'm not the prince you deserve."

"I'm an earl's daughter and I have danced with so many gentlemen, Alfie. I've been to Almack's and the finest balls in Town just like they wanted. Yet, I failed to accomplish what they wanted me to—marriage to a peer—and the worst is that I don't even care about the failure as much as I care about not getting what I want." She crossed her arms over herself and frowned in a way he might find adorable if she wasn't so upset. "I'm a spoiled doll," she declared.

He sobered himself. "You're not a doll, Bea. And you're not failing. You're standing up for what you believe is just, and you've been helping the prince to help my friends. That's strength of character. And you're quite the diplomatic genius!" Alfie said firmly, his voice steady despite the turmoil inside him. "What do you want that you can't have anyway? You can afford anything you want to make you happy."

"Except for you," she whispered.

Except for *you*, his heart echoed. *Bea. My Bea.*

Silence hung between them, heavy and charged with unspoken feelings. Alfie took another step, and then another, until he was standing right in front of her. He reached out, hesitating for a moment before gently taking her hand in his.

"I'm here, Bea," he whispered, his voice full of earnest sincerity. "I'm here, and I'm not going anywhere if you wish for me to stay. But you have to say it."

Bea stared at him, her eyes searching his for some sign of the truth. Truth without truth serum he supposed.

Slowly, almost imperceptibly, she began to relax, the tension in her shoulders easing as she allowed herself to believe him. Alfie squeezed her hand gently, offering her a small, hopeful smile. In that quiet, sun-dappled room, surrounded by the echoes of the past, they stood together, ready to face whatever came next.

"Why didn't you speak to me last night?"

"I did."

"No, you avoided me in the carriage." Bea looked down at her hand in his.

"I had some of the truth serum and didn't want to spill too much… Everybody has secrets."

Her gaze narrowed. "Am I one of them?"

He shook his head. "Not you. Only my feelings for you."

"And you didn't want to admit them? I feared you didn't—" she sucked in air, "I wanted to hear you say it."

"It wasn't my place. Just like it wasn't in India—"

"It is now."

And Alfie's resolve grew. Downstairs was the prince, her parents, and uncountable members of the Ton who'd welcome seeing Bea with the royal. She hoped nobody had seen her return to the building since they took a rarely-used side door. But here, she was with him.

Finally alone.

Chapter Thirty-Three

"You said that everybody has a secret?" She cocked her head and eyed Alfie from her head down.

He nodded.

"Even you?"

Now he shrugged.

"Tell me."

Alfie flattened his lips and gave a faint shake of his head.

Bea narrowed her eyes. "You don't trust me then?"

"I trust you to accomplish many impossible feats, Bea. You have the delicate touch of a great diplomat. It was plain to see at the Langleys when you made List talk. And you were the one who made sense of it."

"You made the truth serum for him," she said.

Alfie raised his brows and inclined his head. "But it was you who made it work."

"Except I didn't have the skill to discover *your* secret."

Now he gave a mischievous tilt of his head. "Ah, but if I hadn't known about the truth serum…You'd be excellent as a spy, I think."

"My mother would expire at the thought." Bea couldn't suppress a smile. "Perhaps I should enlist at the Foreign Office."

"Then you should test your skills to uncover truths." Alfie widened his stance and Bea realized that he was hiding something about his persona.

"Based on your defensive stance, it's not something around you that you're hiding. It's something *about* you."

He didn't move.

"You're not really Alfie Collins but the lost pirate son of Jean Lafitte and you're smuggling opium."

Alfie gave her a crooked smile. "If I had as much money as Jean Lafitte, I wouldn't mix ointments for the Ton in London."

"True. You're also not sunburned enough to have spent much time in the open sea."

"How do you know?"

Bea crossed her arms but then lifted one hand and patted her mouth with her index finger. "You are strong, not sunburned, and you always have enough supplies. I know!"

He narrowed his gaze.

"You're a smuggler at the docks! So you work at night, lifting heavy crates with pulleys and climbing from ship-to-ship."

He grinned. "As enticing as that sounds, I don't like to get my hands quite that dirty. And the docks smell like fish."

Bea stepped closer.

Then, as he stood his ground, even closer.

She knew his scent already and had spent hours in bed conjuring it up. He had tasted fresh and minty when she'd kissed him and his scent was earthen, real, and oh so masculine that she wished to strip his clothes off him and taste every inch of his body.

Then a thought grabbed her, and she couldn't wriggle out of it with any argument of propriety and being a lady.

What did his body look like?

One more step and she could smell him again. His freshness mixed with something that was just him. Bea hesitated for a moment, but he just stood there, his arms now hanging from his sides. So she grabbed his collar and tugged gently. He leaned in and she evaded his face, nuzzling his neck instead. He smelled so wonderfully like Alfie. "You smell smart."

"Smart?" He looked down at her with a combination of manly cockiness and boyish vulnerability. "Like books at a library?"

"Like reading one thick book in front of the fire on a snowy day."

"I'm not sure what this scent is," he whispered, still holding her gaze.

"Call it the scent of my intuition."

"Is that your female intuition?"

"Perhaps."

"And what would confirm your suspicion of how smart I am?"

"An examination."

"I assure you that I have passed all my exams with highest grades."

"Not a paper exam, a physical."

After a moment's blink, there was a glint in his eye of a man who'd been naked before many women. He looked like a warrior who'd used many a sword and always returned from battle victorious. At least, that's what Bea thought. He'd certainly seemed to know his way around the female anatomy after her oatmeal bath.

"What gives you the credentials to perform such an exam?" he asked, but he'd already tucked his index finger under the cravat and loosened the knot. It was a simple knot *à la sentimentale* and Bea pulled one end, watching it slowly unfurl, and then she pulled the white fabric out of his collar.

"My female intuition."

"Of course," Alfie nodded, letting his eyes fall to her cleavage. "You have a great supply of that."

Now he was speaking to her décolleté, and Bea should have been scandalized, but she felt heat rushing to her head instead.

Caught in a wave of brazen courage, she unbuttoned the top of his shirt.

She didn't dare look in his eyes now and focused on the buttons. After all she'd permitted after her bath, she tried to tuck away that pesky thought that she had effectively ruined her reputation already regardless of whether anyone else knew.

Then his hands came to her upper arms, and he gave her a gentle squeeze. "Bea?"

"*Hm-hm.*" She focused on button number four and then five, avoiding his gaze.

"If you want me to take my clothes off for you, all you have to do is ask," he rasped.

She swallowed and tried to remember to breathe but she couldn't concentrate anymore. His shirt was split in the middle and from underneath, masculine perfection emerged. The effect of seeing his skin, so much of it, sent her mind into a hazy space as if she'd stepped onto a cloud and was about to reach for the next.

"I mustn't."

"If you asked, I wouldn't say no, so why not try?"

If she was flushed before and heat rose to her head, she was now about to incinerate.

"I've lost my only virtue—or what's left of it. If I say it aloud, it becomes too real." She focused on button six, pushed the little white circle through the hole and exposed another section of chiseled abdomen. A slight tuft of dark hair covered his skin, and Bea stroked his chest carefully, almost afraid to touch something so beautiful for fear of breaking it—no, of losing the moment.

Then his hand covered hers and she flattened her palm against his body. "Your reputation is by far not your best virtue."

She dropped her head. "It's what matters to the Ton."

"To stupid men who don't deserve you and don't see you for who you are, perhaps. But I hope that none of them will ever have you."

She tried very hard not to look at him because even though he was half naked, she felt more exposed than she had when she was nude and wet in his arms.

"You are not... I mean, you're learned, and you have diplomas, honors, and apprenticeships that make you far more worldly than me."

"Then let me tell you that your qualities far exceed even your reputation as a diamond of the first water. Your beauty goes beyond being the belle at every ball. And the fortune a man would have if he married you cannot be diminished to your beauty alone."

Bea swallowed hard and tried to calm her thrumming heart. "You think so?"

"I know so."

She sniffled and moved her hand on his chest when he moved his own, giving her complete access to his torso. "About the physical exam…"

"Do you know what this muscle is called?" he asked, flexing it beneath her palm so it grew hard and rounded.

She shook her head.

"Pectoralis major."

"Does it cover the heart?" She instinctively met his gaze as she awaited an answer. Somehow, her physical exam had turned into a tutoring lesson on male anatomy, and she was the student.

Well, she was.

And she wanted nothing more than to learn from him.

⫸⫷

ALFIE WOULD MODEL for her and teach her whatever she'd be willing to learn about the human body, and especially how to experience the most exquisite pleasures. But he was no fool and knew that she'd teach him about making love, for it didn't matter how well-versed he was at the mechanics of it, Bea was a new discovery and an experience he wasn't sure he could ever stop learning from.

If simply kissing her had changed his mind, holding her had changed this heart, and whatever followed now would change his fate.

He pulled his shirt out of his breeches and then removed it entirely, exposing even more of his body.

The black pupils nearly eclipsed her lovely green eyes, but she didn't step back. She looked at him, getting her fill, and he would die to know what she was thinking. She bit her lower lip.

Oh how he wanted to bite it a little bit, too.

But not now.

Not yet.

"What's this one called?" She moved around him slowly, taking him in with huge eyes as she trailed her fingers along his upper back.

"*Trapezius.*"

"Like a trapezoid?"

"It's that shape if you isolate it."

She furrowed her brow. "And this?" Her fingers brushed down toward his upper arm and over his shoulder.

"*Deltoid.*"

"And why the ridges?"

Alfie pinched his eyes shut. She was too sweet, too naïve, and he had to control himself to not lift her up, lay her on the bed, and give her a taste of how well he knew the female anatomy, too. He regained that control by thinking about the male anatomy instead.

"The *fascia* connects muscle groups and if there's no fat to mask it, these ridges appear."

He flexed his biceps, but her hands trailed to his abdomen. She lay both hands flat.

"There's no fat here. Are these abdominal muscles?"

Then her hands went to his sides and although it tickled a little bit, he didn't laugh. "And that is a large muscle, the *oblique abdominis.*"

She held him for a moment and then stepped squarely in front of him, as if she tried to measure her frame against his.

Nothing like this had ever happened to Alfie before and he wasn't sure how to reconcile the lust throbbing through his middle with the tenderness overcoming his heart. If she stepped away, it would hurt more than a blow to the gut. So he waited for as long as he could—which wasn't very long, he reckoned—and then wrapped his arms around her.

He just wanted to hold her tightly.

Preferably forever.

But she seemed to have something else in mind and turned her face toward his chest, placing a butterfly kiss on his skin.

Then another.

Alfie's breath hitched when she gave his nipple a little lick.

"Bea!"

"You said you tasted me and thought I was delicious. Now *I* want to know."

Alfie's vision blurred and he nearly finished in his breeches, but he somehow managed to stand still.

She kissed a trail from his pecs to his shoulder, trailed her hands down his arms and back up over his back and then stepped behind him.

"Do all the muscles on your back have names, too?" She asked from behind him.

Alfie squeezed his eyes shut and tried to cool the heat in his crotch. "The superficial muscles of the back and flank are the *trapezius, latissimus dorsi, levator scapulae*, and the major and minor *rhomboids.*" Her hands followed his from his neck downward. "The deep muscles are erect—" Alfie coughed, "*Erector spinae*, the *transvers spinalis* group consisting of *semispinalis*—"

"And this?" Her hands slipped into his waistband, and she tried to grab his bottom.

Alfie sucked his lips in but dutifully untied his breeches in the front.

From behind him, Bea pulled them down, underwear and all, until they pooled below his knees.

Then she grabbed his bottom tightly.

"*Gluteus maximus.*"

"Is it made for sitting only?"

Too sweet. Too naïve. Dangerous.

"It supports the pelvis. It's responsible for movement of the hip and thigh, playing a crucial role in extending, rotating, and abducting the hip."

She was an apt student, following his words with her hands as she came back around to face him, her hands on the ridges above his hip bone. He gave a little flick, and her gaze fell to his manhood. At that, she sucked her lower lip in.

She lingered there and Alfie knew that he'd long left the island of propriety and was setting sail to a scandalous ocean of passion with the woman he loved—if only he'd manage not to drown.

"Can I touch you?" she asked, her eyes still on his middle.

"Anywhere you want Bea. I'm all yours."

She reached down and wrapped her fingers around his shaft. He couldn't help but gasp. And when her eyes met his, Alfie barely managed, but he said it anyway, "I've loved you even when you were just the girl in the veil in Delhi, but now that I know you, and now that I know how you feel, I could never be whole without you."

She narrowed her gaze. He pressed his hand over hers on his most sensitive part.

"Bea, do with me as you wish. But I won't go further unless—" he swallowed his words. This was exactly what he wasn't supposed to say.

"Unless what?"

"You marry me." Alfie blinked at her as if she were the sun blinding him, necessary for his survival and yet sure to burn if he stared too long. "I love you so much." She was so precious, the simple words didn't do the feelings he harbored for her justice.

"And I love you." Bea's voice came out with a squeal. She inhaled sharply and a slow smile built on her face. "I want to marry you," she whispered onto his mouth and wrapped her hands around the back of his head. Alfie's heart swelled with something he'd never experienced, and he vowed to wait until their wedding night to continue. But first, he had to kiss her.

Chapter Thirty-Four

Alfie and Bea had missed the wedding breakfast but after a short nap and a bath, Alfie returned to the ballroom in time for the evening's festivities. It was unusual to extend the celebrations past the breakfast, but Pippa's father felt he owed a ball to the Ton. And Bea said she had to face her parents.

He wasn't quite sure what to call what they'd done in her bed chamber though. Not a ribbon from her dress had come off, and she'd touched him until... well... had she seduced him? Alfie had put a stop to it just in time before he lost the last modicum of control. She was a woman to cherish, not to seduce. And most importantly, he hadn't proposed to her formally with a ring and her father's permission. Now he thought he ought to secure her parents' blessings.

He chuckled and rubbed his palms together. Oh, how soft she'd been in his grasp.

After dinner, when Alfie walked into the ballroom, the music swelled, a symphony of strings and woodwinds painting the air with anticipation. Alfie knew that Pippa was cherishing being the hostess and the bride of the ball at the same time, a well-deserved honor. In the center of the ballroom, Pippa and Nick, the newlyweds, commenced their waltz. The assembled guests encircled them, a tableau of the realm's finest, their approving murmurs a gentle rain.

Alfie's mind swirled with the intoxicating pleasure of the moments he had shared with Bea. Every touch, every whispered word replayed in his thoughts like a cherished melody. But then, across the room, he saw her—Bea, radiant and ethereal, moving with fluid grace and uninhibited joy. His heart plummeted as doubt crept in, a cold dread that tightened around his chest.

In Alfie's heart, a thunderstorm brewed when the next pairing drew a collective breath from the crowd as Bea stepped onto the parquet, her hand finding the prince's with practiced grace. Why wasn't it him leading her onto the dance floor? The world seemed to pause for Alfie as he watched them, the prince leading Bea into the dance; his elegant bow and her graceful curtsy made Alfie's insides clench.

A violin solo gave Bea the moment to assume the position and a hush descended upon the ballroom, the assembled guests' attention fixed upon the center of the ballroom. It was then, in that breath between silence and song, that Alfie's gaze found Bea. She smiled and appeared pleased. Alfie wanted to scream. He was in hell. The moment her slender hand slipped into the prince's, an invisible thread pulled taut around his heart, drawing forth an ache he had not anticipated, sharp and unyielding.

Bea moved with an effortless grace, her steps measured and sure as she positioned herself beside the prince. Alfie watched, transfixed, as if the very act of her taking the prince's hand was an intricate dance all its own—a prelude to the waltz that promised to entwine their fates more closely than he could bear. Her palm lay gently atop the prince's, a silent testament to the bond being forged in the glow of sparkling chandeliers and expectant eyes.

The way Bea glanced up at her partner, a soft smile gracing her lips, struck Alfie with the force of a tempest. It was a look of cordiality, perhaps even of budding affection, reserved for those destined to orbit within the same illustrious spheres.

"What a sweet match," a woman's voice came from behind Alfie.

"The perfect couple," another added.

Her lithe form found its place within the circle of the prince's arm, and as they assumed the starting position, the air around Alfie seemed to thin, each breath a struggle against the weight of realization. The elegance of her stance, the delicate arch of her neck as she prepared to move to the music's rhythm, was a portrait of radiant confidence, casting a glow that seemed to illuminate her from within.

Alfie felt shabby, unable to ask for a dance with her, especially if her parents were there. It was the symbolic crossing of thresholds of classes that were never meant to merge and he had nothing to offer if her father asked—besides his heart. It couldn't be enough, considering that her parents smiled approvingly as Bea swayed in the prince's arms. Even though Bea may have given him her heart and agreed to marry him, her father could stop their union.

Bea, in her resplendent beauty and grace, belonged to this dance, to the grandeur that surrounded her. As the music swelled, carrying them away on its lilting wave, Alfie remained anchored in place, adrift in a sea of unspoken love and unreachable dreams. His heart was lost in the darkness of the storm that would wreck his last hope and break his heart, drowning his naïve hopes that perhaps she could someday be his.

When Bea swayed in unison with the prince to the haunting melody, she moved with an ethereal elegance, her gown billowing softly with every turn, the candlelight flickering against the luster of her hair, now perfectly coiffed yet no less captivating in its beauty. To the onlookers, it was a vision of potential alliances, bright futures with promise. They saw the bride's beauty, the prince's majesty, and the dance's splendor. But Alfie saw only Bea, her fingers lightly resting in the prince's hold, her waist encircled by his arm. Each step they took together was a dagger to his heart, each smile she bestowed upon her partner a twist of the blade.

The jealousy that churned within him ran wild. He watched as Bea leaned into the prince's lead, her laughter mingling with the music, a sound more melodious than any aria. She inclined her head and whispered something to him.

Alfie's heart fractured with each beat of the music, each pulse echoing the shattering realization of his own silent yearning. Amid the grandeur of the ballroom, under the watchful eyes of the elite, he stood alone, a solitary figure grappling with the specter of loss. The dance before him unfolded like a dream from which he could not wake, a poignant reminder of the chasm between what his heart desired and what the morrow would bring.

And as the music dwindled to its final, lingering note, Alfie was left with the bitter taste of envy, and a heartache that whispered of love unspoken, and dreams undone.

⁂

"I NEED YOUR help again," Stan whispered through clenched teeth while the crowd watched them dancing. "List is here."

"I saw," Bea responded with the same practiced ease of continuing the graceful dance. It was a chance to speak, hiding in plain sight.

"There's an Austrian official, Richard Nagy."

"The bailiff?" Bea asked, meeting Stan's eyes for a moment. Violet and Henry had mentioned him, he was just as bad as Baron von List.

"Yes. You never cease to amaze me, Lady Beatrice. I hope that you will continue to work with me." Stan gave a curt incline of his head to show his respect.

That was when Bea realized that she wanted his respect. Being a spy or whatever it was called, using her connections to assist his diplomatic mission—that was what she wanted.

Where was Alfie? She wanted to work with Stan but be with Alfie.

The music rose and Bea felt as if thunderclouds drew apart

and light returned to her heart. All she had to do was tell her parents the truth. She'd marry Alfie, no matter his station and her parents' opinion. If she could work with Stan and marry Alfie, she no longer needed the Ton's approval. She'd found a path in life that excited her.

"Nagy has a stake in this but I'm not clear yet what it is," Stan spoke softly.

"And List is smuggling the gold that the Austrians think should be sent to them?" Bea asked.

"I suspect that Nagy doesn't know where List is keeping the gold."

"And the Russians want it, too?" Bea asked.

"Perhaps."

Chapter Thirty-Five

Alfie's breath hitched, the grandiosity of the ballroom suddenly oppressive, squeezing the very air from his lungs. Directly ahead, as the prince led Bea off the dance floor, Bea's parents fluttered about him and their daughter with the eagerness of bees around the season's first bloom. With hands that bespoke of a life untouched by toil, her mother fussed over Bea's hair, attempting to tame what was never meant to be restrained. Each time a curl escaped its confines, it seemed to Alfie as though a piece of her soul was asserting its freedom, the soft tendrils kissing her skin in silent rebellion.

And he wanted that spirit wild and untamed in his arms, moaning with pleasure, and screaming his name. She was never one to bow to others and Alfie hated that her spirit stifled under her parents' watchful gazes. Wasn't it the responsibility of parents to help their children blossom with their full potential rather than prune them like a boxwood in a maze to cripple them into convalescence?

Bea stood resplendent amidst the chaos, a serene smile playing on her lips, unaware or perhaps uncaring of the commotion her mere presence caused. Alfie's gaze lingered on the way a loose strand of hair brushed against her collarbone, trailing down the delicate expanse of her décolletage—a sight more enthralling than any play he'd witnessed at the theatre.

Then, with the formality reserved for transactions of great import, Bea's father drew the prince aside. Though their words were lost in the cacophony of the gathering, Alfie's heart sank with imagined conversations of dowries and ancestral estates, of special licenses and family jewels that would pass if Bea married—Alfie convulsed at the thought—the prince. Such were the currencies of the aristocracy, bargaining chips in the game of matrimonial alliances and he was not factoring into this equation.

How ironic to think of since he failed to account for the carrier oils or alcohol in a dilution. Even when he labeled the vials of his concoctions, he mentioned the essential oils, powdered teas, or distilled essence of medicinal plants but he never mentioned the base of talcum powder, alcohol, or sunflower oil. Rose oil was five percent rose and ninety-five carrier, yet it was labeled as rose oil. That's what he was, the carrier oil, or the diluting alcohol. And it stung. He'd taught Bea what a real kiss was, how to embrace the pleasure of a climax, and how to give pleasure to a man. Yet, he was never to reap the fruit of his passion—the prince was.

And even though Alfie wanted nothing more than to hate Stan, he couldn't even accomplish that. Stan had a noble cause, an even nobler title, and he could offer Bea a far better life than an apothecary. Yet, it left a bitter taste in his mouth to think of it.

Alfie couldn't bear the sight in the ballroom any more. Fleeing the stifling atmosphere for the cool reprieve of the gardens, he found himself among the imposing silhouettes of the orchard. Quince trees loomed large, their extended branches like trolls with long crooked fingers. The waxy sides of the leaves glistened in the moonlit night, and the farther Alfie got from the building, the silence that beckoned him was ripped apart, startling him as a twig snapped. He kicked it into the darkness, cursing under his breath, wishing his broken heart could be as easily dispatched. Heartache was a cruel contradiction, leading him out there among the quince trees and shadows, but the farther he went from the building, the less he could escape the throbbing image of

Bea swaying in the prince's arms. He was a suitor everyone approved of, and Alfie was simply not.

"Alfie?" A man's voice came from behind him. "Alfie, is that you?" It couldn't possibly be any worse. Stan's voice pierced the silence like a nightmare gripping him. "Alf-i-e!"

"What do you want from me, *hm*?" Alfie pivoted and walked back through the row of trees and found the stately prince, backlit from the yellow glow coming from the ballroom. Alfie took a wide stance and crossed his arms.

The prince quirked a brow. "What's the matter? I came to tell you something."

"*Hmpf!*" *If you're announcing your engagement to Bea, I'm not going to congratulate you.*

It would be too cruel.

"Bea sent me," the prince said, touching Alfie's shoulder. He slammed him away, royal or not. Stan didn't react to his action. Instead, he appeared calm—even understanding—as he said. "She has to tell her parents first, but she said it couldn't wait and sent me to you."

"I'm not happy for you, just so you know. I don't think you'll love her a fraction of how I do."

"Who?"

Now Alfie stopped and blinked at the prince. It was dark but his eyes glistened in the moonlight and Alfie was seething. "How dare you ask me that?"

"*Aaah*. Bea? Yes, you love Bea! I know that. I'm happy for *you*."

Alfie balled his fists. If he knew, then how could he pursue her? Alfie might be below him in station, but he was a human being and had helped him. He deserved at least some respect. "That's why she sent me to tell you right away. Her parents didn't let her so I—"

"What?"

"She'll receive an official secret mission."

"That's a contradiction in itself. If its official, it's not secret."

"No. Well, yes. She'll work with me, as a spy. Didn't you see us at the ball? She's brilliant."

Yes, she is. And she danced with you. Alfie swallowed hard but his insides churned with anger, jealousy, and the worst feelings he never knew he was capable of.

"I'm sorry I stole the dance from her, but we had to keep up the ruse for Nagy and List," Stan explained.

Alfie narrowed his eyes. That was the problem with Stan; he wasn't Alfie's friend, but he had the same enemies. "Explain yourself." But he kept his fists balled, ready to defend Bea's honor and restore respect for himself if necessary. He'd never punched a prince before but there was a first time for anything…

Stan cleared his throat and then leaned in to Alfie. In a low tone, he explained that they needed to extract some information and lead Nagy and List into a certain direction which he couldn't say more about. Comprehension dawned.

"So Bea will spy for you?"

"Well, she'll be on clandestine diplomatic duty as an English citizen to support the autonomy of the Transylvanian people."

Alfie waited.

"Yes, *hm*…" Stan took a step back. "But I hear that congratulations are in order. She told me you proposed."

"And she accepted." Alfie took a wide stance and crossed his arms. The fact that Bea told Stan was a beacon of hope. Perhaps he ought to hear the prince out. "She said she loved me."

"Oh, finally!"

"I beg your pardon?"

"It was so obvious at the Langleys, I was afraid List would comment on it. We had made a plan to extract the information from him but the way you two looked at each other, I wasn't sure List wouldn't focus on another scandal altogether. She was supposed to have come with me, you know."

"I do. That's the problem. I gave her a love potion for you to… wait! I saw you in the carriage at the park together. Are you saying you *don't* like her?"

"Oh, but I do. She's brilliant, as I said. I can't wait to work with her more closely."

Alfie cocked his head. "Just work?"

Stan swallowed audibly and scratched the back of his neck. "Yes. I'm not going home for some time though. I hope you won't mind it if she works with me?"

Stan had the tone Alfie recognized instantly; it was the same one patients used when they didn't give away all the symptoms or the origins of an embarrassing condition. "Is there someone else?"

"Oh well, yes, she's... oh she's..."

"Not Bea?"

Stan shook his head. Relief washed over Alfie. Not Bea, at least not for Stan.

But for Alfie, she was everything!

Chapter Thirty-Six

Bea felt as though life had received its second wind when she left the ballroom in search of Alfie. Stan had paid her the best compliment, enlisted her for a greater cause of justice and diplomacy, and Bea couldn't wait to tell Alfie. But she knew she had to face her parents first. She finally came into her own and felt useful.

Bea walked through the grand hall, the echo of voices drawing her to an alcove off to the side. Her parents' familiar tones were unmistakable, but it was the third voice that made her pause—a voice filled with a haughty elegance, unmistakably that of Baron von List, the man whom Stan had wanted her to target as her first mission. And he was hiding in a corner with a woman Bea couldn't see. She couldn't make out their words, but the intensity of the conversation piqued her curiosity and ignited a spark of suspicion.

Steeling herself, Bea approached with measured caution, staying close to the shadows cast by the ornate columns. But to her surprise, it was her mother with the baron. The sight of her mother, animated and engaged, only deepened her sense of unease. What could they possibly be discussing? As she stepped closer, her mother's gaze shifted, locking onto her with a mix of surprise and concern. The baron, noticing the change in demeanor, turned to see Bea and immediately excused himself, gliding away with an air of practiced suave lies.

The sudden departure left Bea standing at the edge of the conversation, her mind whirling with questions and a gnawing sense of betrayal. What secrets were being kept from her, and why did her presence cause such a swift exit? The fragments of doubt and suspicion coalesced into a determined resolve as she faced her parents, ready to uncover the truth behind the clandestine meeting.

"Mother?"

Her mother cast a look toward the curtains of the tall windows in the hall and Father emerged. "Father?"

Her parents stood with expressions carefully composed, betraying none of the affection she had hoped to see. It was as if she had interrupted them in the middle of an important task, an unwelcome intrusion rather than the return home to a beloved daughter.

Her mother's smile was tight, her father's nod curt. Both exuded an air of polite detachment. Bea searched their faces for some sign of warmth or understanding, but found only cold professionalism. In their eyes, she was not the daughter they had raised, but a nuisance who could not fulfill the one thing they needed most—an advantageous connection within the Ton. She could practically feel their disappointment, an invisible weight pressing down on her shoulders.

The silence stretched uncomfortably, each second amplifying the distance between them. Bea fought to suppress the rising tide of emotions, the hurt and frustration that threatened to spill over. She squared her shoulders, determined to maintain her composure, even as she felt her heart breaking.

Bea stood there, feeling more alone than ever, as the reality of her parents' priorities crystallized before her.

"Your match with the prince will become you." Her mother finally nodded with a flicker of approval as if she'd made peace with the delay of the union.

"I take it Henry and Violet made the introduction?" Father

asked.

Bea furrowed her brows. "You knew?"

Her parents cast each other a look and then her mother put a hand on her shoulder. "Stan needs your help and said you've already done very well."

"What did you discuss with Baron von List?" Bea asked, unable to hide the suspicion coloring her voice.

"We passed on a message," Mother said.

"A threat he can take to his allies." Her father spat as if the baron disgusted him. "Didn't Stan tell you? We've been working to unravel List's schemes for a while."

"And your union with Stan will help achieve our goals, darling. I'm sure of it. And then we can open the port in Singapore for more precious goods."

At that moment, her mother lost Bea's trust. "You're using me as an instrument for your business?"

"Darling, you must take your position in society," Father said as if it went without saying that she would marry to further his cause. Bea's life, her love, her heart—it was all a bargaining chip in Society.

No more!

"I'm not a parcel you can sell, Father. I can be useful in ways other than a wife."

Her mother blinked incredulously. "Yet, you haven't even accomplished that tiny milestone of a betrothal. Even Pippa has!"

"Once we cure the beast, Stan will offer for her," Father said. "Leave the rest to me."

"You're offering him a dowry, paying him to take me, and then what?" Bea couldn't hide the exasperation in her voice. She didn't want any of it and she felt the need to please her parents crack and break off like brittle paint.

→→→»«←←←

ALFIE HAD LEFT Stan in search of Bea and ran back to the

ballroom. Amid the splendor of a wedding that was not his own, Alfie had never felt more out of place. In the shadow of the ballroom, Alfie was surrounded by all the reasons he couldn't be with Bea. She was the granddaughter of one of the wealthiest men in England, at her ancestral estate the size of a small town, with her father, an earl, and her mother, a countess. Though the wedding guests around him were wrapped in the light-hearted revelry befitting such a joyous occasion, inside Alfie, a battle raged.

Every nerve in his body screamed for him to claim Bea, to declare his love boldly. Where was she?

Alfie had to leave the music behind and found a balcony. He closed the double doors behind him, and the nightly darkness gave way to the bright lights from the wedding. Instead of the bouquets of white flowers, he now looked at the landscape, shrouded in blackness just as his heart.

He stood among riches where he didn't belong, and it was as plain and as ancient as the rolling hills that cradled it. Downstairs and around the balcony, flowers bloomed with reckless vibrancy in the gardens, and he could smell the nonsensical mixture. They were arranged by color in a garden focused on the shapes and sizes of the blooms rather than their properties. Even though the people who seemingly tended to the garden had created something beautiful, Alfie knew that the rose bushes had taken root next to vines that would allow for an elixir that mixed harmoniously. If he ever created a garden, he'd sort the plants by medicinal properties and seasons of the best harvest. In this garden, the cacophony of scents irritated him as much as their fragrance—a heady mix that clashed with the storm brewing in his heart.

As he stood on the dark balcony, he thought he'd heard Bea's voice in the gardens below.

"I don't think it's necessary, Mother." Alfie could hear her more clearly now.

"Darling, we found a healer with much experience in this,

and it is the only way." Her mother's voice was soft but adamant.

"We are trying to say that you cannot marry and surprise your husband with those episodes. If he thought you'd tricked him into marriage, he could call for an annulment, and you'd be cast aside."

Alfie leaned over the plaster-coated balusters and felt the cool hardness as much as the harsh words from Bea's parents.

"Darling, please." Her mother handed her something that appeared to be a metal flask, but Alfie wasn't sure, for all he could see was a metallic reflection from the lights that emanated from the ballroom.

"If you take this, you have a fair chance with the prince," her father said.

"I don't want a chance with him, Father," Bea said, the fear audible in her voice. She wasn't happy her parents had returned, Alfie knew that. She'd told him so during their afternoon together. But now he could hear in her voice that she was terrified of them. "I love another."

"As long as you don't tell him, it shall be all right," her father said without even acknowledging that Bea had declared her heart.

Alfie's internal conflict was abruptly eclipsed by a more immediate danger. Bea's mother uncorked the flask.

"This is cinnabar, and it is a very strong cure." From his perch on the balcony, Alfie saw the metal flask. His heart dropped. He knew the truth of that so-called medicine; it was poison, a danger cloaked in the guise of care.

As Bea's slender fingers wrapped around the vial, he watched, every sense heightened. The beauty of the setting—the lush green of the garden, the delicate arrangements of flowers, the music that floated on the air—all of it dulled to a mere backdrop against the peril Bea faced.

In that moment, Alfie's resolve crystallized. His love for Bea, the depth of his feelings, demanded action.

"Please drink—" but Alfie didn't hear the rest of Bea's father's words.

He left the balcony and dashed down the ancient stone stairs, his heart pounding in his chest as though it sought to escape. The grandeur of the castle blurred into a streak of indistinct shapes and shadows. With each step, his urgency grew, his boots slipping on the worn edges of the steps.

After mere seconds that felt like hours, he hoped he wasn't too late.

"Bea!" he called. "Bea!"

Bursting through the double doors, he emerged into the garden and saw Bea standing between her parents, the metal flask in hand and close to her lips. She was a vision of innocence and grace, her hand trembling as it clasped the vial, its contents a sinister shadow amidst the splendor of the gardens and the golden glow cast upon them from the ballroom.

"Bea!" The garden around him was a blur, the fragrance of the blooming flowers a distant note beneath the pounding of his heart. As he neared, the world seemed to narrow to the space between them, every step charged with the weight of his resolve. The closer he got, the clearer he saw the confusion in her eyes, the slight tremor of her hand. Alfie's mind raced with the gravity of what was to come, the act that would expose the poison for what it was, an act that would irrevocably alter the course of their lives.

With a final, desperate burst of speed, Alfie closed the distance, reaching out to snatch the vial from her grasp. The motion was swift, decisive, leaving no room for hesitation or doubt.

"Don't!" Alfie threw it into the darkness. By the sound of it, bushes stopped its fall with dense foliage. Alfie cupped Bea's cheeks and examined her. A pallor, stark like the moon above wrung his heart. "Please tell me that you didn't drink any of it!" He pressed his mouth to hers, desperate, for he couldn't bear to live a day without her.

But Bea barely returned the kiss, her arms hung limp from her sides.

Had he come too late?

He deepened the kiss and dropped his hands to her back, pulling her toward him lest she faint from weakness of the poison.

"Alfie!" She mumbled onto his mouth. "Alfie?"

He broke the kiss, breathless. He didn't taste the poison on his own lips or smell it on her breath, but couldn't be sure. He needed to know.

"What has gotten into you?" Bea asked, licking her lips as she turned to her parents with the look of a schoolgirl caught in the act of stealing the headmistress' quill.

Alfie's breath caught in his throat as he took in the scene, time stretching into an agonizing eternity. The music and laughter of the ball inside seemed to fade into oblivion, leaving only the sound of his own heart racing in tandem with the realization of what he'd done.

"Didn't you drink the cinnabar?" he asked, for her well-being was the only thing that mattered to him now.

"No," she waved toward the bushes behind her. "How dare you throw away my only chance at a cure?" An estranged look in her face gave way to a redness that wasn't at all a blush but sheer anger. He'd never seen Bea like this before.

"Who is this rogue?" Her mother exclaimed in a high voice that made Alfie wince.

"Young man, this is between my daughter and us. That was a rare and highly-concentrated mixture you just tossed away!" Her father was a little shorter than Alfie and still managed to cast him a superciliary glance that instantly reminded Alfie that his station was far below him—nonexistent, to be precise.

"You didn't drink it?" Alfie asked Bea who'd stepped away from him.

"No, I told you. How could you do this to me?" Hurt flickered in her gaze.

"I thought you'd been poisoned, and I wanted to... I don't know, cinnabar is dangerous... I cannot imagine a life without you, Bea. If anything happened to you, I would rather die than suffer the pain of losing you."

The air tensed among the assembled and Bea's mother's countenance was dark with suspicion. But Alfie could only watch Bea, waiting for her to trust him, to believe in the sincerity of his warning.

When Bea hesitated, her mother's impatience grew palpable. Alfie did what he must. In choosing Bea's wellbeing over his safety, he'd crossed a line from which there could be no return.

The garden, with its intoxicating blend of aromas, the castle with its centuries of legacy—all faded into a backdrop for a moment defined by sacrifice and love.

Chapter Thirty-Seven

Bea stood, frozen with shock and disbelief, as Alfie's sudden dash toward her culminated in the snatching of the vial from her grasp. Once filled with the harmonious symphony of the wedding, the garden now seemed eerily silent, save for the racing thoughts thundering through her mind. She watched, helpless, as the vial—a symbol of her desperate gambit for freedom—was unceremoniously discarded, its contents seeping into the earth, lost forever. Her parents had procured a cure for her on a journey to Asia that she couldn't repeat.

They'd brought her a medicine that they promised provided the only chance to tame the beast within her.

Confusion reigned as she tried to grasp the implications of Alfie's actions. Upset mingled with astonishment; how could he dismiss her plans and fears with a single, swift motion? Yet, amidst this tumult of feelings, a part of her couldn't deny the protective fervor in his eyes, a fervor that both alarmed and strangely comforted her.

The garden, with its verdant beauty, suddenly felt like a constricting cage, as she became acutely aware of her parents' eyes upon them, witnesses to Alfie's brazen act of devotion. The scandal of it all—the sheer impropriety of Alfie's kiss—left her speechless, her mind a whirlpool of questions with no anchor.

Just as she gathered the frayed edges of her composure, attempting to string together a coherent thought, Stan stepped through the double doors. His arrival, commanding and poised, sliced through the tension like a knife.

"Bea," he called, his voice a beacon in the stormy sea of her thoughts.

Bea's heart lurched, torn between duty and desire, her future hanging in the balance. In that moment, she knew the eyes of every soul in attendance were fixed upon her, waiting for her to take the next step in this unforeseen dance of destiny.

"Oh, Alfie, hullo." Stan had reached the spot in the garden where they stood, Bea's future teetering between the life she'd been groomed for and the life she'd secretly forged before her parents returned.

"Your Royal Highness." Her father's eyes grew wide, and he stood in front of Alfie, his back to him and Bea as if their presence brought him shame.

"Stan, you know my parents?" Bea stepped in front of her father and curtsied. It was an act more informal than her interaction with Stan required since they'd become friends and colleagues—an unmistakable signal to be cautious.

Stan's eyes met hers for a moment and he gave a faint nod, then bowed and greeted her parents. "We have been formally introduced already, Lady Beatrice. We've been working together."

"Messengers. Supervisors. He's the better diplomat." Father raised his eyebrows in appreciation of Stan. Bea's eyes shot to Stan.

"It's complicated and I will tell you in time. But I don't mind the dangerous parts," Stan said.

"Dangerous?" Alfie wrapped his arm around Bea and pulled her to him.

Bea shook her head. But she didn't know how to act and where to begin to explain to her parents that she worked with Stan and had fallen in love with Alfie. It was too much to package into words with her fear that her parents never forgave her transgressions. Everything they'd taught her, everything they'd hoped she'd become, she'd twisted into something to suit her own whims and was sure to disappoint them. And this was Pippa's wedding day, not the moment to break her parents' hearts.

"Your Royal Highness, it is with—"

But Stan interrupted Bea's father. "Alfie, we are ready to cut the cake. Bea, Pippa has asked for you." It seemed as though Stan and Alfie had exchanged unspoken words and reached an understanding.

"Who is this man?" Bea's mother called in a shrill voice as if she couldn't fathom the scandal of Alfie's arm around Bea after he'd kissed her boldly before them.

"Certainly, Lady Wetherby. He's the best apothecary in England, perhaps even in all of Europe," Stan said.

Alfie cleared his throat, but his gaze was as dark as Bea had feared it to be when he stood behind her.

"Have I interrupted anything?" Stan's eyes jumped from Bea's to Alfie's and then he narrowed this gaze when he saw the pallor on Mother's face. "Oh dear, he was asking for your hand and I… oh, I am so sorry I intruded." Stan inclined his head, unaware he'd misinterpreted the situation. "Lord Wetherby, I assure you that there isn't a better man in the world for your daughter, and I hope that you will accept my well-wishes if I am the first to congratulate your family."

Oh dear, Stan thought Alfie was asking for her hand while her parents wanted Stan… *oh dear, oh dear…*

Father inhaled sharply, and his eyes grew so big it was as if they were about to pop out of his head.

"He ruined your last chance to tame the beast," Mother cried, fanning herself frantically. It was as if she hadn't heard Stan speaking at all, or noticed Alfie's arm around her waist. "There's no other cure and none we can find for you before you're too old to marry!"

"Which beast?" Stan asked Alfie over Bea's head, grimacing as if none of her mother's outburst made any sense.

"Beatrice, explain yourself," her mother demanded.

"Allow me." Alfie stepped forward. "You almost killed her!"

"What happened here?" Stan asked, unable to hide his confusion.

Bea was frozen to the spot on the grass, her heels sinking into the earth as the blades ripped underneath and she wished she could disappear into the earth like a raindrop falling onto dry soil never to be seen again.

"I overheard you. I was upstairs." Alfie pointed at the balcony on the upper floor. "Cinnabar is a source ore for refining elemental mercury. It's been used since the ancient Romans made vermillion-red with it, and I've used it many times in tinctures to cure syphilis."

"Who is this?" Father seethed.

"Syphilis?" Stan asked, giving Alfie a grave look.

"Yes, it's also used for exorcisms in traditional Chinese medicine." Alfie gave Bea's parents a look more dangerous than the vial they'd brought. "It's a lethal poison and you could have killed your daughter with it."

"Poison?" Bea's mother stuttered. "The healer said it never fails to take effect and that the beast... Bea would—"

"Your daughter is not a beast, nor does she have one. It's a simple correlation of what she eats." Alfie straightened his back and took a wide stance. "I analyzed her journal and charted the occurrences. Her breakouts have nothing to do with the balls, nor her temper. I've never met a person with a kinder nature and a sweeter heart than Bea. How could you lock her away and punish her for something that's not her fault?"

"Beatrice, what is this man speaking about?" her mother asked.

"She kept a record—" Alfie started, but the earl raised his hand.

"She asked my daughter. Not you."

"Yes, Father." Bea kept her back ramrod straight, but she

lowered her gaze, and her voice quivered. "I kept a journal with everything I exposed myself to, food, scents, soaps, everything at Cloverdale House."

"Don't tell me that you handed such an intimate record to this man?" Her mother fanned herself even faster, as if she were ready to take flight.

"What did your analysis of the record show?" Stan asked, not paying attention to Bea's parents.

"That there's a pattern of the onset for every breakout within a short delay of approximately two to four hours after she eats pineapple," Alfie explained.

"Pineapple?" Her mother spat. "It's the finest of all fruits, and serving it behooves my daughter. She will not refrain from offering pineapple once she marries."

"She doesn't need to stop serving it. She could have her own orchard if she wanted," Alfie said, "but when she eats it, she breaks out in hives and suffers a painful and itchy rash."

"That's the cost of life and luxury you wouldn't understand," her mother snuffed at Alfie.

"But it could get worse, and she might suffer more grave consequences if she's repeatedly exposed to it." Alfie announced.

"Really?" Bea asked, "But I love pineapple!"

"And so you should. You're a hostess of the Ton," Mother said. "My daughter was raised to maintain a certain station in society."

"That doesn't matter if eating it could make her tongue swell to the point of suffocating her." Alfie's anger pierced his voice. "And even if it doesn't, she suffers the breakouts. And you've forced her to remain locked up for weeks. How could you make her feel ashamed instead of consoling her? You weren't here for her, your own daughter! Do you know how lonely she's been? Don't you care about her feelings more than her appearance in society?"

Bea's father cleared his throat and seemed as if he were about to say something when Stan interrupted him. "What do you mean 'locked away'?"

"Every time Bea had the hives as a reaction to eating the pineapple, she was forced to remain in her chambers until they passed. And she suffered so badly then that she starved herself. Or *you* starved her," Alfie almost shouted at her parents. He reached into the back of his breeches and retrieved the journal. "Look here." He turned to a page with several entries. "Her handwriting was different; she didn't push the fountain pen onto the paper as on the days she ate more. She was lightheaded and faint. And then there wasn't an entry that day between four o'clock and eight the next day." Alfie turned to another page. "And here, she had tea in the evening. For dinner," Alfie snarled. "And then nothing until afternoon tea at Lady Violet's house the next day."

He turned to another page. "There was pineapple marmalade. Four hours later, she started to grow red-faced and flushed. Later that evening, she was covered in hives. It happened again after she tasted the wedding cake samples."

"Your Highness, I must apologize for my daughter's lack of judgment. I was unaware that she'd hand a stranger her diary, let alone that she had no better sense than to record her meals." Her mother made no effort to hide how her daughter embarrassed her.

"That's brilliant," Stan said to Alfie, paying no heed to her mother's words. "You mean that you analyzed the pattern in her exposure to certain foods, and the correlation of pineapple and her hives emerged as the causality for her condition?"

"I assure you, Your Highness, that her condition is curable with a small dose of cinnabar, and that would make for a most satisfactory bride," Father muttered.

"Satisfactory bride?" Alfie seethed. He grabbed Bea's hand, interlaced his fingers with hers, and held on tightly. "She won't be satisfactory after she's dead from the poison you want her to swallow after the fruit you expect her to consume—that could also kill her!"

"Nobody asked you," Father said.

"*I* am asking." Stan crossed his arms. "Bea?"

Bea nodded and leaned against Alfie, drawing his arm over her shoulder with their fingers still linked, and nestled into Alfie's embrace.

"She's the most beautiful, brilliant, and refined woman I've ever known, and I've traveled the world. You won't find anyone with a sweeter heart and a sharper wit, or speedier understanding of the most complex issues." Alfie placed a kiss on the top of her head, his nose brushing the coppery gold of her hair.

"I second that. She has a better grasp of European diplomacy than I do," Stan confirmed.

Her father shook his head in disbelief. "Beatrice? Diplomacy?"

"Yes, she knows the borders of the empires and understands where the foci of friction lie. She's a most valuable asset…" Stan stopped as if he'd misspoken.

"Asset?" Her father said.

"I've helped Stan with a little observation work," Bea said, returning the tight grip of Alfie's hand. "And I shall continue to help him."

He looked at her now, blazing conviction in his eyes. And she nodded at him.

"Thank you for standing by me."

"I will not give my permission, Beatrice," her father said.

"I haven't asked for it," Bea said quite firmly.

That was it, it all came down to station. There was no reasoning with the Ton. He'd known it all along.

Alfie growled and turned away.

Chapter Thirty-Eight

THE GARDEN OF Bea's grandfather's country estate was bathed in the harsh sheen of moonlight, the sharp edges of leaves the only feeling in Alfie's skin as he passed through the orchard. The air was thick with the scent of blooming roses; the only sound breaking the night's tranquility was the occasional chirp of a distant cricket. Alfie's footsteps were heavy, each step pressing into the dewy grass as if the earth itself was pulling him deeper into the enveloping darkness.

"Why are you running away from me, Alfie?" Bea's voice pierced the night air, trembling with a mix of determination and desperation. She quickened her pace, her silken gown whispering against the grass, the hem collecting droplets of morning dew.

"I'm not running away," Alfie called back, his voice strained as he pushed through the low-hanging branches of the orchard. The leaves brushed against his face, their cool touch a stark contrast to the rising heat of his turmoil. Each branch seemed to reach out, as if nature itself were trying to hold him back, to force him to face the inevitable.

"Then why am I chasing after you in the dark?" she demanded. Her breath came in short, sharp gasps.

Alfie stopped abruptly, pivoting to face her. Her exertion was evident in the flushed hue of her cheeks.

His own breath came in ragged bursts, the moonlight catching the beads of sweat on his forehead, illuminating the anguish etched on his features. Bea's eyes, wide and glistening, reflected the confusion and hurt that mirrored his own.

Bea huffed, closing the distance between them, her hands trembling at her sides. "It's unseemly for a lady to go after a man like me," Alfie muttered, his voice laced with bitterness. His gaze dropped to the ground, unable to meet her searching eyes.

"Like you? What's that supposed to mean?" Bea's voice was sharp, cutting through the night's stillness. Her eyes, however, beseeched him, desperate for an explanation.

"Bea," he exhaled, his shoulders sagging under the weight of unspoken words. "Don't pretend like you're blind to the cleft that divides us. We might as well be different species—didn't you see how your father looked at me? It's like I am an ape to him."

Bea's expression softened. She reached out, her fingers brushing against his forehead with a tenderness that made his breath hitch. "You're hot," she said, a gentle smile attempting to lighten the mood.

"Stop jesting," Alfie snapped, stepping back. His voice was raw, the edges frayed with the strain of held-back tears. "It's not funny when my heart is broken because I cannot be enough. I may be just an apothecary to people like you, but I still have worth. And a heart. And it hurts."

"People like me?" She frowned. "And... a broken heart?" Bea whispered, her voice barely audible, the words trembling in the cool night air.

"Yes, Bea, a broken heart!" Alfie's voice cracked, the raw pain evident in every syllable. "What did you think? That I can just shrug it off? Fall in love with you with a passion that cuts my breath and go on as if nothing ever happened?"

Bea's eyes grew wide, shimmering with unshed tears.

Alfie ran both hands through his hair, his frustration palpable in the way his fingers clenched the strands. "I saw it coming and had no defense. You may have agreed to marry me but without your parents' permission... if your father won't..."

"I don't need their permission. They barely know me anymore, and they don't see what matters to me—who matters to me."

"You'd defy the Ton and everything they want for you, if we marry."

She shrugged and gave a mischievous look over her shoulder. "I'll be a spy and do as I please. If you still want me—"

In a sudden, impulsive movement, Alfie reached out and scooped Bea into his arms, cradling her against his chest. She gasped but did not protest, her heart pounding in sync with his. He carried her effortlessly through the garden, the soft glow of the moonlight casting ethereal shadows around them. He entered the castle from a side door. Up the grand staircase and into his chamber—a room that now felt like the epicenter of his torment and longing.

He laid her gently on his bed, stepping back as if afraid his presence might shatter the fragile moment. The room was dimly lit by a solitary candle, its flickering light casting dancing shadows on the walls. Alfie's breath was ragged, his chest heaving with the effort to contain the torrent of emotions threatening to overwhelm him.

He knelt beside the bed, his eyes locking onto Bea's. "It's tearing me apart," he whispered, his voice barely more than a breath. "Loving you is the most excruciatingly beautiful sentiment I've ever felt. I know I'm not what society deems worthy of you, but I can't help it. My heart chose you, and now it's broken because it feels like I'm living a forbidden dream."

Bea reached out, her fingers trembling as they touched his cheek. "Alfie," she whispered, her voice a delicate mixture of wonder and sorrow.

He closed his eyes, leaning into her touch, savoring the warmth and softness of her skin against his. "I thought I was pouring my heart out in vain," he confessed, his voice shaking. "I thought you could never return my love." He held her journal up from the nightstand. "But then I read this."

Tears spilled from Bea's eyes as she cupped his face with both hands. "You're wrong, Alfie," she said, her voice breaking, the words choked with emotion. "I love you too. With every beat of my heart, I love you."

Alfie's eyes snapped open, disbelief mingling with an overwhelming surge of hope and joy. "But can you marry me against your father's wishes?"

"Yes," Bea nodded, her tears mingling with a radiant smile. "I don't care about societal norms or what my father thinks. All I care about is you."

In that moment, the world outside ceased to exist. The garden, the estate, the societal expectations—all faded into oblivion as Alfie leaned in and captured Bea's lips in a searing kiss. It was a kiss that held all the passion, longing, and love they had both kept locked away for so long.

In each other's arms, they found solace and strength. It was a love that defied the boundaries of their world and promised a future where they could be together, no matter the odds. And in the quiet sanctity of that room, Alfie's and Bea's hearts finally beat as one, united by a love that was destined to withstand the tests of time.

Chapter Thirty-Nine

Two months later at Silvercrest Manor...

EVERY SUNDAY FOR several weeks now, all the doctors from Harley Street had come to the country estate. Pippa and Nick had taken their honeymoon there and their Sunday reunions were a welcome pleasure. Plus, Bea and Alfie had been there when the banns were read. And this morning, they'd married in a small church among their closest friends. Stan, Violet, and Henry had been there, too, even though Violet had grown a bit round with child and fanned herself during the entire ceremony in the small and stuffy church.

"I have a wedding present for you," Alfie said when the door to Bea's bed chamber shut with a click. He leaned back and held something behind his back in his left hand, while he turned the key with his right and left it in the lock.

"What are you hiding from me?" Bea cocked her head and took a step toward him. She could tell it was wicked by the look on his face but didn't dare ask. A mischievous glint in his eyes mixed with a grin that bubbled from within him and then his face brightened, and he beamed.

"This is the key. No, it's your jewel."

"Jewel?" She had enough jewelry. What Bea had in mind for this night was different.

He stepped closer, still hiding something behind his back. And as he walked toward her, Bea couldn't suppress her glee that this extraordinarily handsome man was hers. The curl that draped over his forehead a little, the short dark lashes rimming his teal-green eyes—everything about him was perfection.

When he smiled, Bea's insides melted. When he kissed her, she was ablaze. His voice resonated through her very core and when she lay her hands on his chest to feel his heart, she knew it beat for her. Plus, his fingers were wickedly capable—not merely in his apothecary.

Bea sucked her lower lip in.

"Do you wish to say something?" Alfie asked.

I want to feel you inside me.

"I mustn't," Bea mumbled.

"Ah! That's exactly what I thought." He faced her, a small green glass bottle in his hand.

"Is this for me?"

"It's for me," he said but held the little bottle out to her. "A map."

"Perfume."

"No, this is not perfume because it has a taste and a scent. It's sweet almond oil with vanilla and a little of the neroli oil from Pippa's orangery. I added some pine honey."

"Most certainly for me." Bea reached for it and lifted the glass stopper from the bottle. It smelled floral and sweet, like a freshly-baked almond torte.

"No. Some of my friends are jewelers, and they have stories about each piece they craft. I wanted to give you something precious, but more private. So, I mixed this for you, and I vow to make you as much as you need, a lifetime supply at your pleasure."

Bea narrowed her eyes. *Pleasure?*

"Why do I need this and how is it a map?" Bea asked.

"You don't ask for what you want, so you can show it with this."

This was not going as she'd hoped. Bea crossed her arms in front of her body.

"See? Right now, your body language says that you're not pleased with me and yet you won't say anything."

"I'm a lady, it's not my place—"

"*Shhh.*" Alfie came close and pressed a gentle kiss on her lips. "I know you were raised not to ask a husband for certain things. But nobody knew that husband would be me," Alfie whispered, but flames sparked in his eyes and set Bea's skin ablaze with the need for his touch. "In a marriage with me, you're my equal." He cocked his head. "Perhaps my superior in many ways." Then his mien darkened, and he spoke with a sincerity that left Bea breathless. "You are my love and my life. Always speak your mind with me. Please never hold back, for I need to know what's in your mind to make you happy in your heart."

She bit her cheek.

"Right now, I can see, you want something, but you won't ask for it. So, I made this oil for you." He picked up the flask and turned it upside down, then back. He lifted the dauber out of the flask and handed it to her. "Show me where you want me to kiss you. Telling me what to do doesn't have to be with words." Alfie's eyes softened, revealing a vulnerability that spoke volumes, a silent plea wrapped in desire.

At first, Bea hesitated. She had no words.

He'd known that, and that's why she was holding the dauber with the sweet almond oil.

She touched her collarbone gently with the glass dauber; the cold hardness was like ice on her skin.

Alfie's eyes tracked the dauber's path with rapt attention, his gaze lingering on the glistening spot where it touched her skin before he leaned in, his lips brushing softly against the fragrant skin. Bea held the dauber as if it were a key while Alfie kissed her collarbone slowly and with such reverence that she burst into goosebumps.

When he lifted his head, casting her a look that was loyal and yet fierce like a wolf, another wave of courage washed over her. She dabbed a little of the oil on her shoulder. His unwavering gaze, full of longing, followed her every movement, making the room feel smaller and their connection deeper. With the flicker of a mischievous smile, Alfie bent down and kissed her there, too.

"It's working." Bea couldn't suppress a grin. *This would be fun.*

Alfie nodded and licked his lips as his gaze dropped to her mouth. He tugged at his cravat and loosened it. It was really too bad because he had been such a dashing groom dressed in crisp white and black.

He pulled his cravat off and shrugged off his boots.

Hm, on second thought, Bea had to gleefully admit to herself that the only thing better than her elegant groom was her naked husband.

He unbuttoned his shirt, his pupils dilated, reflecting a quiet devotion and an unspoken promise as they locked onto Bea's, unyielding and warm. He was waiting for instructions.

Bea inhaled deeply and shifted the dauber to her left hand, with which she was holding the flask. Then she tilted the flacon and poured a little of the fragrant oil onto her right palm.

Alfie's brows narrowed, and he stilled. The way his gaze followed her every movement, unwavering and full of longing, made the room feel smaller, their connection deeper.

She rubbed the oil on the back of her neck and spread it as low as she could reach on her back.

Alfie's gaze grew more intense.

Without a word but with a proud grin like a peacock, Alfie stepped behind her and lowered his mouth onto her neck. He followed the path she'd painted closely, kissing the scented area with increasing passion, each kiss lasting just a moment longer than the last. The contact of his hot mouth on her skin made the tiny hairs on her neck prick up and a wave of chills rolled over her arms, instantly replaced by the heat of her longing.

He kissed her tenderly while she tilted her head forward, giving him greater access. Bea reached up and started to pull the pins from her upswept hair. Without stopping to kiss her back, Alfie's hands slid up her sides to her arms, over her elbows, and up toward her wrists.

When Alfie's hands met hers, he drove his fingers through her hair, letting it fall like a silken drape as he spun her around. His eyes were black with desire, and Bea's breath hitched when she saw his expression. This was not admiration for the diamond of the first water, nor was it the expectant gaze that usually met her; it was raw and honest love—the unconditional and generous kind that Bea knew deep in her heart only Alfie was capable of.

※

OF ALL THE beauties in the world, Alfie couldn't fathom his luck to have the brightest, sweetest, and most sizzling one of all in his arms. His heart was flooded with so much love for his bride that he marveled at the sturdiness of his ribcage as his heart was thrumming so wildly, it might jump out.

He untied the laces at the back of her dress, reveling in the depth of her breath as the tight corset fell from her delicate frame. Her wedding dress slid to the floor and pooled at her feet. He didn't know how to even begin gathering the fabric, but he suspected that her dress was sinfully expensive, so he merely put it over the chair behind him. And the woman before him was unspeakably precious. Alfie put his hands on her waist over the sheer white chemise and pressed her against him. He was finally allowed to do this. That was a relief, and yet his blood boiled with the urgency to feel more of her and plunge into her. The desire raging in his veins was overpowering his vision and yet, he couldn't close his eyes because he wanted to memorize this night, and every moment thereafter, with his love.

Oh, his love.
His bride.
His wife.
Alfie swallowed hard.

Bea still held the flask and poured some more oil onto her hand, then rubbed it on her chest, down onto her stomach, and then, Alfie forgot to breathe. He bent down to press a tender kiss onto the anointed spots, his lips lingering as if savoring the scent and sensation. She tugged at her chemise and Alfie allowed just enough distance between them to disrobe.

Alfie nodded and pulled his shirt over his head, letting it fall to the floor. Bea hooked her fingers into his breeches, tugging at the waistband.

"You first," Alfie rasped. Apparently, his bride was the exact amount of beauty that turned him into a stammering green boy, so in awe was he of her allure.

Bea crossed her arms, picked up the hem of her chemise, and elegantly pulled it over her head. Then she removed her stays and stockings.

She was naked perfection. And she smelled like a dessert, tasted like honey, and felt like the finest silk.

Before long, they were both naked and Bea sank onto the bed, wrapping her arms around Alfie's neck and pulling him down. He climbed over her, his cock throbbing. This time, finally wed, he'd allow himself to go all the way. As if pulled by a magnet, his tip found the apex of her legs, but he didn't allow himself to move farther.

Not yet.

"Do you want me to use protection?"

"But we are married," Bea said, arching a brow. "Do you need it?"

Alfie stroked a few strands of hair from her forehead and then dug his hand into the silky lushness of the mane upon which her head rested. She was so precious and so beautiful that it hurt to look at her.

"I won't be able to hold back, and I want to feel you climax around me." He knew it sounded harsh, but he needed her to be aware. He wouldn't ever do anything without her permission. "If I pour myself into you, you might get pregnant."

Alfie chastised himself for the clinical touch he'd brought into their wedding night but there was so much she didn't know. He just didn't want any surprises for her that she didn't welcome.

"I know what will happen, Pippa told me."

Alfie rolled his eyes and pursed his lips. "She and Nick …?"

Bea nodded and grinned as if she'd been privy to the most delicious secrets. "She told me in London already."

Alfie cocked his head. He had to hand this to Nick, he didn't miss a moment. Good for them.

Tonight was his turn.

"I'm not afraid of having a baby. We have enough doctors who can help." Bea smiled and something changed.

"Babies are very small when they are born, they need help with everything," Alfie said, plopping on his side and off Bea. He propped his head up on his hand and she turned to face him.

Naked, atop the covers as husband and wife.

She was ready.

He placed a hand on her flat abdomen. "Are you certain you are ready? We can take our time before we—"

But she didn't let him finish. She thrust her lips onto his, sucked his tongue into her mouth and shook her head. "I don't want to wait."

Alfie opened his mouth for her as she gripped his face.

He grabbed her bottom and nudged her to the tip of his cock.

Well, if she was ready, then he most certainly would be.

She adjusted her hips, and he felt the hot need of her wet folds on his shaft. Then she slid up on his and broke the kiss. She pushed him onto the bed and climbed onto him.

Alfie opened his eyes to a siren sitting on him astride.

With her hands on his chest, she adjusted her position. Alfie's fingers ventured to her center, and he parted her folds.

"Here," he managed, arching his neck to look at the erotic image.

She gripped his shaft, flexed her thighs, lifted her center, and then he was at her opening.

His mouth agape, Alfie watched her as she looked down and rubbed her pearl with the tip of his cock. His vision blurred and he blinked, unwilling to give in to the need to thrust in and he waited, slack-jawed at how curious, brave, and delicious his bride was.

Oh, if this was the wedding night only, their marriage would be grand indeed.

He couldn't wait.

But he did.

"It might hurt," he said, using both hands to part her.

She looked down to where their bodies were meeting, about to unite, and her hair fell into her face. Her lush curls draped over her shoulders and Alfie needed to see her eyes. So he let go of her folds and reached for her, brushing her tresses away so he could see her face.

And that's when she dropped onto him, and he slid into her with one swift motion.

She made an adorable hic, her eyes grew big, and her mouth fell open. They both looked down and Alfie was buried inside her to the hilt. She was so wonderfully tight all around and his cock twitched inside her. He didn't mean for it to happen; he had wanted to give her time to adjust to the invasion.

But she just felt so wonderfully perfect and amazing that he dropped onto the covers and tried to steady his breath.

"Are you hurting?" he whispered.

"*Eh-eh.*" She shook her head and placed her hands on his hip bone. "This is big."

Alfie couldn't breathe and speak at the same time.

His virgin—*ahem*, not virgin bride *anymore*—sat on him, enveloping him, and she marveled at his size. If he didn't keep his wits, he'd come on the spot.

"You. Feel. So. Good." *Made for me.*

Then she clenched inside.

He felt her liquid desire spreading around his cock as she moved.

Perhaps he could help her now, teach her even?

Alfie lifted his head and reached for her bottom, nudging her up and down.

She bit her lower lip and looked at where they were joined. Learning.

Exploring.

So sweet.

"You are so deep inside me," she rasped. "And I want more."

"Deeper?" Alfie asked.

She nodded, giving him a puzzled look.

Oh yes, it is possible my love.

He wrapped his right hand around her left thigh and pulled her leg up until her ankle rested on his shoulder.

Her initially puzzled look quickly gave way to astonishment and then amazement. But Alfie still gave her time. She was so very tight, and he didn't want to hurt her.

And he most certainly didn't want her to be too sore in the morning for more marital bliss.

She moaned and pressed her center against his middle, seeking the friction of their united bodies.

"More?"

Was that a question?

Alfie reached for her pearl, and she quivered.

Just when he wanted to retreat his hand, she clasped his with her hand and pushed him down.

"Are you really ready?"

Her breathing came labored, and she licked her lips as she nodded.

So she allowed him to take the lead.

She let out a little yelp and he instantly missed being inside her.

He looked down. No blood.

Good.

Now he took his time and ensured that she lay comfortably on the soft covers, her head on a pillow.

She reached for his torso, touched him everywhere, and when she cupped his balls, Alfie spread her legs.

Slowly but deliberately, he moved toward her.

"May I now?" he asked, his cock at her entrance.

She parted her folds with her fingers just as he had before. One last time, Alfie reached down and was rewarded with a generous drop of her slick desire.

Then he placed the tip of his cock at the opening, wet and hot.

But he didn't push.

He needed to kiss his bride first.

His Bea.

When his mouth came to hers, her tongue darted to his, and she opened up for him. That was when he plunged in and pressed on.

Her hands clasped his bottom this time and she pulled him closer. "You feel... oh Alfie!" She let out another adorable sound and then purred, sucking him in for a deeper kiss, deeper inside her.

His vision blurred and he just shut his eyes.

At first, he moved slowly, in and out.

But she met his every thrust until he pumped harder.

She clenched around his cock and held on to him.

"I have you," Alfie said, then he wrapped everything he had around his wife. They were one, intertwined, and forever united.

Bea was a dream come true. He never wanted to wake up.

⫸⫷

BEA'S ENTIRE BEING swirled with a storm of emotions, every sensation magnified. Alfie moved within her, each motion sending waves of warmth and pleasure through her body. As she reached the peak, he pulled her close, his embrace a fortress of security. In that moment, she found a profound sense of safety she had never known.

Her breath caught as another wave of pleasure surged through her, even more intense than the first. The world around them faded, leaving only their shared intimacy. When she finally returned to herself, she found Alfie's hands cradling the back of her head, his touch tender yet firm. Their bodies remained connected, a physical testament to the bond they had forged.

She gazed into his green eyes, now clear and unguarded. Gone was the headscarf that had concealed him in India; gone was the veil she had worn. They had stripped away all pretenses, offering themselves wholly to one another. Bea's heart brimmed with gratitude, overwhelmed by the completeness she felt.

Alfie brushed a stray lock of hair from her face, his fingers lingering on her cheek. "We are one," he whispered, his voice a soft caress. His words resonated deep within her, affirming their unity.

She smiled, a tear escaping down her cheek. "Forever," she replied, her voice steady with conviction. His lovely green eyes shone with happiness, and she knew she'd been the one to put the light there.

"I'm just sorry I didn't find you sooner," he said, his voice filled with sincerity and warmth. "But now that I have you, I will never let you go."

Tears of joy welled up in Bea's eyes. "I love you, Alfie. More than words can ever express."

His gaze softened, filled with an emotion she knew mirrored her own. "I love you too, Bea. With all my heart and soul."

They lay there, entwined in each other's arms, the room filled with the quiet aftermath of their passion. In that silent communion, Bea knew without a doubt that they had found their truths in each other's embrace. Basking in the afterglow of their union, their future stretching ahead like a golden path... Bea's heart soared with the possibilities ahead.

"We should start planning our new life," Bea said, her voice tinged with excitement. "There's so much I want to do with you."

"And so very, very much I want to do *to* you," Alfie said with a raised brow as he gently peeled the cover off Bea. He kissed a trail from her mouth to her chin, down her neck and over her chest, down farther and she giggled. Alfie made her quiver, laugh, and he healed her; he made her whole.

Epilogue

BEA AND ALFIE walked hand in hand back to the dining room at Silvercrest Manor, and she could see his face flushed with happiness. When they entered, the chatter quieted, and all eyes turned to them. Bea felt her face heating again, but Alfie's gentle grip of her hand steadied her. The wedding breakfast had long since ended, leaving only the remnants of a joyous celebration. Through the tall windows, the sunlight filtered through the tall windows, casting a warm glow over the room filled with close friends and family.

Wendy approached with a smile, her dark curls bouncing with each step. "There you two are! We were beginning to wonder—" but she couldn't finish because Nick gave a brotherly nudge with his elbow.

"There's food for you, tea, cake and everything you need," Pippa said when she came to Bea's side, intertwining her arm with hers. "I'm so happy for you, cousin."

Alfie chuckled, his grip on Bea's hand tightening affectionately. He had an air of a proud rooster, and his chest seemed puffed up, joyful, to present his bride to his friends.

Oh, that was her, Bea reminded herself, as she surveyed the room of smiling faces. The sense of belonging warmed her from within because here, she didn't merely shine and fit in as in the Ton's ballrooms, while vicious people mocked her cousin—no, this was different—here she shared the love for her cousin with people who had big hearts and welcomed them into their tight circle of trust, Nick and Pippa, Wendy, Felix, and Andre.

Bea's heart swelled with love as she glanced around the room. These were the people who had supported her.

Then her face fell. Her parents stood solemnly in the doorway, her father clearing his throat.

Alfie wrapped his arm around Bea.

"Is it done?" Mother asked. "Have I missed your wedding?" She rushed to Bea.

"Yes," Bea said more softly than she'd intended.

Her father, who'd remained a step behind her mother, approached Alfie. He extended his hand and hesitated before he said, "Thank you."

Alfie blinked at Bea and then back at her father. "For what, my lord?"

"For saving my daughter's life."

Mother reached for Bea's hand, and she gave it to her. "We don't expect your forgiveness for years of foolishness, but Stan told us everything you've done to help with Baron von List." She shook her head, "I was too blind to see the truth beyond my mission but you—" her voice broke and she patted Bea's hand as a tear rolled down her cheek.

"What we are trying to say is that we thank you for your wisdom and protection when we were gone. There's no better man for our daughter and even though it is too late, we hope you'll receive our blessing." Her father's voice sounded a little unstable and Bea's mouth fell open. She had no words.

The room remained silent for a moment but then a metal clank on glass chimed. It was Pippa, who came to stand with her glass raised.

Nick stood, too, and lifted his glass. "A toast!" he declared, drawing everyone's attention. "To Bea and Alfie! May your lives be filled with love, joy, and unending adventure."

Glasses clinked together, the sound echoing through the

room like a harmonious symphony. Bea felt a surge of gratitude and happiness as she looked at Alfie. His green eyes shone with love and pride.

Alfie lifted his own glass. "And to Nick and Pippa," he said, his voice strong and clear. "For being the dearest of friends anyone could ask for."

Pippa grinned, her blond hair catching the light.

"Welcome to the family, Bea," Felix added warmly. "Though I suppose you've been part of it for quite some time."

Pippa laughed, nudging Bea playfully. "Indeed, cousin. You've always been family, but now it's doubly knit."

The room erupted in laughter, and Bea felt a deep sense of contentment. These were the people who had stood by her side, who had laughed and cried with her, and now they were here to share in her joy.

As the laughter died down, Alfie leaned in and whispered in Bea's ear, his breath warm against her skin.

Her father cleared his throat again. "Your mother and I would like to present you with a small gift for your wedding." He produced a folded document from his waist pocket. "We are to leave again for another mission. I trust Stan shall give you the details soon. But with Cloverdale House being converted, your mother and I thought this might be a useful beginning for the newlyweds." He handed the document to Alfie.

Alfie opened it and read it, then handed it to Bea.

"A deed to a house on Harley Street?" she gasped.

"It has four chambers, a dining room and a parlor. You can host Society and still remain close to the practice." Father looked proud and smug, bobbing his head with glee that the surprise had been effective.

Pippa squealed with joy in the background. "They will be our neighbors!"

"We will live on Harley Street? In our own house!" Alfie spoke as if he couldn't believe the good fortune the day had brought him.

"It's where you bring about miracles in medicine I've heard," the earl said.

"And in matters of the heart," Bea smiled.

"To the bride and groom!" Andre called from his spot at the table. "One final toast," he announced, gathering everyone's attention. "To love, friendship, and the future."

Everyone raised their glasses, the room filled with a chorus of voices. "To love, friendship, and the future!"

⇝⇜

The series continues with Andre's story in *A Touch of Charm* and Prince Stan's in the *Sound of Seduction*. Find out how the next doctor on Harley Street finds love. For more stories, audiobooks, and new releases, visit www.SaraAdrien.com.

Author's Note

Apothecaries, alchemy, and chemistry versus pharmacy in 1819

In 1819, apothecaries held a vital role in London's medical landscape, functioning as the predecessors of modern pharmacists. Like Alfie, these skilled practitioners not only dispensed medicines but also diagnosed ailments and crafted remedies using a blend of herbs, minerals, and other ingredients. In fact, apothecaries were often the first point of contact for the sick, offering medical advice and treatment. Their shops were bustling hubs of activity, filled with the fragrant aroma of dried herbs and the clinking of glass bottles like the fictional one at 87 Harley Street.

The Regency period was a fascinating transitional era where the ancient art of alchemy began to give way to the burgeoning science of chemistry. Alchemy, with its roots in mysticism and the quest to transform base metals into gold or find the elixir of life, still influenced many apothecaries. They relied heavily on ancient texts and traditional knowledge passed down through generations. However, the early 19th century also saw the rise of modern chemistry, characterized by systematic experimentation and the application of the scientific method. This is why Alfie knows the difference between a truth serum and a love potion, versus concoctions that merely heighten attractive traits, such as a woman's scent, or mixtures that would loosen the villain's tongue, like the one given to Baron von List.

Apothecaries straddled two worlds, blending the mystical

elements of alchemy with the empirical approach of chemistry. Their workspaces were intriguing places where one could find both ancient alchemical symbols and the latest scientific apparatus. When Alfie distilled the neroli oil for Bea's wedding present and perhaps the myrtle for the truth serum, he used a distilling machine, which was commonly referred to as an "alembic." An alembic was a type of distillation apparatus used to purify liquids or create concentrated extracts. It typically consisted of two main parts: the cucurbit, which was the vessel containing the substance to be distilled, and the cap or head, which captured and condensed the vapor produced during heating. The collected liquid would then be directed through a tube into a receiving vessel. The alembic was an essential tool for apothecaries and alchemists alike, allowing them to create a variety of medicinal tinctures, spirits, and other concoctions.

This duality between alchemy and chemistry made the practice of an apothecary both an art and a science, rich with tradition yet open to innovation. As the century progressed, the role of the apothecary would eventually evolve into that of the pharmacist, laying the foundation for the sophisticated pharmaceutical practices we rely on today. This blend of old and new made the world of the apothecary in Regency London a truly captivating subject for historical romance, and made writing Alfie's story all the more enjoyable as there was plenty of fact I could add to the fiction.

So what did Alfie know and how did he use these elusive substances?

Digitalis

Digitalis, derived from the foxglove plant, holds a significant place in the annals of medicine, particularly during the Regency era. In 1819, apothecaries in London would have been familiar with digitalis as a potent remedy for heart conditions. The use of digitalis in medical treatments can be traced back to the late 18th century, when Dr. William Withering popularized its use after observing its effects on patients with dropsy, a condition we now recognize as congestive heart failure. He documented that digitalis could help increase the strength of heart contractions and thereby improve circulation, making it an invaluable tool for treating heart-related ailments.

From the perspective of botany, the foxglove plant, with its tall spikes of tubular flowers, was both a common sight in English gardens and a source of fascination for herbalists. Apothecaries would carefully extract the active compounds from the plant, creating tinctures and powders used to treat their patients. However, digitalis is a double-edged sword; while it can be lifesaving, it is also highly toxic if not administered correctly. The margin between a therapeutic dose and a lethal one was perilously thin, which was why Alfie was so nervous about the truth serum given to Baron von List and why he downed the rest of it before the mixture could become dangerous to the villain.

Nagapushpa flower

In this story, a special place is held by the Nagapushpa flower, also known as Mesua ferrea or the Indian rRose chestnut. This unique blossom symbolizes not only rare beauty but also cherished memories and unspoken connections for our heroine.

The Nagapushpa, native to India, is celebrated for its exquisite, pristine white petals adorned with a subtle blush of pink at their base. The texture of its petals is velvety and soft, making it a delight to touch. Its fragrance is particularly captivating—a sweet, heady aroma that lingers in the air like a whispered promise, enchanting all who encounter it. This flower blooms on the Mesua ferrea tree, which is often found in the lush forests of the Indian subcontinent.

In traditional Indian culture, the Nagapushpa is revered not just for its visual appeal but also for its spiritual significance. It is frequently used in religious ceremonies and offerings, symbolizing purity and devotion. The delicate beauty of the flower, coupled with its lasting fragrance, makes it an enduring symbol of love and memory—perfect for encapsulating Bea's precious recollections.

By incorporating the Nagapushpa into Bea's story, I wanted to highlight how even the smallest, most delicate elements can hold profound significance in our lives. Just as Bea cherishes her pressed flower, we too often find ourselves holding onto tokens of our past, which remind us of the people and moments that have shaped us.

Cinnabar

Cinnabar, known for its strikingly bright red color, holds a fascinating place in medicine and art history. Cinnabar is a form of mercury sulfide and has been used since ancient times. In 1819, apothecaries in London might have encountered this mineral primarily as a pigment, and sometimes as a medicinal substance. The Chinese long prized it for its ability to create the vibrant vermilion pigment in art and decoration. However, its applications extended beyond aesthetics into the realm of medicine—and that's where trouble brewed for Bea.

Apothecaries would sometimes use cinnabar in treatments for various ailments, believing it had purifying properties. For instance, it was employed in the treatment of syphilis, a common yet severe condition of the time. The theory was that mercury, the primary component of cinnabar, could help purge the body of impurities. Unfortunately, while mercury did have some antimicrobial effects, its toxicity often caused more harm than good. Patients treated with cinnabar could suffer from mercury poisoning, leading to severe neurological and physical damage.

The dual nature of cinnabar as both a potential cure and a poison highlights the precarious nature of medical practices in the early 19th century. The understanding of chemical compounds and their effects on the human body was still developing, and many treatments involved a significant degree of risk. Despite its dangers, the use of cinnabar persisted due to the lack of better alternatives and the prevailing belief in its efficacy. This mineral's historical journey from a revered substance to a recognized hazard marks an important chapter in the evolution of medicine, reflecting the trial-and-error approach that characterized the era's medical advancements. Aren't you as glad as I am that Alfie stopped Bea from taking it?

The Prince

To craft a realistic backstory for Prince Ferdinand Constantin Maximilian Hohenzollern-Sigmaringen ("Stan") in a Regency romance, I blended historical context with plausible fiction. Given that the Hohenzollern-Sigmaringen dynasty did not rule Romania until 1866, I took some creative liberties while attempting to maintain historical plausibility.

Thus, Ferdinand Constantin Maximilian is a fictional member of the Hohenzollern-Sigmaringen family, a younger son born into nobility but not in direct line to the throne. In the early 19th century, European royal and noble families often sought prestigious roles for their younger sons, who would not inherit significant titles or lands. As a prince, Ferdinand would hold a high social rank but would need to find a role that allowed him to contribute to his family's prestige and his country's diplomatic efforts.

Given his noble status and the necessity for royal families to forge alliances, Ferdinand could realistically be assigned to a diplomatic mission. It was common for younger sons of noble families to pursue military or diplomatic careers. His education would have included languages, politics, military strategy, and the arts, preparing him for such a role.

In the context of a Regency romance set during the early 19th century, Ferdinand could be sent to England to strengthen ties between the Hohenzollern-Sigmaringen family and the British monarchy or to negotiate a specific alliance, possibly related to the Napoleonic Wars or their aftermath. We will find out in book 4, *The Sound of Seduction*, what his mission is and who caught his heart. His mission might involve delicate negotiations, attending social events to build relationships with British aristocracy, and possibly even espionage or intelligence gathering, given the turbulent political climate of the time.

About the Author

Bestselling author Sara Adrien writes hot and heart-melting Regency romance with a Jewish twist. As a law professor-turned-author, she writes about clandestine identities, whims of fate, and sizzling seduction. If you like unique and intelligent characters, deliciously sexy scenes, and the nostalgia of afternoon tea, then you'll adore Sara Adrien's tender tear-jerkers.

For more information and exclusive sneak peeks, audiobooks, new releases, and more, sign up for Sara Adrien's newsletter at www.SaraAdrien.com

Catch up with Sara Adrien here:
linktr.ee/jewishregencyromance
saraadrien.com
instagram.com/jewishregencyromance
facebook.com/AuthorSaraAdrien
bookbub.com/authors/sara-adrien
goodreads.com/author/show/22249825.Sara_Adrien
youtube.com/channel/UCK9OLp1wN6IaGkXe7OugfHg

Also by Sara Adrien

Books with the doctors on Harley Street:

A Sight to Behold
(Nick and Pippa's story)

A Touch of Gold
(Felix's story)

The Sound of Seduction
(Wendy's story)

A Touch of Charm
(Andre's story)

Don't Wake A Sleeping Lyon
The Lyon's First Choice
The Lyon's Golden Touch
The Lyon's Legacy
and many more!

Acknowledgements

Thanks to Andrea, Emily, Cynthia, and everyone at Dragonblade. My gratitude also extends to Susan, who helped me back up much of the historical medical research for this story and the series as a whole.

Special thanks go to my readers whose kind reviews and responses to my stories are a wonderful source of inspiration.

Milton Keynes UK
Ingram Content Group UK Ltd.
UKHW020909291124
451807UK00013B/826